WIDOWS COVE

PAUL ROONEY

WIDOWS COVE

A ROB RAGUSA
THRILLER

PALMETTO
P U B L I S H I N G
Charleston, SC
www.PalmettoPublishing.com

Copyright © 2023 by Paul Rooney

All rights reserved
No portion of this book may be reproduced, stored in a retrieval system, or transmitted in any form by any means–electronic, mechanical, photocopy, recording, or other–except for brief quotations in printed reviews, without prior permission of the author.

Hardcover ISBN: 979-8-8229-3230-2
Paperback ISBN: 979-8-8229-3231-9
eBook ISBN: 979-8-8229-3232-6

ACKNOWLEDGMENTS

I appreciate the assistance of my wife, Paula Rooney. I would also like to acknowledge the
contributions of Steven Poole, Michael Peters, Sergeant, Massachusetts State Police (Retired), Beth Ann Seastrand, Coast Guard Petty Officer Second Class, Tina Yule, Alison Savicke, editor, Mariam Mustapha, and Warren Hall. I also wish to thank the fishermen of New Bedford and the patrons of the Narrows who helped inspire me to write this novel.

TABLE OF CONTENTS

Chapter One 1
Chapter Two 6
Chapter Three. 9
Chapter Four. 12
Chapter Five 16
Chapter Six 25
Chapter Seven. 30
Chapter Eight 32
Chapter Nine. 36
Chapter Ten. 39
Chapter Eleven 48
Chapter Twelve 53
Chapter Thirteen. 58
Chapter Fourteen 63
Chapter Fifteen. 69
Chapter Sixteen. 72
Chapter Seventeen 78
Chapter Eighteen 86
Chapter Nineteen 88
Chapter Twenty. 97
Chapter Twenty-One 104
Chapter Twenty-two 111
Chapter Twenty-three. 118
Chapter Twenty-Four 131

Chapter Twenty-Five 135
Chapter Twenty-Six 140
Chapter Twenty-Seven 149
Chapter Twenty-Eight 153
Chapter Twenty-Nine.................... 158
Chapter Thirty 162
Chapter Thirty-One 166
Chapter Thirty-Two 177
Chapter Thirty-Three 181
Chapter Thirty-Four.................... 190
Chapter Thirty-Five 197
Chapter Thirty-Six 209
Chapter Thirty-Seven 215
Chapter Thirty-Eight 220
Chapter Thirty-Nine.................... 229
Chapter Forty 240
Chapter Forty-One...................... 247
Chapter Forty-Two 252
Chapter Forty-Three.................... 257
Chapter Forty-Four..................... 261
Chapter Forty-Five 267
Chapter Forty-Six...................... 275
Chapter Forty-Seven.................... 278
Chapter Forty-Eight.................... 287
Chapter Forty-Nine 294
Chapter Fifty.......................... 311
Chapter Fifty-One 317

Chapter Fifty-Two 325
Chapter Fifty-Three 330
Chapter Fifty-Four 340
Chapter Fifty-Five 352
Chapter Fifty-Six 356
Chapter Fifty-Seven 361
Chapter Fifty-Eight 368
Chapter Fifty-Nine 371
Chapter Sixty 376
Chapter Sixty-One 378
Chapter Sixty-Two 383
Chapter Sixty-Three 392
Chapter Sixty-Four 397
Chapter Sixty-Five 404
Chapter Sixty-Six 421
Chapter Sixty-Seven 430
Chapter Sixty-Eight 434
Chapter Sixty-Nine 436
Chapter Seventy 439
Epilogue 447
Glossary 451
About the Author 453

The Fisherman's Prayer

I pray that I may live to fish
Until my dying day
And when it comes to my last cast
I then must humbly pray
When in the Lord's great landing net
And peacefully asleep
That His mercy I be judged
Big enough to keep

-Anonymous-

CHAPTER ONE

The explosion was deafening. One minute, all was quiet on the Emma Jean, and then all hell broke loose. Smoke and flames poured out of the galley. The heat was so intense I thought my face was on fire. I flew out of the pilot's house and grabbed a fire extinguisher, but it was too late. The flames and heat drove me backward as I approached the galley; I could see three of the four crew on deck.

"Abandon ship!" I yelled.

I headed back through the billowing smoke to the pilothouse to get off a "Mayday!" As I climbed the stairs, I could see the silhouette of three men jumping overboard. I am captain of the Emma Jean, and she was sinking.

"Manny, Manny, I can't swim!"

Manny Sousa was holding on for dear life to a life ring. Barry Gomes was doing the dog paddle to stay afloat

"Hang on, Gomes, I'm coming for you," Manny said.

"Hurry, man, I'm going to go under. I'm getting tired, man."

The sixty-degree water was a shock to the system. Manny made it over to the struggling Barry with every inch of strength he had. They both held on to the life ring, for their dear lives.

"What now, Manny?"

"Say a prayer, Gomes, say a prayer."

In the distance, a bright orange life vest could be seen drifting away.

The call came into the Coast Guard station, Boston, at 2400 hours on July 6th. Ensign Robert Edwards answered. The voice on the other end of the line was Gil Galloway, the captain of the fishing trawler, the Olivia Rose.

In a hurried voice, Captain Galloway reported, "One of my crew spotted a bright orange glow in the distance at 2300 hours. We responded to the location and found a trawler, the Emma Jean, engulfed in flames. We found three men in the water and pulled them into our boat. A fourth man, Captain Frank Medeiros, is still on the deck of the burning trawler and refuses to abandon ship."

Ensign Edwards questioned Captain Galloway.

"Is the boat still on fire?"

Captain Galloway responded, "It looks like the fire has been extinguished, but the boat is a smoking wreck."

"What is the crew's condition.? Do they need medical attention?" Ensign Edwards asked.

Captain Galloway replied, "I spoke to the three crew members, Manny Sousa, Christian DeJesus and Barry Gomes. They have minor burns on their hands and arms; but, otherwise, seem to be in good shape." "Have you accounted for all the crewmen?" Captain Galloway replied, "No, there is a fourth man, Henry Gonsalves. He appears to be missing."

Captain Galloway reported, "My position is 41.2060 latitude and 67.3753 longitude." Georges Bank. The Emma Jean is listing twenty degrees starboard and is taking on water. We need a cutter out here ASAP for medical attention, fire control, and rescue!"

Ensign Edwards told Captain Galloway, "Hold your position. Help is on the way. A cutter is being dispatched to your position from Boston. Expect two helicopters from Air Station Cape Cod. They should be at your position in thirty minutes."

Before ending the call, Captain Galloway yelled, "Get here as quick as you can. Captain Medeiros won't abandon his boat, and it's going down fast."

Chief Warrant Officer (CWO) Eric Mallory gave the order to dispatch a cutter to the coordinates provided by Captain Galloway. The Coast Guard's forty seven foot Motor Lifeboat is built to withstand rough seas and can travel at a top speed of sixty knots. CWO Mallory contacted Air Station Cape Cod for assistance.

After hanging up, Captain Galloway stood in the pilothouse alone. A wave of emotions hit him hard. A strange mix of anger, sorrow, and unease. Gil Galloway knew Frank Medeiros well. They had worked at the New Bedford docks for over thirty years. Both started out as "shackers" eventually "getting off the deck" and becoming captains of their boats. A shacker is a new inexperienced crewman. They are usually given the most demanding jobs on the boat.

The Olivia Rose and the Emma Jean were formerly owned by Carlos Rafael, better known as "The Codfather." Carlos had immigrated to the United States, settling in New Bedford, and through hard work and a ruthless business ethic, rose to the top of the New Bedford fishing business. Carlos owned a fleet of twenty-four fishing vessels in New Bedford. He also owned the biggest fish house in the city. He had been in business for over thirty years before his empire crashed. The Codfather was certainly a controversial figure along the New Bedford docks.

New Bedford is the number one fishing port in the United States for landed fish. It was rumored that the Codfather's fleet accounted for 25 percent of groundfish landings. He was a larger-than-life character. Carlos could often be found holding court in the city's bars, restaurants, and Portuguese social clubs, places where Madeira wine flowed freely, and a Portuguese steak was always on the menu. He was one of the town's richest men and rumors swirled around him. So, what was his game?

The genius of the Codfather was that he owned a large fleet of boats but was also a seafood dealer, making it easier for him to cook the books on his catch. When he caught fish subject to strict catch limits, like grey sole or cod, he would report that the catch consisted of more plentiful fish, such as haddock. He would pay himself for the higher priced fish and then sell the fish as a dealer to local restaurants and retailers as legitimate species, knowing that the business owners couldn't be fooled into buying cod that was haddock. Carlos would proudly refer to himself as a "Pirate" and mocked his competitors as "Mosquitoes."

His empire unraveled when agents from the Internal Revenue Service, posing as fish buyers from New York City, taped him describing his illegal activities. He was also bold enough to show the agents a ledger labeled "cash," which he explained was used for the off-the-books transactions. Ultimately, the Codfather pled guilty to charges of conspiracy, tax evasion, bulk cash smuggling, false labeling, and falsifying records. He was sentenced in Massachusetts US District Court to a four-year term in federal prison. Carlos refers to his new digs as a "federally funded gated community." The Codfather's fleet went up for auction, and Gil Galloway and Frank Medeiros each won bids on two of the newer trawlers in the fleet. Both men had achieved their dreams on finally owning their fishing boats.

CHAPTER TWO

Boston Harbor in July can be busier than the rush hour Southeast Expressway. The harbor is packed with an eclectic mix of vessels of all shapes and sizes. Everything from cargo ships to sailboats, pleasure boats, and even kayakers, ply the waters. The 210-foot Black Hull stood out as it cut a wake through the harbor enroute to the Emma Jean's position in Georges Bank. The Black Hull is a Medium Endurance (WHEC) Class Cutter that the Coast Guard uses for search and rescue missions.

The Black Hull navigated the obstacle course of boats in the harbor and reached the relatively uncrowded waters of Cape Cod Bay. Then the order was given by Lieutenant Commander Nicholas "Nick" Dutra for "all engines on." The two modified twin diesel airplane engines roared to life and the Black Hull began to cut through the bay's choppy waters, reaching a cruising speed of thirty knots. A course was plotted for the last reported position of the Emma Jean. It was 165 nautical miles from the Boston Coast Guard Station to the Emma Jean. At thirty knots, Lieutenant Commander Dutra estimated that the Black Hull would reach Emma Jean in four hours with a "following sea."

At the same time the Black Hull was dispatched from the Boston Coast Guard Station, a call was placed to the Coast Guard Air Station at Joint Base Cape Cod. The operator answered the call and was immediately put through to the Commander of the Air Station, Jason Ludowsky. After being informed of the status and position of the Emma Jean, Commander Ludowsky ordered two MH-60 Jayhawk helicopters in the air to assist in the rescue operation. The two Jayhawks quickly scrambled toward the coordinates of the last known position of the Emma Jean. The helicopters were piloted by Lieutenants Harold Hale and George "Cookie" Cooley. The Jayhawks each carry a crew of four--the pilot, copilot, and two rescue swimmers. The choppers traveling at top speed, 160 miles per hour, could reach the Emma Jean within thirty minutes.

The MH-60 Jayhawk is a twin engine, medium range helicopter. The Jayhawk can land on the deck of a Coast Guard cutter. It can stay in the air for six to seven hours before needing to be refueled. The Black Hull was equipped with a landing pad, so the Jayhawks could airlift crew members onto the cutter if necessary.

It was a hot, muggy night. The kind of night where your clothes stick to your skin like Saran Wrap.

Even so, everyone involved in the recovery operation knew that, without a survival suit, nobody lasts very long in the cold waters of the North Atlantic. The clock was ticking.

Georges Bank lies sixty-five miles due east of Cape Cod. The rich fishing ground measures 150 miles in length and seventy-five miles in width. Georges Bank, often mistaken for the Grand Banks located farther north, is the world's second most productive fishery. The first is the Grand Banks. Georges Bank has been heavily fished for cod, halibut, and other species for 400 years because it is the closest fishery to the mainland. Bottom trawlers based out of New Bedford and other East Coast fishing ports drag the bottom of the sea like giant vacuum cleaners. New Bedford harbor is filled with these trawlers, scallopers, and other fishing vessels, making it the number one fishing port in the United States for the dollar value of landed fish.

CHAPTER THREE

The weather was crystal clear, perfect flying weather. The two Jayhawks arrived at the Emma Jean's position. Lieutenant Dutra radioed back to Air Station Cape Cod, that Emma Jean was "dead in the water" and was listing about thirty degrees. The boat was smoking badly, but no flames could be observed on deck.

An order was given by Captain Ludowsky for the two Jayhawks to conduct a grid search. It would be another three hours before the Black Hull arrived on scene. Captain Galloway had reported that the three injured fishermen did not appear to have life threatening injuries, and it was determined that they would be transported by the Jayhawks onto the cutter when it arrived for further medical evaluation and treatment.

Lieutenants Hale and Cooley began the grid search. The seas were smooth as glass; visibility was excellent. Cookie was known as one of the best spotters in the Coast Guard. He grew up in a small town near Lexington, Kentucky, and had never seen the ocean until he reported to boot camp at New London, Connecticut. He spent his youth hunting and fishing with his dad in the backwoods and hollers. He became an expert tracker and hunter, bagging a twelve-point buck when he was just twelve years old, making him a minor celebrity in the local newspaper. Those tracking skills and 20/10 eyesight made him a natural at search and rescue. Cookie would often boast that he could spot a pimple on a tick's ass at 500 yards.

• • •

The two Jayhawks had continued the grid search covering about 200 square miles of the North Atlantic when Lieutenant Cooley radioed Lieutenant Hale and reported that he spotted what appeared to be a body at his ten o'clock. Both Jayhawks banked left for a closer look. Cookie hovered over the scene at an altitude of just thirty feet, the rotors rocking the life suit violently back and forth. It was quickly determined that the life suit did not have an occupant.

About twenty yards from the life suit, Lieutenant Hale spotted what appeared to be a small, black suitcase and what appeared to be a pair of jeans drifting aimlessly on the surface of the ocean. Lieutenant Hale radioed Lieutenant Dutra, and a decision was made to send out a rescue swimmer (RS) to retrieve the items. Lieutenant Hale ordered RS Bryce Harper into the water to retrieve the three objects. The helicopter door was opened, and the rescue swimmer jumped into the swirling backwash made by the Jayhawk's rotors. Lieutenant Hale ordered that the basket be lowered. RS Harper gathered all three objects, which were then subsequently put in the basket and lifted onto the helicopter. The retrieval was textbook, and the Jayhawk continued its grid search.

What appeared to Lieutenant Hale as an ordinary retrieval made no sense to Cookie. He had gotten to know a lot of local fishermen on Cape Cod, and it was well known to all who put to sea that suitcases, particularly black ones, were bad luck, a sign of death or illness. The origins of this myth are murky, but sailors believe that black is the color of death and a metaphor for the depths of the dark, cold sea. How had a black suitcase made its way onto the Emma Jean?

CHAPTER FOUR

A crew member from the cutter spotted the Emma Jean at 1200 hours. Commander Dutra decided to first airlift the three injured men rescued from the sinking Emma Jean onto the landing pad of the cutter. They would then proceed to airlift Captain Medeiros off the Emma Jean. Lieutenant Hale hovered over the Olivia Rose and lowered the basket onto the trawler's deck. Christian DeJesus gingerly got into the basket, hoisted onto the helicopter, and transported to the cutter. Next was Manny Sousa and last in the basket was Barry Gomes. All were transported over to the cutter without incident. Once on the cutter, the men were immediately sent to sickbay for medical attention.

Lieutenant Cooley's next rescue would be more difficult. At this point, the Emma Jean was listing about forty degrees. The backwash from the Jayhawk's rotors knocked the boat back and forth making a rescue off the ship's deck almost impossible. Cookie signaled to Captain Medeiros, who was wearing his life jacket, to jump into the water. An

RS would jump into the sea and help the captain get into the basket. Cookie couldn't believe his eyes. Medeiros was refusing to abandon ship and was signaling he wanted the basket to be lowered to him on deck. The Emma Jean was about to capsize.

Rather than prolonging the stalemate, Cookie decided to retrieve the captain from the deck. The helicopter rotors made for a treacherous rescue. The boat was rocking back and forth, making getting the basket into the proper position difficult. The basket jerked wildly, hitting the captain, and nearly knocking him over. Finally, the basket was able to stay in place long enough for Captain Medeiros to leap in and be hoisted onto the Jayhawk. Once in the chopper, Cookie told the captain that he had put everyone at risk by not abandoning the ship.

Captain Medeiros replied, "Sorry for your troubles, but a real captain stays with his ship."

Cookie did all he could not to tell Medeiros he was an asshole, but he just sighed and proceeded to transport him onto the deck of the cutter.

Health Services Technician (HST) Lara Engalls had already begun medical treatment of the three crew members. Gomes had no injuries. Both DeJesus and Sousa had second degree burns on their hands and arms. All were hooked up to IV drips to prevent dehydration. Ensign Engalls also applied Silvadene, a topical antibiotic ointment used to treat burns and prevent infection. Ensign Engalls could tell both men were in obvious pain but declined pain medication.

"Are you sure you don't want anything for the pain?" queried Ensign Engalls.

"No. No drugs," said DeJesus. "I've seen too many junkies on the boats."

Just as DeJesus's injuries were addressed, Captain Medeiros entered sickbay. Ensign Engalls asked the captain to remove his wet clothes.

Captain Medeiros bellowed, "I don't take off my clothes for any woman but my wife." He then demanded to be seen by a male medic. Ensign Ingalls calmly told the captain that she was in charge, and he would have to be seen by her. The captain shrugged his shoulders and muttered something in Portuguese under his breath. Then to Ensign Engalls' surprise, the captain began to take off his clothes, which appeared to have a noticeable amount of blood on the sleeves. Blood on the crew's clothes wouldn't be unusual, but the captain spent most of his time in the pilothouse, which was not normally a bloody job. The captain's clothes were bagged, and he was given a johnny and blanket for the examination.

Engalls asked the captain, "Are you in pain or injured?"

"I'm just a little sore, but thanks for asking," replied the captain.

Ensign Engalls did not observe any burns on his body, only minor cuts to his hands and lower arms.

She noted that throughout the examination, Captain Medeiros kept muttering to himself, repeatedly.

"I don't know how the hell that fire started, a grease fire doesn't flash like that."

Ensign Engalls cleaned up the captain's minor cuts and applied bacitracin to prevent infection.

With impatience in his voice, Captain Medeiros said, "I need to get back to my men. Are you done yet?"

With one eyebrow cocked, Ensign Engalls replied, "You know, you're not making my job any easier. All right, you're good to go."

The cutter radioed the Emma Jean's position to Sea Tow so she could be towed back to the Boston Coast Guard Station. Sea Tow arrived on the scene about an hour later and began towing the smoking hulk back to Boston for further investigation.

A northeasterly wind was kicking up. The skies darkened as the cutter plowed through the chop and back to port. The air was thick, and the forecast called for possible thunderstorms. The return trip to the USCG Station Boston took four and a half hours due to a stiff twenty mile per hour headwind. The cutter docked at the Boston Station. An ambulance was waiting at the dock, and the three crew members were to be transported to Massachusetts General Hospital for further evaluation.

CHAPTER FIVE

The captain, who had been examined and medically cleared by Ensign Engalls, was escorted off the cutter by two special Coast Guard Investigative Services Division agents. Captain Medeiros was led to a small conference room on the first floor of the main building at the Coast Guard station to be interviewed. Petty Officer First Class Robert Halloran and Petty Officer Roger McCloskey would conduct the interview.

Petty Officer Robert (Bob) Halloran graduated from Boston Latin with honors. After graduation, he worked a series of odd jobs, including construction and security guard, before deciding to join the Boston Police Department. Bob graduated from the Police Academy and was stationed at precinct B-2. The precinct included Roxbury and part of Mattapan, two of the highest crime districts in the city. The ethnic makeup of the district is mostly African American. Officer Halloran worked hard at getting to know the locals and their culture and was mostly accepted into the community. The Crips and

Bloods claimed turf in the area, and there were constant shootings. Bob liked the job but was tired of arresting criminals only to see liberal judges release them the next day at court.

The last straw came after putting in a long shift where Bob chased down a career criminal who had three outstanding warrants. He tackled him hard on Mass Avenue, cuffed, and stuffed him into the cruiser for a trip to the station. The guy filed a complaint for excessive force, and the internal Affairs Board subsequently investigated Bob. He was suspended without pay for two weeks. That's when he decided it was time for a change. He had always loved the sea and decided right then to join the Coast Guard.

Petty Officer Roger McCloskey also had a police background. He grew up in Gloucester, a famous North Shore fishing port. He spent his teenage years working on the trawlers and scallopers that filled the port. The money was great, but the work was brutally hard and sporadic. The weather could change in an instant. The boats went out in the wind, cold, snow and rain. It didn't matter. Sometimes in the winter, the ice would build up on the boat, and the crew would have to break it up with sledgehammers. After one trip trawling for groundfish off Stellwagen Bank, he slipped on the wet deck and badly injured his back. After the boat got back to port, Roger decided to hang up his slicks and join the police department.

He graduated from the Police Academy with honors and soon joined the Gloucester Police Department as an Auxiliary Officer. The assignments were boring, and the pay wasn't a working wage. After six years of trying to secure a full-time position with no hope in sight, he decided it was time for a change. Roger grew up on the sea, knew how to run a boat, and could read the ocean like a Rand McNally Atlas. After a dull, mind-numbing Friday shift, he gave his notice. He went to the local Coast Guard recruiter the next day and signed up for a four-year stint. The sea's sights, sound, and smell pulled him back to a love that had never left him.

The two investigators and Captain Medeiros gathered around a small table in the conference room. The building had air conditioning, but, in the stifling July heat, it wasn't getting the job done. Before the interview even began, all three men were sweating profusely. Halloran stated the obvious.

"Sorry it's hot as hell in here, but the air conditioning has never been worth a damn in this building."

Captain Medeiros replied, "Maybe you two are just trying to turn the heat up on me." He slumped into a chair, looking more like he was about to watch the Patriots game on Sunday rather than being grilled by two Coast Guard Investigators.

Petty Officer Halloran began the interview.

"How long have you been a fisherman?"

Captain Medeiros replied, "I've been fishing since I was twelve. My old man was a day scalloper. He would take me out with him on the weekends. I didn't grow up playing baseball and Boy Scouts like the other kids. I grew up hanging around the waterfront. The old-timers would teach me the tricks of the trade if they were sober and in the mood. It's a tight-knit group on the docks. Mostly Portuguese. Also, a lot of Cape Verdeans. When I turned sixteen, I dropped out of school, hooked onto a boat, and worked my ass off for ten years. I'm a fast learner. I moved up the ladder until I became a captain. I've had my boat for the last three years."

The questioning began to take on a sharper tone as Halloran asked questions about the crew.

"How long have you known your crew, and how did you hire them?"

Captain Medeiros looked the investigator straight in the eye.

"All of my crew are well known on the docks. Fishermen jump from boat to boat depending on the fishing season. Reputations get made fast. There are few secrets on the docks. All my men have no bad habits that I know of. There are a lot of drugs on the boats. It used to be worse years ago, but the problem still exists. I try to stay out of their personal lives. After a trip, we dock at the fish house, and the catch gets offloaded. The fish get sorted and weighed, and then I get paid. The crew gets paid a share of the catch depending on their job on the boat and experience."

The Captain, eyes narrowed, with his index finger jabbing the air and voice rising, pronounced, " anybody who uses drugs on my boat is a dead man."

"After getting paid, we usually make a beeline for the Widows Cove Tavern. The joint has been a hangout for fishermen and dockworkers for forty years. The only guy who didn't go was Manny Sousa. Once he got paid, you never saw him again until the next trip. I don't know why he never joined us at the bar. From what I heard; he drank plenty at the Portuguese American Club. He didn't have much to go home to. His wife left him last year for an old boyfriend who had just gotten out of jail. She took off with this loser and took Manny's two-year-old daughter. Manny was pissed and wanted to kill the guy. On top of it all, the court was making him pay child support even though he could only visit his daughter on Sundays. It seemed like every time he was back in port, that bitch was dragging him back into court to squeeze more money out of him.

"In a good year, a fisherman can make over $100K, and she wanted all of it. Manny had to work a second job, helping his uncle, Mario, in his plumbing business."

Chief Petty Officer McCloskey asked the captain, "What do you know about the other three?"

Captain Medeiros continued, "Everybody calls him Hank—Hank has been fishing and working on the docks for at least ten years. He is a quiet guy, kind of keeps to himself out at sea. Hank is a hard worker. I never heard anyone say anything bad about him. I don't know much about his personal life. He has a steady girlfriend, Lucy. She tends bar at the Widows Cove. That's how they met. She pours a mean Dark 'n Stormy."

"He has custody of Henry Jr., his nine-year-old son from a past relationship that went bad. He loves that kid. The mother had a drug problem. was in and out of Rehab. It never worked. You still see her in the city, hanging around the bus station, trying to score dope. The courts finally gave him custody of his kid."

"Hank started as a shacker. A shacker is the new guy. He gets stuck with the worst jobs: cooking, cleaning the deck, and other dirty jobs that need to be done on a boat. Shackers also get the smallest share of the catch. Usually, a guy will work as a shacker for a year or so and, if he's good, gets moved up to mate. That's what happened with Hank. The only other thing I know about him is he likes to ride his Harley Fat Boy and hang out at the Widows Cove."

The captain went on, "I don't know much about DeJesus, only that he came from Cape Verde two years ago on a work visa. New Bedford has a

WIDOWS COVE

big Cape Verdean population. They're hard workers. Christian has family in Cape Verde. He stays with a fisherman who lives in the city. I like the guy. He was a quick study and did everything I told him to do. The guy works like an animal. He would join us at the Widows Cove after a trip for a couple of pops. Never saw him drunk, though. No girlfriend that I know of. He would send most of his money back to the old country. I think he was saving his pay and planned on eventually moving back to Cape Verde. You can live well there on $30,000 a year. "Cape Verde is still poor. There is a long tradition of leaving the islands for a better life in America. They still come to work here and many settle in New Bedford. The Cape Verdean Festival is one of the biggest in the city. The festival is in July. It's centered around the docks, and it's chaotic. Those Cape Verdeans really know how to party! You get the best Jag in the world from street vendors at that festival."

Halloran and McCloskey interrupted, "What the hell is Jag?"

With a smack of his lips, the captain said, "It's a mix of spices, rice, and beans. Christian never missed the festival. It was the only time he would ever turn down a chance to go out and fish. If you're ever in New Bedford, look me up. I'll take you to a great Cape Verdean restaurant, Izzy's. The best Jag in the city."

"I'll take it into consideration," said Halloran. "This probably won't be our last conversation. Anything more on DeJesus that might stand out?"

The captain replied, "Not that I can think of."

McCloskey chimed in.

"What about Gomes? What do you know about him?"

"Not much," replied Captain Medeiros. "He came on at the last minute. Freddy Sylvia was supposed to be on this trip, but he called out at the last minute. He said he had the flu. Freddy has been with me since I first bought the boat. Good guy, but he's never been able to work sick. Most of these guys can be dying, but they'll still go to sea. The money is too good but not Freddy. I guess he's not about the money. Barry Gomes was a last minute replacement. I called Gil Galloway, and he recommended him. That was good enough for me."

Petty Officer McCloskey stood against the conference room wall while Halloran questioned Captain Medeiros. Since working together, they developed their technique of interrogation. One would begin the questioning while the other observed from the background. Then they would change places. The observer was focused on body language. Did the person seem at ease? Did they have their arms folded, seem fidgety or unfocused, or sweat profusely?

After the interview, the two investigators got together to compare notes. Psychologists have done research that indicates that 90 percent of communication is nonverbal. You can learn much about the person being interviewed just by watching their body language. McCloskey noted that Captain Medeiros seemed cool as a cucumber. He almost seemed to enjoy the attention.

CHAPTER SIX

Bob Halloran looked Captain Medeiros straight in the eye and said, "Well, why don't we get down to business? What do you know about the fire and your missing crewman?"

Captain Medeiros took a long pause and looked down at the floor after what seemed like an hour and said, "We had finished fishing for the day," Captain Medeiros said. "The nets were in. Christian was in the galley, cooking up a chicken stir fry. I was in the pilot's house and the rest of the crew were on deck because it was a beautiful, clear night. The sky was lit up with stars. When you get far enough out to sea, away from the coast, the stars are so bright and seem so close that you could almost touch them. On my boat, the crew takes turns cooking, but Christian is the best cook I have ever had. He makes a shrimp Mozambique that's to die for."

The captain continued, "Anyway, everything is quiet. Then, suddenly I see Christian running from the galley onto the deck and screaming bloody murder. With his thick accent, I could hardly understand a word he was saying. All I heard was 'grease fire.' Those are words you never want to hear when you're out on the ocean! Everybody starts heading toward the galley. I scrambled down from the pilot's house and got to the kitchen at the same time as the rest of the crew. The smoke was so thick I couldn't tell where the fire started. I grabbed a fire extinguisher and sprayed it all over the galley. Then I saw flames. They were getting bigger and the heat more intense. The next thing I knew, the kitchen exploded, and flames were shooting everywhere. The force of the explosion knocked all of us off our feet. It was chaos. Manny, Christian, and Barry were all screaming and headed back up on deck. I couldn't see Hank with all the smoke. I tried to put the fire out, but the heat and the smoke knocked me back. I could tell we were in serious trouble and gave the order to abandon ship. The crew grabbed life vests and jumped into the water. I thought they all made it off the boat. All my men are good swimmers and in good shape. I was confident they would make it. Meanwhile, I stayed onboard to fight the flames and try to save her."

The captain paused for a moment now and shook his head. He continued.

"The battle finally started going my way, and I got the fire out. I went up on deck to ensure everyone got off the boat. I could see Manny, Christian, and Barry in the water, but no sign of Hank. I went up to the pilothouse, grabbed my binoculars, and did a

360-degree search of the ocean. There was no sign of him anywhere. I tried to yell to the men, but they had drifted about 300 yards from the boat and were out of earshot. The boat was listing badly, and I thought she might sink. I went back to the pilothouse and radioed Gil. I knew he was fishing in the same area. He got on the radio, and I told him what happened and that men were in the water and the Emma Jean was sinking. Gil told me he was on his way, and he could get to our position in about twenty minutes and hold on! I was apprehensive about the crew being in the water. It was July. But that far out in the North Atlantic, the sea is still cold. A man would only last about an hour without a life suit."

Captain Medeiros took a breath and a sip of water and then continued.

"My next call was to the Coast Guard Station in Boston. I told the radioman what had happened and gave him my position. Then I paced the deck and waited. I saw the Olivia Rose come over the horizon. She pulled up about twenty yards from my boat, and I could see Manny, Christian, and Barry on deck. Gil was on deck too, and yelling, 'Where is the other crew member?' I yelled back that I didn't know but that the Coast Guard was on their way and were going to search for him. Gil pleaded with me to abandon ship, but I told him I wasn't going anywhere. He said a few choice words back to me. The next thing I remember was the cutter showing up and airlifting me off my boat. The rest, they say, is history. The Emma Jean is a complete loss. I know that. I just can't make sense of what happened."

"What's bothering you, Captain?" McCloskey asked.

Captain Medeiros replied, "All my men are trained in fire protection. A grease fire on a fishing boat is not an unusual happening. I've probably helped put out a half dozen myself. A couple of sprays from a fire extinguisher, and that is the end of the problem. Christian knows how to put out a grease fire and there is a fire extinguisher right next to the stove. I do not know what the hell happened there. I have never witnessed a fire spread and blow back as quickly as it did. Something just doesn't add up. I hope you guys can get to the bottom of it."

McCloskey replied, "That is the plan. A couple more questions before we wrap up. Is the Emma Jean insured?"

The captain's face began turning a deep shade of red.

"What kind of dumb ass question is that? Of course, she is insured. Do you think I would take my boat out into the North Atlantic with a four-man crew without insurance? You do not know much about seafaring for a Coast Guard man."

McCloskey was not finished.

"We found a black suitcase in the water; what do you know about the suitcase, Captain?"

With an icy stare, the captain replied, "You are not getting any smarter with age, investigator. Every fisherman knows you don't bring a suitcase onto a vessel, especially a black one. It is considered bad luck. If any of my crew tried to pull a stunt like that, they and their suitcase would be sitting on the dock."

To cool down the conversation, Investigator Halloran jumped in.

"Okay, Captain. We're done here for today. Thanks for your cooperation. I'm sure you want to get back to your family. We will be in touch. The FBI may contact you. We will get to the bottom of this, Captain."

Captain Medeiros let out a loud sigh and left the room.

CHAPTER SEVEN

FBI Special Agent Robert "Rob" Ragusa was sitting at his desk at the FBI's Boston office, eating an egg salad sandwich from Finagle a Bagel when the phone rang. On the other end of the line was Investigator Bob Halloran.

"Rob, we have a case that I think would be right up your alley. Have you heard what happened to the dragger, the Emma Jean, out of New Bedford?"

After putting down his half-eaten egg salad sandwich, Rob replied, "Hey Bob, it has been a while. It's good to hear from you. Yes, of course, I have heard of her. It is all over the news. WBZ and other heavy hitters were interviewing the captain outside your Coast Guard station. He seems like a real piece of work."

Halloran chuckled.

"Yeah. He's a salty character. That is for sure. Think of Quint in Jaws, but a little rougher around the edges." Then he added, "The higher ups have decided to turn the case over to the FBI for investigation. I think you would be perfect to be the lead investigator, with your background. The Coast Guard will be there to lend support. We do not mind playing second fiddle."

"I appreciate your confidence in my ability, Bob, but I'm curious, why get the FBI involved?"

"Well, Rob, there is no conclusive proof, but some suspicious items were found at the scene. I'm not sure the captain is telling us everything he knows. My gut instinct tells me there was foul play on the Emma Jean. My partner, Roger McCloskey, feels the same way."

"All right, Bob. Let me clear it up with my supervisor. I will let you know either way."

"Okay. Sounds good, Rob. I look forward to working with you. I think the last time I saw you was on the softball field. It was the final game of the Southie Summer League.

Rob chuckled.

"Yeah, you are right. How could I forget! You dropped that pop-up. It cost us the title."

CHAPTER EIGHT

Special Agent Rob Ragusa was born at City Hospital in Boston's South End. The hospital was built in 1864. Its mission was to provide care for "the poor and those needing public charity." Boston City Hospital served its mission for over one hundred years, finally closing its doors in 1996. Boston University Medical Center bought it, and it is now part of the Boston Medical Center, a first-class facility known for its research.

Rob grew up in a three-decker on East Sixth Street in South Boston (Southie). It's said you're not allowed to call it "Southie" unless you were born and raised there. Nobody knows where this rule came from, but it is strictly enforced by the locals. Rob grew up in this heavily Irish enclave with his younger brother and parents. Italian Americans in the 1960s and 1970s faced challenges that seem ridiculous now but were very prevalent back then. Rob heard slurs while walking home from Gate of Heaven Elementary School on East Fourth Street during his childhood. Greasy guinea, and WOP to name a couple.

Rob's father, Salvatore, owned a pizza parlor, Big Sal's, on Broadway. Best slice in Southie. His younger brother, Vincent, became a Greyhound bus driver and married a local girl, Margaret Shaughnessy. His mother, Regina, stayed home and cared for their close-knit family.

Rob was not much into sports like the other kids in the neighborhood. In the third grade at Gate of Heaven, he took an interest in the piano. When the nuns would occasionally take a break from berating the students and rapping on their knuckles with a ruler for minor infractions, the nuns offered piano lessons after school. Rob began taking piano lessons at the school's convent. It provided him with a retreat and a way to express himself. Rob took lessons throughout high school, eventually landing gigs in a local band, Condiments for Cannibals. They played heavy metal, a lot of AC/DC and Slayer. The band played every dive from Boston to the South Shore and Cape Cod. Rob lived at home and attended classes at UMass Boston during the day. Because he lived at home, he could stay financially afloat with student loans and his meager earnings from the band.

Growing up in Southie, the stronghold of the infamous hoodlum, Whitey Bulger, Rob had taken an interest in law enforcement. Whitey had run Southie like his own kingdom until he went on the lamb after being tipped off by a dirty FBI agent. Rob found this fascinating and eventually earned a bachelor's degree in criminal justice. The FBI just seemed like something special. Doesn't everyone want to belong to something special?

Rob's father had a connection at Boston District Court, and Rob got hired as a probation officer (PO). The caseload was enormous, and Rob found the work to be dull. On one such day, he was bitching with another PO, Phil Hughes, in the lunchroom about the job. Phil told Rob that he was applying to the FBI to be a field agent. Rob probed his fellow PO for more information and decided on a whim to apply. To his surprise, Rob was contacted by the FBI for an interview. Getting hired by the FBI is not an easy feat. After surviving intensive interviews, a full-field background check, work references, and a grueling exam, Rob still had to pass a drug test and physical. He passed with flying colors.

The chief of probation, Wayne Hamilton, gave Rob an excellent reference. He had always been an A student from kindergarten through UMass Boston. He passed the exam with a ninety-five. He didn't use drugs and running five miles daily made passing the physical a breeze. Rob was sent for the twenty-week training course at the FBI Academy in Quantico, Virginia. He packed his bags, hugged his parents, and headed south on Route 95. Rob completed the twenty-week training program and was hired on as a special agent.

His roommate at the Academy, Pete Duenas, was a big fan of the 1970s sitcom, *Laverne & Shirley*. One of the show's characters was Carmine Ragusa, a.k.a. "the Big Ragu." The nickname stuck. Upon graduation, Rob was stationed at the Boston Field Office.

CHAPTER NINE

Rob looked forward to working on the case with his old softball friend, Bob Halloran. Before working on the case with Bob, Rob needed to obtain approval from his supervisor, John Ring. Agent Ring had just been promoted to Special Agent in Charge (SAIC) six months ago. Prior to his new position, he had been stationed in New York as a field agent for fifteen years. He was ten years younger than Rob and a bit cocky in a way that only New Yorkers can be.

Rob had been passed over for promotions in the past. He just was not much of a politician. He was still feeling out John, but his initial impressions were that John was a company man who played by the rules. He would back you up to a point, with the caveat that if an operation in the field went south and it was you or John going down for it, it would not be John Ring.

Rob walked into SAIC Ring's office. John was behind his desk on the phone. He finished his call and signaled Rob to sit in a well-worn leather chair.

John asked, "Have you heard about what happened to the trawler, the Emma Jean?"

Rob sat down.

"Yes, I have. It's all over the news. I even got a call from the lead investigator, Bob Halloran, at Boston Coast Guard Station, and he would like us to get involved in the case. We're old softball buddies going way back. I used to play with him years ago in the Southie Summer League. We still talk."

John had a curious look on his face.

"Rob, why does the Coast Guard want us to get involved in a trawler fire off Georges Bank? I would think that would fall under their jurisdiction."

"Bob told me that one of the chopper pilots out of Air Station Cape Cod found a suitcase, life vest, and other interesting items on the water near the Emma Jean. A crewman is missing, and Bob thinks foul play may be involved. He interviewed the captain and had doubts about his story. Things just do not add up. He also thinks the fire is suspicious. Apparently, it wasn't your ordinary grease fire. It spread quickly, and there was a backdraft. Bob described it as possibly an explosion. I've known Bob a long time. His instincts are good. If he thinks the Emma Jean needs to be investigated, it does. I would like to be assigned to the case."

Agent Ring looked away for a minute.

"Rob, you are only six months away from retirement. Are you sure you want to get involved in a case like this?"

It didn't take Rob long to respond.

"Yeah, I do. I would like to work with Bob Halloran, and I have not been to New Bedford since I played in a band at Widows Cove back in the late eighties. It has been a long time since I have had a good Portuguese steak."

Special Agent Ring studied Rob's face.

"Okay, the FBI can get involved under the Crimes on The High Seas Act. I am assigning you the case. Why don't you head down to Otis? Oh, it's now called Air Station Cape Cod, and get the ball rolling."

"Thanks, John, I'll get right on it. If I leave now, I can beat the Cape traffic."

CHAPTER TEN

Rob made his way through the empty parking lot and jumped into his twenty-year-old Cadillac Deville and headed onto Route 93 for the hour-long drive to Otis. My Caddy is a boat, but I like a big car just in case you get into an accident—more padding around you. The interior of the car smelled like my menu from the week before. An intoxicating mixture of stale corned beef, soy sauce, and spareribs.

It was a Thursday in July. When it came to weekend traffic on Cape Cod, Thursday was the new Friday. It was a typical hot July day in Boston. Triple H: hazy, hot, and humid. I popped a Roy Orbison CD in and settled in for the hour ride to the Sagamore Bridge. Massachusetts was known for its aggressive drivers, fondly known as "Massholes," and I admit, I'm no different. I sped along at eighty miles per hour as I weaved in and out of traffic. Any vehicles traveling under eighty got the treatment. A blasting of the horn, a flipping of the bird and some choice words. Nobody was spared. Old people, delivery drivers, pickup trucks. It didn't matter.

Usually, the Sagamore would be backed up for miles getting onto the Cape. The bridge was a two-lane road built by the Army Corps of Engineers in the 1930s when the Model T still ruled. It was built as access to the Cape across the Cape Cod Canal. The bridge was never designed to handle the thousands of Cape residents and tourists who swarm over it today.

The back-up traffic was only about half a mile long. I crossed the Cape Cod Canal and headed toward the Sandwich entrance to Joint Base Cape Cod. Joint Base Cape Cod, formerly known as Otis Air Base, was a sprawling 22,000-acre complex that housed the Army National Guard, Massachusetts Air National Guard, Cape Cod Air Station, and the Coast Guard Air Station Cape Cod.

I drove to the security gate and gave the Military Policeman (MP) my FBI identification and driver's license. The MP reviewed my credentials, returned them, and then asked, "Where are you going?"

As I returned my ID to my wallet, I replied, "I have an appointment with Commander Ludowsky at the Coast Guard Air Station."

The MP got on the phone and called over to the Air Station. After a brief conversation, the MP leaned through the window of the caddy and said, "You are cleared. Do you know where you are going?"

"I have no clue. Never been on the base before in my life."

"Here. Take this map. I've circled the Coast Guard headquarters."

I thanked him and was waived through. I headed toward the building that housed the Coast Guard commander. The base was enormous. I would drive another ten minutes before arriving at the commander's headquarters. After getting briefly lost, I pulled the caddy into the parking lot. I took a few minutes to get my bearings and think about how I wanted to approach the meeting.

I felt a knot in my stomach as I entered the building. Something about authority figures still does not sit right with me. I still have not gotten over my Gate of Heaven days. A young blonde female was sitting behind the plexiglass partition and talking on the phone. She was dressed in a blue knee-length skirt and white silk blouse. She was obviously a civilian. Too young to be retired from the military. Attractive in a girl-next-door kind of way. I continued to wait, and the receptionist continued to talk on the phone, not looking up. Finally, to get her attention, I mustered up a cough. She glanced my way and nodded. At least she knew I existed. She finally hung up the phone.

"How can I help you, Sir?"

"I have a 1:30 p.m. appointment with Commander Ludowsky."

"Okay. Did you sign in? And may I see some identification?" I slid my FBI ID and driver's license through the opening in the plexiglass.

She gave them a glance and said, "I will let him know you are here. Please have a seat."

After waiting fifteen minutes and reading the sports section of a three-day old copy of the Cape Cod Times, an ensign in uniform opened the door to the waiting room and said, "Right this way, sir."

The hallway leading to Commander Ludowsky's office seemed too clean. It was sterile in a way that reminded me of Mass General, the hospital I visited many times as a teenager when my grandfather was dying of stomach cancer.

The commander's office was at the end of the hallway. His name and rank were prominently displayed in gold and white letters on the office door. Commander Ludowsky was seated behind an enormous dark oak desk, probably worth more than my caddy's Kelley Blue Book value. Though he was seated in a chair behind his desk, it was obvious that he was an enormous man. When he stood up, he had to be at least six-foot-five. His snow-white hair was cropped close in a military style. In full dress uniform with more medals and ribbons than I could count, I could not help thinking, if a military commander needs a commanding presence, this guy has it in spades.

"What the hell are you waiting in the doorway for? Come on in. I'm Jason Ludowsky, Base commander, and you must be Special Agent Rob Ragusa from the FBI Boston field office."

I approached the commander's desk, reached out, and shook his hand. It was a death grip that made me wince. It reminded me of an old time Boston wrestler from back in the sixty's— Killer Kowalski—whose signature move was the "Claw." Killer would grab his opponent with one hand in his adversary's chest until he submitted.

"That's some handshake you have, commander."

"I believe you can learn a lot about a man just by his handshake," said Rob.

The commander looked at Rob and said, "So, what have you learned about me so far?"

"That you are all business, all the time. That is what I think."

The commander looked pleased and queried, "Rob, where's the rest of your team?"

"Unlike movies, sir, or TV, most FBI cases are handled by one agent. It is the Bureau's philosophy because they want the agent to take ownership of the case. The theory being that the agent will be totally vested in the outcome."

The commander nodded as if to agree.

"I oversaw the search and rescue of The Emma Jean. It seemed like an ordinary rescue until one of my helicopter pilots conducting the grid search found some interesting items floating on the sea near the trawler. I'm sure you know by now that one of the crew is missing. They found a pair of jeans, a small black suitcase, and a life vest. I've already debriefed the helicopter pilot, George Cooley, who retrieved the items. He is supposed to be off duty now, but I kept him around. Thought you might want to talk with him."

"I sure would, and I'd like to look at what he fished out," Rob replied.

"We bagged the items, and nobody has touched them other than the rescue diver and Lieutenant Cooley. The suitcase has not been opened."

The commander got on the phone. I could hear him ask whoever was on the other end of the line if they would summon Lieutenant Cooley and bring in the items found at the rescue scene. A few minutes went by, and Lieutenant Cooley entered the commander's office carrying plastic sealed bags containing the items he had found. He gave his commander a crisp salute. Commander Ludowsky returned the salute and signaled Lieutenant Cooley to place the sealed bags on the credenza against the wall. He pointed at the Lieutenant sitting in the other chair in front of his desk. Lieutenant Cooley stood in stark contrast to the commander. Short, about five-foot-seven and wiry, he appeared to be about thirty to thirty-five years old. His dark hair length was just under what the Coast Guard would allow.

"Well," bellowed Commander Ludowsky, "why don't we have a look?"

I gently slipped on a pair of latex gloves and began to open the first bag. The orange life jacket was standard equipment on any commercial fishing boat. Any doubt that it did not belong to the Emma Jean quickly disappeared. Written in indelible marker was the name, Emma Jean. I moved to the second bag and opened it. It contained a pair of well-worn blue jeans, size thirty-four waist and a thirty-inch inseam. The jeans were bloodstained. The blood stains were not particularly unusual. Fishermen had all kinds of stains on their clothes. Since fishing is one of the most dangerous jobs in the world, it could easily be blood from a fish or an injury while fishing. I placed the jeans back on the credenza and went to open the last bag. It contained a small, black suitcase. Not an expensive suitcase, more like the kind you buy on sale at JC Penny. By now, Lieutenant Cooley and Commander Ludowsky had gathered behind me. The suitcase had two three-digit tumblers on each side of the handle.

The commander asked the obvious question.

"Well, Agent Ragusa, aren't you going to open it? You've piqued my interest."

I shot back, "I cannot just tear it open, commander. I could damage evidence."

I had a briefcase years ago that I bought at a Staples store in Dorchester. The standard combination from the factory was 000. Could I get this lucky? Just for the hell of it, I turned each tumbler to 000, clicked both latches simultaneously, and the briefcase popped open. Pure luck! It was immediately clear, though, that seawater had seeped into the case. We all peered into the briefcase like we were the first people to see King Tuts tomb in 2,000 years. We all glanced at each other with the same look of bewilderment. I carefully began to gently remove the items from the briefcase.

I reached into the suitcase and took out a 9 millimeter Sig Sauer P365 handgun. Before moving the gun from the suitcase, I checked that the safety was on. The gun had been exposed to water, but that didn't mean it couldn't still fire. Next to the 9 millimeter was two loaded fifteen-capacity clips. These clips stood out because this was Massachusetts. The state has some of the strictest gun laws in the country. Massachusetts law prohibited magazine capacities over ten rounds.

Nothing else was immediately visible. I carefully scoured all the compartments of the suitcase, and in a small pouch in the right inside corner was what looked like a napkin or tissue. Somehow it had stayed dry. I carefully extracted it and placed it face up on the credenza. It was a cocktail napkin with bold, red print: The Widows Cove Tavern. Scribbled on the napkin was a telephone number, 774-274-5555, and the name Wolfie. The other side of the napkin had sixteen random numbers on it. I ran my hand around the case's lining and hit something solid. Stuck under the lining was a motel key for the Moby Dick Motel, room 12, and a drink chip from the Kings Inn.

I had played with my group, Rob, and the Riptides, at the Widows Cove Tavern in the nineties. I remembered the Moby Dick Motel as a seedy, cheap motel in Dartmouth, an upper middle-class town that borders New Bedford. The motel is located next to a strip joint, the Kings Inn. The Kings Inn is the Dollar Store version of strip joints. I visited it once or twice, years ago, after playing gigs at bars in New Bedford. The high-class strip joints were in Providence. The Kings Inn was for locals on a budget. Low cover charge, cheap beer, twenty-dollar lap dances and with some of the girls, a chance for a little more excitement at the Moby Dick Motel next door.

I bagged each of the items separately.

The commander asked, "What do you make of it, Agent Ragusa?"

"I have no idea, Sir. I'm going to pack everything up and get it to the lab for testing."

With that, I gathered all the evidence, thanked Commander Ludowsky and Lieutenant Cooley for their help, and made my way to the parking lot. I packed the evidence in the trunk of my caddy, thinking the whole time that these pieces fit together somehow. If I can figure that out, it will lead me to their owner and shed some light on what happened to Emma Jean.

CHAPTER ELEVEN

By now, it was 5:00 p.m. The Mid-Cape Highway was moving west at sixty miles per hour, toward the Sagamore Bridge. Traveling east on the Sagamore would be backed up for miles with tourists coming to the Cape for their annual vacations. As I approached the bridge, I could see the passenger cars, RVs, pickup trucks, and motorcycles all moving at a snail's pace coming over the bridge across the canal onto the Cape.

It was amazing that all these people would save their hard-earned money to spend their summer vacations on Cape Cod. The Cape is beautiful, with nice beaches, top notch golf courses, deep sea fishing and the best seafood on the East Coast. Every town on the Cape seemed to have a clam shack, or oceanfront restaurant voted the best lobster roll on the Cape. To pass the time, I started taking note of the cars' different license plates: Pennsylvania, Ohio, California, Maine, New Hampshire, New Jersey, New York, and Connecticut, many with bikes on bike racks, pulling campers, four wheelers, and other expensive toys.

I made it over the bridge and headed back up Route 3 toward Boston, making great time. The line of traffic in the opposite direction was mesmerizing with its endless rows of brake lights. I could imagine the frustration of those drivers sitting in their cars full of noisy kids, in ninety-degree weather all asking, "Are we there yet?" Hell on Earth.

I breezed through the city and headed over the Tobin Bridge toward Chelsea. On the left was the TD Garden. A new corporate name for what would always be known to me as the "Boston Garden." There I had seen countless Bruins and Celtics games with my father. We would get on the Massachusetts Bay Transit Authority trolley or more commonly known as the "T" at Andrews Square in Southie. Then after a stop at South Station where, like clockwork, my father would get a regular coffee with two sugars from the kiosk, we would transfer onto the Orange Line to Haymarket Square. From there, it was about a ten-minute walk to the Garden. That ten minutes could seem like an eternity in January when it was twenty degrees outside.

I thought about my idealized memories of the place's smells, sounds and sights. Sausage vendors on Causeway Street. Hawkers selling memorabilia. So many great memories of my youth's sports heroes played here. On the ice: Bobby Orr, Pie McKenzie, Ray Bourque, Gerry Cheevers, Phil Esposito. On the parquet: Bill Russell, John Havlicek, the Chief

(Robert Parrish), Kevin McHale, and the legend, Larry Bird.

New Englanders still think of the old Boston Garden with romantic nostalgia. The glory days were kept alive by the Boston sportswriters and tales handed down of championships from generation to generation. The reality was quite different. The Garden was dirty, smelly, and hot. It lacked modern amenities like air conditioning. If you went to the game after the circus was in town, there was a good chance you would come out with elephant crap on your shoes. That was overlooked because nobody could forget the magical moments that happened there. Havlicek stole the ball, Bobby Orr flying across the ice as he scored the goal to win the Stanley Cup in 1970, and countless others.

I left my trip down Boston Garden memory lane just in time to change over two lanes without signaling and got off at the Beacon Street exit. Chelsea was separated from Boston by the Mystic River. A movie with the same title was produced in Boston and starred Sean Penn. It was based upon the exploits of Whitey Bulger, best known as the crime lord of Southie, but who also was associated with the Winter Hill Gang in Charlestown.

Unlike Southie and Charlestown, Chelsea had mostly been passed over by the gentrification of the 1980s and 1990s. The three-deckers were still occupied mostly by working class people, laborers, plumbers, teachers, nurses, and the like. The face of the city had changed. It was no longer a haven for immigrants from Europe but now more of a mix of all races seeking the American Dream.

As I returned to the FBI field headquarters on Maple Street, I passed through Chelsea's business district. There was an eclectic mix of nail salons, pizza joints, neighborhood bars, restaurants and too many empty storefronts. I pulled into the parking lot and pondered the events of the day. This case looked more like a marathon, not a sprint. Many interviews needed to be conducted, starting with Captain Medeiros, his crew, and the owner and employees of the Widows Cove Tavern. Two of the three surviving crew had suffered minor burns. If they had been released, I would need to head back to New Bedford quickly before they hooked onto another fishing boat and headed out to sea.

I went into headquarters and caught up to John just as he was about to leave the office.

"Hi, Rob. How did you make out with the Coast Guard?"

"Well, I spoke to the pilot who recovered a few items found in the water near the Emma Jean. I also spoke with the commander. He was cooperative, helpful and had a strong presence. I sure would not want to be on his bad side if, you know what I mean. The evidence is bagged and in my car. I'm going to bring it over to the lab for fingerprinting and forensic testing before I head home."

"Great. I need to get home, Rob. My son has soccer practice tonight, and he needs a ride. We'll talk about this tomorrow."

"No problem, John. If you do not mind, I would like to get down to New Bedford ASAP. If possible, I want to talk to the captain of the Emma Jean and the crew. I do not know if the crew will still be in port or heading out to sea on other boats. Most of these fishermen spend their money as fast as they make it and need to keep working. There is also a lead worth pursuing with a bar in the city, the Widows Cove Tavern."

The Widows Cove was an eclectic mix of fishermen, local businessmen, the occasional tourist, and on weekend nights, students from nearby UMass Dartmouth. I wondered if Steve Poole still worked there all these years later. Being the bartender, Steve would know if there was any worthwhile gossip in New Bedford. With what seemed a genuine sense of concern, John offered some parting advice.

"Be careful down there. The Federal Hill wise guys still have reach around the waterfront. We put the Codfather and Frankie 'the Hammer' Costa behind bars, but Frankie's back out and lives nearby. Nobody knows what he is up to, but he's dangerous. You are not likely to receive a warm reception."

CHAPTER TWELVE

I headed out to my caddy to get the evidence bags to the lab before they locked up for the day. The FBI's Regional Forensic Lab opened at our headquarters in Chelsea in 2019. Before that, we had to send everything to Quantico for testing. They did a great job down there, but it delayed things. The field office can get information much more quickly now that the lab is down the hall. The lab also works with the Massachusetts State Police and local law enforcement.

I grabbed all the evidence bags from the trunk and took them to the lab. Lenny Page, a Forensic Specialist, was about to lock up.

I yelled down the hall, "Lenny, I got a few presents for you before you head home."

Lenny looked tired.

"Come on, Rob. I'm beat. Can't it wait until tomorrow?"

"Afraid not, Lenny. I've got some evidence from the Emma Jean, including a firearm. Can you please secure them in the vault?"

I handed the evidence bags to Lenny. Following protocol, Lenny opened the vault, tagged the items, and put everything in the vault.

"You are a real pain in the ass, Rob. I will get to these tomorrow."

Back to the Caddy. Next stop, the Kowloon Restaurant on Route 1 in Saugus. It's Miller time. Well, more like Mai Tai time and a PuPu platter for one. The place is legendary. It's like the Disneyworld of Chinese restaurants. It is huge, and it's been there forever for two reasons. The best Chinese food around and Benny, the bartender. I am not a big drinker, but I love the vibe at the Kowloon. It is busy and loud. The kitchen door swings back and forth in perfect rhythm. An army of servers and busboys brings some sense of order to the chaos. You never know who you are going to see at the bar. Local comics, singers, and sometimes someone you recognize from TV or movies. Mostly however, its clientele is populated by police officers, firemen, businessmen, blue-collar workers. Like the old television show *Cheers*, a place where everyone knows your name.

Chinese restaurants are my vice. I've visited most of them in Boston, the North Shore, and the South Shore. I sample a Mai Tai at every one of them. Nobody comes close to making a Mai Tai like that of Benny. Just the right mix of rum and pineapple juice. Most people think a Mai Tai is a Mai Tai, and they are alike. I beg to differ. This is a major newcomer mistake. The best ones are made from scratch with pineapple juice, white, and dark rum. To save time, some Chinese restaurants use a Mai Tai mix. It is not the same. I never had a bad Mai Tai from Benny Wu.

After a stop at the Kowloon, I went to my condo, right down the road off Route 1 in Saugus. I moved to Saugus for three reasons. It is a ten-minute drive to the office, the prices for real estate are half that of Boston, and finally, I live five minutes from the Kowloon.

Pulling off route 1 onto my quiet street, I arrived at my condominium complex, Evergreen Hill. The complex has seventy-five units. It's nothing fancy, but the complex has a courtyard, barbeque area, and outdoor space, providing a nice summer space. The landscape crew does a great job. Flowering plants cover the grounds in summer, and the parking lot gets plowed as soon as the flakes start falling in the winter. I love it, no maintenance. There's also an indoor gym with a surprisingly decent mix of weights and cardio equipment. A step up from those cheesy gyms you find at Holiday Inns. The thing I hate the most about going to the gym in the winter is having to pack a gym bag and change at the gym. In the complex, I can just get into my gym clothes and go, which is much easier.

I know my cat, Trixie, will be at the door to greet me. Not because she loves me, but because she wants to get fed. Cats are low maintenance. With my job, a dog wouldn't work. I could leave Trixie for a day or two if I had to. She would just need some extra food, two bowls of water, and a clean litter box.

I do not mind living alone. It's quiet, and I can come and go when I want, walk around in my underwear, drink milk straight from the carton, leave the toilet seat up, and eat Chinese take-out seven days a week if I'm in the mood. There is no significant other, no Mrs. Ragusa. I just never met the right one. Maintaining two loves—the FBI and a woman—is hard. There have been a lot of girlfriends, but it never went to the next level. I have not given up hope, though. The right one is still out there. I just need to find her.

It was about 8:00 p.m. when I opened the door, and Trixie is there meowing. I usually fill her bowl with some Purina Cat Chow Sensitive Stomach. It is the only brand of cat food she'll eat. It was time to hit the recliner and catch up on the local news on WBZ. The condominium isn't much, but it's mine. Most of the furniture came from flea markets and yard sales. That also goes for the kitchenware. The salad bowls are not old Cool Whip containers, but it's close. I spent some money on my Lazy Boy leather recliner and my fifty-inch big screen TV. You must have your priorities straight.

After watching about twenty minutes of the local news and hearing the usual drumbeat of rapes, murders, and car accidents, I drifted off to sleep. I wish

I could say this is unusual but not really. I have not cleaned the sheets on my bed for a month; no need to. They do not get much use.

The sun beamed through the living room window, waking me up. Legs draped over the side of the recliner, Trixie purring in my lap. A quick shower, shave, and clean set of clothes, and it is off to New Bedford. First stop, the Widows Cove Tavern.

CHAPTER THIRTEEN

I last visited New Bedford on my last gig at the Widows Cove Tavern thirty years ago. Traffic was light, and the drive down took about an hour. I didn't need my GPS to point me in the right direction. It had been a long time, but I still remembered the route by heart. As I exited onto Route 18, I noticed the city had changed. Route 18 parallels the harbor and is the main highway into the city. The trawlers, draggers, and scallopers were still in port just like I remember them in the early ninety's. New Bedford is known for fishing, but it was also a manufacturing hub until the 1980s when the shoe and textile industries started moving to Mexico and China in search of cheaper labor.

I continued down Route 18, where some of the factories looked like they had been converted into office space or apartments, but more than one of the ancient brick buildings still resembled decaying hulks of a forgotten time. I turned up Union Street, New Bedford's main drag, and on the right was the Widows Cove Tavern. It sat there with a neon sign blinking OPEN in the front window.

It was like I had entered a time warp. At least from the outside, nothing had changed. The sign was the same. A picture of a mermaid surrounded by the words the Widows Cove Tavern still hung above the front door beckoning in thirsty mariners. Time had taken its toll, and the mermaid looked a little worse for wear than in 1992, with flecks of paint chipping off her brown hair. I do not remember parking meters in the city back in the day, but they seemed to be everywhere now.

The city needs to pay its bills somehow now that the factories are gone. I looked at my watch, and it was 10:15 a.m. Not a problem in New Bedford. Most of the bars were open by 10 a.m. or earlier.

I walked through the front door and was surprised. The inside had changed. It was not a yuppie bar, but some of the character of the place had been lost. When I played there in the late eighties and nineties, half the tables would rock, and you needed mastery in cocktail napkin folding and precision matchbook placement under the appropriate table leg to maintain stability. The tables were the same, but they were now covered with tablecloths decorated with a nautical theme. I looked behind the bar, and I recognized many pictures of patrons, most of them dead by now. Everybody had a nickname. I recognized Mac and Shep circa 1991 each hoisting a Narragansett dressed in old style New England Patriots Jerseys. There was a dusty picture of the harbor after Hurricane Bob, sailboats tipped over like bowling pins and seawater lapping across Route 18, and an eight by ten picture of an old timer, Ernie, sunburned with his shirt off, long gone but not forgotten at the Widows Cove.

Hal, the owner, had decided to venture into the art world. Local artists selling overpriced paintings and framed photographs of local scenes, sailboats, lighthouses, sunsets, and cobblestone street scenes adorned the bar's back wall next to the cash register. I wondered how many had been sold. New Bedford was coming up, but had it arrived yet?

As I approached the bar, I noticed a tall, white-haired man come out of the kitchen. He turned and looked at me, and before I could open my mouth, I heard, "Rob, how the hell are you?"

I could not believe it! It was Steve Poole. He looked a little heavier, and the curly mop of hair was now white, but it was him. The voice sounded the same.

"You're Rob Ragusa, aren't you?"

"How do you remember me after all these years?" I shot back.

"You look the same. I knew it was you right away," Steve replied warmly.

"I appreciate the compliment, but you need your eyes checked. I am twenty pounds heavier, and I don't have to comb my hair as much. I thought the Widows

Cove would be a stopover for you until you figured out what you wanted to do for the rest of your life?"

Steve rubbed his head and said, "Well, I got to like the city and the cast of characters who come here, so I just kept hanging around. Hal still owns the place, and he takes good care of me. What brings you to our fair city?"

"I wish it were a social occasion, Steve, but I'm here on business."

"What kind of business are you in, Rob?"

"I am a field agent for the FBI. I am down here working on the Emma Jean case."

With that, Steve's looked down at the floor. He waited a minute to respond.

"Well, it's great to see you, Rob, but I wish it were under different circumstances."

Steve waived me over to a seat at the bar. "Have a seat. I think you are going to be here awhile."

The bar stools had been replaced, no longer the hard backed stools that challenged your lower back muscles. The new version was all black soft cushioned, and somewhat luxurious, at least for the Widows Cove. The old stools all seemed to slope in one direction or another. I remember the last one at the bar near the bathroom sloped about thirty degrees. Even if you were sober, you looked like you were half in the bag in that stool because you had to hang on with your left hand to keep from sliding to the floor. Hal blamed the building. It was built in the

1880s, Somehow the new stools had magically cured the physics problem.

I sat down at the horseshoe-shaped bar. The bar top looked like it had been refinished with polyurethane but in a testament to the old days, the cigarette burns from another era still shone through the gloss, each one a reminder of a time when the cigarette smoke was so thick it burned your eyes. Steve had to answer the phone. While he was writing up a take-out order, I couldn't help thinking that it was great to see Steve and walk down memory lane, but I wondered, what does he know?

Steve knew everything that went on in the city. Everyone from the mayor to dockworkers felt comfortable talking to Steve. The Widows Cove was a hangout for all walks of life. If word got out that he was talking to the FBI, his life might be in danger.

CHAPTER FOURTEEN

Steve had only been a bartender for about a year when I first met him in 1992. Everybody loved Steve. He was gregarious, always in a great mood, and always up for a good time. The first time I met him, it felt like I had known him my whole life. He has a way of putting you at ease. Anything could happen when he worked. He played guitar and the harmonica, and if he liked a song we were playing, he would come out from behind the bar and jam with us. Of course, the place was packed, and the patrons were looking for food and drink refills. Steve didn't care, and neither did the regulars. It was part of the charm. If you didn't get it, there were plenty of other bars to drink cheaply in New Bedford, but none had the vibe of the Widows Cove. The patrons liked the oldies at the Widows Cove. When I played there, I borrowed a drummer and lead guitarist from another Boston band, and we transformed from my heavy metal band, Condiments for Cannibals, to Rob and the Riptides. There was lots of Jimmy Buffet, Tom Petty, and the Rolling Stones. I liked this music better than heavy metal, but other than the Widows Cove, playing these sets at other bars would get me a beer bottle upside the head.

Many Friday nights after the last stragglers ambled out onto Union Street, Steve would pour me a sixteen ounce Narragansett, and we would talk, at first about how the night went, local politics, the Red Sox, and small talk. Eventually, when he got to know me better and trusted me, he opened up about his life.

Steve was from a wealthy South Shore banking family. He had told the story of his grandfather saving Rockland Trust during the Depression by keeping the bank afloat with his life savings. The bank became one of the largest regional banks on the East Coast. I remember Steve telling me he was in the ROTC in college at the University of Vermont. After college, the family business came calling. He was on the path to becoming the bank's Chief Executive Officer when he suddenly quit in 1990. At first, I thought he was joking, but he wasn't. He never talked about money, but I did get out of him what his salary was when he quit: $200,000.00. I had asked him why he would leave that kind of money behind. I remember him talking about a difficult divorce and his young daughter. He told me that he was living on his 40-foot sailboat and one day called his supervisor at corporate headquarters and just quit.

I recall him saying he had no plan and no money. The divorce lawyers had gotten that. The story sounded like it came from the pages of a dime store novel. On his last day at the bank, Steve took his Movado watch, threw it into Cape Cod Bay as a parting gesture to corporate America, and embarked on an unplanned life of simplicity and adventure. I remember thinking, who does this? I still thought this might be delusional on his part, a work of fiction; but other patrons and workers in the bar backed up his story.

Steve said he sailed from Plymouth into Provincetown harbor the day after Memorial Day, 1991. Memorial Day is the unofficial start of the summer season on the Cape, and Provincetown was a sea of tourists from all over the country and day trippers. Provincetown is a colorful town in the summer. Long a mecca for gays, the main drag in town is Commercial Street. During the summer season, the streets are packed with gay men, lesbians, transvestites, and tourists snapping pictures with their cell phones. He told me that he walked up Commercial Street, taking in the scene, not knowing where he was going nor what the future held. Steve said he noticed a help sign at the Edgy Oyster Restaurant.

Steve walked in and ordered a martini. He asked the bartender about the help wanted sign. She got one of the owners. Anna emerged from the kitchen. Steve said he inquired about the job, and she asked him if he would be willing to wash dishes. He nodded yes. She grabbed his martini off the table and said, "Come with me. You start now."

Two lesbians, Anna, and Anna owned the restaurant. Steve said he just referred to them as Anna One and Anna Two. He spent the summer of 1991 washing dishes, sleeping on the boat, and taking in Provincetown's sights, smells, and sounds.

Before our last gig at Widows Cove, I had asked him how he ended up in New Bedford and why he didn't stay in Provincetown. Of course, there was no simple answer. I remember he said it was mid-August, and a powerful hurricane was coming up the coast headed for southern New England. Steve had told me that the harbormaster told him it wouldn't be safe to remain in the harbor and that he should head for a safer harbor like New Bedford to ride out the storm. The tourists and day trippers had packed up and headed out of Dodge. The only people left in town were a few locals and summer workers who did not have enough money to get off Cape and ride out the storm.

Most of the restaurants and bars in Provincetown were closed or closing, including the Edgy Oyster. Steve packed up, left port, and sailed for New Bedford's sheltered harbor. Steve's boat, the Jennifer Dale, was a forty-foot cutter ketch. She was his baby, and he babied her. Sailing and music are Steve's passions. He worked to live, not lived to work. Steve drank life from a full cup. After mooring in New

Bedford harbor, he headed up Union Street for a beer and a sandwich. The neon sign at the Widows Cove was blinking OPEN. He went in, and the rest, as they say, is history.

The owner, Hal Naworski, was behind the bar that afternoon. Steve asked if there were any job openings. Hal was looking for help and asked Steve what he had made at his last job. When Steve told him $200,000.00, Hal said, "I don't think I can match that!" He was offered a dishwasher position that day. He accepted and eventually worked up to be a bartender and then bar manager.

Steve started his first shift that day, half a step in front of Hurricane Bob. Steve was living on his forty-foot sailboat and rode out the storm alone on the boat. The New Bedford Hurricane Barrier was built in 1962, and when closed, provided excellent protection against such a fierce storm. Steve liked to regale the regulars at the Widows Cove with stories of his man-versus-the-elements tale of riding out Hurricane Bob. In truth, it had been one hell of a storm and wreaked havoc up and down the New England coast. I remember him saying that even with the hurricane barrier, pleasure boats were scattered like bath toys on the New Bedford and Fairhaven side of the harbor. After checking his boat for damage, other than taking on some water, there was none. Steve returned to the Widows Cove and was stunned to find the place packed and hopping. Hal had shown some foresight and bought a generator. The lights were out all over New Bedford, but not the Widows Cove. It became a mecca for those wanting to get out of the house. That was the beginning of the legend of Steve Poole and the Widows Cove Tavern.

After almost thirty years, I could not help thinking I had never met anyone quite like Steve Poole and probably never will. Such a unique guy. Most people I have met in my life lead ordinary and predictable existences. Steve's life is right out of a Hemingway novel. I guess that is why the details of his adventures are still so vivid in my mind.

CHAPTER FIFTEEN

After the one patron in the bar had finished his morning revelation and left, it was time to get past the reminiscing and speak in the present.

"Steve, I know you have a lot of connections in the city, and if it still holds true, the Widows Cove has always been the best place to hear about the latest scuttlebutt on the docks. What do you know about Captain Medeiros and his crew?'

"Rob, you are right about that. Nothing has changed since the '90s in that regard, but wouldn't you do better to speak directly to the captain and crew? They all live in the city. You're with the FBI. I am sure you know how to find them."

"I know where to find them, and I'm going to interview them all, but a couple of pieces of evidence found in the sea near the Emma Jean brought me here Rob pulled out a photo of the burned hulk of the Emma Jean and slid it in front of Steve. Steve looked at the picture intently and just shook his head.

"Floating near the Emma Jean was a suitcase. In it was a cocktail napkin from the Widows Cove.

Written in ink was the name Wolfie; on the other side of the napkin was written a phone number, 774-274-5555. There was also a motel key from the Moby Dick Motel and a nine-millimeter handgun. Does any of this mean anything to you?"

Steve took a minute before answering.

"When the fishermen return to port, their pockets usually are flowing with money. Some of them used to head to the King's Inn for a little relaxation and adult entertainment. The Moby Dick Motel is right next door, and if a lap dance weren't enough, some dancers would further entertain the patrons there. I do not know anything about the handgun. Lots of folks own nine millimeters. I cannot help you with that. In terms of a phone number, doesn't the FBI have the ability to track that down?"

"Of course, and we do. It turned out to be a burner phone—not traceable. Steve, how about the name Wolfie? Does that ring a bell with you?"

"Yea Rob, the name Wolfie does ring a bell. A group of about five guys came in about six months ago. They were not regulars and didn't seem like locals. These men were dressed too well, and they all sat at a table. I only remember them because there was no waitress that day, and I waited on them. They were loud, obnoxious, and they shortchanged me on a $150 tab. One guy was the center of attention. Everyone at the table called him Wolfie."

"Steve, do you remember what he looked like?"

"Yeah. How can I forget? Short, stocky, make that fat, going bald, fifty-five with salt and pepper hair, a poorly maintained beard, and unfortunate teeth. After that I wouldn't say they were regulars; but they came in maybe once every two weeks, same crew, same table."

"Thanks, Steve. Before I head out, can you do me a favor? Give me a call if you remember anything else. Also, would you mind checking that phone number against any work records you still have? It's a long shot, but sometimes long shots pay off. Call me if that long shot comes in. It was great to see you, Steve."

"You too, Rob. Don't be a stranger and stay safe."

CHAPTER SIXTEEN

My next stop was the King's Inn and the Moby Dick Motel in Dartmouth. Dartmouth was about a ten-minute ride from New Bedford. I had the room key in my pocket. A little pop in visit from the FBI might jog some memories.

The King's Inn is an old school strip joint, that as I remember had a kind of corral as a stage. The girls would bump and grind against the wood fencing and exhibit their wares. It was not a particularly classy joint. The Providence mob allegedly ran it but that has never been proven. I pulled into the parking lot at 2:00 p.m. During off hours, only a couple of cars were in the parking lot. The Moby Dick Motel shared the parking lot with the King's Inn; very convenient.

I figured I would start with the motel. The office had a flashing neon vacancy sign with the letter V out of commission, which read ACANCY. I opened the door to the lobby and rang the bell on the counter. Nothing. So I kept banging on the bell until finally, a short dark-skinned man, who looked Indian or Pakistani, appeared from behind the wall.

In a thick accent, which I could barely understand, he asked, "May I help you sir?"

I flashed my FBI badge in front of the plexi-glass, and his eyes nearly popped out of his head. I have no personal issues with either strip clubs or cheap motels. In the past I have been a patron of both and will not get on my soap box. However, these folks are not usually forthcoming with information to law enforcement.

"Yes, mister FBI man, how can I help you?"

I flashed a picture of Hank Gonsalves in the desks clerk's face.

"Do you know this man?" He paused.

"Well, he looks familiar, but I can't quite place him, sir."

With that, I promptly plopped the Moby Dick room key, number twelve, on the counter.

"Oh yes, sir. Now I remember. He was a regular. Always the same room, once a week, always paid in cash."

I pushed further.

"What else do you remember about him?"

"Nothing, sir, but he was usually in the company of a dark-skinned woman, very pretty."

I left him with some reassurance, "Ok. Thanks for your help; you are not in any trouble."

I walked across the parking lot to the Kings Inn. It had not changed much since the 1990s. A bouncer was stationed at the door. If his main job was to scare the patrons into playing nice with the strippers, he fit the part. He stood about six-feet-four, biceps bulging, and tattoos covering both arms. His shaved head was completely covered in purple ink with a tattoo of a spider's web. Wearing a black T-shirt decorated with the Kings Inn name and logo in pink, he made a for an intimidating greeter.

I had not gotten a word out when he murmured, "Five-dollar cover, pal."

I flashed my FBI badge, and suddenly his demeanor seemed to change magically.

"What can I do for you, sir?"

That was more like it. I showed him a picture of Hank Gonsalves.

"Do you know this man?"

With a hand that would fill out an extra-large glove, he grabbed the picture and looked.

"Yeah, I know him. He used to be a regular, but he has not been around in a while, quiet guy, no trouble. He always came in with a girl, not one of ours."

"Ok, can you describe this girl?"

"Yeah, she was like light skinned black, maybe Cape Verdean. She went by the name of Cocoa."

"Anything else?"

"No man, she didn't work here. Look, I am on probation. I do not want any trouble."

"No trouble here, thanks for your help." specialist

I got back into the caddy, and my cell phone was beeping before I turned the ignition. It was Bob Halloran.

"Rob, we have the Emma Jean at the dock. She's in rough shape. They are going to put her in drydock for the investigation. I got a call from one of your guys, Special Agent Henry Avena. Do you know him?"

"Hey, Bob. Yes, I know him. He is our top forensic fire specialist"

"Great Rob. He's coming by the station to meet with me and Investigator McCloskey, tomorrow at 9:00 a.m. Can you make that meeting?"

"I am in New Bedford right now. I will try to interview Captain Medeiros while I am in the city, but I can be there tomorrow at 9:00 a.m. Agent Avena has investigated more than three hundred fires. If it was more than an accident, he is the right guy to get to the bottom of it."

"All right. See you tomorrow then. Good luck with the captain. He's a real joy."

I ended the call with Bob and called Captain Medeiros's home telephone number. A woman with a thick Portuguese accent answered the phone. I asked to speak with Captain Medeiros.

Her reply was, "Who you?"

I identified myself as an agent with the FBI. I do not think she understood a word I said.

After a brief pause, I heard her yell, "Frank, come to the phone. Some agent guy for you." In the background, I could hear the Captain, I assumed, saying what sounded like, "Who the hell is on the phone?"

The woman, his wife, responded abruptly, "Agent guy, agent guy on the phone, come."

The phone went silent for what seemed like an eternity before a voice from the other end of the line almost blew my eardrum out. By Investigator Halloran's description of the Captain, I knew it had to be him. The bellowing voice of Captain Medeiros on the phone greeted me with less than a warm welcome.

"Who the hell are you?"

"I am FBI Special Agent Rob Ragusa. I have been assigned to the case of the Emma Jean."

The captain's reply was quick.

"I already told those two investigators from the Coast Guard everything I know. Why is the FBI involved in a fishing boat fire?"

"Captain, one of your men is still missing, and we believe foul play may have been involved. I'm in the city and would like to meet with you if you can spare some time?"

"I assume you have my address. I'll see you only because it will save me a trip to your office."

Before the captain had a chance to change his mind, Rob blurted out, "See you in five minutes at your house."

As I reached the top of Union Street, I placed a call back to Bob Halloran. He picked up immediately.

"Bob, this is Rob Ragusa. I'm meeting with Captain Medeiros in a few minutes at his home. Any tips you want to share with me?"

"Not really, Rob, just bring a thick skin. You're going to need it dealing with him. He seems like a decent guy after you get past the salty language and rough exterior. By the way, I spoke with the commander. He would like to meet with both of us tomorrow at 1200 hours. He wants to debrief you and ensure the FBI and the Coast Guard are on the same page. The Emma Jean is on the news, and the case has become high profile. All kinds of rumors are flying around, and the commander wants full cooperation."

"I will be there, Bob. Maybe the captain can shed some light on what happened to the Emma Jean. He has had more time to think about it and perhaps remembers more."

"Do me a favor, Rob, mention the black suitcase and observe his reaction. I'll explain it to you tomorrow."

"Okay. Will do. I got to go. I just pulled into the captain's driveway."

I put the caddy on park, turned off the ignition, and before hanging up, remarked, "Bob, I do hope this was a simple galley grease fire, but that sixth sense you develop after years on the job is telling me we need to keep digging."

CHAPTER SEVENTEEN

Captain Medeiros lived off County Street. County street runs across the top of Union Street. It is the highest point in New Bedford. Today everyone wants to live on the ocean, and you pay a premium price for real estate on or near the water. It was just the opposite in colonial times. The wealthy sea captains and merchants lived on the high ground providing some protection from the inevitable nor'easters that batter the New England coast with regularity.

I drove slowly down a long driveway shaded by oak trees that had been saplings when clipper ships plied the harbor. The captain's house sat around a right-hand bend in the driveway—a white colonial with green shutters. If it weren't for the peeling paint, it could have been a set in a Hollywood movie. I pulled into an open space near the front door and put the caddy on park.

Built 1836 was written on a bronze plaque beside the doorbell. The house was two stories with a widow's peak on the roof. (A widow's peak was a small enclosure on the top of some homes where the fisherman's wife would look out over the ocean as the clipper ships came back to port, not knowing if her husband had survived the voyage.)

I rang the doorbell, and what sounded like a pack of wild jackals began barking furiously. I waited for what seemed an eternity as the dogs continued to bark and bang on the door. Finally, the door opened slowly, and the captain stood behind a screen door. The door didn't seem like much protection between me and what appeared to be two pit bulls, both with heads the size of a basketball and less fat on their bodies than an Olympic runner. Neither the captain nor the dogs seemed happy to see me. The captain greeted me with an obvious observation.

"What are you afraid of? A couple of little dogs? Fluffy and Buffy will not bite you."

I blurted out, "Fluffy and Buffy? Their names do not seem to fit the breed."

Captain Medeiros grinned and said, "I named them that because when someone comes over and asks if I have dogs, I say yes, two, Fluffy and Buffy. It's worth a chuckle every time I answer the door, and whoever is there almost shits their pants when they see the dogs. It does not take much to amuse me. They are harmless but good protection. This neighborhood is not what it once was."

I gingerly opened the front door and entered the foyer. The dogs were growling as I slowly stepped inside. I didn't know whether they wanted to be petted or take my right arm off at the elbow. I have been bitten twice by dogs on the job and learned a little from each experience. Do not appear afraid even though you're scared shitless. Move slowly, look at the dog, or in this case, dogs, directly in the eyes, and do not make any sudden movements. Dogs primarily go by smell and movement. Fluffy and Buffy were taking turns sniffing every part of my feet, legs, and balls. I didn't feel the need to rush them. After a minute or two they concluded that I was not a threat and sauntered into the living room.

The captain did not look at all like the stereotypical fishing captain. Somehow, I had visions of Quint from Jaws greeting me at the doorway, particularly after our brief phone conversation. Captain Medeiros looked more like an aging athlete: clean shaven, tanned, tall, and sinewy. He struck me as someone who, though probably well past fifty, could still hold his own in a bar fight. It was July and stifling hot, yet his flannel shirt and stained jeans strangely did not seem out of place. He shook my hand with the strong, well-weathered hands of a fisherman. His ruddy face showed the years he had spent on the sea with a full head of salt and pepper hair. Dressed up, he could have passed for an accountant.

"Well, don't stand there looking stupid; come in."

The captain may not have resembled Quint physically, but their personalities had much in common.

"Follow me into the living room and grab a seat," the captain said with authority. "I do not know why you're here. I already spilled my guts to the Coast Guard guys."

"Mr. Medeiros, I appreciate your cooperation with the Coast Guard, but this is a joint investigation between the Coast Guard and the FBI."

The captain shot back, "I will talk to you, but nobody calls me Mr. Medeiros. Call me Frank or Captain, your choice. I do not know what all the fuss is over a galley grease fire. They happen all the time. This one just got out of hand."

"Well, Captain, which is going to be investigated by our guys and the Coast Guard, but there still is a missing crew member."

Captain Medeiros replied, "I do not know what you know about the fishing business. It is the most dangerous job in the world. I cannot count the number of fishermen I know who have been hurt on boats. The North Atlantic is unforgiving. Bad luck or a mistake will send you to the bottom. I am not the hard ass you may think I am. Of all my years at sea, I have never had a man go overboard that we didn't get back in the boat. I have known Hank for years. He was a good man. I feel bad for this family, but he is probably at the bottom of the sea. The crew didn't have time to put on life vests."

"Captain, you just mentioned that you have seen other grease fires happen in the galley. What usually causes those fires, and how is the crew prepared to put one out?" I asked.

"The galley is small, and most of these guys aren't exactly culinary experts," the captain replied. "It is not much different from a grease fire at home. Someone does not drain the frying pan or cook something too hot on the stove. There is no special training for fire control. We are not in the Coast Guard. We have a couple of fire extinguishers on the boat. Everyone knows how to use them. Usually, within a minute or so, the fire is out."

My next question seemed obvious.

"Then why did this one get out of control?"

The captain looked at the floor and paused before answering.

"I have been racking my brain about that. I must admit a few things do bother me. I've never seen a fire spread that fast. Also, it may seem stupid, but Christian was cooking pork chops that night. They do not produce a lot of grease. Also, when I got down to the galley, it didn't smell like grease fire. It smelled like something else. I cannot quite put my finger on it."

"So, can you describe what you smelled?" I asked.

Without pause, he said, "It smelled like metal. I know that sounds crazy, but that is what sticks with me."

Just then, a petite woman with stark white hair came into the room with a tray of croissants and coffee. The captain looked at her and said,

"Agent Ragusa, this is my wife, Grace."

"Nice to meet you, Mrs. Medeiros," I replied.

She looked directly at the captain and, with a tone that reminded me of the nuns at Gate of Heaven School, said "My husband does not have the best manners. Would you like a croissant and a cup of coffee or tea? The croissants are fresh from the oven."

I quickly answered, "I think I'll take you up on the offer."

Mrs. Medeiros politely asked me, "How do you like your coffee?"

"Black, please, ma'am."

"Do not call me ma'am. It makes me sound old. Please call me Grace."

"Okay, Grace. Thank you. My Nona used to make homemade croissants. I used to love them. I still remember that smell. This experience brings back fond memories."

"Well, I will leave you two alone to finish your business. I will be in the kitchen. Please let me know if you need anything." Grace slowly walked out of the living room.

"I will, ma'am—sorry, I mean Grace," my response garnered a glance of disapproval from the lady of the house. The captain's wife surprised me. After many years as a field agent, I try not to stereotype people or enter situations with preconceived notions. Still, I did not expect such a refined woman to be the wife of Captain Medeiros, a man who being described as "rough around the edges" was an understatement.

I informed the captain, "We found some items of interest in the sea about half a mile from the Emma Jean."

"What type of items are we talking about?" he inquired.

"I cannot tell you everything now as this is an ongoing investigation. Let me ask you this. What type of personal items do the crew usually bring onboard?"

The captain responded, "Usually only their sea bag with their clothes, shaving kit, toothpaste, that type of thing. Of course, everyone now has a cell phone. They can only be used close to shore. No reception out at sea."

I leaned in a little toward the captain and asked, "Did any of the crew bring a black suitcase onboard?"

The captain leaped and yelled, "I told those two Coast Guard guys that nobody brings a black suitcase on a fishing boat. It's considered bad luck, according to an old fishing tale. Why are you asking me the same dumb ass question?"

"I can't tell you right now, but it's important to find out if something other than a grease fire happened on the Emma Jean."

The captain's tone turned hostile.

"Are we done here, Agent?"

"Yes, sir. If I have any more questions, I will be in touch. Thank you for your cooperation and hospitality."

The captain grunted, "I don't know what the fuss is about over a fucking grease fire."

I headed for the front door when Grace appeared and waved goodbye.

"Nice meeting you, Agent Ragusa."

Out the front door, I went and jumped into the caddy. Just as I started her up, my phone rang. On the other end of the line was a familiar voice.

"Rob, it is Steve. Are you still in town?"

"Yes. I was about to head back home. Good to hear from you. What's up?"

Steve replied, "If you have time, swing back to the Widows Cove. I've got something that might interest you on that phone number you wanted me to check."

"Okay, Steve. I'm on my way."

CHAPTER EIGHTEEN

On my way back to the Widows Cove Tavern, I got a call from Bob Halloran. The Emma Jean had been towed back to the Boston Coast Guard Station. The Coast Guard station is located on Commercial Street in Boston's North End. It's known as the Coast Guard's birthplace, the first operational station in the United States. Cutters and other Coast Guard vessels are docked at Allerton Point, which juts into Boston Harbor.

The North End of Boston is considered Boston's Little Italy. It has the distinction of being the city's oldest residential community. It's a bustling jumble of side streets, sidewalk bistros, Italian delis, and bakeries. The smell of freshly baked Italian bread, cannoli's and marinara sauce overwhelms the senses. Hanover Street is the heart of the North End, and it is bursting with Italian restaurants, from the high-end Strega, where a chicken parm will set you back $29, to Regina's Pizzeria, where you can get a large cheese pizza for $17. Regina's is one of the oldest restaurants in Boston, pumping out pies since 1926.

Do you want New York style pizza, deep dish pizza, thin crust, Chicago style? It's all on Hanover Street. Though only 0.36 square miles, the North End is home to over 10,000 locals who are packed into four-story tenements. Streets are narrow, and everyone knows everyone.

During the summer weekends, the North End swells with tourists as well. A staunch Catholic enclave, the residents of the North End celebrate a saint every weekend. They parade the saintly statues through the streets, and people throw money from their windows at the procession. Street food can be had on every corner and these parades are something to experience. Tourists love it. It's considered a must stop for any trip to Boston—as much as the Freedom Trail, Public Gardens, and Swan Boats on the Boston Common.

The FBI and the Coast Guard would conduct a joint investigation of what happened to the Emma Jean. Sea Tow arrived at the Coast Guard station at 6:00 p.m. The charred remains of the Emma Jean were towed into the travel lift, and she was strapped in and, ever so carefully, hoisted out of the water and lowered onto a flatbed truck. The investigation would be conducted in a hangar located right next to the docks. The hangar doors were shut and locked. This location would be the home of the Emma Jean until she gave up her secrets.

CHAPTER NINETEEN

I pulled onto Union St. and was suddenly reminded how hard it is finding a parking space in downtown New Bedford. The whole downtown cobblestone section of the city had only metered street parking. Today was my lucky day. A guy came out of the Widows Cove and jumped into a black pickup right before the entrance. He pulled out, and I pulled in. There was still time left on the meter! Maybe this day would end on a good note after all.

I walked back into Widows Cove, and the clientele had changed from earlier in the day. Now an eclectic mix of construction workers, local businessmen, and, of course, fishermen filled the bar stools and tables. At the two tables nearest the door were tourists armed with cameras. A ferry runs from New Bedford to Martha's Vineyard every day. Some of the tourists would take part of the day and explore the revitalized New Bedford historic zone. Once paved over with asphalt, the cobblestones in the downtown area had been restored to their original state. I noticed that downtown had changed a lot since I played

Friday night gigs at the Widows Cove in the '90s. New restaurants had opened, and there was an organic food store and a sprinkling of galleries. I had read in the Boston Globe that the Whaling Museum had undergone a multimillion-dollar renovation. New Bedford, a tourist destination? Could it be true?

I entered the bar, and Steve was running around like a madman, serving drinks and the usual pub grub as in most neighborhood restaurants. He spotted me and signaled me over to the bar. There was one seat left at the end near the bathroom, and I grabbed it.

"Rob, I think I might have something for you," Steve blurted out. "After you left, I finished setting up for the day and had some time before the lunch crowd. I reviewed all our current employees' files, and no hit on the phone number. You remember Hal, the owner, right?"

"Yes, of course, I remember him. Nice guy. Used to buy me and the guys in the band shots of Jameson if we brought in a good crowd."

"Well, he never throws anything out. He still has the records of the employees he hired when he first opened the joint. So, for the hell of it, I started going through old records starting with the most recent. It took a while, but I matched your phone number with a cook who worked here about a year ago. He got fired after six months because he was caught selling drugs in the bathroom. His name is

Wayne Barrett. Everybody called him Waxy because his skin was so pale, like an Albino. I have got his address if you want it."

I shot back, "Of course I want it."

"Ok, I have his address as 73 Willow Street, third floor. Willow is up in the north section of New Bedford, off Acushnet Avenue.

"'ll find it on my GPS. I'm going to head up there right now."

I let Steve know I appreciated his help. I waved goodbye, and as I walked out the door, I shouted, "Steve, it is great to see you. You have been a big help. This place brings back great memories."

Steve yelled back, "Come back soon when you can stay longer."

A meter maid stood near my car, waiting to put an orange ticket on my windshield.

I pointed at the meter, "One minute left, Sweetheart. Not today."

She glared at me and started walking up Union Street, looking for the next contributor to New Bedford's annual budget. I jumped in the caddy and set my GPS for Waxy's address.

• • •

As I approached Acushnet Avenue, an old familiar landmark came into view. Antonio's Restaurant. It looked the same as in the nineties when I would stop in for the best mouth-watering Portuguese steak in the city. A Portuguese steak is a heart attack waiting to happen. It is a thin pounded steak smothered in a spicy red sauce and a fried egg on top. It comes with fried potatoes. No substitutions. Not a vegetable in sight. The sauce is the key. Every Portuguese restaurant in the city claims to have the best Portuguese Steak and Shrimp Mozambique, but my vote is Antonio's. It was reassuring to see that they were still in business. As I passed the restaurant and turned onto Acushnet Avenue, my mind and my taste buds drifted back to that steak coming out of the kitchen. The smell of garlic and red pepper came flooding back.

I made my way up Acushnet Avenue, through a mix of retail stores and three-deckers in various states of disrepair lining the street. My GPS showed Willow Street coming up on the left at one hundred feet. 73 Willow Street was about halfway down on the left. I approached the address, a three decker with green peeling paint. A Ford Taurus that looked like it had not been on the road since the Reagan administration sat in the driveway.

Waxy lived on the third floor. I slowly made my way up the twisting steps. It was daylight and sunny, but the stairway was dark. It had one small window with a grime-covered shade blocking the light. I reached the third floor landing a little out of breath and sweating profusely. I had not climbed that many stairs in a long time. I could hear the television on in the apartment. I banged hard on the door.

"Mr. Barrett, I am Special Agent Robert Ragusa with the FBI. Can I have a word with you?"

Nothing, no voices, no footsteps, then the TV went silent. My internal radar detector went off, and I banged again hard with my left hand, my right hand on my Glock and still, I heard nothing. Still nothing. I had no legal reason to enter the premises, no search warrant, no reasonable cause. Still, I was running out of patience.

I was about to head back down the stairway when the door opened about an inch. A voice that reminded me of my Uncle Jerry, a three-pack-a-day Camel smoker, spoke.

"Can I see some ID?"

I took out my badge and held it up to the peephole in the door. The door opened slowly, and a gaunt man about thirty years of age stood in the doorway. His pasty white skin and sunken cheeks made me think, he must be Waxy.

I asked, "Are you Wayne Barrett?"

After about a thirty-second delay, the response came.

"Yeah, I am Wayne. Who is asking?"

"I am FBI Special Agent Rob Ragusa. Can I come in?"

"Why? What is this about?"

"It involves the Widows Cove Tavern. Please, may I come in?"

Waxy motioned me in and directed me to a gray threadbare couch occupied by a mangy calico cat. I sat on the sofa with stains that presented a visual history of what Waxy had eaten for the past six months. I positioned myself as far to the sofa's edge as humanly possible without slipping off onto my ass. Waxy was the type who liked to get right to the point.

"What the hell does an FBI agent want with me?"

"Did you hear about that fire on a fishing boat off Georges Bank? The name of the trawler was the Emma Jean. I've been assigned the investigation and am following a lead that involves the Widows Cove Tavern."

Waxy looked away and said, "Yeah, it was on the news. So. What has that got to do with me?"

"I do not know, Wayne. But your telephone number was found in a suitcase floating near the Emma Jean. Why would that be? You're not a fisherman, are you?"

Waxy replied, "Listen, first off, call me Waxy. Nobody calls me Wayne, not even my mother. Hell no. I hate fish. I cannot stand the smell of them, and I get seasick. I don't know why my number would be near a fishing boat."

"Did you ever work at the Widows Cove Tavern?"

"Yeah, I worked there for about six months last summer as a cook. That asshole owner, Hal, fired me. Said I was dealing drugs in the bathroom, but I was not, I swear. A lot of fishermen hang out there, and some of them use drugs, but mostly heroin. I stay clear of the stuff because there are many overdose incidents in the city. Me? I like beer and weed. That's it."

"So, what are you doing for work these days?" I asked.

Waxy replied, "Nothing right now. I am collecting unemployment. I'm looking for another job as a cook, but nobody seems to be hiring. I am behind two months on my rent, and my landlord is on my ass. I got to find something soon. Look, I am no saint, but I had nothing to do with anything that happened on that boat. I have been selling a little weed on the side to stay afloat. One of the customers wrote down my number. Pretty stupid, but some of these assholes are not too bright."

"Ok, Waxy, thanks for your time." I pulled out my business card. "Here is my card. If you hear anything, give me a call."

Waxy glanced at my card and put it in his pants pocket. His next stop, the trashcan.

I made my way down the darkened stairwell and onto the street. As I approached my caddy, I noticed it seemed to sit lower to the ground. As I got closer, it was clear that all four tires had been slashed. A group of about six teenagers were on their bikes nearby.

I yelled, "Did anybody see who was around my car?"

They responded with a deafening silence. New Bedford, even in the '90s had street gangs, real ones, like the Latin Kings. The saying on the street was, "snitches get stitches."

The kids shrugged their shoulders and took off on their bikes toward Acushnet Ave. I went to unlock my car and noticed it was opened. If the car alarm had gone off, I would have heard it from Waxy's apartment. His windows were open, and I could hear cars going by and people talking on the street during my interview. I opened the driver's side door, and there were two bandannas on the front seat, one black and one yellow. This bandanna color was that of the Latin Kings. I knew the North End of New Bedford had been Latin Kings' territory in the '90s. Some of the regulars at the Widows Cove lived there and told me twenty years ago that the neighborhood had gone to hell. New Bedford's gentrification program had not reached Acushnet Avenue.

The Latin Kings were the real deal, not a wannabe gang. They were known for drug smuggling, extortion, and prostitution all up and down the East Coast. Unlike popular belief, the Latin Kings were not strictly a Hispanic gang. Anyone could join if you could make it through the initiation process. So Waxy could be a Latin King, but I didn't think so. I didn't see any signs or symbols in Waxy's apartment that would lead me to believe he was affiliated with the Latin Kings. They had guessed I was law enforcement and were sending me a message that I was not welcome, or maybe there was a tie in with what happened on the Emma Jean. Or someone was trying to send a message had followed me to New Bedford. Was this related to the Emma Jean incident or was this just a coincidence? I did not know, but I was going to find out.

CHAPTER TWENTY

I called AAA and cooled my heels in the July heat for forty-five minutes until a tow truck slowly pulled down Willow Street. Rodrigues Brothers Towing was in big blue letters on the side.

The wrecker pulled up next to my car, and a bald guy with a deep tan yelled, "You call a tow?"

The heat and flat tires diminishing my usually sunny disposition, I snapped back, "Yes, sir. It's hard to drive on four flat tires."

He looked at my car, and you see the fifteen-watt lightbulb go off in his head. His brilliant reply was, "Oh wow, man! Somebody sure does not like you.

He hooked up the caddy, hauled it onto his flatbed, and asked me, "Where do you want me to tow it?"

"Chucks Auto on Route 1 in Saugus," I replied.

Geography was not his strong suit. He asked, "Where the hell is Saugus?"

I answered, "A little north of Boston."

"Have you got the gold card?" he asked.

"Yeah, I do. Here."

I pulled my gold AAA card out of my wallet.

He took a quick look and said, "Ok. That's good. You get one hundred free miles of towing."

With that, I jumped into the passenger side of the tow truck cab, and off we went, heading onto Route 195. I was not in the mood for small talk, but my politeness kicked in, and I introduced myself.

"It's going to be a long ride. Since we are going to spend some time together, I'm Rob."

"Nice to meet you. Sorry, it is under these circumstances. I'm Phil. Any idea who slashed your tires? You are obviously not from around here."

I responded, "No idea. You are right. I am not from New Bedford. I'm here on business. I used to play in a band about thirty years ago at the Widows Cove Tavern."

He surprised me when the tow truck entered the ramp onto Highway 495 North.

"No kidding. I live in the city and love that place. They have the best burger in New Bedford. I'm there all the time. Do you know Steve Poole?"

"Of course, I know Steve."

"Well, we have something in common, don't we?" I was warming up to Phil. At least on the ride to Saugus we could compare Widows Cove stories.

I decided to change the course of the conversation.

"You don't happen to remember a guy named Wayne Barrett, do you?"

"No. Doesn't ring a bell. What does he look like?"

"Tall, thin white guy. Like white, pale, thirties, maybe."

"Oh, you are talking about Waxy. He used to work there, cooking. I stayed away from that dude. He was bad news. A lot of rumors floating around the city about Waxy."

Potbellied Phil was beginning to pique my attention. This ride was going to be more interesting than I had anticipated.

"Would you care to share some of those rumors with me?" I asked. "You are from Boston, right? Why would you be interested in what happens in New Bedford?"

"Well," I replied, "let's just say I'm doing some research."

"You a police officer? Because I should just keep my mouth shut."

"Well, Phil, even if I am a cop, why wouldn't you talk to me unless you've got something to hide?"

"I ain't got nothing to hide, friend. I drive a tow truck. I am a hard worker, and a family man. Maybe I will buy a little weed at the Widows Cove occasionally. You know, it helps me relax."

The tow truck continued to lumber along as we reached the ramp onto Route 24. Traffic was not bad so far.

I said to Phil, "I do not care about your weed buying. Let's talk about Waxy. What was he into?"

It was hot in the cab. Ninety degrees, and humid outside, and the air conditioning in the truck was not keeping up.

Beads of sweat began to form on Phil's forehead, and he stammered, "I do not know much about the man, but I heard he was dealing. Not just weed but some heavier shit, heroin. Supposedly, the connection was in Boston. There have been a lot of junkies dropping dead in the city. Word going around is the dope is being cut with something, and Waxy was the local distributor. I bought only weed from him. Best price in the city and the best quality. Anyway, you didn't hear it from me."

I shook his sweaty, greasy hand and assured Phil, "Promise, I won't say a word."

The truck was nearing the ramp to Route 128 North. Without traffic, it would be another twenty-five minutes to Saugus. With traffic, two plus hours. I decided it was time to touch base with Bob Halloran. I pulled my cell phone out of my pocket as Phil merged into traffic on Route 24. I dialed Bob, and he picked up right away.

"Hey, Rob. Where are you? I'm heading over to the Coast Guard station. They are going to start the arson investigation at 3:00 p.m. I hope you will be there. Your arson guy called me. He is going to be there acting as the lead investigator."

"Well, Bob, the plan may have to change a little. I'm sitting in a tow truck heading up the Southeast

Expressway toward the city with my new best friend, Phil. I was not well received on my return to the Whaling City. No key to the city or Welcome Wagon. Just four slashed tires."

"Well, Rob, you were always good at making new friends. So, what is the new plan?"

"I will have the caddy dropped off at Chuck's Auto on Route 1 in Saugus. It's on the same side of Route 1 as the Kowloon Restaurant, about a mile past. It looks like traffic will be light going through the city. Can you meet me there in half an hour? Call the Coast Guard station and tell them we will to be a little late. I'll call my arson investigator at the FBI and tell him what's happening." "I am sorry to hear about your car. I will make those calls and meet you there."

My next call was to the FBI Arson Investigator at the Boston Field Office, Henry Avena. Henry was going to be leading the fire investigation of the Emma Jean. I had Henry's cell phone number in my contact list. We were making a good time. The usual bumper-to-bumper summer traffic was not happening. It was a typical mid-summer New England weather day: hazy, hot, and humid, the three Hs. We were just passing over the Zakim bridge when I placed the call. Henry picked up immediately.

"Hey Rob, Glad you called. I got tied up at the office. I might be a few minutes late getting to the Coast Guard station."

"Do not worry about it, Henry. I am crossing the Tobin Bridge in the cab of a tow truck, heading to my mechanic's garage in Saugus. Bob Halloran is picking me up at the garage, and we will head to the Coast Guard station from there. Bob is calling the Coast Guard and letting them know we will be late. So, do not rush. I will fill you in on what happened when I see you."

Henry replied, "Sounds good. Glad you are ok. See you in a few."

When I hung up with Henry, we were on Route 1, passing the Kowloon. Man, a Mai Tai would hit the spot right now, but that would have to wait. Phil wheeled the tow truck into the lot at Chuck's. Chuck came out of the garage. He knew the caddy well. He was the only one I trusted to work on her. I could buy tires anywhere, but I was loyal to Chuck and wanted to give him my business.

Chuck was wiping the grease off his hands with a rag. He pointed Phil to a corner of the lot where he wanted the car dropped. Phil obliged. My travels with Phil were coming to an end. I exited the cab, and Chuck yelled across the lot, "What the hell happened to your car?"

I replied, "Let us just say I was less than welcomed in New Bedford. I am going to need four new tires. Top of the line. I do not care about the price."

Chuck responded, "I am busy as hell today. It is going to have to be tomorrow."

Just then, Bob pulled in, driving his Jeep Wrangler. I slipped Phil a twenty and said my goodbyes. I jumped into the Wrangler, wondering who didn't want me in New Bedford. I didn't know whether I was just in the wrong place at the wrong time or was the tire slashing a message from someone involved with the Emma Jean fire.

CHAPTER TWENTY ONE

Before I had my seat belt buckled, Bob gunned it, and we soon headed south on Route 1 back toward the Tobin. Bob was weaving in and out of traffic until I finally leaned over and yelled, "I prefer to arrive a few minutes late than not at all. Slow down."

Bob shot me a look I interpreted as, this is your fault, not mine. I got the message. We passed a Statie on our left, finally getting him to throttle it back a bit. We crossed back over the Tobin and into the city. We exited at Government Center. There must have been nothing happening at the Garden because, as we merged onto Causeway Street, the traffic was light. We hit the traffic lights perfectly—all green—soon we were in the North End heading down Hanover Street. It was a sunny, warm day. Every Italian restaurant on Hanover Street had outside tables on the sidewalk. The smells and sounds made you feel like you were in Italy.

Traffic slowed and it was peak tourist season in Boston. The Duck Boats were out on the Charles River. The Freedom Trail was being explored, and the tourists were dining at alfresco in the North End. I love Italian food. I have eaten at most of the restaurants in the North End. My favorite was Strega, but you could not go wrong with any of them. They all claimed to have the best "gravy" in the city. My friends who were not Italian didn't know that gravy meant red sauce. The recipes would be handed down from Nona to the children, the grandchildren. The recipes were kept secret and guarded like the nuclear codes. Of course, my Nona Estelle thought hers was the best. Every Sunday, the family would gather around the dining room table at her second-floor walk-up on L Street and feast on spaghetti and meatballs. The TV would be off, and the matter at hand was the food and conversation. Some of the best days of my life were spent around that table. There was family present, and there was good food and conversation. Cannot ask for anything more. I still miss her.

We passed through the heavily congested restaurant row and pulled up to the guard station at the entrance to the Coast Guard station. After showing the guard our credentials, we were directed to a hangar near the water.

Bob asked, "Who will be the arson investigator in this case?"

I replied, "Henry Avena. He's our best man. I think you will like him. Nice guy. Knows his stuff."

We pulled into a parking spot near the hangar, got out of the Wrangler, and headed toward the hangar. I could spot Henry next to what I assumed were the remains of Emma Jean. A sorry sight.

Henry saw us and came toward us.

"How are you, Rob? Who's your friend?"

"This is Bob Halloran. He's the lead Coast Guard investigator assigned to this case. The FBI has the lead, so you will oversee the arson investigation. Investigator Halloran will be working with you. He has experience in arson, investigations, and crimes against persons."

Henry seemed slightly startled and said, "I thought this was strictly an arson case, Rob?"

"It may be, but we have a missing fisherman and a few other suspicious items in a suitcase floating near the boat. We are unsure of what happened on the Emma Jean, but it may involve more than a simple kitchen fire."

Henry shook Bob's hand and said, "Well, let's get the show on the road."

With an arson investigation, you are looking for the point of origin and burn patterns to determine how the fire started. It would to be difficult in this case because it quickly became apparent that almost everything that wasn't metal on the Emma Jean had burned. The surviving crew, including the captain, said the fire started in the kitchen and was caused by grease igniting. Grease fires are common, but they are usually put out quickly and do not cause this type of damage.

Henry had brought Astro with him. Astro was a three-year-old long haired German shepherd. He was specifically trained to smell accelerants. Henry, Bob, and I gloved up and carefully climbed onto what was left of the deck of the Emma Jean. Henry had Astro on a leash, and you could tell the dog was dying to be let loose. Astro liked nothing better than to do what he was trained to do. Henry let him loose, and he methodically started sniffing the deck from bow to stern. Astro could climb stairs better than most humans. He made his way up the stairs to the pilothouse. Nothing so far.

The next stop was the galley. As we entered, the smell was overwhelming. It was difficult to describe the smell: a less than enticing mix of burned wood, metal, and rotting food. I did all I could to not to lose my lunch. It did appear that the fire started in the kitchen. There was a burn pattern in the kitchen but not near the stove where it was reported the grease fire started. I noticed what was left of a toaster and pieces of metal on the countertop. Not steel but what seemed like pieces of an aluminum can. I motioned Henry and Bob over.

"You guys are the experts, but I think I found our point of origin."

Henry approached and gently unplugged the toaster. The outlet looked fine. Just then Astro caught a scent. He jumped up and put his front paws on the counter and started barking like crazy.

Henry started examining the toaster. As he looked inside, he said, "This fire was deliberately set. Come take a look."

Both Bob and I took turns looking into the toaster. We both chimed in at the same time,

"What are we looking at? It's a toaster."

Henry replied, "Look down at the bottom. You think you see crumbs. But they are not. I bet you the farm that they are tiny remnants of paper towels that were stuffed into the toaster. The only reason I know this is because I have seen it before. I investigated a fire in Brookline a few years ago. The husband used the same trick. Stuffed the toaster with paper towels, turned the toaster on and left. He thought there would be nothing left to trace. But there was. I got the toaster back to the lab and took it apart. Under the microscope I could make out tiny pieces of charred paper towel."

Bob asked Henry, "What about these pieces of aluminum all over the counter?"

Henry took a brush and began to scrape the pieces together.

He said, "I believe this was part of the plan."

Henry held up a charred piece of the aluminum label for us to see. The word Pam was visible.

"This was no coincidence. Whoever planned this did their homework. Pam is a cooking oil sold in aerosol cans. If left too close to a heat source, it will explode. When the toaster caught fire, the can of

Pam was right next to it. It exploded and that is what caused the flash over. I am going to bag up the toaster and the pieces of the Pam can."

Henry put the aluminum pieces and the toaster into separate evidence bags. We continued the investigation checking every square inch of the Emma Jean. The engine room, bathroom, the captain's, and crew's sleeping quarters and, best of all, the fish. Nothing quite like the smell of rotting fish to clear the senses.

We all climbed off the Emma Jean and headed back to the parking lot. As Henry headed to his car, he shouted, "Rob, I'll call you when I get the results from the lab."

"All right, Henry. Great job as usual." Then I added, "And give Astro a Milk Bone on me!"

I know Bob. He hates to admit that someone may know more than he does but I did hear him whisper, "You were right. That guy really knows his stuff."

Before we got back into the Jeep, I could see there was a text message on my phone. It was from Chuck's Auto. It read, Got lucky, my tire vendor was delivering in Saugus today. Dropped off four new tires, not cheap, top of the line. Come pick up your baby, she is ready.

"Good news, Bob. My car is ready. Can you drop me off at Chuck's Auto?"

"No problem, Rob. Let's roll."

I was nearing the end of a productive day with four new tires and some answers about the Emma Jean. A toaster, paper towels and Pam, who knew. So, it was not an accident. Someone had done their research and meticulously planned the fire. But why, and most importantly, who?

CHAPTER TWENTY TWO

Bob fired up the Wrangler, and we headed off the base, back through the North End and onto the expressway. Traffic was still surprisingly light for the middle of July. We got back on Route 93 North heading toward Saugus. We drove back over the Tobin and north onto Route 1. Route 1 is one of the deadliest highways in the country. It's not even really a highway. It is just two lanes going north and south. It is a death trap because the fifty miles per hour speed limit isn't observed, and the road is lined with all kinds of restaurants, hotels, business parks, shopping centers, and strip malls. You have cars slowing down to pull off the road and into parking lots and cars trying to reenter Route 1 from a standstill. Of course, in Massachusetts nobody uses their signals, and everyone is going at least 20 miles per hour over the speed limit. Then add an obstacle course of potholes that, if hit just right, will blow out your tire, and you're lucky to get to your destination in one piece.

My destination was Chuck's Auto to pick up the caddy if he was still open. Then, to end a perfect day, the #7 combo plate at the Kowloon: boneless spareribs, pork fried rice, and chicken wings, extra crispy. I would wash it all down with one of Benny's Mai Tai's. Then home to a quiet night watching the Red Sox play Minnesota.

We pulled into Chuck's Auto, and I could see Chuck alone inside the office. The garage doors were closed, so I knew he was waiting for me. I jumped out of the Wrangler and opened the office door.

I was greeted with, "Where have you been? I want to go home. My wife is going to be pissed."

I replied, "Sorry, Chuck. I was in the city on business, and it took a little longer than I thought."

I was a special agent at the FBI, and Chuck was a mechanic, but good mechanics are hard to find, especially ones who can work on vintage cars. I needed Chuck a lot more than he needed me. Over the years, I learned to keep my mouth shut when he shot off his. At his core Chuck is really a good guy and, more importantly, a great mechanic.

Chuck replied, "Well, you are ready to go. I got four top-of-the-line tires, but they were not cheap."

He handed me the bill, and as I glanced at the total, I tried not to express my shock. The total was just short of a week's pay, and I make pretty good money. I gave Chuck my credit card, signed the receipt, and thanked him for waiting. Chuck was not cheap, but he was a talented mechanic, honest, and I just plain liked him. I waved Bob off, hopped in the caddy, started her up, and headed south on Route 1. My next stop: the Kowloon.

Five minutes later, I was pulling into the lot. It was a Thursday night, about 6:00 p.m., and the place was jammed. The gold buddha in the lobby greeted me as I entered the restaurant.

My stress level was already coming down. My luck was holding. One bar stool was left at the end of the bar near the door, and it was my favorite barstool. I always felt welcome here. I was a regular, and most of the bartenders and servers knew me. The other regulars were also friendly enough, but years of being on stakeouts in the field left me always wanting to know who was coming and who was going. I was a little disappointed. Benny was not tending the bar tonight. Johnny Wu was filling in.

There was a tradition when Johnny was behind the bar that when you finished your workday and sat down at the bar, you yelled, "Wu Hu!" I followed the tradition, not because I thought it was cute, but because it always got the bartender's attention. The result got me my Mai Tai faster. I got a few shoutouts from a couple of regulars. Johnny came over with my Mai Tai, put it in front of me, and greeted me with the words I had been waiting for all day.

"Hi, Rob. Number seven, right, wings extra crispy?"

"Yeah, Johnny. I'm nothing if not consistent."

The food came out fast, even though the place was mobbed. I never knew how they did it. There had to be two hundred people in the restaurant. It was bedlam, noisy, servers coming and going. They never made a mistake. My drink was always perfect, as was the food. Like a good symphony, it all came together. I wolfed down my food and ordered a second Mai Tai. Two was my limit. After a particularly trying day, I ordered three one night and had to drive back to the condominium one-eyed. Never again! I paid my bill and headed back to the parking lot. Another thing I love about the Kowloon is it is five minutes from my condo.

The traffic on Route 1 was light. I headed south, staying within the speed limit. I pulled up at a red light right next to a strip joint. I was thinking ahead to my date with my recliner when, wham. The force of the crash knocked me into the intersection. I saw a black sedan with tinted windows in the rear-view mirror. Son of a bitch. I just paid a week's salary for four new tires. Now some jerk, texting and not paying attention, slams into me. I got in the right-hand lane and pulled into the parking lot of the strip joint. The sedan followed me. Good, at least they were not going to take off. We could exchange papers and go our separate ways.

I opened my door and was trying to keep cool when I saw the front passenger side window lowering. A little unusual. Why would the passenger lower the window? It was the driver I needed to talk to.

That's when I saw it. The end of a rifle barrel poked out the window. It was about three feet from my car. I do not know why, but I had left my car door open, thank Christ. As I took one leap and landed halfway across the front seat, the shots started coming fast and furious. The back window of the caddy exploded. I could hear the rounds whizzing past my car. One hit the side mirror on the driver's side, sending more glass flying.

A few customers were coming out of the strip club. They were screaming and scattering in all different directions. I had left the caddy running, so I rammed it into drive and took off. The caddy was old, but her engine was a V8, and she could move when she had to. And she had to.

Lucky for me, the shooter was not a great shot. If this had been a professional hit, my life would have ended in the strip club parking lot. Unfortunately, the driver could drive.

As my instincts kicked in, I floored it onto Route 1, heading south. Thank God for the defensive driving course at Quantico. The odometer was hitting eighty. I was weaving in and out of traffic, horns blowing, and people yelling out their windows. The son of a bitch was staying right with me. We were getting closer to the city. I blew through two red lights, somehow avoiding getting T-boned. The sedan was still with me. This guy was good, really good. How can my shot-up caddy and this sedan be speeding over the Tobin Bridge without a frigging police officer behind us? I have been pulled over for creeping through a stop sign, but this doesn't draw attention?!!

I stayed in the left-hand lane on Route 1, knowing the shooter could not get a shot off because of oncoming traffic heading northbound. On the Tobin Bridge, the driver of the sedan took advantage of a breakdown lane on the left. I tried to block him but couldn't.

The sedan pulled up right next to me. I glanced over and got a glimpse of the shooter. Big guy, dark complexion, maybe Hispanic. I could see a partial side profile of the driver. He looked like a white guy, and had thin face, and brown hair. It looked like it might be Waxy, but I couldn't be sure. We were just crossing the bridge. I knew he was lining me up. I took a glance to the right and in the rearview mirror. The exit was clear. I hit the brake hard and pulled the steering wheel hard right. I nearly flipped the caddy as I hit the Government Street exit going ninety miles per hour.

The sedan shot past the exit. I needed to get off the street before the sedan doubled back. I made my way to Causeway Street and pulled into the first parking garage I saw. I found a spot between two pickup trucks on level one. I had my 9 millimeter in my right hand and my cell phone in my left hand. I was about to call 911 when a black sedan approached. I thought there was no way they could have followed me here, but my heart was still racing. I had cut the engine of the caddy so as not to draw attention. Without the AC, the sweat was starting to pour off me. The sedan slowed down. I pulled an extra clip out, just in case. The sedan kept going. I could breathe again.

This was going to be my last stop for today. My car was now a crime scene. The caddy wouldn't be heading home today nor to Chuck's Auto. It was now evidence. I had a few calls to make. First, the Boston Police Department. Second to my supervisor, John Ring. I felt that this had to be connected to the investigation of the Emma Jean. Then a call to Bob Halloran. I was worried about his safety. Had the two mooks in the sedan followed us to Chuck's Auto? There were more than two involved and a second car had Bob in their gunsights. Obviously, I was not welcome in New Bedford. I was not even welcome in my adopted hometown of Saugus. Two things I knew for sure. I was making people angry with my investigation, and the fire on the Emma Jean was no grease fire!

CHAPTER TWENTY THREE

I called 911, and a female dispatcher answered. I try not to be biased, but she sounded about thirteen years old.

"911. What is your emergency?"

I answered her out of breath, "I just got shot at by a black sedan on the Southeast Expressway coming over the Tobin Bridge."

"Somebody was shooting at you. Are you hurt?"

"No. I'm fine, but my car could use a little work."

"Can you describe the assailant's vehicle?"

"A black sedan, newer model, tinted windows."

"Were you able to get a plate number?"

"No. We were traveling at a high rate of speed, and I was too busy trying to evade the shooter."

"What is your name, sir?"

"My name is Robert Ragusa. I'm an FBI agent."

"Where are you now, sir?"

"I am at a parking garage right across from the main entrance of the TD Garden on Causeway Street, level one, about halfway down. You cannot miss me. I am in a later model Cadillac with the windows shot out."

"Are you in imminent danger?"

"Not sure. I believe I lost them. I am going to sit tight until the calvary arrives."

"Okay, Agent Ragusa. Help is on the way. Stay with the vehicle, if possible."

"Ok. Will do."

My next call was to Bob. John could wait. I didn't know if whoever was shooting at me knew that Bob was also investigating the Emma Jean for the Coast Guard. I was not sure if I had been followed to Saugus from New Bedford or if the attempt on my life was unrelated to the Emma Jean investigation. It could be just a coincidence. I've worked hundreds of cases during my career. It could have been some lowlife I helped put behind bars, wanting payback.

Bob's phone went straight to voicemail.

"This is Bob Halloran. I'm unable to take your call right now. Please leave a message."

My heart sank. A sense of dread washed over me.

"Bob, it is Rob Ragusa. I'm in a garage waiting for the police to show. Somebody in a black sedan just shot the hell out of my caddy, trying to take me out. I'm ok. But you need to watch your back. There were two men in the sedan armed with at least one rifle. I do not know if they know you're working with me on the Emma Jean case. I am assuming they followed me back to Saugus from New Bedford. They followed us to the Coast Guard station, so you've probably been made. There were two guys in the car. One big man, maybe thirty, dark-skinned, possibly Hispanic. He was the shooter. The other guy was white, skinny, and about the same age. Stay alert and call me ASAP. I'll be at precinct A giving a statement. Stay safe."

I was about to call my supervisor, John Ring, when I could hear the sirens coming up the ramp. Three cruisers surrounded my car. Six uniformed police officers jumped out, guns drawn, and ordered me out of my car. I left my gun in the passenger's seat and slowly opened the car door, putting both hands in the air. I had my agent ID badge in my left hand.

They all approached slowly, and a sergeant with a heavy Boston accent ordered, "Put your hands on the hood and spread your legs."

He took my ID, and while he was patting me down, barked, "Are you Robert Ragusa? Do you have any weapons on you?"

I replied, "Yes. I'm FBI Agent Robert Ragusa. My 9 millimeter is on the passenger's front seat of my car."

I could see him motion a junior officer to the caddy. With his gun still drawn, he opened the door and retrieved the 9 millimeter. The sergeant's tone softened a bit.

"I am going to reach into your back pocket for your wallet. I want to see your driver's license."

I was in no position to refuse. "Sure, no problem."

The sergeant reached into my pocket, extracted my wallet, and took out my driver's license. He took a long, long look at both IDs, then at me, and released his grip.

"I am Sergeant Hernandez. Sorry I was rough with you, but you cannot be too careful."

"I hear you. We're both in the same line of work. No hard feelings. I'm just glad you're here."

"No problem," the sergeant responded. "That is what we do. We will have your car towed to the precinct. Why don't you hop into the back of my cruiser? We'll give you a police escort back to the precinct."

Precinct A was less than five minutes from TD Garden. The sergeant attempted small talk during the short trip.

"So, you're with the FBI?"

"Yes, I am. Thirty years in fact. I am almost ready for retirement."

"Well, for your sake, I hope you make it. It seems like somebody does not like you."

"No argument there. I just wish I knew who. In this line of work, you ruffle lots of feathers."

The sergeant said, "We will have a couple of our top detectives interview you. They will find the bastards who tried to ruin your retirement party."

The sergeant pulled into the parking lot at the station, and we both got out and headed for the front door. I had been to precinct A more than a few times during my career and knew the layout of the building. The sergeant escorted me to interview room three. I interviewed a suspect in a kidnapping case in the same room five years ago.

I just sat down when two young men in civilian clothes entered the room. I assumed these were the detectives who were going to conduct the interview. They introduced themselves.

"I am Detective Morris, and this is my partner, Detective Sampson. We are going to ask you some questions about the incident that happened today."

Morris was about forty-five, tall, a medium build with a nice summer tan. His brown suit was off the rack. Probably JC Penney. Sampson was about the same age and a few inches shorter than Morris. He was African American and a better dresser. He wore a custom-tailored blue suit, white shirt, and red tie. He looked like an investment banker from the Financial District.

Sampson started the interview.

"Any idea who wants you dead, Agent Ragusa?"

"No idea, but lucky for me, the shooter was a lousy shot."

"Could you see who was in the vehicle?"

"Yes, there were two guys in the front seat. I didn't see anyone in the back seat."

"Were you able to determine what make and model vehicle they were driving?"

"Yes, it was a black sedan, four doors, tinted windows, newer model. I think American-made."

Morris took notes on a well-worn steno pad as the interview continued. Sampson pressed further.

"Can you give me a description of them?"

"Yes, I got a brief glimpse. I was a little busy trying to dodge bullets and lose them. There was one big man, about thirty, dark complexion, and maybe Hispanic. He was the shooter. I got a quick side view of the driver. He was white, with long brown hair, and skinny. He looked familiar to me."

Morris chimed in, "What do you mean, he looked familiar?"

I responded, "I interviewed a guy this morning in New Bedford who looked similar."

"What case are you working on?" Morris asked.

"The fire on a fishing boat out of New Bedford, the Emma Jean. One of the crew is still missing. I interviewed a guy this morning in New Bedford. I cannot say for sure it was him, but it's a hell of a coincidence."

Sampson chimed in, "Yeah, it sure is. Did you get the plate number?"

"No, I was hitting ninety, and they were keeping up."

Sampson said, "Well, we might get a break. The phone lines have been lighting up. Channel 5 ran the story as breaking news. Everyone on the expressway seems to have been a witness. One anonymous caller said he was behind the sedan and had a video from his dashcam that showed the plate number. The problem is he wants a reward to turn over the video. Greedy bastard."

I audibly sighed.

"I hope somebody produces one. I will sleep better."

Sampson replied, "Might not need a reward. We're trying to track his call. It bounced off a cell tower just off the expressway. He might be legit. If we can track his phone, we can bring him in as a material witness and confiscate the video."

Morris wrapped it up.

"It is not much to go on. Anything else you can think of?"

"Not right now. I am still trying to process all of it. I will keep in touch, and you'll keep in touch, right fellas?"

Morris said, "Of course. There are hundreds of black sedans in Boston. Without a plate number, we do not even know if the vehicle is from Massachusetts. It could be from anywhere. The best bet is that video. Hopefully, we can track down the caller. If we can get our hands on the video, our tech guys will work their magic. They will find these guys."

"Well, do not be afraid to ask for our office help. We have got some pretty good tech guys at the FBI, too."

Sampson added, "We know how to reach you, Agent Ragusa, if necessary. Before you leave, we are going to have a sketch artist come in and, with your help, draw profiles of the shooter and the driver."

"All right by me," I said. "But I told you I didn't get a good look at him."

Morris spoke up.

"This lady is pretty good. She's an artist but also has a psychology degree. She might be able to use her skills to help get out of you a more detailed description of these two."

The two detectives shook my hand and left the interview room. I waited for what seemed like an hour, but what was five minutes before the door opened, and in walked a woman who I assumed was the sketch artist. She was a tall, fair skinned woman, in her fifties but looked ten years younger. Her long blonde hair, tied back in a ponytail, was beginning to show some streaks of white. She wore a yellow knee-length dress that fit her lean body perfectly. With high heeled shoes and a simple gold necklace around her neck, she looked like she might be an aging model. I suddenly realized that I was staring at her in a way that might make a woman uncomfortable. I changed my gaze to the wall as she sat across the small conference table from me.

"Hello, Agent Ragusa. My name is Sandy Atlas. With your help, I will draw a sketch of the driver and man who tried to kill you today."

I stammered, "Nice to meet you, Ms. Atlas. I didn't get a good look at them, but I'll try my best."

"Please call me Sandy. Everyone in the station does."

"Ok, then. Sandy, it is. But do not call me Agent Ragusa, call me Rob."

"Fair enough, Rob. Let's get started. What type of skin complexion did the shooter have?"

"He was dark-skinned. I do not think African American. More Hispanic or Arabic."

Sandy had her easel set up and drawing pencils next to her.

"What about his face? Round shaped, oval, narrow? How would you describe it?"

"I'd say it was round shaped with a bit of a double chin."

"How about his hair color?"

"His hair was dark, black, or maybe dark brown."

"Okay. What about the style and length of his hair?"

"His hair was short. Not a buzz cut but close cropped."

"Okay, what about facial hair?"

"He was clean shaven, but it looked like he had not shaved for a few days."

"What about his eyes? Can you describe the shape, color or whether they were close together or far apart?"

"That I remember. He had slit eyes, cold, dark brown color, almost black. For a couple of seconds, we made eye contact. I'll never forget his eyes. Stone cold, lifeless eyes like a shark before it goes in for the kill."

I looked over at the easel, and the face of a killer began to take shape. Sandy continued to lead me through the sketch process.

"What shape was his nose?"

"He had a big nose, pushed in like a boxer who's been hit too many times in the face."

"How about his mouth and lips?"

"He had a small mouth and was not smiling or frowning. He didn't look mad, just intense and determined. Like he had a job to do, and he was going to get it done. The job was to kill me."

"Okay. Is there anything else you can remember? Skin marks, abrasions, acne, anything like that?"

"Nothing that I can recall."

"Take your time, Rob. Sometimes, the mind blocks things out after experiencing a traumatic event."

"Detective Morris told me you had a degree in psychology."

"What else did he tell you about me?"

"Nothing, but I'd be interested in getting to know more."

Her facial expression was surprising. Sandy's face started turning slightly red. She was blushing. I had overstepped my bounds and started apologizing but Sandy kept going.

"Rob, just relax and try to visualize him like a movie in slow motion, frame by frame."

"God, Sandy, how could I have forgotten this? He was wearing a wife beaters. Oh, sorry for using that term. It is offensive."

"I am not offended. I know what wife beaters are."

"I apologize anyway. He also had a tattoo on his neck."

"Can you describe the tattoo?"

"Not really. It was some kind of writing. I could not make out the letters. The tattoo started from his neck all the way up to his chin." I took another glance over, and it was uncanny. I was almost startled. The face she had drawn looked just like the man who tried to kill me.

"Rob, does this look like the man who tried to kill you?"

"It sure does, Sandy. Man, you are good!"

"Would you like me to change anything about the sketch?"

"No. Not a thing. You nailed it! You're quite talented."

"Okay, what about the driver?"

"He was staring straight ahead, so I only got a side view of the right side of his face. He was white, seemed young, mid-twenties, long scraggly brown hair."

Sandy pressed further.

"What about facial features? Did he have any facial hair?"

"Again, I only got a side view for a few seconds. A little scruff around his chin,

but I am unsure. I cannot tell you anything about his mouth or eyes."

"Okay, Rob. How about any distinguishing marks?"

"Oh yes, kind of a pockmarked face, like he had acne in high school or something. I know this sounds crazy, but I interviewed a guy in New Bedford this morning regarding the Emma Jean investigation who looked like this guy. His nickname was Waxy because he was an albino. Pale white skin, I cannot be sure, but it seems like a big-time coincidence."

I glanced over at Sandy, and the image appearing on the easel jumped out at me.

"That is him, Sandy! That is the driver."

"Thanks, Rob. Then I think we are done for today."

Sandy began to gather her drawing materials and was about to exit the interview room when I blurted out, "Are you married?"

Sandy turned around and said, "No, why do you ask?"

"Well, this isn't proper protocol, but I'd like to ask you out."

Sandy looked a bit stunned. She looked directly at me and said what I was hoping to hear.

"I haven't been on a date since my divorce two years ago, but yes, I'd love to."

"I have not been on a date in a long time either. I am glad you said yes. Have you heard of the Continental?"

"I have. It's on Route 1, isn't it?"

"Yeah, Route 1 in Saugus. Great food, and they have live music on Saturday nights, jazz, blues, and oldies. It, however, depends on the night you are there. How about next Saturday, say, six o'clock?"

"I would like that, Rob. I live in Weymouth, so it is probably about a thirty-five-minute ride to Saugus. How about I meet you there."

"It is a date. Are you sure you are willing to be on a date with somebody who just got shot at?"

She brought the conversation to an end.

"I do not scare easy. See you Saturday, Rob. Stay safe."

Well, I thought, this should be interesting. This woman is no shrinking violet. I got up from the folding metal chair and headed to the front desk to retrieve my 9-millimeter, driver's license, and FBI badge. For such a shitty day, the end turned out okay. I couldn't stop smiling. I got to the front desk and, after signing some paperwork, the desk sergeant handed me back my gun ID and driver's license. My next call was to my supervisor, John Ring.

CHAPTER TWENTY FOUR

I called John from the lobby of the police station. I was going to need an Uber to get home as the caddy was being held for evidence. I called John, and he picked up on the first ring.

"Hey, John. It's Rob. How are you doing?"

"I am fine, Rob. What are you doing calling me on a Friday night? They must be worried about you at the Kowloon," chuckled John.

"They should be."

"Whoa, what are you talking about? Is everything okay, Rob?"

"Have you heard anything yet about the shooting on the Southeast Expressway?"

John replied, "Yes. I just turned on the local news a few minutes ago. It is breaking news. On every news station in the city."

"Well, that was me, John. That was me getting shot at. I'm in the lobby of precinct A in the city. The caddy is in the lot here, shot to hell. The Boston Police Department is holding it for evidence. I'm okay. Luckily, the shooter was not very good. I am going to call Uber and go home. It has been a long day."

"No, Rob. Stay put. I'm coming to get you. I do not think going home is a good idea. How do you know the shooter is not still out there? He could be waiting at your condominium to ambush you and finish the job. Why don't you stay at our house tonight? We have an extra bedroom. Mary and the kids would love to see you. It's been a while since you've been by the house. Mary cooked her famous lasagna. There's some left over."

"Thanks, John, but I just want to go home and sleep in my bed."

"All right, Rob if you insist. But I am driving you home myself. We will clear your condo together just in case somebody has further bad intentions. I am going to put a surveillance team on you twenty-four-seven. You obviously stirred things up in New Bedford. There seems to be much to this case than a fire on a fishing boat."

"No argument here, boss. I'll wait for you in the lobby. How long do you think it will take you to get here?"

"I am leaving right now. With light traffic, about thirty-five minutes."

"Okay, I appreciate it, John. We can talk more in your car on the way home. I'll bring you up to speed. See you soon, bye."

John was a good supervisor. He could manage people well and judge their strengths as well as their weaknesses. He had been a field agent for over twenty years before being promoted to supervisor. He was a seasoned investigator, unlike a lot of other FBI field supervisors who got promoted because of who they knew. The FBI is political, just like any other organization. I've seen many good agents get passed over for promotions because they didn't play the game. Not John Ring. He made it with hard work and ability.

John lived in Wilmington with his wife, Mary, and their two kids, Brandon, and Heather. Wilmington was only about twenty miles away from the field office in Chelsea, but it was a world apart. Wilmington was a small, quiet New England town. It was middle-class. The houses were a mixture of medium-sized capes and ranches that were built in the '60s and '70s. In the last ten years, newer 3,000 square-foot plus McMansions had begun to dot the landscape. Nobody built small homes within the Route 495 loop anymore. The land is too expensive.

The station was quiet for a Friday night. A few people came up to the desk to ask questions about filing restraining orders. An officer was bringing in a young twentysomething in handcuffs. The kid was dressed shirtless, in shorts and flip flops. He was swearing like a truck driver. I could hear what sounded like, "you are a fucking asshole," but it came out more like "yo frucking a hole."

The young man had an early start on the weekend festivities. Next stop for him: the booking room, fingerprints, and a mugshot. Nobody ever looks good in a mug shot. Then off to a holding cell and a phone call to the parents after he sobers up a bit.

I had done more than my share of stupid shit in high school, like the time me and Bobby O'Connell hit an ice patch going eighty and plowed his mother's new Nova into a fishpond in Braintree. The guy who owned the home pitied us. After we got the Nova towed out, he told us he wouldn't call our parents if we paid for his broken fence and damaged rose bush. It took Bobby and I two months, but we paid him off. Thank God I never had to make that call from jail. It would not have gone well.

Just as the officer was escorting him past me, my ride arrived. John came into the lobby.

"Let's go, Rob. Your audition for the next Fast and Furious movie is over for today."

I waved goodbye to the desk sergeant and headed out the front door into the still stifling heat. John was able to park right out front. The job does have some perks. We jumped into his Chrysler 300 and headed back to the expressway. Next stop, Home! Hopefully, nobody but my cat would be there to greet me.

CHAPTER TWENTY FIVE

As we made our way through the West End of Boston onto the Southeast Expressway heading toward Saugus, John started to grill me a little.

"Rob, I want you to come into the office tomorrow morning and fully debrief. I want to ask you a few questions before I take you home. Can you walk me through your day in New Bedford? Start from the beginning."

"Okay, first, I stopped at the Widows Cove Tavern to talk to the bartender, Steve Poole. He's been slinging beers there for over thirty years. I have known Steve from back in the nineties when my band used to play there on Friday nights. It was primarily a fishermen's hangout in the nineties, but New Bedford is starting to go upscale. If anything were going on around the docks, Steve would hear about it. The phone number that was found in the briefcase matched the phone number of a former cook there, Wayne Barrett, a.k.a. Waxy. Anyway, I guess Hal, the owner of Widows Cove, fired Waxy because he was dealing drugs in the bathroom. I got Waxy's address from Steve. Willow Street in the north section of New Bedford.

"Then I called the Captain of the Emma Jean, Frank Medeiros, who lives in New Bedford. He agreed to see me. I got to his house and interviewed him for about an hour. Salty old bird, but he answered all my questions. Nothing particularly interesting came out of the interview. He is sticking to his story about a grease fire, but he did admit that the fire spread fast. He couldn't explain why. From there, I headed to Willow Street, Waxy's last known address, hoping I would get lucky. He still lived there. I pulled up in front of the address. His apartment was on the third floor of a three-decker. It looked like the lights were on, so I went up and banged on the door. A thin, pale guy answered. From Steve's description, I assumed this was Waxy. He let me in, and I questioned him for about forty-five minutes. He thought he got a bum deal at the Widows Cove. He would only admit to selling marijuana and denied selling heroin or any other type of drugs. I think he is full of crap. I cannot prove it yet, but I'm pretty sure he's involved in something illegal, and it's more than just selling weed. He had heard about the fire on the Emma Jean but claimed he had no idea why his number would show up in a suitcase floating near the boat. Waxy admitted he sold weed to plenty of fishermen out of the bathroom at the Widows Cove when he was cooking there."

"At face value, his explanation holds water, but my sixth sense tells me there is more going on. After interviewing Waxy, I returned to my car, greeted by four flat tires. I left my car unlocked and a black and yellow bandanna was placed on my front seat. The north section of New Bedford is Latin Kings' territory. Yellow and black are their colors. Of course, nobody saw anything. I called a tow truck and had the car towed to my mechanic in Saugus. I had called Bob Halloran at the Coast Guard Station in Boston and asked him to pick me up at the garage in Saugus. Bob met me at Chucks' Auto around three in the afternoon. We scheduled meeting at 3:30 p.m. at the Boston Coast Guard Station to conduct the arson investigation with Henry Avena. I didn't want to miss that.

"We conducted the investigation. Henry is sure the fire was set. It looks like someone jerry-rigged the toaster, stuffing it with napkins, and then left a can of Pam cooking spray nearby, which exploded from the heat. Henry said he could see little charred remains of paper towels in the toaster. No question. The fire was no accident. Chuck called me just as we were wrapping up the investigation. My car was ready, and Chuck was waiting for me. Bob drove me back to Chuck's Auto and dropped me off. I got the caddy and headed to the Kowloon Restaurant for dinner. Then it was home for the night. I fired up the caddy and headed south on Route 1, and that is when all hell broke loose."

I was about to get to the exciting part when John pulled into the condo complex. He had been over to my place before. He knew where I lived and the general layout of the complex. We drove around the complex to check if anything seemed out of place. It was a little past 8:00 p.m. Dusk was setting in. It was quiet. Almost too quiet.

John looked at me and said, "I am going to follow you in. Take your gun off safety. Let's go."

We both had our hands on our Glocks as we approached the front door. Just as I was about to enter my code to open the lobby door, a rustling noise came from a rose bush to my right. We both wheeled around and aimed at the rose bush. The biggest cat I have ever seen came flying out of the bush and ran right past me.

We both took a deep breath and I whispered to John, "Did that just scare the shit out of you like it did me?"

He nodded yes. I punched in the code, and we entered the building with guns drawn. Nobody in the hallway. I made my way up one flight of stairs with John behind me. I made my way down the hall to number six, my condo. I put the key in the door and opened it real slow. Everything looked to be in order. John and I both cleared the apartment, and I felt like I could finally breathe again.

"Everything looks okay, Rob. Are you all set for the night?"

I replied, "I sure hope so. It's been quite a day."

"Hopefully tomorrow will be uneventful. Rob, I want you in my office at 9:00 a.m. for a full debriefing. And Rob, be careful." John gave me a quick wave goodbye and headed back to the parking lot.

I popped open a Sam Adams Summer Ale and sank into my recliner. I tried to relax, but my mind was still racing. I kept trying to process the day's events, but it was all a jumble. The fire on the Emma Jean was a puzzle, but some of the pieces were starting to fall into place. Trixie jumped up onto my lap. I do not know why but her purring always calms me down. Something rhythmic and soothing about the sound. With my eyes at half-mast, I finally drifted off to sleep.

CHAPTER TWENTY SIX

I woke up in the recliner at 6:00 a.m. with Trixie meowing loudly. Her less than subtle call for food. I fed her and put on a pot of coffee. I usually only make two cups. I like my coffee black, with no sugar, but this was a four-cup morning. I had slept all night in the recliner, so it was time for a shower, shave, and a change of clothes. The corporate dress code seems to have become more relaxed in recent years but not at the FBI. The FBI is still stuck in the fifties, dress shirt, suit, tie, and dress shoes. It does not matter about the weather. You do not show up at the office without the company uniform. I finished my shower, shaved, and dressed in my best navy-blue suit and red tie.

On my way out the front door, I grabbed my Boston Globe and Boston Herald. Most people read their news online these days. I'm still old school. The Boston Globe and the Boston Herald are delivered daily to my condo. The delivery guy leaves the papers at the front entranceway. My name is clearly labeled on both papers, but I need to get downstairs early before they get grabbed. It makes me angry. People who are too cheap to subscribe read the newspaper on my dime.

I like the feeling of having a newspaper in my hand. I grew up reading the sports pages as a kid and I have never changed. The Herald is the conservative paper in the city and the Globe is much more liberal. I lean conservative, but I like to read both to get different perspectives. The fact that both papers were still there was a pleasant surprise.

• • •

Everyone uses Uber these days for a ride. Again, I am old school. I do not know how to download the app, so I called the local cab company in Saugus, Yellow Cab. The dispatcher said it would be about fifteen minutes before they could get a cab to my location. No problem. That would give me some time to leaf through the papers.

My adventure on the expressway was second page news. A quarter page article in both the Globe and the Herald described a shooting that had taken place on the Southeast Expressway on Friday afternoon near the Tobin Bridge. My name was not mentioned. It simply mentioned there was a shooting and that police were looking for two people in a black sedan. I guessed that John had called the station and told them not to provide any details, that an FBI agent was the target.

Ten minutes had passed by when a bright Yellow Cab pulled up. I got up off the bench and headed over toward the cab. A cheery older man with a shock of white hair greeted me.

"You call for a cab, pal?"

"That I did," was my reply. I had the cabbie swing by the Dunkin Donuts drive through on Route 1. Usually, the line at the drive through is a mile long. Today, there was only a Fed-Ex van in front of us.

Over his right shoulder, the cabbie shouted, "What do you want?"

"A large black coffee and a ham and cheese on a plain bagel, and order something for yourself on me."

"Hey, thanks."

The voice from the squawk box came through loud and clear. "Can I take your order?"

The cabbie shouted back, "Yeah, a large regular, large black coffee and ham and cheese on a plain bagel."

You ask for a regular outside New England, and they do not know what you're talking about. Any establishment in Massachusetts that serves coffee knows what a regular is, just like the driver said. Cream, two sugars.

"Hey, thanks, pal. Nobody ever offers me a coffee. So, how are you doing today? My name is Ray."

I responded, "I am good. It should be an interesting day."

"Well, that is good. Nothing too interesting about driving a cab. I got held up at gunpoint once about five years ago, so that qualifies for interesting."

Before I could answer, he pulled up to the pickup area. With food in hand, we made our way back onto Route 1.

"Thanks for the coffee, pal. Where are you heading today?"

"201 Maple Street in Chelsea."

"What's at 201 Maple Street?"

"The Boston Area FBI field office."

"No kidding! So, you are an FBI agent?"

"I am, and if I'm not there by ten minutes to nine my ass is grass, so step on it."

"Not a problem," said Ray. "I have been driving a hack for thirty years. I know every shortcut there is. I'll have you there in plenty of time."

Ray was right. We pulled into the parking lot at 8:45 a.m. I've driven to the office a thousand times, but he took streets I didn't even know existed. I paid the fare, thirty-five dollars, and got a receipt. I tipped Ray, said goodbye, and headed into the building.

I showed my badge to the receptionist, Milly. She knows who I am, but it is protocol. She buzzed me in, and I made my way to John's office. Of course, being the field office supervisor, he had the big corner office. The door was open, and John was sitting behind his desk typing something on his laptop. His office was furnished, befitting his title, with a mahogany desk, mahogany credenza behind him decorated with various pictures of his wife, Mary, and the kids. He motioned for me to sit in one of the two chairs in front of his desk. He logged off his computer and got right down to business.

"Rob, you really stirred it up on the expressway yesterday."

I replied, sheepishly, "Well, that was not my intention. Somebody was trying to kill me, and I do my best to avoid such situations."

"I am just glad you're okay. Tell me what happened."

"Well, I was heading home from Kowloon. I had my guard down. I didn't think that what happened in New Bedford to my car was related to the fire on the Emma Jean. I chalked it up to punk kids or the Latin Kings making a statement about their turf or wannabe gang bangers. Nothing I thought I couldn't handle. I was heading down Route 1 and noticed in my rear-view mirror a black sedan with tinted windows riding my bumper. That did not necessarily raise my suspicions because everyone in Massachusetts tailgates. The next thing I know, the sedan plows into me. I pulled into the parking lot of a strip club to exchange papers. I was halfway out of the door when I saw a rifle barrel pointing at me. I jumped back into the Caddy and took off with the sedan behind me. The next thing I know, the back window of the caddy explodes. I'm shaking glass out of my hair. I still was not sure what was happening. Then I heard gunshots hitting the trunk. My driver's side mirror got shot off. The shooter was using a high caliber round semi-automatic rifle. Then, it was on. I gunned it, trying to lose them. The driver was good. The black sedan stuck right to my tail. He managed to get to my left in the breakdown lane on the Tobin Bridge.

"I'm boxed in by traffic. The shooter looks right at me and takes aim. He gets off a couple of rounds, and my side window shatters. I can barely see. I've got glass everywhere. I did my best to maneuver and gunned it over the Tobin toward the city. I saw my chance. The sedan was boxed in. Just over the bridge, I cut a hard right and took the TD Garden exit ramp at about ninety miles per hour. The sedan shot past the exit. I hooked into the TD Garden parking lot on two wheels. I put the caddy into the first parking spot I found and called for the calvary."

John had been listening intently.

"I called Commissioner Crowell and kept your name off the papers."

Boston Police Commissioner, James Crowell, was a longtime friend of John's. The FBI often works together on cases with BPD, and the Commissioner took an active role. Everybody in the FBI Boston Field Office liked him because he had your back and was not a politician.

"Rob, I want to assign a surveillance team to you. I don't know if this was a contract hit by a perp you put away or has any connection to the current investigation of the Emma Jean. Whatever the history or connection, you were targeted."

My response came quickly.

"You cannot do that, John. I need to work this case alone. They will pick up on the surveillance team if they're pros. I need to get back to New Bedford, interview the fishermen on the Emma Jean and visit Waxy again.

John said, "Remind me who Waxy is again."

"Wayne Barrett is better known on the seedy side of New Bedford as Waxy. He's a local character whose name came up related to the telephone number found in the black suitcase, floating near the Emma Jean. It turned out to be a burner phone. He was employed as a cook at the Widows Cove Tavern. The bartender there, Steve Poole, found the number on an employment application, which included his name and address. I only got a quick side view of the driver, but it sure looked like him."

"BPD faxed over the sketch you gave of the shooter at the station." John slid the sketch over to me.

Seeing it again made the hair stand up on the back of my neck. It looked just like the guy who tried to kill me.

"That is him all right. He was the shooter. The problem is, he looks like a thousand other guys. Black sedans are a dime a dozen, and I was unable to get a license plate. Too busy dodging bullets. The license plate was probably stolen anyway. I'd like to take this sketch down to the docks. If this guy is from New Bedford, somebody will recognize him."

"Rob, you know I don't need your permission to assign you a surveillance team."

"I know, John. But let me handle this alone. I know the city well from my band playing days at the Widows Cove. I've got a good connection at the Widows Cove in Steve Poole. If anything is going down in the city, it is going to be talked about at that bar, and Steve is going to hear about it."

"All right, Rob, but be careful. Whether these guys are from New Bedford or not, they want you dead for some reason, and they are not going to give up."

"I know. The caddy is shot to hell, and the BPD is holding it for a while as evidence. I'll need a rental car, John. Something inconspicuous."

"I am way ahead of you. I called Hertz. I got you a White BMW SUV. You'll look like you're taking the kids to soccer practice. Here are the keys. It's parked by the front door. I am sad about what happened to the caddy. I know she is your pride and joy."

"Thanks, John, I am insured. She will be back on the road before you know it."

I shook John's hand and headed out of his office and out to my new ride. What a letdown from my 1968 caddy in mint condition to this. Oh well,

I needed to contact all the fishermen on the Emma Jean and interview them at their homes. I also want to pay Waxy an unannounced visit and see how he reacts when he sees me.

I started my new ride, pulled out my cell phone, and called the three surviving crew members. I always liked New Bedford. It has the smell of the ocean, history, and old fishing captains' mansions. That was then, and this was now. I didn't know what to expect. I just had to be prepared for the unexpected because I knew the unexpected had already happened and could happen again.

CHAPTER TWENTY SEVEN

I never realized how many black four-door sedans there are in the world. Heading out of Boston and onto Route 24 South, I must have passed thirty cars that fit the description. I just could not help myself. Every black sedan I passed; I glanced over to see who was inside. A middle-aged soccer mom with two kids in car seats. An attractive blonde female with one hand on the wheel, and the other hand applying makeup. Another sedan had a young teenager talking on her phone and one guy looked a little like the driver. I slowed down, my heart beating a little faster. The driver must have thought I was trying to screw with him because, as I stayed on his right, he turned, and I saw a perfect profile of his face as he flipped me the bird and floored it. He looked similar, but his face was too fat, triple chin fat. My guy's face was round but not basketball sized. I continued this exercise of futility all the way to the Route 18 exit off Route 195.

The sketch had also been shown on all the local news stations. I had a few copies with me. After I paid Waxy a visit, my plan was to go back to the

WIDOWS COVE

Widows Cove Tavern to sit down with Steve Poole and see what the word was on the street. Then I wanted to head down to the docks.

Everybody knows everybody on the waterfront. I remember from my days playing at the Widows Cove, fishermen like to tell tales. Some were true but most were bullshit. They do not just talk about the fish they caught. They gossip worse than old ladies in a sewing circle. They know who is on drugs, who spends too much time in the bars, and who is screwing whose wife when their husbands are out at sea. The drama at the waterfront is a real-life version of Marlon Brando's old movie, *On the Waterfront*. The question was, would they talk, especially to a stranger? I was not one of them, and I would be noticed the minute I stepped foot on the docks. I didn't want Steve involved in this mess, but I thought he might be my best bet at identifying the shooter, especially if he was a local. Everybody liked Steve. He was a legend in New Bedford. Everybody knew his story, and though he had been the Vice President of a major New England Bank, he could talk to anyone on their level. The fishermen who frequented the Widows Cove would tell him things they wouldn't tell their wives.

I got off the exit and headed back to the north section of New Bedford and Waxy's dilapidated three-decker. There was a spot in the driveway, so I took it. I was not sure who had flattened the caddy's tires. I didn't think a white SUV would draw any attention. But as much as I came to like Phil, the tow truck driver, one trip was enough. It was local punks from the neighborhood, but I was not taking any chances this time.

I put on my Red Sox baseball cap, dark sunglasses, and unholstered my Glock. Not much of a disguise, but it would have to do. I made my way up the dark stairway to Waxy's third floor apartment. I could hear the TV inside. I did not know what type of greeting I would receive. I could receive Waxy with a scowl on his face or a shotgun blast through the door. I stood to the side of the door and banged loudly with my left hand, right hand on my Glock. I heard nothing. I banged a second time. Again, I heard nothing. Then the TV went silent. That is never a good sign. I was about to knock again when I heard loud clanging. Someone was heading down the fire escape. I ran back down the stairs like hell and flew out the front door. A thin male was booking it down Ford Street toward Acushnet Ave. He was about fifty yards ahead of me, and I was not gaining on him. It looked like Waxy from the back, but I couldn't be sure. He turned around and looked me straight in the eye. It was Waxy.

The odd thing was the look on his face was neither fear nor anger. Curiously, it looked like relief. He took a sharp left and lost me down an alleyway behind a Chinese take-out joint. I stopped and put my hands on my knees, breathing like I had just run the Boston Marathon. It was not illegal to climb down a fire escape and run like hell, but it sure raised Waxy's profile as a suspect.

I walked slowly back to Waxy's apartment, still trying to catch my breath. I figured he had been alone, but I walked back up the three flights of stairs just to be sure. I had no warrant and no probable cause to enter the premises. I listened at the door for fifteen minutes. I didn't hear a peep. If someone were in there, they would keep it quiet. I figured Waxy was street smart. He would not be coming back anytime soon, if ever. Next stop, the Widows Cove Tavern and Steve Poole.

CHAPTER TWENTY EIGHT

I headed down Acushnet Avenue, back onto Route 18 South toward downtown. I took a right onto Union Street and looked for a parking spot. I got lucky again. A guy in a red Ford Explorer was pulling out of a spot about two blocks from the Widows Cove. I pulled in, fed the meter, and began the two-block walk to the bar.

I took a long look around as I made my way up the cobblestone street. The city was on the upswing. Instead of dive bars, hot dog joints, and empty storefronts, downtown New Bedford was starting to look trendy. New restaurants like the Quahog Republic and Moby Dick, organic food stores, and art galleries were populating Union Street. I didn't know if I was happy or sad about the changes. I liked the city, and a piece of me was nostalgic for the old days. New Bedford had been downtrodden for a long time. I rooted for the city to make a comeback, without losing its character. It looked like it was starting to happen.

I made my way to the bar's front door and walked in. Steve was behind the bar. It was 10:30 in the morning. Not yet time for the lunch crowd. Two construction types were sitting at the bar's far end, enjoying a morning revelation—a shot of Jack Daniels and a bottle of Bud.

• • •

Steve spotted me coming in and yelled out.

"Hey, Rob. I didn't expect to see you back in town so soon."

Before I reached the bar, I shot back, "You and me both!"

I sat at the opposite end of the bar from the two patrons. They talked loudly in Portuguese and seemed too busy drinking and yacking to pay attention to me. Just as well.

"Rob, how did you make out after you left here last time?" Steve asked.

"Well, some folks in Waxy's neighborhood were not very friendly, including Waxy. After our chat, I came out to find all four tires of my caddy slashed. A bit more concerning was a yellow and black bandanna on my front seat. I'm thinking the Latin Kings or maybe some wannabes. Steve, I know you are plugged into the gossip in the city, and I can trust you. Have you been watching the news?"

Steve replied, "Yeah. You know I always have the news on unless a ballgame is airing."

"Well, then you may have seen the news story about the shooting on the Southeast Expressway yesterday."

"Of course, I did, it was on every channel."

"Well, those bullets were meant for me."

"Holy cow!" Steve blurted out. "Are you okay?"

"Yeah. I'm fine but a little concerned about my health. I do not know if this is related to the investigation of the Emma Jean or not. I figured I would return to New Bedford and snoop around. I stopped by Waxy's apartment this morning. I do not know who he was expecting, but after I banged on the door, he took off like a bat out of hell down the fire escape. I chased him for a few blocks, but he ducked down an alley and lost me. I brought some copies of the sketch of the shooter. I know it is all over the news, but the quality of the sketch is much better than what you see on TV. There is a $25,000 reward for information leading to the arrest of either the driver or the shooter. I only saw the driver's side profile briefly, and it looked a little like Waxy. I did get a good look at the shooter."

I pulled out a copy of the sketch of the shooter and put it on the bar in front of Steve. "Does this guy look familiar?"

Steve put his blue wire-rimmed glasses on and lifted the sketch to the bridge of his nose.

"I am not positive, Rob, but he looks a lot like a guy that used to hang around with Frankie Costa back in the day. If I take twenty years off this guy and twenty pounds, it looks like one of his cohorts. Frankie and four or five of his posse would pop in here occasionally. Frankie would hold court, talking business. He liked me. Always respectful and a big tipper. I heard all the rumors about illegal activities and the like. I just kept my mouth shut and served the beer and shots. That does not mean I didn't listen. If it is the guy I'm thinking, I never heard his real name. Frankie would refer to him as Rollo. He might have been Frankie's right-hand man."

What Steve told me was not good news. Frankie Costa, also known as "Frankie the Hammer." He was a notorious local enforcer whose heyday was in the '80s and '90s. Frankie was reputed to be an associate of the Patriarca crime family based out of the Federal Hill section of Providence, Rhode Island. The Patriarca family ran a criminal enterprise that included extortion, gambling, and prostitution all over New England. In the mid-nineties, federal officials arrested and imprisoned most Patriarca associates on extortion charges. The arrest left Costa as the dominant figure in the local underworld. He retreated from Providence and set up a series of legitimate businesses, including in the fishing industry in New Bedford. He began building a multimillion-dollar empire over a nine-year period. Costa was arrested in 2002 on charges, including extortion, racketeering, and the forced takeover of a local fishery. He was accused of using fishing vessels to smuggle cocaine and marijuana into New Bedford and Fall River. He pleaded guilty to the racketeering charge and was sentenced and sent to jail.

Frankie was released and dropped off the radar screen. He lives a quiet suburban life with his wife and family in a neighboring town. I had not been directly involved in the case but had followed it closely. Was Frankie Costa back in business on the waterfront? Or maybe some of his associates had decided to fill the power vacuum. Either way, it was not good news for New Bedford or me.

CHAPTER TWENTY NINE

The waterfront was within walking distance of the Widows Cove. It was a nice day. Hot but not muggy. I fed a couple more quarters into the parking meter and headed down Union Street toward the docks. I walked across the walkway over Route 18, the main drag that separated the waterfront from downtown.

A new restaurant across the street was busy with the early lunch crowd dining alfresco on a brick patio on the harbor. The patrons looked to be upscale, some had cameras and tourists in New Bedford. Wow, times have really changed! I crossed Route 18, then passed through the parking lot of a fish house and into the main harbor area. I had driven by the harbor a hundred times but had never actually walked around the docks. I had no reason to. I was in New Bedford to play music, not buy or sell fish. I like fish. Sometimes I will order fish and chips in a restaurant. But this was different. The smell of fish was overpowering and combined with screeching, dive-bombing seagulls, the atmosphere was not as romantic as in the George Clooney movie *Perfect Storm*. More like Steinbeck's *Cannery Row*. Fishing boats were loading up with ice and supplies for their next trip out to sea. Other boats were offloading their catch. Fishermen were cursing, yelling, running back and forth. A symphony of controlled chaos.

I remembered the local fishermen at the Widows Cove in the nineties talking about a fish house with a secret backroom. Like the speakeasies of the twenties in Chicago, you walked through a phalanx of workers, chattering in Vietnamese and Portuguese, cleaning and sorting the day's catch. In the back of the building was a heavy metal door. A keypad near the door allowed anyone who knew the code access. Once through the door, it was like Caesar's Palace on a Saturday night. The clanging of coins being dropped into hungry slot machines, blackjack tables, craps, roulette, and a fully stocked bar. A guy nicknamed Ra Ra ran the place. The police officers knew about it, but magically, it never got raided. Fishermen fresh off the boat would get paid their share after a trip and head straight over. Working girls were more than happy to lighten the fishermen's wallets. Drug dealers, it was one stop shopping. Word had it that the Codfather was behind the whole thing, but no one could prove it. For all I knew it was still going. I knew enough to avoid these joints in New Bedford in the nineties and that had not changed.

I knew that everyone knew everyone on the docks. I would stand out like a sore thumb. I did not expect a warm reception, but a $25,000.00 reward was being offered for information on Emma Jean. That might loosen some tongues. Most of these guys made well over $100,000.00 a year, even in a bad year. The sad part was most of them also spent that much on bad habits such as drinking, drugs, and women. They spent their cash as quickly as they got it. $25,000.00 might be enough to attract a fisherman who may be behind on his child support payments or owed a local dealer.

I made my way up and down the inner harbor, speaking to anyone who would stop. I showed the sketch of the shooter to at least thirty to forty fishermen, asking them if they knew the guy. I got a lot of head shaking, "Don't know him" and the occasional "Go fuck yourself." I was getting ready to head back to the Widows Cove when I felt a tap on my shoulder from behind. It was a kid, thirteen or fourteen. He looked too young to be a fisherman or one working in the fish houses. He had a dark complexion, probably either Cape Verdean or Hispanic. He handed me a crumpled piece of paper.

As I started to unwrinkle the paper, he took off through the fish house parking lot toward downtown. The kid was fast as hell, and I had already lost one foot race today. There was no sense in getting into another. I yelled for him to stop. He didn't turn around. I saw him jump over the guardrail and cross Route 18, almost getting creamed by a black pickup truck and disappear down a side street.

I slowly flattened out the piece of paper, and one line was written on it:

Be at Mike's Restaurant at 7:00 p.m. tonight.

That was it. Mikes was a restaurant in Fairhaven, a small, middle-class town across the drawbridge from New Bedford. Primarily a steak house, Mikes was known for their prime rib, steak sandwiches and huge portions. I had not planned on dining out, but a prime rib medium and baked potato with sour cream suddenly sounded appealing. I am not a fan of this "cloak and dagger" crap. It was just some fisherman screwing with me, but I had to be sure. Mikes at 7:00 p.m. it would be.

Right now, it was lunchtime, and I was starving. Since I stopped playing at the Widows Cove, I had not had Portuguese food. I loved Antonio's on Coggeshall Street. I shoved the paper in my pocket, walked back to my rental car and headed for Antonio's. It had been a busy day so far, but right now, all I had on my mind was a cold Sam Adams draft beer and a Portuguese steak sandwich with fries.

CHAPTER THIRTY

I headed back up Route 18 toward the North End of New Bedford. I pulled into Antonio's parking lot a little before Noon. The lunch crowd was in full swing, and the lot was almost full. I had not eaten there in thirty years. The restaurant was legendary in New Bedford. Family-owned, Antonio's had been a staple in New Bedford for decades. The exterior of the building looked the same. Newly painted, but otherwise, it was exactly as I remembered it. The entrance to the dining room was on the left. The bar entrance was on the right. I figured I would try my luck at the bar. I walked in, and it was like time had stood still. The same dark stained bar. The same high-backed bar stools and probably many of the same patrons drinking madeira wine or espresso. The last time I ate at Antonio's, smoking was still allowed. The bar would be filled with cigarette smoke. After you left, the smell of smoke would linger on your clothes until they found their way to the washing machine.

I do not smoke and am grateful that it's no longer allowed in bars and restaurants in Massachusetts.

Though, I must admit, in some strange way, the smokers added a certain level of atmosphere to the bar. Wisps of white smoke circled in the air. I was waxing nostalgic, but it sure smelled much better in Antonio's, without the stink of cigarettes.

The white menu board with the daily specials was posted at the end of the bar. Today they had rabbit for $14.99. Tempting, but I had a Portuguese steak sandwich on my mind. One seat was left at the end of the bar, near the kitchen door. The dining room was jammed. Waiters and waitresses were coming and going like bees building a nest. The smell of olive oil and garlic wafted out of the kitchen every time the door opened. I sat down on the ancient stool, and every eye in the bar turned my way. Antonio's was the kind of place where everyone knew everyone. Locals primarily frequented it. Think of a Portuguese version of *Cheers*. I could hear Portuguese conversation as much as English. I know a few swear words in Portuguese. "Foda-se," (fuck it), "merda," (shit). As I moved past the regulars, I heard a muffled "merda policia." I am not bi-lingual, but I'm pretty sure the translation is "shit; the police." How had I been made so fast? It was a lucky guess or someone who had seen me at the docks was in the bar. After giving me the once over, everyone returned to their espressos and conversation.

The bartender, a thickly built, middle-aged man, dropped a menu in front of me. I was greeted with,

"Specials are on the board. We're out of littlenecks today."

Before I could order a beer, he walked back down to the other end of the bar and started talking in Portuguese to two older guys who had been there from the first day the joint opened. I was parched and tried everything short of waving my arms like the sailors do on the deck of a cutter, guiding fighter pilots. Finally, I caught his eye, and he slowly strolled back in my direction.

"Know what you want?"

I quickly replied before he had a chance to escape. "Yeah. I want a Sam Adams draft and a Portuguese steak sandwich."

No reply. But I did get an ice-cold beer plopped in front of me and a setup. What the hell? Not very friendly. But I was not here for the conversation anyway.

The service was always fast at Antonio's, and that had not changed either. Within ten minutes, my sandwich was sitting in front of me. The difference between a Portuguese steak sandwich and your average steak and cheese was the steak, the seasoning, and the sauce. It was a thin steak, and not shaved. A sauce that is hard to describe, garlic, olive oil, and a hint of mustard. Visualize creole meeting garlic. Topped with onions and red peppers, Heaven was on a Portuguese roll and always served with Portuguese fries. The fries were not like your standard fries at a chain restaurant. These fries were thin, circular slices of potato, fried to a light brown.

I inhaled the contents of my plate, washed it down with another Sam Adams, and asked for the check. It was well under twenty dollars. The meal was a money well spent. I paid my bill, leaving the bartender a generous tip. I had a feeling I would be back in New Bedford again. Maybe I could build some good will. I said, "Thanks," then headed out the front door.

I had not planned on spending the night in New Bedford, but plans had changed. I needed to find a hotel room for the night. I would call John Ring to let him know what was happening and call my neighbor, Lily, at the condominium complex to feed Trixie. I hated leaving my cat alone overnight. Unlike most cats, Trixie was a social creature. She likes Lily. So that helps. My dinner date at Mike's Restaurant was set, and I could not be late.

CHAPTER THIRTY ONE

I called John first, and my call went straight to voicemail. I left a message letting him know I would be spending the night in New Bedford, continuing to follow leads, and would call him first thing in the morning with an update. I needed to find a hotel room for the night. In the nineties, the only lodging available were cheap motels whose clientele consisted of prostitutes, drug addicts, and various other unsavory types. I pulled out my smartphone and googled hotels in New Bedford. Surprisingly, a couple of new hotels popped up on the screen. The Fairfield Inn and Suites was a four-star chain on New Bedford harbor. It seemed a bit pricey at $250 per night, but I had an expense account.

This was an unexpected expense, but after all, Emma Jean was a high-profile FBI case with top priority. I didn't think John would mind. I called the 800 number, and a woman with a distinct Boston accent answered. They had two rooms available. I booked a room with a king bed. I still had time before my 7:00 p.m. meet and greet at Mike's. I had the phone numbers of the crew members of the Emma Jean on my cell phone. I had not planned on interviewing any of them on this trip, but I had the time, and I was in the city, so why not make some calls and see if anyone was available to talk to me?

New Bedford Scallopers were having a good year. The prices were high, and the catches were great. Fishermen must make their money when they can. The season is limited, and the Division of Marine Fisheries rules are always changing. The Emma Jean was a single-bucket scalloper. That is why there were only five fishermen: not the usual seven for a two-bucket. It made my job a little easier.

My first call went to Emma Jean's mechanic, Barry Gomes. The mechanic on a fishing boat is the most important crew member besides the captain. He would be responsible for anything mechanical such as refrigeration, hydraulics, electrical, and diesel engine repairs. A boat with a bucket that does not work, or refrigeration gone awry would be a major problem. Scallops do not keep fresh for long, particularly in the summer heat.

I called Barry's phone number, and it went straight to voicemail.

"Hi, this is Barry. I probably do not want to talk to you, but if you insist, leave a message, and maybe I'll call you back."

A real charmer. I left a message identifying myself as an FBI agent, that I was in the city and would like to talk with him. I hung up and was about to make my next call when an incoming call appeared on my screen as Unknown caller.

"This is Agent Ragusa. Who am I speaking with?"

A growling, low pitched voice said, "Are you really with the FBI?"

"Yes, I am Special Agent Robert Ragusa. Who are you?"

After a long pause, the reply came, "This is Barry Gomes. You wanted to talk with me?"

"Yes, Mr. Gomes. I'm in the city and would like to meet with you about the fire on the Emma Jean."

"Dude, I already talked with those guys from the Coast Guard. I told them everything I know. One minute, everything is fine. The next minute the ship is on fire, and I am jumping into the ocean."

"Well, Mr. Gomes, there have been some new developments. I would really like to talk to you in person." I pushed a little harder. "Your cooperation with the FBI would be greatly appreciated. Where can we meet?"

"Okay, okay, I want to cooperate, of course. I'm at home. Feel free to come by. I'll give you the address."

"I already have it, sir. I'll be there in fifteen minutes."

• • •

Barry lived on Hathaway Road near New Bedford Municipal Airport. Hathaway Road was in one of the better sections of the city. Populated by Middle-class homes with manicured lawns, it was about as close to suburbia as you could get in New Bedford. I set my GPS to Barry's address, 149 Hathaway Road, and headed toward Route 140 north. The first exit was Hathaway Road. I took a right off the exit, and about a mile down on the right was Barry's house, a nondescript ranch on a quarter acre lot. Nothing special. What stood out was a newer model Porsche 911 Carrera S sitting in the driveway. It did not fit with the neighborhood. Fishermen make a good living, $100K to $200K in a good year, and this was a good year. Fishermen make good money but not Porsche Carrera S money.

I had already conducted extensive background checks on every crew member of the Emma Jean. Barry was married with two kids. His oldest son, Bruno, was in college. His wife, Lydia, was a homemaker. Something did not add up, unless he hit the lottery, inherited money, or had a little side action going on. If Barry was trying to keep a low profile, he was doing a lousy job.

I walked up the concrete driveway, weeds sprouting out of the cracks here and there, and banged on the front door. I was greeted by a petite, attractive, dark-haired woman dressed in a brightly printed sundress.

"I am Lydia. You must be Agent Ragusa from the FBI. Barry told me that you would be by. Come in, please. Have a seat on the couch. Barry is in the garage. I'll let him know that you're here."

The house was your typical one-level ranch. Nicely furnished. Nothing fancy. Pictures of the kids and who I assumed were other family members on the walls. Mrs. Gomes went toward the kitchen, where there was a door leading out to the garage. I could hear a radio on that sounded like a sports radio station. A caller was screaming about how the "Sawx" should blow up the team and bring up the kids from the minors.

Out of the garage emerged Barry. He towered over his wife by at least a foot. Barry's attire was, shall we say, casual. He has on grease-covered jeans, a white T-shirt, and old school Converse sneakers, which had seen better days. Barry was still wiping grease from his hands when he reached out to shake my hand.

"Sorry about my appearance. My hobby is restoring old cars. I'm working on a 1966 Mustang Convertible in the garage. She is a sweet car, red with a tan interior. Care to look?"

I reached out and shook his hand. I noticed a smudge of grease left behind on my palm.

"Sure. I'm a bit of a car buff myself."

Barry led the way to the garage and what a sight to behold! It looked like one of those cars they auctioned off on that TV show, Mecum Auto Auctions. The one where guys with white gloves gingerly push perfectly restored cars onto the auction floor and wealthy car enthusiasts with money to burn bid exorbitant prices to own a piece of automobile history. Barry's Mustang was a beauty.

"What do you think?" crowed Barry, obviously proud of his work.

"I think with a Porsche Carrera S in your driveway and this '66 Mustang in your garage, fishing must be good this year."

Barry replied, "Unlike most fishermen, my only vice is cars. Not women, drugs, nor alcohol." Barry continued; You would be surprised how much money that saves"

I slowly walked around the Mustang, careful not to touch it. I could see my reflection in the shiny paint job. This car was a dream car. The Mustang was a work in progress now but will be a showstopper once restored. A 1966 Mustang Convertible in excellent condition can sell for over $50,000.00.

After slowly circling the car, I said, "She is a beauty, Mr. Gomes. Thanks for letting me see her. Is there somewhere we can talk?"

"Please, everyone calls me Barry. Let's go into my office. We'll have some privacy there."

I followed Barry out of the garage, through the kitchen where Mrs. Gomes was stirring a simmering pot of kale soup on the stove. His office was a converted bedroom at the other end of the house. Miniature classic model cars lined the shelves on all four walls. It was obvious that cars were his passion.

"Barry, I understand you were the mechanic on the Emma Jean the day she caught fire."

"Yes, that is right, but that's not my only job on the boat. I am a fisherman, just like every other man on the Emma Jean. Scalloping has been excellent this year, and everyone, including myself, works hard on deck shucking scallops. At the New Bedford auction, prices go for over $20.00 per pound. I do not know how much you know about fishing Agent Ragusa, but that's record pricing. Every crewman gets a share of the catch. We work an average of fourteen hours a day in all kinds of conditions. We go out from ten to fourteen days at a time. It's exhausting work, but you can make what a factory worker makes a year, in a couple of good trips. My main job as the ship mechanic is to check the engines, hydraulics, refrigeration, and anything mechanical on the boat. If everything works well, I am on deck working just like everyone else."

"Do you have a background in marine mechanics?" I inquired.

"I spent two years at Mass Maritime. I never graduated. I had to drop out after my sophomore year. I ran out of money. I knew there was money in fishing. Most of the guys I went to high school with went right to the docks after they graduated. Hell, half of them never graduated. I've worked a few boats with guys that can't read or write, but they're making 100K a year, shucking scallops. I started as a shacker twenty years ago and have been at it ever since. My background in mechanics gave me an edge over the other guys, and I quickly moved up the ranks to mechanic. Every minute lost due to mechanical malfunctions is money lost. The captains know that and take good care of me. I have always had work on the docks."

I was starting to build a good rapport with Barry. I thought the time was right to push a little harder.

"Barry, what do you think caused the fire on the Emma Jean?"

"I do not know. It all happened so fast. I was on deck. The next thing I know, smoke is billowing out of the galley. I grabbed the nearest fire extinguisher and rushed downstairs to extinguish the fire, but the smoke and heat knocked me back. I saw the flames coming at me. Next thing I knew, the captain gave the order to abandon the ship.

"I dropped the fire extinguisher, grabbed a life jacket, and jumped into the sea. I've never been so scared in my life. I am bobbing like a top in three-foot swells, hoping the captain got off a mayday. We were not due back in port for a week. I was not going to last that long. I could see Manny and Christian also drifting in the water. I thought the Emma Jean would sink, but she didn't. I saw the captain come out of the pilothouse onto the deck. I felt relieved. I knew Captain Medeiros must have got off a mayday, and we would be saved. The current took me slowly away from the boat. I'm not a good swimmer and I drifted apart from the rest of the crew. Without that life jacket, we would not be having this conversation. About half an hour later, I saw a fishing boat approaching the horizon. It was the Olivia Rose, thank God. They were heading right for me. A few minutes later, I was on the deck of the Olivia Rose, a blanket around me. Next, they fished out Manny and Christian. I felt so overwhelmed and grateful. A real miracle. I feel awful about Hank. He had a young son. It's a shame that a kitchen fire was to blame."

I wanted to gauge Barry's reaction to my next question, so I leaned toward him and slowly said, "What if I told you the fire was no accident?"

"Barry bolted out of his chair. "What are you talking about?" His helpful demeanor had turned to rage. "Are you accusing me of setting the fire?"

"I am not accusing you of anything, Barry. But the FBI lab in Boston has determined the fire was set on purpose." I am a pretty good poker player and thought a little bluffing might be in order.

"It was an electrical fire, Barry. Someone messed with the outlet in the kitchen to make the fire look like an accident."

With a blank look of disbelief, Barry said, "Come on, man. Do you think I would risk my life and the lives of the crew? For what? What motive would I have to burn down my ship? Do you know how much money that fire cost me, not to mention the captain and the rest of the crew?"

I had to keep pushing. Barry's reaction of outrage was what an innocent man usually projects, but he could be just a good actor.

"You have an expensive hobby for a fisherman. You own a Porsche in the driveway and a classic Mustang in the garage. You're the boat mechanic, Barry. I assume you know a lot about electrical work."

Barry glared at me like he wanted to teach me a lesson with a filet knife. Now it was his turn to push me. He leaned into me until we were nose-to-nose.

"Listen, you FBI motherfucker. I have worked twenty years to get what I got, all legit. I told you already I do not have any bad habits. Cars are my passion and only vice. After the bills are paid, that is where my money goes. Now, get out of my house."

I tried to cool down the temperature in the garage a bit.

"You seem like a hard-working guy. Sorry if my questions made you angry, but a man may have died on the Emma Jean. I am sure you want me to get to the bottom of this."

No response from Barry, just an icy stare and a finger pointing toward the front door. I made my way out of the garage through the kitchen, past his wife. She must have heard the yelling. Lydia gave me a look at a mixture of anger and concern as I headed out the front door. I could not rule Barry Gomes out, but my gut told me he wasn't involved.

I started up my rental and headed back to Route 140 South, toward downtown. I wanted to check into the Fairfield Inn before heading to Mike's Restaurant for the rendezvous with Mr. or Ms. Anonymous. I had a couple of hours until the meeting and was getting nervous. Against FBI protocol, I planned to go to the rendezvous at Mike's alone. No backup. It was not textbook, but it had to be this way. No matter how much training you get at Quantico, you cannot be prepared for every contingency. That was about to be proven true.

CHAPTER THIRTY TWO

The Fairfield Inn and Suites are located just off Route 18 on New Bedford harbor, another sign that this was not your grandfather's New Bedford. New Bedford was still a working harbor, but it had taken on a much different vibe since the last time I was here in the '90s. Upscale harbor front restaurants such as The Black Whale dotted the inner harbor. The mayor and the Chamber of Commerce were pitching the city as a tourist destination, and it was working to some degree. The quaint, cobblestoned downtown was transformed from fishermen's bars, pawn shops, and dive bars to a trendy mix of restaurants and art galleries anchored by the New Bedford Whaling Museum. The museum had recently undergone a multimillion-dollar facelift and anchored the downtown. Nearby was the Zeiterion Performing Arts Center. The "Z" was opened in April 1923, when New Bedford was known as "the richest city in the world."

New Bedford then was home to two dozen theaters, attracting all the day's top acts like George

Jessel. One of its most notable openings was that of *Moby Dick* in 1956, with Gregory Peck in attendance. The art deco theater, with marble walls and stately chandeliers, was a throwback to a bygone era. The Z had undergone a facelift and continues to provide culture and entertainment to the city today.

Ferry service provides roundtrip travel to and from New Bedford and Martha's Vineyard, the island where celebrities and presidents are frequent visitors. Former President Barak Obama had recently purchased a twelve-million-dollar estate on "the Vineyard." The ferry terminal is within walking distance of the cobblestone section of New Bedford, and more tourists are discovering its history and growing art scene. I needed to let John know that plans had changed. I called from my cellphone and the call went immediately to voice mail. I left a vague message about staying over the night in New Bedford and new developments in the case. I knew this was not going to satisfy John and that he would want a full debriefing when I got back to the field office.

I pulled into the parking lot of the Fairfield Inn and walked into the empty lobby. A young desk clerk with purple hair and a sleeve of tattoos on her left arm greeted me.

"Yes, sir, can I help you?"

"You should have a room for me. Robert Ragusa."

She checked on the computer and looked it up at me with a smile.

"Yes, sir, I have you here for one night. Your total for one night is $269.15, which includes taxes. How will you be paying?"

"With my credit card," I replied. "Okay, I just need your driver's license and credit card."

Her name tag said Tallulah. Tallulah pushed a piece of paper in front of me.

"Could you please complete this form with your vehicle type and plate number?"

I had no idea what the plate number was on the SUV, so I headed back into the parking lot. I returned, completed the form, and she handed me the magnetic card key to room 332. Tallulah then pulled out a map of the property, drew a circle around my room and directed me to parking nearby. She asked if I needed help with my luggage.

As I had none, I replied, "No thanks."

"Mr. Ragusa, breakfast is free. Breakfast is served from 7:00 a.m. to 10:00 a.m. Have a nice stay."

She was cheerful enough. Free breakfast at a hotel usually means watery scrambled eggs, watered down orange juice, and sausages that Jimmy Dean would not put his name on. Well, there is always toast and coffee.

I ambled into the hotel's little souvenir shop and passed by the coffee mugs with whales painted on them and T-shirts that read New Bedford the Whaling City. In the corner of the shop was a small section devoted to toiletries. I grabbed a toothbrush, toothpaste, a package of disposable razors, and some shaving cream. I plopped them on the counter. A surly, overweight Hispanic woman rang me up. She clearly did not like her job. The register read $28.30. About three times what it would have cost me at Walmart. I put it on the company card. What the hell? This was an important case, and some things you just cannot plan for. I didn't think John would complain about the money.

Next stop was my room, and a nap before showtime. I entered my room, tossed the bag of toiletries on the bathroom sink, and plopped down onto the king-sized bed. The view was quite stunning. A steady parade of draggers, trawlers, colorful sailboats at full mast, and power boats headed past Fish Island, Crow Island, and the open sea. It all looked so peaceful. I love the ocean. Watching the waves, the smells of the sea, the gentle rocking of a boat. It mesmerizes me. It hits all the senses. Pleasure boating would have to be another day. I had a date at Mike's Restaurant. Who would my dinner date be?

CHAPTER THIRTY THREE

I was lying on the bed looking out the window, watching the fishing boats come and go. New Bedford is a working harbor, but the hustle and bustle of the waterfront, the smell of the ocean, the cries of the seagulls, and the variety of characters working on the docks made it a strangely romantic backdrop. I realize that now. Back in the '90s I came down to play my gigs at the Widows Cove, packed up, and headed back north, week after week. I never took the time to enjoy the beauty and history of the "Whaling City."

I didn't have much of a game plan for my meeting at Mike's. Was this a setup? Is some fisherman messing with me? Or someone with a conscience would provide valuable information that would help me break the case of Emma Jean wide open. New Bedford is a small city, and even smaller in the fishing community. Word must have gotten around that I was an FBI agent and had been snooping around the docks. I had been made at Antonio's. That and my four flats at Waxy's and my Caddy getting shot up on the Tobin was not coincidence.

I had been to Mike's for dinner several times in the '90s. It was the kind of place where everyone knew everyone. The bartender and the waitstaff never changed. That was because the place was always packed. Not just on Friday and Saturday nights but every night. It had a tremendously loyal lunch crowd as well. They were known for their Italian food and prime rib. The entrance led you directly to an L-shaped bar. The hostess stand was to the right, and behind the hostess stand was the dining room. The only bathroom was to the left of the bar. I wanted to get there early and get a seat at the bar, preferably one of the three seats in front of the bathroom entrance. The angle would give me a clear line of sight for anyone entering the restaurant. It was 5:00 p.m. and time to go.

New Bedford is connected to Fairhaven by a working drawbridge. If the bridge were up, you could sit on Route 6 for at least fifteen minutes, especially in the summer. I didn't want to take the chance. I took the safety off my Glock, holstered it, and headed out of the hotel lobby. I started the car and drove down Route 18. The exit for Fairhaven was to the right. I could see that traffic on Route 6 was moving, which meant the bridge was down. I passed over the bridge and into Fairhaven. Though separated from New Bedford by only three hundred feet of water, Fairhaven is a world apart. Fairhaven is a small town with single-family homes, open green spaces, good schools and mostly a lily-white population.

As I remembered, Mike's was about a mile down Route 6 on the left. At 5:15, I pulled into the parking lot, which was already half full. I didn't want dinner at Mike's to turn into the gunfight at the OK Corral, so I unholstered my Glock and left it in the trunk. The FBI has standard protocols for these types of meetings with informants or suspects in a case. I was following none of them. I had no real surveillance, no backup team, and no backup plan. I was on my own. A real piss poor idea, but it was worth the risk.

Mike's was exactly as I remembered. I do not think they had painted the place since I last had dinner there in 1998. I entered through the front door, and the layout was the same. Nothing had changed. The same L-shaped bar, same hostess stand, and probably the same waitresses, with a little grayer hair. I spotted one seat near the bathroom on the left side of the bar and made a beeline to it. An elderly couple, engaged in a conversation that seemed to center around the pros and cons of Donald Trump, was to my left. Apparently, nobody told these two you don't talk religion or politics in a bar. The bartender, an overweight, middle-aged woman with dark, short-cropped hair and a tattoo of barbed wire wrapping around her right wrist, looked at me.

"I will be right with you. I got to get some food from the kitchen first."

She briefly disappeared and returned with a plate of veal parm that she placed in front of a construction worker seated at the other end of the bar. She waddled her way toward me, plopped a well-worn menu in front of me and asked, "What you are drinking?"

"Jim Beam Manhattan rocks on the side."

The Manhattan came in a glass twice the size I was used to. It also came with a side car that amounted to half of another drink. The menu had not changed. There was a mix of American and New England Classics, open faced steak sandwich, prime rib, half pound lobster roll, pizza, chicken parm. You get the idea. I flagged down the bartender and ordered the shrimp and garlic appetizer. Something to help absorb the alcohol. The biggest piece of meat I have ever seen, called the Cattleman Cut, did a drive by on its way to a table of four executive types in the corner booth. Fifteen minutes later, I could smell it coming. The garlic and oil were an intoxicating mix that filled the senses. An appetizer masquerading as a meal. The portions were always huge at Mike's. That had not changed either.

I watched and waited for my contact to appear. I kept looking down at my Timex as the minutes slipped by. The place was getting busy. I didn't know who the hell I was looking for or how I might be approached. I had a view of anyone entering the bar, but for all I knew, whoever was my contact could already be here or out of my line of sight in the dining room. I thought about looking in the dining room, but whoever wanted to meet knew who I was. I just needed to sit tight and let whomever it was make their move.

I was getting tense as the minutes ticked by. A steady stream of men and women passed by me on their way to the restrooms. Halfway through my Manhattan I got a gentle tap on the shoulder. I turned around, and a young, attractive woman was on my right. She was wearing a cream-colored short sleeve blouse, a short black skirt, and a tattoo on her left shoulder with the initials WM inside a heart. She was an eye turner with her bleach blonde hair pulled tight into a ponytail.

The blonde leaned in and asked me, "Is your name Harrison? You look just like the father of a guy I dated in high school." She looked so young. High school might have been last year. Curious.

I replied, "No. My last name is not Harrison."

I didn't know what was going on. Was she a go-between to my contact or just a simple case of mistaken identity? I was waiting for a follow-up question, but it never came. She casually strutted through the bar, precariously balanced on stiletto heels with another older brunette behind her. Why do women always go to the bathroom in twos? If men did that someone would be calling the manager. They passed by the entrance and disappeared back into the main dining room. My heart rate returned to normal, and I kept surveilling the restaurant.

It was now close to 8:00 p.m. The dining room had mostly cleared out. A few barflies remained on their favorite stools. I was on my second Manhattan, and things were getting a little blurry. The bartender gave me a look like "buddy, it's time to go." It was time to call it a night. I paid my tab of $39.50. Cheaper than Boston prices for sure. I left a 30 percent tip and headed back to the parking lot. My SUV sat alone on the far side of the parking lot.

I felt dejected as I opened the driver's side door and slid in. I thought this was a setup, or some fisherman was just screwing with me. I knew Mike's would be a dead end, but I had hung onto a small glimmer of hope that this contact might help me break the case wide open. I was about to push the ignition button when things started spinning. I had had two Manhattans over the course of three hours plus dinner, so a little buzz was possible, but not this. Then everything went dark.

The next thing I knew, I could hear pounding. Was it my head? No, a beefy guy with a scraggly beard was banging on the driver's side window. In a fog, I could hear him screaming,

"Hey, buddy. You cannot sleep here in the parking lot. If you cannot drive, I'll call you a cab."

I could barely think straight. My head was pounding, but I nodded my head, said no, and waved him off. He lingered for a few seconds, then headed toward a red Camaro. He jumped in and took off east on Route 6. I looked at my Timex, and it read 1:00 a.m. Incredulously, I looked again. I'd been out of it for five hours. What happened?

I was starting to regain my faculties when I noticed the car had been tossed. My wallet's on the floor on the front passenger side. The glove compartment is open, with the rental agreement hanging halfway out. I reached down and grabbed my wallet. Someone had gone through it, but nothing was missing. Even my cash, a couple of hundred dollars, was still there. I'm still just starting to feel normal when I notice a cocktail napkin stuck under the windshield wiper. I slowly open the door and step into the muggy air. I'm still wobbly but I managed to lift the windshield wiper and retrieve the cocktail napkin. The napkin is from Mike's. I turned it over, and in blue ink was written:

We know who you are; we know why you're here; you're looking in the wrong direction.

Who were they? Are there even they? Or was someone trying to send me and my investigation in the wrong direction? I felt embarrassed. With all my training and field experience, someone was able to get to me. I had not left my barstool all night. I watched the bartender pour my drinks. I had only picked at my food. If someone had put something in my food, I wouldn't have eaten enough for any knockout drug to take effect.

It had to be the bottle blonde. When she approached, she tapped me on my right shoulder. I had turned my head to the right to talk to her. No way she could have slipped anything into my drink. I had my eyes on her the whole time. She had to be working with an accomplice. The bar was crowded, and a steady parade of people came and went to the restrooms. Somebody could have slipped me a mickey on my left side, and I would never have seen it. The older brunette had to be working with the blonde. She had to have been behind me, to my left. I never even saw her until they passed in front of me as they strolled through the bar. It was a perfect spot. All she had to do was wait till the bartender was not looking, and bingo.

All I got from my night at Mike's Restaurant was a pounding headache and more questions than answers. My head was starting to clear. I was about to start her up and head back to the hotel when a moment of clarity struck. Holy shit, what about my Glock?

The keys were still in my pocket, but they could have opened the trunk just by pushing the trunk button on the dashboard. I opened the trunk, and it was still there. I checked it. Still loaded with the safety on, thank Christ! Losing your weapon is a serious offense in the FBI. This offense could end one's career. I did not want anyone to know what had happened at Mike's.

The restaurant was closed tight. Mine was the only car left in the lot. I would have to wait another day to return visit to Mike's. I doubted the blonde or the brunette were regulars, but I had to check with the staff to see if anybody knew them. The good news? I was still alive. The bad news? What happened to the Emma Jean was more than a simple kitchen fire. Whoever slipped me that mickey knew who I was and the reason I was in New Bedford. They were sending me a message to back off from the investigation. Or I was looking in the wrong direction. But one thing was abundantly clear. I was wearing out my welcome.

CHAPTER THIRTY FOUR

My head was still clearing as I pulled into the parking lot of the Fairfield Inn. My Timex read 2:00 a.m. One lone desk clerk reading the New Bedford Standard Times. He gave me a quick once over and then returned to the sports page.

I went to my room still trying to process what had happened at Mike's. I was feeling a mixture of fear and anger. All my training and years of experience, and someone had been able to get to me. I had been thinking about retirement. I had enough years in to receive a full pension. Maybe it was time, but I didn't want to go out like this. I had no more idea now what happened on the Emma Jean than I did the day I got the case. All I knew was it was not a simple grease fire. There was something much bigger going on here. I needed to keep digging and I needed a break. I took my loafers off, set the alarm for 7:00 a.m. and crashed. I was asleep before my head hit the pillow.

The alarm went off at 7:00 a.m. I leaned across the bed, tempted to hit the snooze button, but I had to get back to the field office in Chelsea and debrief John. I called his cellphone and left a voicemail that I would be in the office by 9:00 a.m. I was going to hit rush hour traffic. So, I bought a corn muffin and a large black coffee to go from the lobby coffee shop and made my way to the office. Traffic was lighter than expected. I had forgotten that it was Saturday. I made it to the parking lot by 8:00 a.m., an hour earlier than planned. The FBI field office was mostly a Monday through Friday operation, but there were always a few agents working on open cases on the weekends.

John usually came into the office on Saturdays. He would stay until about Noon and then head out to one of his kid's endless soccer or baseball games. The door to John's office was open. I was not looking forward to this meeting. Lying to an FBI supervisor could get you fired, but I couldn't tell him what had happened at Mike's Restaurant. I had gone way off the reservation. Probably not enough to get me fired but certainly suspended. I needed to stay on the case. I was hoping nothing would get back to him. Whoever had slipped me that mickey had no cause to contact the FBI. Nobody in the bar knew me, and the guy who banged on my window thought I was just another drunk guy who decided to sleep it off in their car.

I kept trying to convince myself it would all work out, but the knot in my stomach kept tightening as I approached John's office.

"Rob, you must be taking a real liking to New Bedford. I hardly see you around here anymore. I hope you have some good news. What's happening with the Emma Jean investigation? Our travel budget is not what it used to be. I hope last night's stay at the Fairfield Inn was worth it?"

"Well, John. I'm still digging. Word has gotten around the waterfront that the FBI is working the case."

"How do you know that Rob?"

"I was approached, anonymously, on the docks, and a kid handed me a note and took off before I could talk to him. The note read, meet me at 7:00 p.m. at Mike's Restaurant. I thought it was a dead end, but you never know. That is why I stayed the night. I was hoping someone would come forward with more information. I spent the most of last night sitting at the bar at Mike's nursing a Manhattan. The bar was packed, but nobody approached me. It ended up being a no-show."

I conveniently omitted the part about my four hours of unconsciousness in the SUV. I knew it was important, but I couldn't tell John what happened there. At least not yet.

I was about to tell John I had nothing more to report when Vinny Chen, our resident computer nerd, came bursting through the door. I had not consulted with Vinny on the case but knew he was working on that number found in the suitcase. Vinny could program, write code, restore deleted files, and do anything with computers. The FBI had recruited him right out of MIT. Top of his class, Vinny could have gone anywhere. He could have been one of those internet millionaires, working at Google or Facebook but that was not his style. Vinny enjoyed the chase. He liked solving puzzles and I hoped he had discovered a piece.

"Rob, I have been working around the clock on that number in the black suitcase. I thought it might have been an international phone number. I worked that angle and kept coming up empty."

"Okay, Vinny. You look excited. You're getting me excited. Do not keep me in suspense."

"It is an IP address. Out of the blue, it dawned on me that maybe I was on the wrong track. The numbers didn't match any known international phone numbers. The more I looked at it, the more I realized it was not a phone number. It was an IP address. An IP address can go from 0 to 255. From 0 0 0 0 to 255 255 255 255. Your number is in a group of four. So, I went on my desktop and started searching the dark web using the Tor Browser."

I jumped in, "Vinny, you are speaking a foreign language. I can barely send an email. What's the Tor Browser?"

"Oh, sorry, Rob. I forgot you were born in the Jurassic period. The Tor Browser, also known as an Onion Router, hides your IP address and browsing activity by redirecting web traffic through a series of routers. It's used by legit people, who want to stay anonymous, but it's rumored to be used by others for illegal means.

"I have been at it for days but kept getting timed out. I finally tracked the IP address to a website based in London, The Red Crescent Trading Company. I downloaded and printed the contents of the site. It is in code. I sent it down to our codebreakers in Quantico. It is a cover for a smuggling operation. An operation smuggling drugs into the United States using fishing boats as cover. New Bedford is not mentioned by name, but there is a reference to East Coast fishing ports. I've got the printout and what Quantico sent me back in my office. I will go get it so you can have a look."

I could see John's face turning a bright shade of red.

He yelled, "Vinny, you have worked here long enough to know the chain of command by now. Why is this the first I am hearing of this code?"

The look on Vinny's face was a mix of surprise and terror. He stammered.

"I–I am sorry, sir. I should have brought it to you immediately. I do not know what I was thinking."

"You were not thinking. This code could be the key to the Emma Jean case, and it is sitting on your goddamn desk. Get it now!"

Vinny slinked out the door and headed to his office. He must have run because, in what seemed like ten seconds, he returned with a twenty-page printout of the website, 'rocalvm2z1976onion.

Vinny handed the printout to John, who looked at it quizzically. John shouted at Vinny.

"Make another copy for Rob. I'm going to call Barry Easley in Quantico. He heads up the code-breaking lab. I want to go over the print-out word-by-word with Barry and make sure he is kept in the loop."

Vinny hurried back to his office and printed out another copy for me.

"Rob, I want you to read this over the weekend and see if you recognize any names, places, or anything that might give us a clue as to who is behind this Red Crescent Trading Company and what they are up to. You have spent some time now in New Bedford. Maybe some characters you have met are tied up in this."

"Ok, John. I will. Maybe some of the crew on the Emma Jean are involved."

"All right. Be in my office at nine o'clock on Monday morning, and we will compare notes. You too, Vinny. I want you to stay on this, and from now on, everything goes through me. Got it?"

Vinny was avoiding eye contact but replied, "Yes, boss." Vinny did a 360 and headed back to his office.

John said, "I am going to contact Interpol in London and see if they know anything about this site. Maybe we can draw a line from London to New Bedford."

"Okay, John. Unless there is something else, I would like to go home and feed my cat."

"Sure, Rob, see you Monday."

Tonight was my date with Sandy. I sure was not going to impress Sandy with a white SUV. The caddy had been released from evidence, but I had it towed to Chuck's Auto for some much-needed repairs and bodywork. I shook John's hand, grabbed the printout, and returned to the SUV.

CHAPTER THIRTY FIVE

I had not been on a real date in about ten years. The plan was to meet at the Continental Restaurant in Saugus at 7:00 p.m. I called and made a reservation. Since it was a Saturday night, I anticipated that the venue would be crowded. Even though the Kowloon was my favorite watering hole, it was a bit too casual for a first date. Plus, I didn't know if Sandy liked Chinese food. The Continental was a sure bet to impress. A couple of miles down Route 1, it was ten minutes from my house. The Continental was a landmark. The place had been there forever. A classic steakhouse with that old dark elegant mahogany interior, dim lighting, and romantic ambiance. White linen tablecloths and servers dressed in crisp white shirts and black pants, real class.

The Continental is a little pricey, so I do not go there often, but I wanted to impress Sandy. Other than going to Boston, it was my best option. I had some time to kill. I needed to get home, feed Trixie, and pick up a fifty-dollar gift card from the Kowloon for my neighbor, Mrs. Clancy, for feeding Trixie and changing her litter box while I was in New Bedford.

I needed to process the last forty-eight hours. Finally, we had a break. The case was starting to come together. I needed to coordinate with John, Vinny, and the computer nerds in Quantico, and Interpol in London. It was complicated, but I was starting to feel more confident that all roads were leading to the Emma Jean.

I pulled into the parking lot of my condominium at 4:00 p.m. The timeframe gave me a couple of hours to feed and get reacquainted with Trixie. I walked through the door, and there she was. She greeted me with a look of indifference, as only cats can do. It was like she was pissed that I had left her for a couple of days. I heard a saying once: If you want to be adored, get a dog, and if you want to be ignored, get a cat. Trixie could be fickle. She had been well taken care of. She still had some wet food in her bowl, and her water dish was full. The cat box was immaculate. Thank God for Mrs. Clancy. After she stared at me for a few minutes, I called Trixie and she slowly sauntered up to me and started rubbing against my leg, purring. This act was Trixie's sign that all was forgiven, and we were friends again. I slipped the gift card into an envelope with a note of thanks and slipped it under Mrs. Clancy's door. I knew that if I gave the envelope directly to Mrs. Clancy, she would not accept it.

It was time to get ready for my date with Sandy. After looking through my closet, I settled on a black shirt, tan pants, and my only pair of brown dress shoes. Casual but stylish was going to be the theme. I showered, put on the only cologne I own, Old Spice, got dressed and cracked open the last beer in the fridge. I sat in my recliner, my mind bouncing from what happened at Mike's, to my date with Sandy. Nerves, I guess. I had not been on a real date for almost ten years. I didn't know much about Sandy, only that there was an instant attraction between us. Anyway, at least, I hoped that was the case. Maybe it was just a projection on my part. She accepted my offer for dinner, so that is a start. I wanted to get to the Continental by six o'clock, get a seat at the bar, and wait for her arrival. I've always tried to be a little early rather than late. I had high hopes for our date and wanted to get off on the right foot. It was 5:45 p.m. The Continental was about ten minutes from my condo. Time to head out.

The Continental was the gold standard for restaurants in Saugus. It had been there since I was a kid. Generations had passed through its doors. It was an understated, and classy place. Maybe a little dated, but you knew you would get good food and great service. The same servers and bartenders had been there for years. That is always a good sign. The kind of restaurant where the piano player in the lounge would be playing songs like Summer Wind and other classics, and the patrons would be sipping on drinks you do not see served much anymore, like Rob Roy's and Old Fashioneds. I didn't know Sandy's tastes in either food or music, but I felt the Continental was probably the safest bet for both.

I pulled into the parking lot at about five minutes to six, parked the SUV, and headed in. The hostess was an older woman, with stark white hair that hung down to her waist. She recognized me. I could not remember her name, but she remembered mine.

As I approached the hostess station, she said, "Hi, Rob. It is so good to see you. I noticed you have a reservation for two in the book. I have not seen you here for a long time. Where have you been?"

I was not a regular at the Continental, but when I did go there for dinner, I was always alone and sat at the bar.

I muttered, "Well, work has been really busy."

"I hope you're not working too hard." Then she winked at me and said, "I have got a table for two reserved for you in a nice quiet corner. Who is your guest? Anyone special?"

"Well, I sure hope so. I'm going to grab a seat at the bar until she shows up."

"Okay, Rob. Let me know when you are ready."

That is what I love about the Continental. They try to know all their patrons, regulars or not. I took a seat at the end of the bar. The restaurant was starting to fill up. I ordered a Manhattan from the bartender, who introduced himself as Bill. Bill was an older guy with white hair, glasses, and a bit of a paunch. I didn't recognize him, but I don't consider myself a regular here. Bill suggested a new bourbon that had just come in, but I stuck to Jim Beam. Why mess with the old "tried and true."

I was sipping on my Manhattan, keeping an eye on the front door, 7:00 p.m. came and went. I had not been stood up since Julie Boyce told me she couldn't go to the senior prom because she had to take care of her sick dog. Turned out she did not have a dog. She just wanted to hang out with her friends instead of me. I had to return my powder blue tuxedo to the rental shop, still in the plastic garment bag, ouch! That was almost forty years ago, but it still bothered me.

Just as I was losing hope, she walked through the front door and, man, it was worth the wait. She was dressed in high heels and a black, knee-length cocktail dress. Her hair was pulled back in a ponytail. She has just the right amount of makeup and a simple strand of white pearls around her neck. I was really taken aback. She had transformed from the girl next door to a supermodel. I took one last sip of my drink, left a twenty on the bar, and slowly walked up to her.

I stammered.

"Hi, Sandy, you look great. I didn't think you were going to make it."

She looked at me in such a way that I thought this date might be over before it even started. I could tell she was upset, but I didn't know why. I was not underdressed by the Continental's standards, although I was clearly a step behind her.

She looked at me and said, "I am sorry I'm late. I forgot how bad the traffic is going over the Tobin."

My heart got back into rhythm. It was not me or my casual attire. This night still had promise. The hostess gave me a knowing smile and signaled us toward the dining room.

The table for two was in the back of the restaurant, tucked into a corner. The dinner crowd was loud, but you could converse. I told her she looked sensational and apologized for being underdressed.

"You look great, Rob. I'm a little nervous. I have not been on a date for a long time."

"You and me both," I replied. "I feel like I'm back in high school."

Our waiter, a tall, dark-haired younger guy, in his early thirties, came over and lit the candle on the table. He handed us both well-worn menus.

"My name is Mario; I will be your server tonight. Would you like a drink this evening?"

Sandy ordered Johnny Walker black on the rocks, and I ordered my second Jim Beam Manhattan. Johnny Walker Black: I liked this woman already. My preconceived notion that she would order a Cosmo went right out the window.

I hate pretentious restaurants that have ten specials on the menu, nine of which I cannot pronounce.

After a few minutes, Mario returned with our drinks and asked if we would like to hear about the specials.

He referred to a piece of paper and said, "Tonight, we have smothered steak tips with peppers and onions, served with your choice of potato and seasonal mixed vegetables. In addition, we have a bone in pork chop, served with a demi glaze, also served with your choice of potato and seasonal mixed vegetables." We both took a quick glance at the menu. Sandy ordered the steak tips, medium rare baked potato with sour cream. The night was looking better and better. I ordered the same.

The conversation started a little awkwardly. We talked about police business, ongoing cases, and that sort of thing. I was intrigued by this woman and wanted to know more about her.

"So, enough shop talk. Tell me about Sandy."

She looked down at the table and then slowly raised her eyes to meet mine.

"What would you like to know, Rob?"

"Well, Sandy, I do not really know anything about you. What do you like to do when you are not working?"

She replied, "I love art, literature, the Red Sox, and the Patriots. I follow all their games. I love to travel and try new things. Right now, I am taking a class in woodworking at Massasoit Community College.

"My father was a carpenter. I watched him as a kid in his shop behind our house. He's retired now. I want to pay homage to him and learn more about his craft. I have been all over Europe. The next trip I am planning is to Israel. I am not Jewish but love history, and it seems like a fascinating place."

She paused, leaned forward, and whispered, "You seem like a sweet guy. Nobody's ever asked me about me before on a date. Most of the guys I dated after my divorce only wanted to discuss themselves. I usually could not get a word in edgewise. You are different. It is refreshing," she said with a smile.

"Well, I would like to know who I am having dinner with," came my reply. "How did you get into being a sketch artist?"

"I graduated from Massachusetts College of Art and Design in 1985. I pictured myself becoming a famous artist with shows in prestigious galleries in New York City. I tried to get my work into galleries but didn't have much luck. I did have one showing at a gallery on Newbury Street in Boston. I sold a couple of landscapes, but it is hard to live on $400.00." Sandy chuckled then.

"I have two brothers, one of whom is a sergeant with the police department in Hartford, Connecticut. He told me sketch artists make pretty good money and that he knew a few people in the Boston Police Department. One thing led to another, and here I am. I like the work and get some sense of reward knowing that sometimes my sketches help catch the bad guys. My family is close. Mom and Dad are still together after fifty-five years of marriage. I've had a good life. No complaints. I still have hope of finding that special someone."

My inner voice was loudly saying, "I hope that's me." I could see the waiter coming with our steak tips. The conversation would have to be put on hold. I was famished.

Sandy said, "I haven't had anything to eat today since my morning bowl of oatmeal."

The stack of blackened steak tips was enough to feed three people. Alongside was a steaming baked potato and a medley of fresh veggies including summer squash, zucchini, and red peppers. We both looked up at each other and simultaneously nodded approval. All conversation ceased for about twenty minutes until both plates were empty. Our waiter, Mario, checked in on us a couple of times. Both plates were clean. It was obvious we had enjoyed our meals. We ordered two coffees as he put the dessert menu on the table. The Continental's Crème Brulé is outstanding, but I was too stuffed. Sandy gave the menu a glance and pushed it away. Mario promptly returned with our coffees.

Sandy restarted the conversation.

"That was the best meal I have had in a long time. How come I have never heard of this place?" Sandy asked.

"Saugus is kind of a flyover country." I said. "Everyone seems to head directly to Boston to try out the newest, trendy restaurants. If you are willing to drive ten minutes north over the Tobin, you can get a great meal at the Continental for half the price of a Boston steakhouse." I quickly corrected myself.

"Not that I am cheap. Driving in Boston can be hazardous to your health. Then there's the parking. Try getting a parking space this time of night in the North End, fuhgeddaboudit."

"Well, I am sold, Rob. I will come back to this place."

I smiled at Sandy and said, "I hope so, and maybe I can keep you company."

"I would like that. So, I told you the Sandy story. Tell me about the Rob story."

For the next twenty, minutes I talked with Sandy about my family, my childhood in Southie, and how difficult it was being an Italian, growing up in an Irish neighborhood. I gave Sandy the abbreviated version of my law enforcement career that eventually led me to become an FBI Special Agent. I touched on my brief failed marriage and limited dating history. Sandy leaned forward and seemed genuinely interested. I'm pretty good at reading people. I can tell when someone is paying attention or tuning me out. Sandy was paying attention. I signaled to Mario for the check. That kind of universal pretend signature sign that everyone seems to understand.

He put the check face down in front of me. Sandy reached for it.

"Let me pay, Rob. I've had a really good time."

I was a little taken aback. I had never had a woman offer to pay a dinner tab before. Never even offer to pay the tip. I could tell Sandy was genuine, not just making a show of it. I snatched up the check, gave it a quick once over, and handed it back to Mario with my Visa.

"Rob, times have changed. Women pay their own way these days."

"Sandy, I am a bit of a dinosaur. Anyway, I asked you to dinner, remember? Like I said, I have not done much dating. Things have changed. That's going to take me some time to get used to. Sandy, I had a great time too. I was nervous as hell about this date, but I feel comfortable around you. I hope I can see you again."

"I like you, Rob. I had a great time, and yes, I want to see you again."

I thought the night had gone well, but you never know. I really liked Sandy. She was genuine, smart, interesting, and quite a looker.

Mario came back with the bill. I added a 30 percent tip. I slipped the Visa back into my wallet and handed the bill to Mario. This had been a special evening. Mario picked up the bill, took a glance at it, gave me a big smile, and said, "I hope to see you again."

"Do not worry, Mario. We'll be back."

I got out of the black leather chair, leaned over to Sandy, and gave her a peck on the cheek.

She grabbed my neck, pulled me closer and said, "You can do better than that I hope."

Sandy then kissed me on the lips.

"That's better."

I held her hand as we walked out into the sticky July air. I walked her to her car. She hugged me tight, gave me a long goodnight kiss, and got into her car.

"Thanks for a wonderful night, Rob. Call me. The next dinner is on me."

"You are on," I replied.

Sandy got into her Mini Cooper and, as she let the window down, slowly nodded, yes. I watched Sandy drive away before making my way to my SUV. Maybe I was thinking way too far ahead, but I felt my life had just changed.

As I drove back to my condominium, I couldn't get that old song, Singing in the Rain, out of my head. I felt like Gene Kelly splashing in that puddle. I was on cloud nine. I had not felt this way about a woman in a long time. It was going to be hard to focus. Back to reality, though. The rest of the weekend would be work-related. I had to review Vinny's printout, read my notes, and prepare for my Monday morning meeting with John.

CHAPTER THIRTY SIX

I opened the door to my condominium, still on cloud nine. Trixie was waiting for me with that look of benign neglect only a cat can provide. I love Trixie. She's great company, but I always feel I must keep trying to win her approval. A shrink could find some deeper meaning in all this.

I spent Sunday mostly in my recliner reading Vinny's printout. Whoever was on the site was talking in code. I'm no expert on the dark web, but the FBI and other government agencies constantly monitor activity. It always seems like the bad guys are one step ahead of our techs, and our techs are the best in the world. It shows you how sophisticated these bad actors are.

I was about two-thirds through the document when it started getting a little more interesting. The names Emma and Jean appeared. Not together in reference to a ship, but separately on different pages like they were names of real people. Lots of subtle references, too, regarding travel and the East Coast.

This placement was no coincidence. There were references to the fact that Emma and Jean might be unreliable.

It took me the entire day to get through the document as I read and re-read it, not wanting to miss any of the subtleties. I studied in my recliner with the TV on low volume and Trixie purring on my lap. The Red Sox were playing the Orioles at Fenway. The Orioles, a once proud franchise that sadly, were cellar dwellers for the last few years. The Red Sox were up nine to one in the fifth inning.

Most of what I was reading was boring as hell. I needed the occasional break to keep my eyes from glazing over. I needed to use the bathroom, but I knew Trixie would scratch me if I tried to get up. So, I held it. Such a princess. My mind sometimes wandered to last night's dinner date with Sandy, pleasant thoughts. Then a shift would happen. My mind would wander back to Mike's Restaurant and how I had let my guard down. I had made a newcomer mistake, and I'm not rookie. I was lucky. So far, word had not gotten back to John about what happened at Mike's Restaurant.

I planned to head back to New Bedford on Monday morning after the meeting with John. I wanted to stop by the Widows Cove Tavern and see Steve Poole. There were few secrets on the waterfront. If there were any talk about an FBI agent asking questions on the docks, it would eventually get back to Steve. I also wanted to take a side trip over the bridge to Fairhaven to interview the waitstaff at Mike's. I did not have high hopes of anyone recognizing the bottle blonde, but it was worth a shot.

I had the phone numbers for the other two crew members of the Emma Jean, Manny Sousa, and Christian DeJesus. They had caught on with other boats, but I was going to be in the city anyway, and they needed to be interviewed. It was worth a shot. I called them and got voicemail for both. I left Manny and Christian a message identifying myself as an FBI agent and that I would be in New Bedford on Monday to conduct interviews and ask that they make themselves available. Usually, unless you are dealing with hardcore criminals when people hear "FBI," they pay attention. I did not know what I was dealing with here. New Bedford had already thrown a lot of surprises at me. I guess these two were either hard-working fishermen or one or both were wrapped up in whatever happened on the Emma Jean.

I fell asleep on the recliner as usual. Trixie spent the whole night on my lap. I had not fed her, and she was meowing loudly while biting my ear. She wanted to be fed. I showered, shaved, and put on khaki pants and a polo shirt.

I called John and got his voicemail. I left him a message about my intentions for today. I headed out the door at eight o'clock. My first stop was

Enterprise Rental Car. My SUV had been tossed at Mike's. I needed a new rental to avoid detection. The Enterprise lot was on Route 1 just before the Continental. Route 1 South was already bumper-to-bumper with blurry-eyed commuters heading into Boston. I was heading north, so traffic was light. I pulled into the Enterprise parking lot and entered the tiny office. The FBI had a national agreement with Enterprise. I liked the convenience of Enterprise. Unlike other car rental agencies, Enterprise had small offices in cities and towns nationwide.

I approached the counter, and the same young guy, Sam, with heavily tattooed arms, was behind the desk.

He smiled and said, "Good morning, Mr. Ragusa. Is something wrong with the car?"

"No, Sam. The car is just fine, but I need something a little roomier. Can you help me?"

"Of course. No problem. Do you want a bigger SUV or a sedan?"

"I'd prefer a sedan if you have one." Sam led me to the lot's front door and pointed to a blue Chrysler 300. "This one just came in. Low mileage and loaded with options, including GPS."

I gave the Chrysler a quick once over and said, "I'll take it."

We went back into the office, and Sam drew up the paperwork. Within fifteen minutes, I was out the door and headed south down Route 1 and over the

Tobin Bridge. I knew that changing cars would not hide my identity, but any little advantage was worth the effort. As I crossed the Tobin, my cell phone began buzzing, it was John. I picked up on the first ring.

"Good morning, John. I am on my way. I'm on the Tobin. I should be there in fifteen minutes."

"There has been a change of plans, Rob. Quantico called, and they want me in on a conference call at 9:15 a.m. Why don't you just go straight to New Bedford? We can catch up later in the day."

I crossed over the Tobin onto the Southeast Expressway.

"Ok, John, I'll head to New Bedford and contact you when I'm finished there."

John's reply came with a hint of concern in his voice. "Be careful, Rob."

• • •

It was another hot, hazy day with a layer of brown smog over the city. I made good time getting to Route 24. With any luck, I would be in New Bedford by 9:00 a.m. I had not had breakfast yet, and my stomach was making noises. I stopped at the Burger King on Route 24's Bridgewater Plaza. I usually use the drive-thru, but I had some time to kill, so, I went inside and grabbed a table. I ordered a black coffee, with a ham and cheese croissant to kickstart my day. I finished the croissant and grabbed my coffee for the half hour ride to New Bedford. I rolled up at the

Widows Cove at five minutes to ten. A line of guys were already waiting for Steve to open the front door.

It never ceases to amaze me how anyone could drink at that time in the morning. It looked to be a mix of third-shift factory workers and fishermen who had probably just unloaded their catch. Steve would be in high gear as soon as the door opened. The alcohol would loosen a few tongues. Steve had been slinging beers and shots at the Widows Cove forever. He was not a fisherman, but he was an experienced sailor who knew the sea. Steve had sailed from Florida to New England in all kinds of weather. He could talk the talk. Steve was trusted and liked by the locals. Anyone from the mayor of New Bedford to fishermen with their deck boots still on, could be found at the well-worn bar. The first time I met him in the early nineties, it seemed like I had known him my whole life. He just had that gift. He could mutitask, pouring drinks and conversing with a regular while overhearing a conversation at the end of the bar. Useful skills to have. What had he heard? I would soon find out a lot.

CHAPTER THIRTY SEVEN

Steve opened the door at precisely 10:00 a.m. I waited a few minutes to let the crowd enter and get their drinks before entering. I did not know what the word on the docks was, but Steve would. I hoped he had something that would steer me in the right direction. The barstools were occupied by a mix of locals, from the factories and fish houses who worked the third shift.

Seven fishermen right off the boat, still dressed in deck shoes and greasy sweatpants, were sitting at a table at the end of the bar. The smell coming from their table was a foul mix of grease, fish, and diesel fuel. I remembered from my conversations with fishermen in the nineties that their scruffy look and smell was a source of pride for their dirty, dangerous work. A few construction types were at a table near the front door. They were well into their shots and beer when I entered the door.

Steve was pouring shots for five loud fishermen at the end of the bar. I recognized them from the docks. They were the crew on a single-bucket scalloper, docked two boats down from the Olivia Rose. They all gave me the once over and quickly returned to their shots of Jameson. Steve glanced toward the front door and spotted me as I made my way to the only open seat left, next to the kitchen door.

Steve shouted above the crowd noise, "Good to see you again, Rob. Let me get these drinks poured and I will be right with you. We need to talk."

"Sounds good. I'm going to grab this bar stool. I will take a cup of black coffee if you have some."

With a smile, he said, "I just made a fresh pot. These guys are not coffee drinkers, so it's all yours."

I sat on the ancient wooden stool, and Steve plopped a steaming hot cup of black coffee in front of me. The aroma was heavenly. I cannot even look at a beer until at least late afternoon. A sign behind the bar read It's 5 o'clock somewhere.

It was always 5 o'clock at the Widows Cove Tavern.

It was safe to talk. I knew the fishermen had spotted me at the end of the bar, but they seemed more intent on spending their money from their last catch than listening to me. Steve poured another round of shots for the fishermen and made his way down to my end of the bar.

"Rob, everyone on the docks knows who you are, and some of them aren't too happy about you snooping around."

"I know, Steve. Some kid handed me a note on the docks on Friday. The note was anonymous and said to meet at Mike's Restaurant in Fairhaven at 7:00 p.m. It did not go well. I think a good looking blonde, mid-twenties, with a rose tattoo on her left wrist, slipped me a mickey at the bar. The next thing I know, I am waking up in the front seat of my rental in Mike's parking lot at 2:00 a.m. Whoever knocked me out tossed my car and wallet. They must have been amateurs because they didn't search the trunk. Thank Christ because my Glock was in there. And it was loaded. I just got shit lucky for being so stupid.

"Steve, what about the girl? Does that description match anyone you know?"

"No, Rob. A good looking blonde with a rose tattoo would stand out. We do not get too many women in here, period. I am sure you remember that adventurous college kids from UMass Dartmouth would sometimes come in on Friday and Saturday nights to listen to the bands. When I first started here, the only ones with tattoos were fishermen and the occasional servicemen. Now everyone has them. I'll ask around. Somebody knows her."

"Okay, Steve, but be careful. I do not know who is involved. She was with a brunette, but I didn't get a good look at her."

Then Steve said, "Word on the street is that something more than scalloping has been feeding the local economy for more than a year or so. I do not know anything specific, but I think it involves more than one boat. You are on the right track. But as they say on the docks, you must widen your net. Waxy is in it up to his ears."

"I know, Steve. Waxy and I had a little foot race last week. He won. I was chasing him down Acushnet Avenue. Suddenly he turned his head around, and we made eye contact. It was weird that he almost looked relieved to see me. I do not get that look from suspects often."

"Rob, be careful. I don't know how deep this runs or who exactly is involved in what, but it's big. From what I am hearing, it makes the Codfather's escapades seem minor in comparison. Whatever is happening in the harbor involves more than just the local fishermen."

Steve added, "I got to be careful myself. I've been in the city long enough for the locals to trust me, but it could raise suspicion if I ask too many questions. It wouldn't be out of the question that I end up taking a one-way fishing trip. It is a big ocean out there. It can be hard to find a body in the blue expanse. Rob, I have your number. It's probably best not to come to the bar for a while. At least until things settle down a bit. If there is anything I think you need to know, I'll call you."

"Okay, Steve, thanks for your help and advice. I will try to interview the rest of the crew today, starting with Manny Sousa. I left voicemails for them. So, we will see who's in a talking mood."

"Rob, if you do not catch up to Manny at home, check out the Portuguese American Club. It is on Holly St. He spends time together there, usually playing cribbage and drinking espresso."

I slowly got off my barstool and scanned the room. The locals were busy boasting about their catch and getting a buzz on. I headed out the front door. First stop, I will be going to Manny's home in the South End of New Bedford.

CHAPTER THIRTY EIGHT

I was beginning to learn some of the lingo spoken on the docks. Captain Medeiros says Manny is known around the harbor as a shacker, or new guy, usually young and inexperienced. The captain told me these guys hang around the docks hoping to hook on with a boat. Many of them were high school dropouts or had a GED if they were lucky.

New Bedford had long ago fallen on hard times. With most of the factories having moved down south or to Mexico, or China, employment prospects in the city were bleak. Fishing was the only industry in New Bedford where someone without a trade or an education could make a living wage. Even a shacker in a good year could make close to $100,000.00 per year. That's a lot of shifts at a supermarket or making glazed donuts at Dunkin's. The shackers got the worst jobs. If they stuck it out and were good workers, word would get around the docks, and they could catch on as permanent crew.

Bob Halloran had interviewed the crew of the Emma Jean, and nobody seemed to know much about Manny. His reputation was that he was a good worker who kept to himself. He told the captain that he was originally from Dorchester and had followed his girlfriend, Linda, down to New Bedford. She had a five-year old son named Frankie from another relationship. The father was out of the picture. In and out of prison, drugs. His current whereabouts are unknown. Bob had told me Captain Medeiros mentioned that Manny often talked on fishing trips about Frankie. He seemed to have taken to the job of instant father and really loved the boy. They lived in the south end of New Bedford across from the hurricane barrier. By luck, Manny had been on the docks the day the Emma Jean was heading out to sea. Captain Medeiros had just learned he would be down a crew member because of illness. Manny had been on two prior trips on the Emma Jean. He had proven to be a hard worker who took direction well. Manny had his seabag with him. Captain Medeiros offered him a job as a shacker. Manny jumped at the chance. Scalloping had been good this year. He made a phone call to his girlfriend and hopped onto the Emma Jean.

Bob Halloran told me that Captain Medeiros admitted he had not done any background checking on Manny. Not conducting background checks was not unusual. Most of these guys had checkered pasts. The captain needed a body, and Manny was it.

I called Manny on my cell phone before heading out to his apartment. I was greeted by a friendly female voice on the answering machine. I pulled out onto Union Street and headed down Route 18 toward the south end of New Bedford. The south end is a mixture of expansive former Whaling Captains' homes and three decker tenements in various states of condition. The ferry to Martha's Vineyard docks there, and there was an oceanfront restaurant, Davy's Locker. The best clam chowder in the city.

I went down Route 18 and turned left toward the hurricane barrier. It was another warm, humid day. Along the walkway, atop the hurricane barrier, were a mixture of joggers and people walking their dogs. All were enjoying the breeze and fresh sea air. Tourists were boarding the ferry for the Vineyard. On their way to spending twenty dollars for a hamburger and eight dollars for a draft beer. Oh well, it was Martha's Vineyard, after all. The summer retreat of presidents and other celebrities. It provided interesting conversation back home if you were from Des Moines, Iowa. I passed the waterfront restaurant that used to be Davy's Locker. The restaurant was under new management, The sign read Cisco Brewers, and the building had been remodeled. I could not believe my eyes. A thatched roof tiki bar was in the back of the parking lot by the water's edge. A tiki bar in New Bedford. What next? A rooftop fern bar?

Manny lived on a side street, 14 Bayside Avenue. I turned right onto Bayside Avenue and parked on the street in front of a well-manicured, white three decker. He had told Bob Halloran that he lived on the first floor. It was just before Noon on a Monday, so not much was happening. A couple of teenagers are shooting hoops in the driveway next door, and an old man is sitting out on the front stoop of Manny's apartment building.

I approached the front door, and an old man with a stained flannel shirt asked me, "Do I know you?"

I replied, "I do not think so, sir. I am looking for Manny Sousa. Does he live here?"

The man looked me up and down and said, "Who's asking?"

"My name is Robert Ragusa. I'm with the FBI." I flashed him my badge so he wouldn't think I was bullshitting him.

"Do you live here, sir?"

"Stop calling me sir. My name is Ed, and yes, I live on the third floor. Manny and his girlfriend, Linda, live on the first floor."

"Do you know if Manny or Linda is home today?" I asked.

Ed paused and said, "Linda left for work with her son Frankie. She usually drops him off at daycare. That Chevy Camaro is Manny's car. If it is in the driveway, he's probably home. I am just curious. Why would an FBI agent be looking for Manny? Does it have anything to do with Emma Jean? I spent my life fishing before I retired last year. I still frequent the docks. Lots of rumors floating around there about the Emma Jean. Nothing I care to pass along to you as they are only rumors, as far as I can tell."

I thanked Ed for his time, brushed past him, and entered the hallway on the first floor. Unlike Waxy's abode, the hallway was clean and well lit. I knocked on the door of apartment 1A. No answer. I pounded harder the second time. Still no answer. I could hear what sounded like news on a television set. I had left Manny my number on his voicemail using my regular cell phone. I'm sure I showed up on his caller ID. I decided to try a new strategy. I had a burner phone with a phone number that I didn't give to anyone. I dialed his number using the burner phone, and surprisingly, a male voice answered.

"Yeah, this is Manny. Who is this?"

"Open your front door, Manny, and you will find out."

A long silence followed. Slowly the door opened and a tall, young, dark-haired man with an iPhone in his hand emerged into the doorway.

"Hi Manny, I am FBI Agent Robert Ragusa. Can I come in?"

The look on his face told me he was contemplating either letting me in or slamming the door shut. Before he had made up his mind, I said, "This is about the Emma Jean."

Manny gave me a slight nod indicating that it was okay to enter. He signaled me over to the kitchen table without saying a word. A hot cup of black coffee was sitting on the table with steam rising. He still had not said a word as I sat at the table directly across from him. The apartment was nicely furnished with a nautical theme, with pictures of Manny, Linda, and Frankie on the walls and end tables in the living room.

Finally, I had had enough of the staring match and decided to break the ice.

"Manny, I know you were on the Emma Jean when she caught fire. What can you tell me about that day?"

Again, another long pause. Apparently, Manny was the quiet type.

"Nothing, man." came the reply. "I'm just a shacker trying to make a buck. I keep my mouth shut and do whatever the captain asks me to do on the boat."

I let that response hang in the air, hoping Manny would add to it. When he didn't, I asked, "What do you know about the captain and the crew?"

"Not much. I've only been in New Bedford for a year. I followed my girlfriend down here from Boston."

"How does a guy from Boston meet a girl from New Bedford?"

"I met Linda during a lunch break while working construction in the North End. I chatted her up at Regina's Pizzeria. She was ahead of me in line at Regina's and turned around and talked to me. She was with her son checking out the city, doing the tourist thing. I didn't even know where New Bedford was, just that it was south of Boston. Anything outside of Route 128 is a foreign country to me. Anyway, we had dinner that night at the Union Oyster House. I made the trip to New Bedford for a couple of dates, and we hit it off. The next thing I know, she asks me to move in with her and Frankie. I was living with my parents in Dorchester and working odd construction jobs. No luck getting into the union. I figured what the heck, and moved in. I learned quickly that fishing is the only work in New Bedford that pays."

Manny added, "The only boat I had been on in my life was my cousin's twenty-foot Boston Whaler. The locals told me the best way to break in was as a shacker. I didn't know what the hell they were talking about. You hang around the docks when boats are in and hope you get called on to fill in if a boat is short a man. I hung around there for at least a month before Captain Medeiros, the captain of the Emma Jean, called me over. His shacker had gotten arrested for a DUI, and he needed a body. That body was me. I went on my first fishing trip out to Georges Bank scalloping. Got seasick as hell. The crew thought that was a riot. I cleaned the bathroom, cooked, scrubbed the deck, and did any crap job that needed doing. I never complained. I eventually earned the crew's trust and respect. Word on the docks travels quickly. I've been working steadily since. Even as a shacker, I am making more money than I ever did. I am not a bar guy, and I don't do drugs, except Dramamine. Most of these guys have bad habits. They spend their money as soon as we hit port. Not me. I have a plan. I like fishing. It's hard work, but I will work my way up to Captain someday. That is where the big money is."

At first, Manny would not say a word. Now I know his life story.

I asked, "Do you know how the fire started and what might have happened to Hank Gonsalves? He's still missing at sea."

"I have no clue. I was on watch when I saw smoke pouring out of the kitchen. It all happened so fast. I had a little training in fire prevention, but my mind went blank. Everyone was running around like lunatics. The captain jumped off the pilothouse, ran toward the kitchen, and disappeared in the smoke. By now I could see flames. The next thing I knew, the captain is giving the order to abandon ship. My sixth fishing trip and I am grabbing a life ring and jumping into the Atlantic. I did not have time to put on a life vest, never mind a survival suit. I was scared. Really, Agent Ragusa, this is all I know. If I knew something more, I would tell you. I rarely spend time together with the crew in port. I know their names and that is about it. I barely knew Hank. As far as I know, it was a kitchen fire. I never saw Hank on deck. Me, Christian and Barry jumped overboard. I never saw Hank in the water."

Manny struck me as being sincere. I was getting ready to wrap up when I noticed a small, framed picture almost hidden on the top of a bookshelf. It was a picture of an attractive young woman with long brown hair kneeling beside an Irish Setter. She had different colored hair, was younger and a had curly hair style but she bore a striking resemblance to the blonde at Mike's. I could not see the whole picture from the kitchen table, so as I got up to leave, I went over to the bookshelf.

"So, you like to read about World War II, Manny?" I picked up a hardcover book titled D-Day. I studied the picture of the woman. In the picture, she was wearing a long-sleeved blouse. There appeared to be part of a tattoo poking out beyond the sleeve on her left wrist. A rose petal? I couldn't tell. I gently put the book back on the shelf and thanked Manny for his cooperation. As I returned to my rental, I could not help thinking, was it her? My radar was up. I was not crossing Manny off my suspect list. Not just yet.

CHAPTER THIRTY NINE

I had left a message for Christian DeJesus, but like the other crew members of the Emma Jean, he had not called me back. Christian lived a few streets over from Manny in the south end. I figured I could kill two birds with one stone. I called again, and the voicemail picked up. The message was in Spanish. I could understand "DeJesus," but that was about it. I left a message in English. I didn't know Christian's understanding of English, but Bob Halloran had interviewed him, and he would have told me if he had needed a translator.

I had his address on Cove Road, so I figured I would take a chance and pay him a surprise visit. I pulled in front of the small cottage at 1410 Cove Road. The cottage was sandwiched between two triple-deckers in various stages of disrepair. In contrast, The DeJesus home seemed to be well cared for. The front yard burst with color, hibiscus, azaleas and two of the most beautiful cherry trees I have ever seen. Somebody in the household had a green thumb. The home had a natural Cape Code style with shake shingles on the exterior. I made my way up a flagstone walkway to the front door. There were no cars in the driveway or lights on in the house. I rang the doorbell and was greeted with the loudest, scariest barking I have ever heard. A pit bull with a head the size of a basketball stared at me through the living room picture window. The dog was better security than any system made by ADP.

I rang it again. Same response, more barking, more snarling. No signs of human life. I pulled out a business card and wrote 'Call me' on it. I stuck it in the front door and waved goodbye to the friendly family pet. The barking finally subsided when I got into my rental and drove away.

I didn't want to head back to Saugus just yet. I figured I would head over to Mike's Restaurant and see if somebody knew the blonde or brunette who, I was pretty sure, had caused me to go lights out. I headed back over the drawbridge to Fairhaven about 3:00 p.m. I googled Mike's Restaurant just to make sure they were open on Mondays. It was a good time to go. Monday is usually a slow day for restaurants, and mid-afternoon is the slow time any day. Fifteen minutes after leaving the DeJesus home, I pulled into Mike's parking lot. There was a sprinkling of cars in the lot. I hoped the bartender who had served me Friday night was working.

I walked into Mike's, and it was a much different scene than Friday night. A couple of construction types in dirty jeans and T-shirts sat at the bar. Another two middle-aged businessmen in suits sat in a booth near the front door. I peeked around the corner. The dining room was empty. I grabbed a seat at the end of the bar and waited. Finally, after what seemed like eternity, the bartender came out of the kitchen. Lucky me. It was her. The same bartender who had served me. She did not make eye contact, instead making her way to the construction workers who needed another couple of Buds. She opened the bottles, without saying a word, and put them on the bar.

Then she slowly turned toward me and gave me that "I think I know you look."

As she approached me, I was greeted with, "Jim Beam Manhattan. Right?"

"You have got a good memory. I have only been here once."

Her comeback was, "It is my business, honey, to know my customers' drinks. It makes people feel special, and it usually pumps up my tips."

"I am impressed, but I'm not drinking today. I have got a couple of questions for you." I pulled out my FBI ID and flashed it in front of her. That got her attention. She looked at me like I was about to put the cuffs on her.

"Relax, I am not here for you. The night I was here, there was a young, attractive blonde, hair pulled back in a ponytail with a rose tattoo on her left wrist. She was with a brunette about the same age. She went to the ladies' room and then stopped beside me to ask me a question. Do you know who she is?"

"I remember her and her friend," she replied. "The blonde ordered a Chocolate Martini. She was with another woman, dark-haired, young. Sorry, honey, but I have never seen either one of them before or since. I work over sixty hours a week here as a bartender and server. If either of them were regulars, I would know it."

"How about the kitchen crew or any of the other bartenders?"

"You can talk with them if you like. It's a skeleton crew on Mondays. There is one line cook here today and one server. The line cook never comes out of the kitchen unless he must use the bathroom, and the server started yesterday. I think you would be wasting your time."

"Okay, well, thanks for your time."

"Come back when you're in the mood for the best prime rib around."

"Sounds good. That's a date." Somehow her rough exterior had started to fade away as we talked. I believed her. She didn't know anything, and it was unlikely that any other staff at Mike's did either.

I was walking slowly back to my car when my cell phone lit up. I picked it up on the first ring. I heard in a thick Spanish accent, "You want to talk to me?"

"Who is this?"

"This is Christian DeJesus. I just got home and saw your business card on the front door." I thought about trying out my limited knowledge of Spanish. I had gotten a D in Spanish at Gate of Heaven High, so I decided to stick with English.

"Thanks for calling me back, Mr. DeJesus. I can be at your home in fifteen minutes. I have some questions for you about the fire on the Emma Jean."

In broken English, Christian replied, "I already talked to some Coast Guard guys. I told them all I know."

"Yes, I know; but I still want to talk to you. Can you give me a little of your time?"

"Okay, okay. Come to my house. My wife gets home in an hour. Talk before she gets here. My injuries, Emma Jean destroyed, and Hank missing are too much for her. I do not want to upset her any further."

"I hear you. I am on my way. Like I said. I will be there in about fifteen minutes."

I hopped back into the Chrysler and headed over the city's drawbridge. Christian was not at the top of my suspect list, but this case was full of surprises. I arrived at his house at 4:00 p.m. I pulled up behind a newer model red Ford F-150 pickup truck. One of our tech guys owns one. I remember him saying he had gotten a deal at one of the dealerships on Route 1 in Chelsea. He paid $70,000.00, brand new, right off the lot with all the bells and whistles. Some deal.

Fishermen have always made big money. The few that do not have bad habits can afford the luxuries of life. Christian DeJesus was one of those few.

I kept my Glock holstered with the safety on and slowly exited the Chrysler and approached the front door. The barking and snarling got louder with every step closer. I reached the front porch and opened a screen door that had a jagged rip down the middle. I reached for the brass door knocker when I noticed a bright blue eyeball. Staring at me from the peephole. I heard, "Shut the fuck up, Walter." The barking suddenly stopped. The dog's name was Walter. Really? It seemed like Satan would have been a better fit.

With the eyeball still staring at me intently, a voice rang out in a thick Spanish accent, "You the FBI guy?"

I replied with a question of my own.

"Are you Christian DeJesus?"

"Yeah, that is me. Show me your badge."

Fair enough, I supposed. I pulled out my official gold FBI badge and stuck it in front of the peephole. I got the response for which I was hoping.

"Okay. Come in."

The heavy wooden door creaked open. I was greeted by who I assumed was Christian DeJesus. He was holding Walter by the collar. The dog was sizing me up. The barking had stopped and had been replaced by sniffing. I knew that a dog's sense of smell is at least a thousand times stronger than that of a human. Trixie's smell was all over me. I hoped Walter liked cats. I also knew from personal experience that pit bulls have a strong bite. I am not against the breed in general. With the right training, I know they can be terrific guard dogs and family pets. However, in the wrong hands, like any dog, they can be dangerous.

I still had burned into my brain a late-night drug trafficking bust in Mattapan three years ago. After breaking down the front door with a ram, I entered a dimly lit living room and was greeted by a pit bull that clamped onto my left arm. I thought my left hand had been severed. It took another agent eight bullets to kill the dog. A trip to the Mass General Emergency Room and twenty-one stitches later, I was sent home for a little unplanned vacation time. Once was enough for me.

"Mr. DeJesus, could you please put the dog in another room while we talk?"

"Walter good dog. He no bite."

"I'm sure he is, but please, this won't take long, so please."

He looked unhappy, but Mr. DeJesus pointed at Walter and then to a bedroom. Walter gave me a parting glance, turned, and slowly jaunted into the bedroom. Mr. DeJesus closed the bedroom door and waved me in. After glancing at the bedroom door. It was shut. I breathed a little easier. I followed DeJesus to the kitchen. The house looked like a typical Cape style cottage. The furnishings were newer, and everything was in its place. Framed pictures of Mr. DeJesus and what must have been some of his friends or relatives on a Boston Whaler proudly holding up Striped Bass ran the length of the hallway.

I could not help thinking, if you fish for a living, would golf not seem a more appropriate hobby? I guess not. The kitchen was at the back of the cottage. A glass slider opened out onto an expansive deck. With his back facing me, Christian pointed me toward the kitchen chair closest to the slider. It was a sunny day, and the sunlight was beaming through the glass door, lighting up the cluttered table. There were four kitchen chairs. Christian sat directly in front of me. A recent copy of The New Bedford Standard Times and a half-eaten meatball sub on his right.

Before I could get a word out, he picked up the meatball sub and took a huge bite. With marinara sauce still dripping out his mouth, I heard him mumble.

"So you are here. What you want to ask me?"

I did not know whether to wait until he finished the sub or just jump right in. I decided on the latter.

"What was your job on the Emma Jean?"

With a mouthful of meatballs came the reply.

"I'm a cook, but I clean scallops on the boat, like everyone else."

I had to focus for a seasoned FBI agent; I must admit, the meatball thing was throwing me off my game.

"I know what that means, so you haven't been fishing that long?"

"Not long, maybe two years."

With a beaming smile and a thumbs up, Mr. DeJesus announced, "I just became US citizen. Before that, it was hard to get work. I worked mostly construction."

"How long had you been on the Emma Jean?"

"I have known Captain Frank for one year. He is a good man, fair. Anytime he needs a cook, he calls me. If I am not on another boat, I go."

"Do you know the other crewmen well?"

"Not really, I keep to myself. They like to go to bar after fishing." He laughed. "Not me. I go home, cheaper that way."

"What happened to the Emma Jean that night? The night of the fire."

"No idea. I was on deck washing down the bucket. Next thing smoke pouring out of kitchen. I ran to help but it was too hot. Captain Frank gives the order to abandon ship. I grab my life vest and jump in the ocean. I was afraid. I no swim good. Another boat, the Olivia Rose, picked me up. Why did you ask me these questions? Kitchen fires happen all the time. This one got out of hand."

"Mr. DeJesus, this fire was started on purpose."

My statement got a response from Mr. DeJesus. With a stunned look, he put what was left of the meatball sub down on the table.

"No way, man."

"Yes, someone set that fire. Was it you?"

"I no answer any more questions. You leave my house now."

He pointed at the front door. I got the message. I got out of my chair and went down the hallway to the front door. I stopped at the last picture and took a close look. One of the men on the Boston Whaler fit Steve Poole's description of Wolfie. He looked like a stocky dark-haired, balding middle-aged man. He was holding up what must have been a 40-inch striper. In the picture, there were three other guys surrounding him and smiling for the camera. I pointed at him.

"How do you know this man?"

"None of your business. Now go."

I headed out the front door and soon could hear Walter making his presence known. I turned around, and all that separated Walter from me was a worn-out screen door. My pace accelerated as I approached the driver's side door of the Chrysler. I jumped in just as the front door opened. Walter bounded out and headed straight for me. I slammed the car door, started the engine, and rammed the shift into reverse. It was a gravel driveway, and as I hit the gas, pebbles kicked up, showering Walter. The dog stayed on the front lawn and didn't chase after me as I went back down Cove Street. Was that guy in the picture Wolfie? I didn't know. There were plenty of stocky, dark-haired guys in New Bedford. It was just a coincidence, maybe not. It was time to get back to the Widows Cove and Steve Poole.

CHAPTER FORTY

I started heading back down Route 18 toward Union Street. As I approached the traffic light at the corner of Union, my phone rang. I recognized the number. It was Steve Poole. I picked up just before the call went to voicemail.

"Rob where are you?" came the familiar voice.

"I didn't think I'd hear from you so soon, Steve."

"I was about to get onto 195 and head home. What's up?"

"I'm at the Widows Cove, and I have been asking some locals about the Emma Jean. I've heard some interesting information from a couple of good sources. It's about Frank Medeiros and Gil Galloway. They aren't quite as squeaky clean as they would have you believe. I get off my shift in half an hour. Swing by, and I can fill you in."

"Absolutely, I'm two minutes away. I'll be there in a few. Is it busy in the bar?"

"No, Rob, just a couple of fishermen here, downing shots of Crown Royal," Steve added, "Grab the table near the window. We should be able to talk there."

"Okay, Steve. I'll head right over. See you in a few minutes."

When Steve first came to New Bedford, he didn't know haddock from a scallop, but the locals took to him immediately. He had an interesting back story that he would tell anyone who would listen. Steve also made anyone he was talking to him feel like they were the most intelligent, interesting person he had ever spoken to. The locals trusted him, and after providing a little tongue lube in the way of beers and shots, he could get even the wariest fishermen talking. I knew he wouldn't call if he didn't have something good. I would finally get a lead pointing me in the right direction.

I swung the Chrysler back onto Union St. and headed up the hill past the now defunct National Club, a new trendy new brewpub, Moby Dick Brewery, and an arcade bar called Play. Classic games like Pac Man and pinball. Sadly, I had played Pac Man when it wasn't considered a classic game.

The city was in transition. The National Club was from a bygone era. Local fishermen right off the boats would fill the place, smoke lingering in the air and the smell of stale beer ever present. Other long-gone establishments like the Sea Breeze and the Cultivator had become victims of New Bedford's Historic District gentrification. A local developer had just purchased the National Club and was about to be refurbished and reborn as another trendy hotspot. The Widows Cove was one of the last survivors from the old days. I think the owner and Steve Poole were a big reason why. The Widows Cove was also not strictly a fishermen's bar. It was considered safe, and businessmen and other merchants were regulars just like the fishermen. It was clean, and the food was good. The weekend bands always drew an eclectic crowd. An interesting mix of students from the local colleges, businessmen and blue-collar types. It was a circus, with Steve Poole playing the role of the ringmaster.

My parking karma was still holding up. A metered spot with thirty minutes still on the meter was available right in front. I parked, put another quarter in the meter to buy an extra fifteen minutes, and headed toward the front door. The door flew open as I approached, nearly knocking me over.

The two fishermen blew by me, the taller of the two said, "Sorry man. Didn't see you."

I felt like saying, "No shit, Sherlock," but thought better of it. I kept the thought to myself. I didn't need an altercation with two soused fishermen. I opened the door, and the place was empty. Good timing.

"Rob let's grab this table and talk. I've got someone I want you to meet. As we sat down at the four-top nearest the window, a woman who I thought I recognized came out of the ladies' room. Light skinned black, probably, Cape Verdean. Tall, thin, dressed in blue jeans and a white halter top. She sashayed her way toward our table and gave me a wary look like, who is this guy?

Then the light went on. It's been quite a few years, but I remembered this woman. Cocoa Brown was a regular on Friday nights when Rob and the Riptides played. She was a local character, and never really got in trouble with the law, but there was always something mysterious about her. I didn't know if she remembered me.

"Rob, do you remember Cocoa Brown?"

I looked at Cocoa and said with an outstretched hand, "Cocoa, I'm Rob Ragusa. I've changed quite a bit. You don't recognize me. It's been years since I played here with my band. Cocoa, is Summer Wind still your favorite song? Few twenty-somethings were into Sinatra back in the day."

"I remember you, Rob. You look great. The graying hair becomes you. I miss your band. Nobody else that played here in those days knew Sinatra. I can't believe you remembered my song. Now everyone is covering his hits. The greats never really go away. So good to see you."

Cocoa hadn't changed. She could charm the rattles off a rattlesnake.

"Good to see you too. You haven't changed a bit. Sinatra never goes out of style."

She slowly pulled out a chair and slinked into it. There was always something distinctly feline about her. I never really had a thing for her, but she was intriguing. Cocoa grew up in New Bedford. She was equally at ease with the Latin Kings as the fishermen on the docks. I liked her, but I never really felt I could trust her.

With a voice slightly above a whisper, Cocoa said, "I'm taking a chance talking to you, so let's make this quick. Word on the street is that you've been snooping around the docks looking into what happened to the Emma Jean. Have you talked to the crew yet?"

I responded, equally using my best stage whisper, "Yes, I've interviewed the crew members from the Emma Jean, including the captain, Frank Medeiros."

Cocoa leaned in.

"Did you interview anyone on the Olivia Rose that night?"

"Why do you ask? I thought they were simply in the area and came to the rescue of the Emma Jean when the distress call went out."

Cocoa leaned in further, making us nose-to-nose.

"You probably know that Gil Galloway and Frank Medeiros were friends, right?" Well, you might want to dig a little deeper into their relationship, particularly regarding finances."

"Okay." I responded. "What are you getting at?"

"Gambling. The word is that they both make frequent trips to the fish house when they're in port. The boys from Federal Hill still have a presence on the docks. Galloway and Medeiros are behind in their payment plan."

The wheels were churning in my head. There was a sizable insurance policy on the Emma Jean but nothing unusual. Most fishing captains would rather sell off their first-born than sink their own boat, but it wasn't unheard of. It could be a motive. But other than gambling, how were the two men linked? Was the missing crewman, Hank Gonsalves, involved? Or was he collateral damage? I had never linked the two boats. Not linking them was an oversight on my part. Maybe it was time to pay Captain Galloway a visit. I could catch him off-guard. He had already talked to Bob Halloran at the Coast Guard station, but he wouldn't expect a call from the FBI. I could shake his tree and see what would fall out.

Cocoa stood and pulled her chair back with slow deliberation.

"You owe me one, Rob. Are you married?"

I shook my head no. Cocoa smirked, "Next time you're in town, I want a dinner date with you at Antonio's. I'm dying for a good Portuguese steak. I had a thing for you back in the day, but you never picked up on it. Steve has my number. Call me next time you're in the city." With that, she strutted through the front door.

After Cocoa exited the bar, I turned to Steve.

"Steve, what do you think? Is she solid?"

Steve tugged at this chin when he replied, "She could steal a hot stove from the kitchen, but she wouldn't make up something like this. She's taking a helluva chance talking to you, and so am I."

He slipped me a Widows Cove cocktail napkin with a 508 number on it.

"This is her cell. I would take her up on that dinner date. My guess is she's holding back on you. With Cocoa Brown, everything comes with a price. If you want more information, you'll have to pay, one way or another."

I gently folded the napkin and slipped it into my pants pocket.

"Thanks, Steve. I'm going to do some digging. I get tired of eating alone. A dinner date at Antonio's sounds good." I added, "Steve, be careful. I'll call when I'm back in town."

I had a lot to think about on my way back to Saugus. Although pieces were still missing, I felt like the puzzle was starting to come together.

CHAPTER FORTY ONE

I planned to head back home, feed Trixie, and get my thoughts together. What I did know was that the relationship between Gil Galloway and Frank Medeiros was more complicated than two captains who had come of age around the docks simultaneously and rose the ranks to own their boats. What kept bothering me was the missing fisherman, Hank Gonsalves. It's a big ocean, but his disappearance just seemed too convenient. Did Hank Gonsalves know too much and pay the price? Or was he involved in whatever secrets the Emma Jean held? I was sure the Emma Jean was involved in more than just fishing. But what?

Rumors were flying all over the harbor about the demise of the Emma Jean. It was the Mafia, "Frankie the hammer's" gang had reformed, that the Codfather was operating from behind bars. The docks are never short on gossip. New Bedford had a long history of less than honorable behavior in the harbor. It was reported that New Bedford was a major smuggling point for rum runners during the

Depression. The FBI and local law enforcement had long been aware that New Bedford was a major trafficking area for heroin and, more recently, the deadly drug, fentanyl. The drugs had traditionally crossed Interstate 95 from the south to New York and New England. Recent major drug busts and stepped-up enforcement have significantly reduced the trafficking. Maybe the bad guys were taking a chapter out of the rum runners' book and going back to using ocean travel to smuggle drugs.

• • •

I made my way through heavy rush hour traffic. A low layer of haze hung over Boston. It was another typical "Triple H" July day: hazy, hot, and humid. I liked Boston in the summer. Eating alfresco in the North End, the Red Sox on TV. Pretending to read a paperback at Revere Beach, with the parade of bikinis strolling by. Ending the day with a sunset over the Atlantic, eating a roast beef sandwich from Kelly's Roast Beef and washing it down with an ice-cold Narragansett. Kelly's is an institution on the North Shore. They claim to have invented the roast beef sandwich. There's only one way to order a roast beef sandwich at Kelly's. A "three way:" thin sliced rare roast beef, mayo, cheese, and their special barbeque sauce on a toasted bun. Heaven.

I crossed the Tobin Bridge and back onto Route 1 North. I pulled into the parking lot of my condo and headed inside to feed Trixie and catch my breath. Trixie was waiting for me when I opened the door. I don't know if a cat can scowl, but whenever I came home after leaving Trixie a little longer than she liked, I would get "that look." It's a combination of disdain and disappointment. The look made me feel like I was a bad parent. I always feel guilty. Goes back to my Gate of Heaven days. I fed her a can of cat food and put water in her dish. She started to come around, and I was off the hook until the next time. She began purring and rubbing my leg. A sign that all was forgiven.

I turned on the tube, opened a bottle of beer, and plopped into the Barcalounger. I was three gulps into my beer when the events of the last few days caught up with me, and my mind and body drifted off to sleep. I woke up, and the clock on the end table said 2:00 a.m. Then it hit me. I hadn't called John. Well, tomorrow's another day. I had been asleep for eight hours. This case was taking a toll on me mentally. I felt like progress was being made, but it was painfully slow.

During my slumber, my cell phone fell off the end table onto the hardwood floor. Trixie knocked it off. When she wanted attention, that's what she would do. I had fed her, and that was about it. She wanted to be petted, so I picked up the phone, and she settled into my lap, purring like a high-speed motorboat. I had three voicemails on my iPhone.

Reluctantly, I upgraded two months ago from a flip phone at the insistence of my boss. John wanted me to join the 21st Century. I didn't even know what half the functions were for. I thought Safari was some kind of kids' game. The first call was from Chuck's Auto. The caddy had been pieced back together and was ready to be picked up. Hallelujah! That put some pep in my step. I loved that car. So many memories and milestones; weekends down the Cape, cruise night at Revere Beach, sneaking my friends, Joey, and Billy Rossini, into the drive-in in the trunk. I also made it to second base with Susie Shannon in the summer of 1979 at Wollaston Beach, a.k.a. the Irish Riviera.

The second call was from John Ring. He was looking for a progress report on the case. There was a sense of urgency in his voice. He wanted to share additional information from Interpol to get me up to speed. John wanted to meet me at the office tomorrow at 9:00 a.m.

The last message was from Steve Poole. He wanted to talk. His voice seemed rushed, and there was a lot of background noise. Men were talking loudly and swearing. I guessed that he was calling from the Widows Cove. I could barely make out what he was saying but heard, "Hank Gonsalves was spotted in Hyannis."

My heart began pounding. I felt this was the break I had been waiting for. I also knew that Steve had gotten way too involved in this case. Steve wasn't a cop. He was a bartender, and I had brought him in. He was in this way over his head. It was known that Steve was feeding me information. He was in uncharted waters, and I was worried.

CHAPTER FORTY TWO

It was late, but I was starving. I grabbed a Hungry Man TV dinner and plopped it in the microwave. I'm a pretty good cook. Italian is my specialty. I would put my stuffed shells up against anyone's. Tonight, though, I was exhausted. The kind of exhaustion just taking the cover of the TV dinner and setting the timer was a struggle. I have never figured out what fruit compote is made of in a TV dinner. It looks like something the military eats in the field because it won't go bad for at least a hundred years. I ate a quick dinner and jumped into bed, setting the alarm for 7:30 a.m. I fell back asleep as soon as my head hit the pillow. I've been told I snore loudly. The kind of snore where the thin walls of my condo rattle. Trixie doesn't seem to mind. She was curled up beside me.

The alarm went off at 7:30 a.m. I shaved, showered, poured a cup of Folgers into my thermos, and headed to the office. I desperately wanted to go by Chuck's Auto and pick up the caddy, but he didn't open until 8:00 a.m. I had to return the rental first, so there wasn't enough time. The caddy would have to wait 'til later. I made good time and parked in the FBI lot. Headed in to meet with John. I was five minutes early. Dad's mantra: "Better to be five minutes early than five minutes late." He was a wise man. I should have listened to him more often. John was behind his desk with his feet up, reading the Boston Herald.

"I can see you're hard at work as always, boss."

The top of his head and then the top of his horn-rimmed glasses appeared above the top fold of the newspaper.

"Good morning, Rob. Right on time, as usual. You didn't call yesterday, but I admit it's good to see you. I mean that."

"The Interpol techs in London have been working with Vinnie and our tech guys in Quantico on tracking activity on the website. The Cyber Division found a series of contacts from the Red Crescent Trading Company IP address to another IP address on the dark web—the Dragon Trading Company. Dragon is a street name for heroin. I think we may have found our smugglers."

John added, "Interpol has been monitoring traffic on the site. Much traffic has been coming from New York City and Massachusetts, particularly Hyannis and New Bedford. The conversations were all in code, but as you know, our codebreakers are the best in the world. They have broken the code and exposed a drug smuggling operation from Cape Verde to Georges Bank. The drugs are smuggled from Cape

Verde on private planes. The planes drop the drugs near Georges Bank. Then commercial fishing vessels transport the drugs to port. The drugs are offloaded in New Bedford at night before the fish houses open in the morning. The boats then unload their catch as usual. What have you come up on your end?"

I could hardly contain the excitement in my voice.

"John, this is finally starting to make sense. My gut told me this case had to be bigger than the fire on the Emma Jean. I got a voicemail from a good source in New Bedford that the missing fisherman, Hank Gonsalves, may have been spotted in Hyannis."

"Rob, this is more than your typical drug smuggling operation. It's much bigger. It looks like they are smuggling carfentanil. We think the operation is being directed out of New York City and London. The drugs are likely being sent from the docks to cut houses in the city and then shipped to dealers all over the East Coast. We're not sure yet how Hyannis fits into the picture."

"This drug is bad news, John. Carfentanil is scarier than fentanyl. In the last three months, there has been a major spike in overdoses in Fall River, New Bedford, and Providence. It's got to be linked. If you think about it, the harbor is perfect for smuggling at night. A handful of security guards, mostly kids or old-timers, watch the fish houses. Usually, they're either asleep or playing games on their cell phones.

I picked up a copy of The New Bedford Standard Times yesterday, and there was a small blurb about a security guard found dead at one of the fish houses. It was suspected to be an overdose, but who knows. Maybe this poor bastard stumbled onto something he wasn't supposed to see."

Carfentanil is a synthetic opioid usually used by veterinarians to sedate large animals like bears and elephants. It's 1,000 times more potent than morphine and 100 times more potent than fentanyl. Only two milligrams can be fatal to a human being. If heroin is being laced with carfentanil, it would make the crack cocaine epidemic of the '90s look like child's play.

My pulse quickened. I needed to get back to New Bedford to talk to Steve Poole. I was already worried about him. Carfentanil added a whole new layer of danger to the equation. It was time for Steve to lay low. A nice peaceful sail to Provincetown might be in order. At least 'til the picture in New Bedford got clearer.

The Edgy Oyster had reopened. I couldn't tell Steve everything, but he needed to know he was likely in danger and that the fire on the Emma Jean was just the tip of the iceberg. I trusted Steve, and his information was solid, but I needed to know his source on the Hank Gonsalves sighting in Hyannis. After a sit-down with Steve, Hyannis was next on the docket. It was the height of the season. Hyannis would be packed with sunburned tourists. Finding

Hank Gonsalves would be the longest of long shots, but I had to try. If he was alive and involved in this thing, I couldn't believe that he would come out in public so soon.

John handed me some recent pictures of Gonsalves. I stuffed them in my shirt pocket and headed for the door. I turned at the door and yelled to John, "I'm heading back to New Bedford to talk to my contact, and then I'm going to take a side trip to Hyannis and shake the tree there."

"All right, Rob, be careful. You're getting close to retirement. I'd like to be at your retirement party."

"You'll be there," I replied, with more than a hint of self-doubt.

CHAPTER FORTY THREE

I was tempted to head back to Chuck's Auto first to pick up the caddy. Probably not a good idea. The caddy had been made. It stuck out like a sore thumb. So, I decided to head south to New Bedford instead, in the Chrysler. It was 10:30 a.m., and the morning rush was nearly over. I was making a good time. With any luck I would get to the Widows Cove before the lunch crowd ramped up.

Traffic was light to New Bedford. It was 11:30 a.m. when I took a right off Route 18 and onto Union Street. The Widows Cove was only three blocks up on the right. Three New Bedford cruisers were parked right in front of the bar. I parked at the first open space about a block away and quickly approached the front door. The sight of yellow police tape draping the front entrance set my heart racing. I approached the uniformed patrolman looking at me intently as I continued walking up Union Street. He was yelling something unintelligible at me and waving me off furiously. Undeterred, I pulled out my FBI badge and plowed on. The cop was intimidating, about six foot three and not more than twenty-five years old. He was screaming at me.

"Get on the other side of the street. This is a crime scene."

I didn't say a word. Police don't like their authority challenged, and he saw me as a challenge.

I calmly put my badge about an inch from his nose and announced, "FBI. Agent Robert Ragusa. Can you please tell me what's going on here?"

My badge did not impress him. His response was "Why is the FBI involved in this?"

Already on edge, I was beginning to get annoyed with this cop. I knew Steve was working at the bar today, and my concern for his safety had grown. Maybe the yellow tape covering the entrance to the Widows Cove had nothing to do with Steve. It was not unusual for some junkie to rob a convenience store or bar for some quick money for a fix.

I gathered myself and said to the officer, "I'm a friend of the bartender, Steve Poole. Is he okay?"

The officer's tone softened, and he replied, "Sorry. I shouldn't have flown off the handle. I'm Officer Pereira, New Bedford Police. I know Steve, too. I stop in sometimes with a couple of my fellow cops after our shifts to see Steve. He's such a character and a great guy."

"I know that, but is he all right "Officer Pereira looked me directly in the eyes and said,

"The ambulance just left for St. Luke's, and Steve is in it. He's okay, but he's pretty banged up."

Now, my mind was racing into overdrive. With my eyes fixed on Officer Pereira, I asked, "What happened?"

"We're interviewing witnesses now. Steve was behind the bar when three guys in ski masks entered the bar. Three fishermen were drinking at the bar. The masked suspects pulled guns, marched the three fishermen into the refrigerator walk-in, and jammed the door.

"Our guys had gotten a call from a fourth patron who had tried to enter the bar. The front door was locked, and he heard glass breaking and yelling, so he called 911. When we arrived, my sergeant and I were the first to enter. We could hear screaming from the walk-in. We unjammed the door and let the three fishermen out. They were hysterical. The place was in shambles. Tables were overturned, and broken glass was everywhere. We found Steve in the kitchen next to the grille. He was conscious but not in good shape. It looked like he had been worked over pretty well. Cuts to his face and what looked like defensive wounds to his hands. My sergeant kept asking him, 'Who did this to you?' but Steve kept drifting in and out of consciousness. All he kept saying was, 'Wolfe.' Does that mean anything to you?"

"It might," I replied. Then the officer continued.

"Then the EMTs showed up and took him to St. Luke's. I don't know his condition."

I was tempted to pull rank and enter the Widows Cove, but I had no real authority here. As far as the local police knew, this was a robbery gone wrong.

"Thanks, Officer. You've been very helpful. What's the name of your sergeant? I'd like to talk with him when things settle down."

"Sergeant Fielding, Sir. Please give him some time. The paperwork these days is ridiculous." I handed Officer Pereira my card and asked him to call me with any new developments.

I started walking back down Union Street to my car. I felt like a sledgehammer just hit me. My next stop was Hyannis, but I needed to take a side trip to St. Luke's to check on Steve. I was feeling guilty. I should never have gotten him involved in this mess. I was so anxious to solve the case that I let our friendship from the old days cloud my judgment, and Steve had paid for it. I jumped into the Chrysler, and Officer Pereira waived me through. I blew through a traffic light, my mind on Steve and his injuries. I got to County Street at the top of the hill and took a left. I had to pull over as an ambulance screeched by. The hospital was less than five minutes away. It was the longest five minutes of my life. I parked sideways into the first parking spot I found and headed for the hospital's front door. I was not prepared for what I would see.

CHAPTER FORTY FOUR

I sprinted into St. Luke's front door, badge in hand. The receptionist was behind the glass partition with a surgical mask covering her face. She was at least fifty pounds overweight and looked like the type who didn't suffer fools lightly. I flashed my badge and asked for directions to the emergency room. Startled with an FBI badge flashed in her face, she pointed behind me to my right. I must believe she was trying to give me directions to the ER, but her voice sounded as if it were underwater. I yelled at her again to direct me to the ER. She kept talking, and I wasn't understanding a thing she was saying.

My patience had worn thin, so I yelled, "Take that damn mask off and tell me where the ER is!"

She finally pulled the mask down to her chin and said, "Down the hall, second corridor to the right."

I nodded and left the woman there, now apparently speechless. I must have startled her because her face was five shades of red. I blew past people in wheelchairs, patients using walkers, and anyone else who got in my way. I made it to the ER in record time.

I was out of breath when I approached the receptionist. She looked up from the chart she was reading and asked me if she could help me. She was a young attractive brunette with her hair pulled back in a scrunchy. She seemed taken aback when I pushed my FBI badge against the glass partition. I thought, here we go again. She was double masked across her face. I understood that face coverings were mandatory in hospitals since COVID-19 became the modern-day Bubonic Plague, but trying to understand someone talking through one was like trying to understand the low talker on that episode of Seinfeld.

I asked her if a tall, older man with white hair had recently been brought in by ambulance.

I was pleasantly surprised when, clear as a bell, she said, "They just brought him in. He's in Room 4, but you can't go back there unless your family."

I ignored her warning and headed past the receptionist desk toward Room 4. I heard a man's voice yell, "Hey, you stop."

It was the hospital security guard. He couldn't have been more than twenty. I flashed my badge and identified myself as an FBI agent. I almost felt bad for the kid. He was stumbling all over his words, apologizing. I asked him where Room 4 was. He walked with me to Room 4. The curtain was closed.

I could hear a lot of commotion in the room. I yanked back the curtain, and two nurses and a doctor gave me a look like, "Who are you?"

Steve was awake and talking to the doctor. I was surprised that no New Bedford Police were here, but that was okay with me. They had jurisdiction in this case and would not be thrilled by an FBI agent sticking his nose in.

Steve immediately recognized me, and like nothing was happening, yelled, "Rob. Great to see you." I showed my badge to the nurses and doctor and asked the doctor how he was doing.

A young guy in a white lab coat with a stethoscope draped across his neck took a step toward me. He reminded me of Neil Patrick Harris, the actor who played Doogie Howser in the old TV show.

"I'm Dr. Anderson." He turned to look at Steve in the hospital bed said, "This is one lucky dude. He has many cuts and bruises, and his right hand incurred second degree burns. We will patch him up here and then take him down to imaging for x-rays to ensure nothing is broken. He will have to spend at least one night here for observation before he can be discharged. You can have a few minutes with him. We'll step out."

Dr. Anderson and the two nurses stepped out and closed the curtain behind them, giving us some privacy. I was grateful that he was going to be okay. I still felt like crap for getting him involved.

"Steve, what happened? Do you know who did this to you?"

He looked like he had been hit by a bus. He had two black eyes, lacerations on his hands and arms. Just a mess. He had every right to be pissed at me but, that's not Steve.

In a hoarse voice came out, "Rob, I was cutting up fruit, not really paying attention. A couple of fishermen were doing shots and beers. Next thing I know, I hear the front door open, and three guys were walking in wearing ski masks. They all had guns and were screaming and waving their guns all over the place. The fishermen were frozen in place. One guy, tall and burly, seemed in charge. Their guns were pointed at the fishermen. The leader screamed at the fisherman to get up and get into the walk-in refrigerator. Thank God nobody tried to play Rambo. A second guy got behind the fishermen and pushed one of them hard, forcing them into the walk-in, then closed the door and locked it from the outside.

"At first, I thought this was a robbery. Then realized these weren't your common junkies or gangbangers. They seemed like they had done this kind of thing before, well scripted. I had the cash drawer open and was practically throwing money at them. They didn't seem interested in the cash. The next thing I know, I hear the big guy say, 'You've been talking to the wrong people. I didn't have a chance to respond when a small, wiry guy jumped over the bar and slammed my head down onto a pile of glasses. I'm stunned, blood pouring out of my face. He drags me out from behind the bar, throwing me down on the floor and the three-start kicking the crap out of me. I'm curled up just trying to protect myself. The big guy then tells me to get my ass off the floor. I managed to stagger to my feet, and two of them, one on each arm, started dragging me toward the kitchen. The wiry guy hit me on the side of my head with the dull side of a meat cleaver. Then everything got fuzzy. The big guy gave me some parting advice, 'stop talking to the Feds, or next time, you won't be so lucky.' Then they took off out the back door. Rob, the big guy sounded a lot like Wolfie. He was only in the bar that one time, but he made an impression. I think he was the leader of this crew. The other two seemed to follow his lead. It wasn't a robbery. Those fishermen probably had thousands of dollars on them. These guys never asked for money. No. It was a warning to me. Believe me, I got the message."

"I'm sorry, Steve, that I got you into this. I'm going to find these bastards, and they will go down. You can't go back to the Widows Cove for a while. Do you have someplace to stay?"

"Yeah, I can stay with my sister in Marshfield. It's not your fault, Rob. I wanted to help you. I still do. Try to find this guy Wolfie. He's the key to the Emma Jean."

"I will, Steve. Just get some rest and recover. We'll talk soon."

I opened the curtain, and no one was there. On my way out, I told the receptionist the man in Room 4 needed attending. She shook her head, saying yes, and I headed out toward the front entrance. I felt lousy. Steve lived check to check, and he would be out of commission for a while. No way could he go back to the Widows Cove, not until this case was solved.

Hopefully, Hyannis would offer up some secrets. I didn't have much to go on, just a few grainy pictures of Hank Gonsalves. Summer tourists would have overrun Hyannis. It was a long shot that I would turn up anything. But you never know. Maybe my luck would change. I thought of my grandmother, who used to say to me whenever she could sense something was bothering me, "Everything will work out just fine. I'm sure of it." I thought, Nona, I hope you're right.

CHAPTER FORTY FIVE

The traffic on Cape Cod in the summer was always heavy. It was Thursday afternoon. Thursday had become the new Friday on the Cape. It was 2:00 p.m. when I left St. Luke's and headed east on Interstate 195 toward the Bourne Bridge. Since the Cape Cod Canal was completed in the 1930s, there were only two bridges you could traverse to get you "On Cape," the Bourne Bridge and the Sagamore Bridge. Traffic was no longer the occasional Model T heading over the bridge for a weekend on the Cape. Now every summer was a cavalcade of cars and recreational vehicles of all shapes and sizes heading for their place in the sun.

I knew that both bridges would be backed up for miles. I like the Cape. I visited often as a teenager with my family. My parents would rent a cottage for a week in Falmouth for our annual family vacation. As I've gotten older and look back on it, the Cape seems overrated. The New England weather often didn't cooperate. Sometimes, you'd get a whole week of rain. Mom, Dad, and kids in a small cottage for a week. You could only see so many movies or go bowling. There were overpriced lobster rolls, fisherman platters, and fried clams. I guess if you were from Iowa, it all seemed cool. As an adult, I started going to the coast of Maine for summer vacations because there are fewer tourists, and the lobster rolls are cheaper.

I had done a few gigs as the piano man at a local restaurant in Hyannis, the Black Cat, during the mid-80s. The Black Cat was still around. It had the best location in Hyannis—right across the street from the ferry terminal to Martha's Vineyard and Nantucket. Hundreds of thirsty, hungry, sunburned tourists walked off the ferry and into the Black Cat's front door. The place was packed from Memorial Day until Labor Day. I had fond memories of the Black Cat. A classy joint with a long wooden bar, rich mahogany, and leather stools. A big step up from the Widows Cove. You could smell the fried clams within one hundred feet of the restaurant.

While my mind wandered down memory lane, I made steady progress in my journey. I had made my way through Buzzards Bay and across the Bourne Bridge to the rotary. It was always amusing to see how tourists, who had never experienced a rotary, would handle it. In the middle of the rotary, flowers spell out Welcome to Cape Cod. What a welcome it is. Like a traffic circle in some third world country. Cars are trying to get into the rotary, trying to get out of the rotary. Drivers seem like they just want to survive the ordeal. There are no rules. It's killed or be killed. Never make eye contact with another driver. You might feel sorry for them and let them in. You must be aggressive if you want to survive.

I banked hard right and cut off a red SUV loaded with kids, bikes, and a kayak on the roof. The driver blasted his horn, but I stuck to my strategy and kept going, merging to the right, and exiting onto the road that parallels the Cape Cod Canal. Traffic was bumper-to-bumper along the canal. I finally made it onto the entrance ramp to the Mid-Cape Highway at 3:30 p.m. To my surprise, the traffic had thinned out a little. I made good time and rolled into Hyannis Center at 4:00 p.m. The city was packed. It was a typical July day. I slowly made my way down Main Street. Parking was at a premium during the summer, but I had a secret spot. The Department of Children and Family Services had an office in a strip mall at the end of the commercial part of Main Street. There was always parking there. Unless you seriously overstayed your welcome, the police didn't bother you.

I had no real plan. Just a bunch of pictures of Hank Gonsalves that I could flash around town to the store owners, bartenders, and other summer helpers, hoping someone might recognize him. It was the longest of long shots, but it was all I had. Anyway, spending a beautiful summer day in Hyannis wasn't the worst thing in the world. The sidewalks were packed. Outdoor dining, which had always been popular in the summer on the Cape, was even more so now. During the COVID-19 pandemic, to stay in business many restaurants had cleverly blocked off sections of their parking lots, sidewalks, and alleyways. Anywhere you could set up an umbrella, table, and some chairs.

I slowly weaved in and out of T-shirt shops, ice cream stores, restaurants, and bars, going down Main Street to the end of the commercial district and back up past the Post Office and the John F. Kennedy Museum. The Kennedy's were American royalty, particularly in Massachusetts. The clan would gather at the Kennedy Compound in Hyannis port during the summer months. Touch football games and sailing on Buzzards Bay occupied the clan. They mostly kept to themselves, but back in the day, Ted Kennedy was known to drop into the Black Cat and other Hyannis establishments for some summer refreshment. Scotch on the rocks, "three fingers."

I had flashed Hank Gonsalves' picture in front of every waiter, waitress, bartender, busboy, and retail clerk I could find. I was greeted with a shrug of shoulders and an occasional, "Don't know the dude." My expectations were low, so I wasn't that disappointed. The sighting of Hank Gonsalves was likely another dead end. It was well beyond the dinner hour, and I was hot and thirsty. I was in the mood for a lobster roll, and nostalgia was drawing me back to the Black Cat. I hoped the menu hadn't changed too much since the '90s. The Black Cat had a terrific lobster roll. The bun was freshly toasted, and the lobster was piled high with all claw and knuckle meat. Other restaurants used mostly tail meat but not the Black Cat. You could get it with hot drawn butter or with mayonnaise. I liked mine with hot butter. Why would anyone pay thirty dollars for a lobster roll and only be able to taste the mayonnaise? It seems like it should be against the law.

I ambled down Main Street toward Ocean Street and the harbor. The ferry boats were not in port. That was a good thing. I might have half a chance at getting a seat at the bar. I walked through the front door, and the place looked exactly like it did in 1992. The aged walnut bar still looked regal, stretching the length of the dining room. The bar stools looked new, with thicker padding than the old hard wooden ones I remembered. Seeing that the Black Cat was not one of those legacy restaurants that was getting by on their reputation was comforting. The piano bar had been remodeled, but the same baby grand Steinway still held court. I spent many a Saturday night at that piano, taking requests for Sinatra and Tony Bennett standards like "New York, New York," and "I Left My Heart in San Francisco" from blurry-eyed, middle-aged tourists who had one Mudslide too many.

Two seats open at the bar, and I grabbed the one closest to the kitchen door. The bartender looked familiar. It had been thirty plus years, but I could swear he had worked a few Friday nights when I played here. His hair, then blonde, was now stark white, and some crow's feet were evident around his eyes. Twenty pounds heavier. I knew I knew him. He came up and put a cocktail napkin in front of me.

"How are you doing on this beautiful day? What can I get you?"

"I'm sure you don't remember me, but you look familiar. How long have you been a bartender at the Black Cat?"

His reply came with a wry smile, "Longer than I care to remember."

I shot back, "My name is Rob Ragusa. You don't remember me, but I played piano here on Friday nights in the early '90s."

"Holy cow! Rob! Sure, I remember you. It's been a long time. You look great. What have you been doing all these years? Obviously, not much has changed for me other than the prices on the menu."

"I'm a field agent with the FBI out of the Boston office."

"Good for you, that's awesome. Do you still play piano?"

"I have an occasional gig here and there up on the North Shore. I'm usually not good with names but Willy, right?"

"You have a great memory, Rob. Are you here for pleasure or on business?"

I replied, "Business. I'm working on the case of the Emma Jean, out of New Bedford."

"Oh yeah. I heard about that. It was all over the news. I read about it in the Cape Cod Times. Something about a fire on the boat and a missing crewman."

"There might be more to it than what's in the papers. I can't say much more about the case, but the missing man's name is Henry Gonsalves." I pulled out a picture of him and handed it to Willy. "He was reported to be seen recently in Hyannis. Do you know this guy, or does he look familiar?"

Willy took the picture and stared at it intently through his black wire-rimmed glasses.

"I wish I could help you, Rob, but I don't know him."

"Willy, would you mind if I leave a few copies of his picture with you? Maybe one of your customers knows him or has seen him. Here are some of my business cards. If you come up with anything, give me a call."

"Sure thing, Rob. You look thirsty. What sounds good?"

"I'm hot and tired. How about something tropical?"

"Well, it's not tropical, but have you ever had a strawberry Mudslide? It's all booze, fresh strawberries, and whipped cream on top. It tastes like a strawberry milkshake but with a punch."

"Sounds good, Willy. I'll also take one of your famous lobster rolls, butter with fries."

"Coming up, Rob. It's great to see you."

The dinner crowd was starting to pour in. Another bartender came in at 5:00 p.m. She looked like a young girl, early twenties, big boobs, blonde hair with a green streak. Times had changed. When I played at the Black Cat in the '80s, all the bartenders were male, and the only people with tattoos who patronized the place were servicemen stationed at Otis Air Base. Now most bartenders are female. One crude remark heard from a young bartender say at the Kowloon was, "tits get tips." I guess Willy was the last of a dying breed.

Willy served me my strawberry Mudslide, which went down fast. The lobster roll showed up ten minutes later. It was just as I remembered. I savored every bite. Willy was slammed by now. The check came, sticker shock, $36.95 for a lobster roll. Last time I ate one at the Black Cat it was $9.95. Inflation. I left a generous tip, waved goodbye to Willy, and headed to Ocean Street.

CHAPTER FORTY SIX

I returned up Ocean Street to Main Street and the strip mall parking lot to retrieve my car. My car was still there, no ticket. I hopped in and started making my way back down Main Street toward the Mid-Cape Highway and then back to Chelsea. Traffic on Main Street was bumper-to-bumper. I heard someone yell something to my right. I was right in front of the Post Office. There was a man dropping a letter into the mailbox. When he turned and faced the street, I could swear it was the Captain of the Olivia Rose, Gil Galloway. He wasn't the reason I was in New Bedford, but what a weird coincidence. He hadn't been on my radar screen until just recently.

A hero in this saga, the Olivia Rose had been the first boat to reach the sinking Emma Jean and had plucked the crew out of the ocean. We had nothing tying him to the fire on the Emma Jean, other than he and Frank Medeiros were friends and had come up through the ranks together. Recent revelations of him and Frank Medeiros being behind on gambling debts had raised his profile.

My mind started churning. Maybe he was just in Hyannis for a summer weekend with his family. My curiosity was piquing, and I wanted to follow him but had no way of pulling over or turning around. I had to keep moving with the traffic. I could see him walking back down Main Street. I finally got to a side street and could turn around and head back down Main toward the Post Office. I drove down Main Street and other side streets that connected to Main Street but no luck. He was gone. I was frustrated. I didn't know what Gil Galloway was doing in Hyannis, but I wanted to find out. Was he the good Samaritan who saved the crew of the Emma Jean, or was there a backstory?

I made my way past the summer crowd and onto the highway. I was going against traffic now, and I was finally making good headway. I had just popped in a CD, The Best of Nat King Cole, when my cell phone began to hum. I didn't recognize the number, but I picked it up anyway.

"Hello, this is Rob."

"Is this Agent Ragusa?"

"Yes, it is. Who am I speaking with?"

"This is Richard Pereira with the New Bedford Police Department. You told me at the Widows Cove that you were working on the Emma Jean case. I thought you might want to know that the captain of the Emma Jean was murdered today. He was shot as he came out of his house. Our detectives are interviewing witnesses now. I don't know much else, but you may want to call Detective Rick Raymond. He's been put in charge of the investigation. His number is 774-644-2669. I can text that to you. I can give him a heads up that you'll be calling, Agent Ragusa."

"Thanks for keeping me in the loop, officer. I'll call him right now."

I stared at my iPhone trying to absorb what I just heard. I needed to call John Ring and fill him in on this latest twist in the case. The casualties were starting to pile up. First, Steve Poole got roughed up now Frank Medeiros gunned down at his home.

I stared out at the windshield, my mind going a million miles an hour. I'm thinking, My god. One of my prime suspects is dead. Then I heard a loud honking and looked to my right. I had drifted into the next lane and almost hit a silver pickup truck. I pulled over into a convenience store parking lot and called John. He didn't pick up, so I left a voicemail giving him an update. I knew he'd want to debrief tomorrow. I had thought the pieces were starting to come together, and now this. Time to talk to Captain Galloway.

CHAPTER FORTY SEVEN

I put the call to Captain Galloway. It went straight to voicemail.

"Hi, this is Gil. I'm currently on vacation in Northern Maine. I'll be back on Monday. Please feel free to leave a message. I will return your call once I return. The cell reception up here sucks. Bye."

I left a message.

"Hi, Captain Galloway. This is Special Agent Robert Ragusa of the Boston FBI Office. I hope you're enjoying your summer vacation in Maine. Beautiful country up there. When you get back to town, please give me a call. I would like to talk to you about the fire on the Emma Jean. Nothing urgent, just a routine follow-up."

If Galloway was involved, I didn't want to spook him. Convenient that he was on vacation in rural Maine. I remember the cell reception in Hyannis as being just fine.

When most people go on vacation, they either don't change their greeting, or they just say they're on vacation. Why bother telling you where they're vacationing? Having a voicemail greeting that says you're in Maine when you're in Hyannis isn't a crime, but it sure seemed suspect. I needed to meet with the New Bedford Police to learn more about the murder of Frank Medeiros. I was tempted to head to Medeiros's house and poke around the crime scene, but experience has shown that pulling rank over the local police often backfires. Everyone wants to protect their turf. This was their city, and there was no need to jump to the conclusion that the murder of Frank Medeiros was connected to whatever happened to the Emma Jean.

It looked like I would be heading back to New Bedford on Monday. I hoped to meet with the Police Chief. If anything pointed to Gil Galloway being involved, the element of surprise would work in my favor. If Galloway called, I planned on letting it go to voicemail. I wanted to drop by his house unannounced and see how he would react. They say 90 percent of communication is nonverbal. You can get a lot of information just from body language. Well, enough sun and fun for one day, back to Saugus and Trixie.

I made steady progress headed west on the Mid-Cape Highway. Traffic was moving at a steady fifty miles an hour. For those seeking a Cape Cod experience heading on cape, it was a different story. As I approached the Sagamore Bridge, an endless caravan of vacationers dotted the horizon. They were driving everything from Harleys to forty-foot RVs. Bike racks and Kayaks adorned the SUVs, passenger cars, pickup trucks, and motorhomes. The weather forecast for the upcoming week was hot and humid. Perfect vacation weather. I knew that, for some of these families, their annual one-week stay on the Cape was their only reprieve from the daily grind of life. I had nightmarish images reliving that rainy week as a ten-year-old, stuck in a small cottage with my parents, who were trying to make the best of it. This group would be going home happy with sunburns and overpriced I Love Cape Cod T-shirts.

I didn't know what to expect when I started this morning. I planned on touching base with Steve at the Widows Cove in New Bedford and getting lucky flashing Hank Gonsalves' picture around Hyannis. Now, poor Steve had been worked over. Frank Medeiros had been murdered outside of his own home. I knew that New Bedford PD would take the lead in the captain Medeiros murder, but I wanted to see if his wife would be willing to talk to me. I didn't know what she knew about who might have killed her husband, but sometimes people tell their spouses things they wouldn't tell anyone else. Sometimes they don't even know they're doing it.

Gil Galloway had initially been portrayed as the hero. I'm not saying he isn't. If not for his action of coming to the aid of the Emma Jean, men likely would have died in the ocean of exposure.

The relationship between Gil Galloway and Frank Medeiros went way back, but I just had a feeling that there was more to their relationship than two aging sea captains who had come up the ranks together. I had Captain Galloway's phone number. He lives only three streets over from Frank Medeiros. I could kill two birds with one stone, I thought. A bad analogy, I suppose.

Early in my FBI career, I learned not to try to steer a case in a particular direction, but to go where the evidence takes you. I felt in my gut that all these developments were related but I didn't know how. I just wanted to get back home, care for Trixie and get some rest.

I called John again and got his voicemail. I wouldn't be getting back to Boston until rush hour. The debriefing could wait until tomorrow unless John had other plans. My phone didn't ring until I was about to pull into the parking lot of my condo. To my delight, it was Sandy. I picked up immediately.

"How are you doing, Rob? Is everything okay? You were supposed to call me to firm up our plans for Saturday tonight."

In the day's chaos, I had forgotten about our plans for a second date. I wasn't getting off to a good start.

"I'm sorry, Sandy. It was a little crazy today. I'm just heading home from the Cape. Do you like Chinese food?"

"It depends on the restaurant. What did you have in mind?"

"The Kowloon is right down the street from my condo. We could go there for dinner tomorrow night and then to Giggles right down the street. That's a comedy club on Route 1. Steve Sweeney is there tomorrow night. He's one of my favorite comedians. I can make a reservation there if you like."

With what seemed like enthusiasm, she replied, "I love Steve Sweeney. That sounds great. When and where did you want to meet?"

"How about 6:00 p.m. at my place? Maybe a quick glass of wine and we'll head out. The Kowloon's five minutes away. What do you like to drink?"

"Chardonnay or Pinot Grigio would be great."

"I have just the Chardonnay in mind, 2020 Sea Slopes, light, crisp, buttery, and refreshing. Great for a sultry summer night."

"Okay, Rob. You talked me into it. I'm really looking forward to seeing you again."

I felt guilty for not having put more forethought into our date, but I had made a nice recovery. I should have offered to meet Sandy somewhere on the South Shore this time since she had come to Saugus for our first date. Steve Sweeney was a good bet. He was a local guy, and his comedy was centered on Boston culture. One of his bits was about the Southie men's softball league. Sully on first base, Murph on second base, and Fitzy on third. That type of stuff. If you were from New England, you got it. If you were from Iowa, not so much. Sweeny's bit rang home with me. I played in the Southie men's softball league in the eighties. The only player whose last name ended with a vowel. It was a good experience. I got ragged on a lot, but that was how these guys communicated. You wouldn't be part of the crew if you weren't getting ragged on. After the game, winners and losers alike would head to Foleys, where Guinness and the bragging would flow freely.

I'm no prude, but when a comic must rely on swear words in every joke, it gets old with me. One thing I like about Steve Sweeney is his comedy is clean, and there is audience participation. If you heckle Steve Sweeney, watch out. He's been on the comedy circuit forever, and will come back at you, hard and relentless. A few years ago, I was at one of his shows at Nick's Comedy Stop. Steve told one of his standard jokes about Boston and a guy in a three-piece suit in the back yelled, "Boston sucks." In a calm voice Steve asked him where he was from. The guy yells back Louisville, Kentucky. He didn't stand a chance. Next thing you know, a stream of jokes about Kentucky came flying out one after another. My head was spinning. The one I remember was, "What do you say to a girl in Kentucky when you break up? Can we still be cousins?" This guy turned nine shades of red. Steve went up to him after the show and bought him a drink. They shook hands, and that was that.

I remember in college, making the mistake of taking a first date to a comedy club. The headliner's vocabulary consisted of two words: asshole and motherfucker. He also would throw in an occasional racist or sexist joke. There was no second date. Steve Sweeny was a safe bet.

It was early, but Sandy was stirring feelings I hadn't experienced in a long time. She checked all the boxes. Stylish, attractive, smart, and accomplished. The fact that she liked Steve Sweeney, Chardonnay, and Chinese food also went into the plus column.

I pulled into my assigned parking spot and went up to my front door. Trixie was there waiting with her usual look of disdain. A full dish of food, water, and petting would get me back in her good graces. I changed into a pair of shorts and my Red Sox T-shirt, popped open an ice-cold beer. I plopped into the Barcalounger and grabbed the remote to see what was on the tube. I found the Red Sox playing the Baltimore Orioles. It was the third inning, and the Red Sox were behind 3 to 2. Trixie ate her dinner and made her way to my lap. Her rhythmic purring told me all was good in her world.

My mind kept bouncing like a ping pong ball from my upcoming date with Sandy to the confusing events of the day. I was looking forward to brainstorming with John tomorrow. I was hoping that Interpol might have even more information on the two websites connected to the IP address and tie together what the connection was between London, New York, New Bedford, and Hyannis.

• • •

There are puzzle pieces and more suspects but few answers. I knew the New Bedford Police would want to take the lead role in the assault on Steve Poole at the Widows Cove and the murder of Frank Medeiros. I had already pushed back once on working with other agents on this case. With everything that happened today, John would insist that more agents join me in the investigation. I didn't want that. It's not that I want all the glory or didn't play well with others. I just work better alone. Plus, New Bedford is a small city. Bringing in more agents would further stir the pot, and the bad guys would go underground. Well, that was a battle to be fought tomorrow.

I drifted to sleep, waking up with Trixie still in my lap. It was 10:00 p.m. The Red Sox had gone into extra innings. I wanted to see the end of the game, but I was exhausted. I turned the TV off, set the alarm for 7:00 a.m., and went to bed. Tomorrow would be a day to regroup. I had to get John up to speed on my day in New Bedford and Hyannis. The assault on Steve Poole, the IP address, Gil Galloway and maybe Hank Gonsalves in Hyannis, Frank Medeiros being killed, Wolfie, Mike's Restaurant. It was a lot to digest.

It was overwhelming, with so many moving parts. I felt we were always a day late and a dollar short, and I needed that to change. I felt that most of the pieces were there. It was just a question of fitting them together. We were close.

CHAPTER FORTY EIGHT

The alarm went off at 7:00 a.m., much to my dismay. I reached over and knocked the clock onto the floor, trying to shut it off. I rolled out of bed and went through my usual weekday morning routine of feeding Trixie and putting on a pot of coffee. I jumped into a steaming shower, put on my summer light blue suit, and was ready to go by 7:45 a.m. I have eggs, cereal, and toast in the kitchen, but I hardly ever make breakfast. Dunkin' Donuts is just too damn convenient. I've developed a love affair with their ham, egg, and cheese on a whole grain bagel.

The line at Dunkin's was four cars, short by weekday standards. I was through the line in under five minutes, leaving a generous tip for the older lady who took my order. I was heading back over the Tobin Bridge to the FBI office for my 9:00 meeting with John. Summers in Boston are usually hot and humid, but unlike, places like Washington DC, you occasionally get cooler, drier air that comes down from Canada. These are the days I live for. Seventy-five degrees and low humidity. Today was not one of those days. It was the typical triple H.

I turned the air conditioning on high. I made my way through the twisting, narrow roads of the North End. All the restaurants were closed, and the streets were relatively empty. A few stray tourists wandered around looking at the maps they handed out at the tourists' kiosks. These last few days had been hectic, to say the least. I wanted to compare notes with John and get him up to speed on my New Bedford and Hyannis adventures.

The complexity of the case had grown exponentially. I figured John would want additional agents assigned to my case. I could use the help, but I knew that anyone involved with the Emma Jean would go off the grid if the FBI invaded New Bedford or Hyannis.

It was Saturday, so other than the cleaning crew and a skeleton office staff, the building would be deserted. I parked in the near empty parking lot and entered the main building. Rose Gallagher had been the Boston FBI field office receptionist since the early 90's. An always friendly face in a building that was often filled with intensity. I didn't recognize the young woman with jet-black hair behind the glass. I assumed Rose must be on vacation. It was July, peak vacation season. I showed my badge and smiled, "You must be filling in for Rose. Is she on vacation?"

The receptionist gave me a puzzled look. Her reply stunned me.

"Didn't you hear? Rose is at Mass General. She had a heart attack yesterday afternoon. She's doing all right from what I've heard."

I stared blankly at the woman, unable to reply. I barely acknowledged her question.

"I'm Sarah. How can I help you?"

"You just said that Rose had a heart attack, right?"

"Yes sir, it happened right here, at her desk. From what I was told she was fine one minute and, on the floor, the next. Paramedics came and performed CPR. She was transported to Mass General yesterday afternoon. From what I've heard she's in intensive care but stable."

"Thank you, Sarah. I didn't mean to be rude. I'm just a bit stunned. I've known Rose forever." I gathered myself and pulled out my ID. "I'm Special Agent Rob Ragusa. I have a 9 a.m. appointment with John Ring. I was out of the office yesterday. No wonder I couldn't reach John last night."

Sarah seemed at a loss for words. She glanced at my ID and beeped me in.

I was already a little on edge about my meeting with John. The news about Rose threw me. She is one of those people who is always in a good mood. Always had a smile on her face in a building where that was a rare commodity. You could always count on Rose to lighten the mood. I'm sure she had her issues at home. Everyone does. But she never brought them to work.

The door to John's office was open. I knocked gently and entered. John was sitting in his leather chair with his back to me. He was on the phone, and the conversation seemed heated. I slowly sat in one of the two chairs in front of his oversized mahogany desk. After another minute or so, he hung up the phone and swiveled around to face me. His face was quite flushed.

"Do you know, Rob, who I just got off the phone from?"

"No, I don't, but you don't seem happy."

"You're damn right. I'm not happy. That was the Police Chief of New Bedford, Ron Dellicker. He's not happy, Rob, that the FBI is investigating the fire on the Emma Jean, in his city, without his knowledge. The trashing of the Widows Cove Tavern, the beatdown of Mr. Poole, and subsequent threats to Mr. Poole have centered attention on the Emma Jean. Now Frank Medeiros is dead. He's connecting the dots. He's figured out that this was likely not a simple kitchen fire. He's angry that the New Bedford PD was left out of the loop. The captain of the Emma Jean was murdered in front of his home. When did you plan on filling me in on all this? What exactly have you been up to down there?"

I had never seen John like this. He was the most measured man I had ever met. His voice was booming, and the veins in his neck were bulging out. John liked to pride himself on keeping local law enforcement in the loop. He was not one of these macho types who liked to throw the FBI's weight around. He liked cooperation, not conflict. I stammered my disjointed response,

"John, I didn't mean to step on anyone's toes. I've known Steve Poole since my band days at the Widows Cove in the '90s. Yes, he's plugged into the city and fed me useful information. I drove up on the scene as the ambulance was driving him to St. Luke's Hospital. I know I got him involved. I feel like crap over what happened to him. I take personal responsibility. In terms of the Frank Medeiros murder, I didn't see that coming. He was involved in the fire or was involved in drug smuggling or knew too much. All the above.

"Steve had given me a lead about a recent sighting of Hank Gonsalves in Hyannis. So, I was there yesterday checking it out. I showed Hank's picture all over town. No luck. I left you a voicemail. Didn't you get it?"

John's voice began to modulate. "I'm sorry, Rob. You're right. I did get your message, but yesterday was a crazy day here. Rose had a heart attack, and that just threw us all for a loop. I followed the ambulance to Mass General. Rose is like a second mother to me."

"John, she's like a second mother to all of us. I get it. The receptionist told me she's in intensive care but stable."

"Yes, nobody can visit her but immediate family. Her husband, Phil, has been keeping me updated about her condition. She's going to make it, thank God."

"You're not the Lone Ranger, you know. Following FBI protocol is how I run this office. This case has gotten way too big for one agent to handle. I'm coordinating with the New Bedford Police Department on any further investigation and developments on this case. The Coast Guard is going to be taking the lead on this case. I know you and Bob Halloran are friends. He's going to be working with you from here on in. The Coast Guard had been nice enough to lend Bob to us.

"Interpol has traced chatter on the Red Crescent Trading Company website to a flat on the East End of London. They have staked out the flat and will move in when the time is right. I want you in the office today. You need to call Bob Halloran, get him up to speed, and coordinate all future operations going forward. You also need to call Chief Dellicker. An apology would be in order. No more solo trips to New Bedford or Hyannis. Chief Dellicker has put out a BOLO order on Hank Gonsalves. Rob, I want daily briefings on your progress. I want your paperwork on my desk by the end of the day including your expense report. I feel like the FBI is supporting the local tourism business in New Bedford."

No words came out of my mouth. I simply nodded, yes, and slinked out of John's office. I headed down the hallway toward my office, wondering what just hit me. I realized I had been out of line. I was lucky John didn't suspend me. It would be a coordinated effort from here on it. My days of being the Lone Ranger were over.

CHAPTER FORTY NINE

I was dying to return to New Bedford, but the game plan had changed. I didn't want today's interaction with John to affect my date with Sandy. I was looking forward to seeing her again. I had to put today's dress down by John into the dark recesses of my mind and switch gears to second date mode.

In my dating experience, which isn't much, the second date is the most important. You've made it past the first date. So, that means your date considers you as datable material, but you are far from out of the woods. On the second date, a spilled drink, having too much to drink, an off-color joke, or something completely out of left field can put a swift end to your romantic endeavor. I speak from experience.

Sandy seemed like the easy-going type. She had a good sense of humor and could talk on a wide range of topics. I thought the Kowloon and a comedy show was a safe bet. The Kowloon and giggles were less than a mile from the condo. Sandy agreed to meet me at the condo and have a glass of wine before we went out. I'm glad she agreed to meet me at the condo. I wanted to show her I didn't live in my mother's basement. I owned a respectable dwelling that was clean and nicely furnished. I was sexually attracted to her, but I had no intentions of going anywhere near there on the second date. For most woman, going that far on just the second date was a deal breaker.

The only thing I worried about was that I was a regular at the Kowloon. I knew I'd be greeted by a round of, "Hey, Rob, how are you doing?" from Benny and the regulars. I didn't want Sandy to think I was lush. It was a calculated risk I was willing to take.

I had a full day at the office. I made my calls, completed my paperwork, and headed out the door at 4:00 p.m. I wanted to return the rental and pick up the caddy at Chuck's Auto. The Caddy wasn't a limo, but it was a little more impressive than the Chrysler 300. I pulled out of the lot and headed back to Saugus. Chuck didn't close the shop until 5:00 p.m., so I had time. I could drop the rental off first, and one of the salesmen could drop me off at Chuck's.

I swung into the Enterprise lot at 4:30 p.m. A tall, thin Hispanic man with coke bottle glasses was behind the counter.

"Can I help you sir?"

"I want to return the Chrysler 300. My name is Rob Ragusa. I'm with the FBI. We have an account with you."

He banged away on the computer keyboard and looked up.

"Yes, sir, I have you right here. Let me check the mileage and take a quick look at the car."

After a few minutes, he returned and printed out the paperwork. Before he could hand it to me, I asked, "My car is at Chucks Auto. It's only a few minutes from here. Could anyone give me a ride?"

"Yes, sir, my name is Trevor. I'm about to close and afterward I'll give you a ride." I shook his hand.

"Thanks, Trevor, I appreciate that."

"I hope you don't mind riding in an old pickup truck, sir."

"Please call me Rob. No, I don't mind driving in a pickup."

I called Chuck on my cell phone and told him I was on my way. He told me not to rush, but it was Saturday afternoon and I assumed, like me, Chuck had air conditioning and a cold one in mind. Trevor shut off the lights, closed up shop and drove me the five minutes to Chucks Auto in a blue Toyota Tacoma pickup truck that looked like it was on its last legs. We pulled in at five minutes of five. I tried to hand Trevor a ten-dollar bill, but he refused it. I shook his hand, and he sped off back down Route 1.

Chuck was standing next to my caddy. I walked over, and he greeted me with a hand covered in a day's work—grease, oil, and some other black matter I wasn't quite sure of. The caddy looked brand new. By outward appearances, Chuck looked like the kind of guy you wouldn't want to meet in a dark alley. A hulk of a man with hands that looked like they could lift a transmission. Once you talked to him, though, he put you at ease. His love of all things automotive came through quickly. He was a masterful mechanic.

When other mechanics in the area couldn't fix a problem, they called Chuck. I signed the paperwork. The insurance company would be paying. I was putting my $500 deductible on my expense account. My caddy had suffered work-related damages as best as I could tell. I didn't think someone had just decided to test their new nine-millimeter on my car. I hoped John would see it my way, but I wasn't his favorite currently. Still, we had a lot of history together. Most of it good.

I shook Chuck's beefy hand and jumped into the Caddy. I love this car, and Chuck made it rise like a phoenix from the ashes. I was ecstatic. I headed south down Route 1 back to my condo. I wanted to relax a little before my big date. I had a nice light gray silk shirt that had been sitting in my closet for two years. It was a Christmas gift from my sister. A little too fancy for everyday use, but I thought the silk shirt and a pair of tan pants would fit the bill for my date with Sandy. I pulled into the condo. The caddy was running beautifully. Chuck had even had it washed, waxed, and vacuumed.

I'd be styling tonight. I washed up, changed, and put the dirty dishes from the sink into the dishwasher. I tidied up the house and fed Trixie. As a final touch, I put on some Calvin Klein cologne I had bought for the occasion. Now the waiting game. The plan was for Sandy to come to the condo around 6:00 p.m., have a quick glass of wine, and then off to the Kowloon. The air was full of promise. Here we go.

I sat on the recliner, watching the seconds tick on the clock. Trixie kept trying to sit on my lap, but I had to keep putting her down. I didn't want any stray fur on my pants. I didn't know if Sandy was a fan of cats or not. It was now five minutes past six. I had given her the passcode to the building, and she hadn't called to say she was lost. Then there was a gentle knock on the door. I jumped out of the recliner and toward the front door. I opened the door. She looked stunning. She wore a red silk knee-length dress, high heels, and a simple strand of white pearls around her neck. She must have been out in the sun because her skin was a perfect bronze color, like the models in the Coppertone commercials.

"Please come in. I was a little worried you got lost." I wasn't looking for an apology. I was just relieved to see her.

"I'm sorry I'm late, Rob. I passed the turn-off for your parking lot. I haven't been on Route 1 in a long time. I forgot how scary a road it is. I had to enter the left lane and turn around at the traffic light. Of course, nobody lets you in. Anyway, it took a few minutes to make my way back."

"You look like you could use a drink. I have a nice Pinot Grigio or Chardonnay."

"I'll take a glass of Pinot. Thanks Rob."

I went over and uncorked a chilled bottle of Pinot Grigio. I poured two glasses and brought one to Sandy, who was now sitting on the couch. She was joined by Trixie, who wanted to know who this new guest was. She must have liked Sandy because she was rubbing on Sandy's silk stockings and purring.

While leaning over to pet Trixie, she said, "I love cats. I had a Siamese for fifteen years, but it died last year of cancer. I haven't had the heart to get another cat yet. It's the first time since college that I haven't had a pet. She seems so sweet, Rob. So, what's her name?"

"I named her Trixie after Vivian Vance's character on *The Honeymooners*. I love the old TV shows—*Hogan's Heroes*, *The Dick Van Dyke Show*, and my favorite, *The Honeymooners*. I'm sure you don't remember these shows."

"Sure, I do. I like the old game shows. *The Match Game* is my favorite. 1970s orange shag carpet, the guest stars smoking on the set. A different time. A simpler time."

She had the wine glass halfway to her mouth when I said, "Here's to the weekend."

Not the most romantic thing to say but, it was all I could think of. We clinked glasses, and each took a sip. Sandy nodded her approval. So far, so good. I could see her starting to relax.

We made small talk about work. She asked how the Emma Jean case was coming along. I couldn't say much, just that some things were starting to break in the case. I gave her the nickel tour of my two-bedroom condo, and we finished our glasses of wine. The Kowloon doesn't take reservations, so I wanted to get there before the rush. I put the empty wine glasses in the kitchen sink and opened the door for Sandy. We headed out to the parking lot.

"Wow, Rob, what a classic, and it's in beautiful condition. I'm always jealous when I see an old Cadillac, Mustang, or Chevelle. They knew how to make cars back in those days. This car must be a V8. Right?"

"I'm impressed, Sandy. You know your cars. She's fast, and I can get out of the way in a hurry."

The news of the shoot-out on the Tobin Bridge had been all over the local news. John had called in some favors with the management of the TV stations and managed to keep my name out of the reporting. Sandy didn't know I was involved. She would have had a different opinion if she had seen the Caddy at Chuck's before, he worked his magic. Some things are better left unsaid. At some point, I would have to tell her, but tonight was not the night.

Sandy climbed into the passenger seat, and I switched the radio to an Oldies channel. The song playing was "Summer Wind" by Frank Sinatra. It seemed perfect for tonight. It was a beautiful night. Like a wet blanket, the humidity that had hung over the city for days, had lifted. There were gentle breezes blowing in from the Atlantic. I rolled my window down. Sandy followed suit and we headed north on Route 1 to the Kowloon.

The Kowloon Restaurant is enormous. Besides the restaurant, there is a long bar, banquet rooms, and their comedy club. It's like a Chinese amusement park for adults. The parking lot was about two-thirds full. Since the pandemic, many restaurants have closed, and the ones that managed to survive saw their business drop. In normal times, the Kowloon would be packed on a Saturday night.

We entered through the gigantic twenty-foot gold colored front door, and the bar was completely full. I knew most of the patrons. Benny was behind the bar. He spotted me and indiscreetly yelled out, "Hey, Rob. Where have you been?" About half the bar turned around and gave me a knowing wave.

"Wow, Rob. You must be some kind of celebrity here."

"Well, I've been known to stop by for the occasional Mai Tai."

Sandy shot me a glance like I think it's a little more than occasional. I wondered if I had made a mistake taking her here. Oh well, too late now. The manager pointed us to a booth in the back.

Sandy was looking around like an eight-year-old at Disneyworld.

"I've been in plenty of Chinese restaurants, but I must admit, I've never seen anything like this. This place is crazy."

"You're only seeing a small part of it. There are banquet rooms around the corner, an entertainment venue with live bands every weekend and they have their own comedy club. They get all the top comics to come here. I've seen Steve Sweeney here a few times. Tonight, he's playing Giggles. It's only a few minutes down Route 1. I think it will be a good show. "

Our waiter came by. He looked like an ancient Asian man with thinning white hair. He glanced briefly and plopped two glasses of water and menus in front of us. He asked in perfect English if we wanted something to drink. Sandy deferred to me. "This seems like your hangout, Rob. What do you recommend?" "Benny is a great bartender. All the Polynesian drinks are excellent. I'd go with a Mai Tai. I need to warn you, though. Benny makes a strong drink."

Sandy reviewed the drink menu and said, "It's been a long week. Strong sounds good to me." The Mai Tai's arrived, little umbrellas and all. I was waiting for Sandy's reaction as she took her first sip. A long smile slowly lit up her face. "Where has this drink been all my life?" I chuckled, not expecting that comment. I replied, "At the Kowloon and about any other Chinese restaurant with a bar. Although I must admit, I've probably been in at least thirty Chinese restaurants in my life and always ordered a Mai Tai. I've never had one that compares to Benny's. Benny will spoil you."

Sandy looked over the menu. There were so many options. Dozens of entrées including Szechwan, sushi, at least thirty plus combo plates, Pu Pu platters and American food. After a few minutes, she glanced from the menu to me and said, "I'm guessing this isn't your first visit to the Kowloon. "It's overwhelming, Rob. There's so much to choose from. What are you in the mood for?"

I suggested the Pu Pu platter for two. It's loaded with many of the standard Chinese food staples like beef teriyaki, boneless pork ribs, chicken wings, egg rolls, fried shrimp, and crab Rangoon. With a side order of fried rice, you have enough food to feed a family of six. The Kowloon does it old school, in a wooden serving tray with a lit sterno canister in the middle. You could warm up your beef teriyaki over the flame. It wasn't Crème Brulé at a fine French restaurant but still fun.

I asked Sandy if she liked rice. She said yes.

"So, you're okay with the Pu Pu platter for two? What type of rice would you like? They have lots of choices."

She replied, "I'm not the connoisseur of Chinese food that you are, but I used to go to Bob Lees

Islander in Chinatown back in the day. Have you ever tried the house rice here?"

"No, I'm more of a traditionalist. Pork fried rice: but I'm willing to throw caution to the wind."

She let out a giggle. That was a good sign. I'm not much of a comedian, but people have told me I have a good dry sense of humor. At the FBI, it's called gallows humor. With what the average field agent sees in a career, you need that to survive. It's amazing what one human being can do to another.

I signaled our waiter over. He walked slowly and stooped over. I wondered if he had been here decades ago when the Kowloon first opened.

"You know what you want?"

I ordered the Pu Pu platter for two and a small order of the house rice. I looked at our drinks, and Sandy had drunk about half her Mai Tai. I was down to the bottom of the glass with a few lonely melting ice cubes. I hesitated but then ordered another Mai Tai for myself. Sandy had already witnessed the *Cheers*-type greeting I received from the bar crowd when we walked in. If she thought I had a drinking problem, this would be our last date. I vowed to milk the second Mai Tai until we had finished dinner.

Sandy was easy to talk to. We had many of the same interests: the Red Sox, the Patriots, jazz music, the beach. I was already smitten with her but was fighting the law enforcement instinct to keep digging. I felt like this was too good to be true; that there must be some serious flaws in her personality. I loved working for the FBI, but you tend to see the worst in people. It was a hazard of the job. You get jaded. You tend not to trust people. I didn't want that mindset ruining what might be one of the best things that's ever happened to me.

At the Kowloon, your food comes out of the kitchen fast. Even when the place is packed, I've never had to wait more than ten minutes for my food. True to form, the flaming Pu Pu platter arrived, and Sandy's eyes bugged out of her head. The Pu Pu platter for two could easily feed six of the Patriots offensive linemen.

I had never heard her swear but when the Pu Pu platter hit the table, she gasped and said, "Holy shit. That's a lot of food!" Somehow, this further endeared her to me.

"Rob, I think we'll need a couple of doggie bags." She had finished her first Mai Tai and ordered another one. Now the playing field was level.

The conversation got a little more serious between munching on chicken wings and boneless spareribs. She asked, "When was the last time you were in a serious relationship, Rob?" I wasn't sure if she was sincerely curious or testing me out. In my experience, women can be suspicious of a man who hasn't been in a serious relationship for some time. The first couple of dates are like two boxers searching for the other's deficiencies. She might be wondering, well, he has a great job, owns his own condo, and is decent looking. Why isn't he with someone? It's a legitimate question, so I replied honestly.

"It's been a few years." I knew what her follow-up question would be.

"Why so long?"

"Well, my job takes up a lot of my time, and I guess, to be honest, I haven't been looking."

The conversation drifted between our work and hobbies. We both kept it light. It was only the second date, after all. In my past dating life, I always got suspicious when the talk got too serious too soon. I was grateful that this wasn't Sandy's style. Our waiter gave me the check and bagged up the mound of leftovers. In true traditional Kowloon style, the waiter also brought a dish of pineapple chunks and two fortune cookies. I read my fortune out loud.

"Good things come to those who wait." I asked Sandy to read hers aloud.

She looked at her fortune and said, "Are you sure you want me to? It's kind of deep."

"Yeah, sure," I replied.

"Okay. Every new beginning comes from some beginning's end. What do you think, Rob? Are we at the beginning of something or the end?"

Wow. I didn't expect a fortune cookie to put me on the spot.

"I don't know where the road will lead, but I hope you'll be along for the ride." I inquired. "Sandy can we stop conversing in fortune cookies?"

"I think that would be a good idea, Rob. Let's quit while we're ahead."

I grabbed our doggie bags, and we headed out. Steve Sweeny appeared at 8:00 p.m. It was 7:30, so we had plenty of time to get there and grab our seats. So far, everything has been going well. I hadn't gotten drunk. Sandy hadn't gotten drunk. Neither of us spilled a drink or spilled duck sauce on our clothes. The fortune cookie threw me for a loop, but I thought I had handled it well.

The trip to Giggles only took five minutes. Traffic on Route 1 had thinned out. Top local comedians played at Giggles, but it wasn't much to look at. Inside was a small stage with a dated neon sign that spelled out Giggles in red. It reminded me of the signs at cheap motels where the "no vacancy" sign would be blinking.

We walked through the dated front door and approached the hostess station.

A youthful brunette dressed in a way too short black skirt asked, "Are you here for the show?"

"Yes. My name is Rob Ragusa. You should have a reservation for me."

She gazed intently at the sheet of reservations in front of her. The list was little too long for my liking.

Now I'm thinking, damn they don't have my reservation. Finally, she looked up,

"Yes Mr. Ragusa, I've got you right here." The hostess sat us at a table near the front. In my experience, this can be dangerous.

Years ago, when I lived in Boston, I was visited by my gay cousin and his partner from Florida. They wanted to see a comedy show, so I took them to Giggles. The first comedian told a series of off-color gay jokes to the point where I wanted to crawl under the table. When the show was over, I apologized to both. They shook it off. My cousin said there was no way of predicting their bits. The comedian usually reads the audience. If you're upfront, you're more likely to draw attention. Steve Sweeney was great at improvisation and could tear a heckler apart. I wasn't going to heckle. I just hoped he didn't decide to zero in on me during his act.

He came out to a rousing round of applause. He sat on a wooden stool with a glass of water and started his routine. I've heard most of his bits at least five times, but they're still funny. He asked where people were from. One guy said New Jersey. That turned into a ten-minute volley of jokes about New Jersey. One of his jokes was about the joys of driving through Newark and how the city smelled like Boston Harbor at low tide. He kept on this guy until I wanted to throw my white cocktail napkin onto the stage like a boxing manager throwing in the white towel. Finally, he gave up and moved on to the classics like the player's names in the Southie summer softball league. Everyone was roaring, even the guy from New Jersey. The humor is local and biting but not mean. That's a hard balance to keep, but Steve Sweeney pulls it off.

I occasionally glanced over at Sandy. She was having a great time. She was sipping on her ginger ale, laughing loudly. She had a genuine laugh that came right from her toes. Her laugh was the kind that would make other people laugh, even if they didn't get the joke. I hate a fake laugh. I can pick up on it instantly. Steve thanked the crowd for coming and retreated backstage. We both finished our drinks at the same time and headed back to the car. Now came another critical decision. Do I ask her up to my place for a nightcap? If I do and she says yes, what then? We pulled into the parking lot at 10:30 p.m. Still early for a Saturday night.

"Sandy, I had a great time tonight. Would you like to come up for a nightcap?"

"Thanks, Rob, but I must get up early tomorrow for a meeting."

I was disappointed and relieved at the same time. I reached over to give her a goodnight peck on her cheek, and she startled me by grabbing me by the front of my shirt.

She said, "You can do better than that, I hope."

A long, slow kiss and hug ensued. I felt like a high school kid who just made out for the first time.

I was tempted to grab her hand and lead her toward the condo, but something told me not to.

Instead, I slowly pulled away and asked, "Will I see you again?"

"Rob, that's a dumb question. I wouldn't have kissed you like that if this was our last date. Call me." She jumped into her Mini Cooper and beeped as she left the parking lot.

A million things were going through my mind, and for the first time in a long time, they were all good. Whew, I had made it through to the second date. There would be a third. Feelings I hadn't felt in years were bubbling to the surface. I had finally met "the one." I had a bounce in my step that I hadn't had for a long time.

CHAPTER FIFTY

I walked back to the condo staring at a moonlit sky. For the first time in a long time, I felt raw emotion. As a field agent in the FBI, you learn to hide and push down your emotions, distance yourself from a situation. I was feeling exhilarated and, at the same time, anxious. My personal life was looking up. My work life was a different story. I was bogged down in the investigation of the Emma Jean. I prided myself on my experience and professionalism, and somehow, this investigation had veered way off course. Steve Poole was recovering from injuries at St. Luke's Hospital as a direct result of my involving him in this case. I hadn't made any friends in New Bedford, including the Police Chief.

As I entered my condo, Trixie greeted me, as always. She seemed in a better mood than when I usually returned after leaving her alone. She immediately began rubbing on my pant leg and purring. Sandy liked her, and Trixie seemed to warm up to Sandy. That was a plus.

I needed a break. Tomorrow, I will pack my cooler, grab a good book, and head to Singing Beach in Manchester by the Sea. They called it Singing Beach because you can hear the sand singing when you walk across the beach. It was my favorite beach on the North Shore. The sand was powdery white, and it was usually not crowded.

The water was cold, but that was par for the course in New England, even in July. I love New England. There are so many historic and beautiful places to see. The Berkshires, the rocky coast of Maine, the Green Mountains of Vermont and Newport, just to name a few. Boston, the self-proclaimed "Hub of The Universe," was a combination of the new and the old. It was a vibrant seafront city that combined new world sophistication with the old charms of Beacon Hill and the Back Bay. It had great restaurants in ethnic neighborhoods like the North End and East Boston. I loved living here, but at least once every winter, when I was stuck in traffic in a snowstorm in January with the temperature outside in the twenties, I would vow to put the condo up for sale, retire and move to a sunny beach in Florida.

Then in February, on local TV the truck leaving Fenway for the Red Sox Spring Training home in Fort Meyers Florida, would provide some hope that the long winter was coming to an end. St. Patrick's Day would come, and the parade in Southie would happen with all the local pols making lame jokes about each other at the annual St. Patrick's Day Breakfast.

Opening Day is the real start of Spring in Boston. Hope springs eternal for the Red Sox until they break your heart. I always went to opening day. It was a tradition during my childhood with my folks and even later in life with my chums. My friend, Richie DeMond, still lived on L Street in Southie. Every opening day since high school, the two of us would sit in the bleachers, hot dog and beverage in hand, and root on the "Sox." By now, the crocuses would start popping up through the soil, and Red Sox opening day at Fenway would be a week or two away. Boston would then be back in my good graces, and Florida would have to wait another year.

I was tired and decided to skip my usual turn-on-the-TV-and-conk-out-in-the-recliner nightly routine. I hit the sack at about 11:30 p.m., didn't set the alarm, and drifted off. I woke up and, through blurry eye. saw the alarm clock read 9:15 a.m. Whoa, this was sleeping in for me. I prepared my favorite breakfast of scrambled eggs. Sandy had insisted I take the leftovers from the Kowloon. I pulled out a steak teriyaki and cut it up. My version of steak and eggs. Sunday, for me, was always the same routine. I cooked either pancakes or scrambled eggs, and read the Boston Herald and the Boston Globe, cover to cover. After reading the Sunday papers, I packed my cooler with a few diet cokes and grabbed a paperback off the bookshelf that I had been meaning to read. The title was Burn by James Patterson. I didn't know what the book was about, but the title seemed appropriate given my current investigation.

What a great day at Singing Beach. Perfect weather. The water was above sixty degrees, balmy by North Shore standards. I relaxed, read six chapters of *Burn*, and was getting the beginning of a pretty good sunburn. I know it's not smart, but I hate suntan lotion. Whether you spray it on or lather it on it doesn't matter. It makes me feel like a greased pig. So, after a day at the beach, I usually resemble a cooked half pound lobster on a fisherman's platter. I thought back on my date with Sandy. I was pleased with how things were progressing. She laughed at my jokes. We had a much in common, and the conversation didn't focus on work. I love law enforcement, but it can be depressing. You see the dark side of humanity. That's why I like to see a comedy when I go to the movies. If I decide to watch a play, it's usually a musical. Can't go wrong with *My Fair Lady*. I've seen it five times. I got back in the Caddy about 2:00 p.m. and returned to the condo for a little more down time.

I was grateful the two major Boston newspapers were still in business. The newspaper business was dying a slow, deliberate death. The internet and social media are the culprits. There were still enough dinosaurs like me to keep them going a while longer. There was something about the sound and feel of a newspaper in your hand that I enjoyed. The crunching of the newspaper when you thumbed through it. Even the black ink stains on your hands. Reading the paper online just wasn't the same.

I thumbed through the papers and was about to start dinner, meatloaf, green beans, and mashed potatoes when the cell phone lit up. It was John. He didn't usually call me on the weekends unless it was important. I picked it up right away.

"Rob, I've assigned another agent to work with you on the Emma Jean investigation. Do you know Rick Raymond?"

"I remember Rick. We've met a few times. I've never worked a case with him, but we've talked at a few conferences and trainings over the years."

John said, "Well, he's on vacation now, but will return in a week. I called around, and the Bureau Chief in Portsmouth, New Hampshire, recommended him. Rick grew up in New Bedford and still has contacts there. I think he might be a good fit. In the meantime, I want you to call Agent Raymond.

"Chief Dellicker is going to assign his best detective to the case. The three of you will work together as a joint task force. He has some new information on the Widows Cove and the murder of Captain Medeiros. I want you to get down to New Bedford tomorrow. I want you to compare notes with the local detective and Chief Dellicker. I've assured him that this will be a joint effort. You're a good agent, Rob.

But no more lone wolf heroics. Agent Raymond's phone number is 603-524-6697. He's expecting your call. Get him up to speed, and we'll meet at my office when he returns."

"I'll be there, John. Thanks for sticking with me. I won't screw this up. Don't worry. I'm good at smoothing ruffled feathers. It's all going to be fine."

"Ok, keep me in the loop. I expect daily briefings from you."

Well, my days of working the case alone were ending. I was grateful for the help. Nobody knew the city better than the local police, and now, Rick Raymond who had ties to the city. I needed all the help I could get. I planned to go to bed early and return to New Bedford early in the morning.

I had one week before Agent Raymond joined me. I had a couple of ideas about how I wanted to spend the upcoming week. Nothing illegal, but Rick has a reputation for being a straight shooter and following strict FBI protocol. I only had another week to push the envelope a little. John surprised me a bit. He didn't tell me the name of the New Bedford detective assigned to the case. I didn't know if that was on purpose or an oversight. Well, I've worked with all types in the past, by the book types, cowboys, social climbers. I could handle it. I wanted whoever this detective was to stay off the case until Rick Raymond joined the team. One more week alone, that would be all it would take.

CHAPTER FIFTY ONE

I was up bright and early Monday morning. I was crossing the Tobin Bridge with the skyline of Boston panned out in front of me. A cold front from Canada had moved in and would hang around New England. That meant a few days of seventy-five to eighty degrees and low humidity. These weather ranges were the normal summer pattern for Boston. There were a few days of the triple Hs, followed by a few days of cool Canadian air. There were some summers when the cool Canadian air decided to stay home. I remember these days as a kid. I spent long days at Carson Beach, playing ball with the neighborhood kids. Those were fond memories. No one had air conditioning in those days. Nights were not so pleasant. There was sweltering heat, the whir of fans blowing around hot air and sweating through multiple shirts at night. The only breeze you could get would be at Castle Island. Sometimes we even went in our pajamas. I loved the cooler summer days, and today was picture perfect for another trip to New Bedford.

It was 7:00 a.m. I had given myself two hours to make what should have been a one-hour ride to New Bedford. You could never count on traffic. There was always road construction. It seemed like the highways were always under repair. I got it, though. New England isn't San Diego. New England winters could be snowy and bone chilling, followed by the spring melt and blistering summer heat. It took a toll on the roads. Road crews spent the spring and summer patching up the knee breaking potholes that kept many a tire store and car repair shop in business.

John had arranged a meeting with me and the New Bedford chief of police, Ron Dellicker. I needed to smooth over some ruffled feathers. I should have gotten New Bedford Police involved in the Emma Jean case right from the beginning, but I had no idea what long tentacles this case would have. I now had a missing fisherman, murdered fishing boat captain, beat up bartender and a possible international drug smuggling ring. It was time for reinforcements.

The ride to New Bedford went smoother than expected. Light traffic for a Monday morning. I got off 195 and onto Route 18 an hour early. I had time to kill so I stopped at a breakfast place on Purchase Street. Portuguese style hash and eggs, black coffee, and a quick read of The New Bedford Standard Times, and it was showtime. I had two hours on the meter. Two hours is plenty of time for a sit-down with the chief. It was a beautiful day, and, from where

I parked, it was five minutes to the police station, so I decided to walk. Purchase Street was about half a mile from the water. You couldn't see the water, but you could smell it. I love the smell of salt water. I never could imagine living in the Midwest with no ocean for a thousand miles at least.

I passed the new art galleries, fancy coffee shops, and new ethnic restaurants on my way. I got to the station with ten minutes to spare. The police station was an imposing old granite building right in the city's center. Police cruisers were parked at the front entrance letting you know where you are. I got there right after shift change. Patrolmen scurried in and out of the front door. I entered through the front door and was greeted by the desk sergeant. He was a younger, distinguished looking man with bright, piercing blue eyes.

"Can I help you?"

I pushed my badge up against the plexiglass.

"I'm FBI Special Agent Robert Ragusa. I have a 9:00 a.m. meeting scheduled with Chief Dellicker."

"Okay, sign in, and I'll buzz you through."

I signed the log and was buzzed in. The station was a beehive of activity. Police officers passed by me in the narrow hallway. The usual police banter was going on. I overheard talk about ongoing cases mixed in with more mundane talk about family, the Red Sox, and summer vacation plans. I was escorted to the chief's office by a young officer who looked like he was hired last week. Was I getting older or was everyone else just looking younger? He couldn't have been much more than twenty. It was getting harder to recruit quality police officers. A combination of bad press, scrutiny by the public, and a decline of respect for the police made joining the Fire department more appealing to many. Most of the public associate firemen with saving babies from burning buildings. With the police, it was more like pulling them over and presenting them with a hundred dollar speeding ticket. The local police do so much good, but they never make the papers. I give these new officers a lot of credit. Despite all this, they are willing to put their lives on the line every day of the week.

"So, you're with the FBI? I heard you're here about the fire on the Emma Jean. To give you fair warning, the Chief is angry that you didn't include us in the investigation from the beginning. I think many guys in this building feel like the FBI looks down on local police work. I would think you would want our help. After all, we live and work in the city."

"Look, Officer—"

"Sorry, I should have introduced myself. I'm Officer George Santos."

"Nice to meet you, Officer Santos. You're right. I should have contacted the Chief right from the get-go. It was a mistake. A big one. The Chief is going to get an apology."

"I appreciate that, Agent Ragusa. I hope from here on the FBI and the New Bedford Police can work together to solve this case."

Officer Santos led me to the Chief's office on the second floor. He opened the door and left me with some parting advice.

"Don't try to bullshit him. He'll see right through you."

I stepped into Chief Dellicker's office and was impressed with the organization. Unlike John's office, which usually had papers and folders scattered about, everything in Chief Dellicker's office seemed to be in place. He was sitting behind the biggest mahogany desk I have ever seen. The middle-aged man with jet-black hair got up from his black leather chair and approached me. At first glance, the chief looked too young for the job. He was about six foot tall, in excellent physical shape, and looked like he could easily run the Boston Marathon. Not intimidating, but more intellectual. Police Departments were changing. Maybe he was one of the new breed.

Chief Dellicker smiled and greeted me.

"Welcome. You must be Special Agent Ragusa. I've been expecting you."

He gave me a firm but not bone crushing handshake and pointed me toward one of the two black leather chairs in front of his desk.

"I've heard a lot about you, Agent Ragusa. Mostly good. You have a habit of visiting our fair city and conducting FBI business without our knowledge. Don't you feel local law enforcement is worth consulting with, especially on a high-profile case like that of the Emma Jean?"

This moment seemed like a good time to offer an olive branch.

"Yes, Chief. I know I didn't follow proper protocol when coordinating with local officials. The FBI always welcomes the help of local law enforcement. I'm sorry we didn't get your department involved right from the beginning. This case started simply and when it started to get more complicated, I should have reached out to you. I apologize for that and look forward to working with your department to solve this case."

Chief Dellicker extended his right hand and shook mine in a way that let me know we were on equal terms.

"Good, Agent Ragusa. I'm glad we're both on the same page. I want you to meet someone. I've assigned our best man, Detective Mosey Bedard, to this investigation. He's been on the force for twenty-five years and is fluent in Portuguese, Creole, and Spanish. His language skills come in handy in the city."

Just then, a well-dressed man in a blue Brooks Brothers blazer, gray slacks, and red tie walked into the office. He looked like he was pulled from central casting from an episode of the TV show *Law and Order*. He was about six feet tall, had a dark complexion and jet-black hair with not one hair out of place. He extended his well-manicured right hand.

"You must be Agent Ragusa. I'm Detective Mosey Bedard. I believe we're going to be working together on the Emma Jean case."

I shook his hand firmly and said, "Yes. It's nice to meet you. Your Chief speaks very highly of you."

With an air of superiority, Detective Bedard added, "Your Bureau Chief, John Ring, and Chief Dellicker have arranged a meeting at the FBI office in Chelsea for 3:00 p.m. today. Investigator Bob Halloran from the Coast Guard will also be attending. I also hear that Interpol has deciphered communication from computers seized in a raid in London's East End. There is going to be a shipment of carfentanil dropped by air tomorrow night. The coordinates for the drop put it right in the middle of Georges Bank. Cape Verdean Police have been working with Interpol in London. A Beechcraft Super King Air 300 has filed a flight plan for tomorrow night to Martha's Vineyard. A surveillance team in Cape Verde has been watching the aircraft and, with the help of an inside source, has determined a large shipment of carfentanil will be on that plane. A joint operation involving the Coast Guard, the FBI, and the New Bedford Police will intercept the boat and plane after the shipment has been delivered."

I was stunned. I looked at Chief Dellicker and Detective Bedard. They both gave me a knowing smile. I thought I would be getting them up to speed on the case, and they were telling me new information and laying out operational plans that I knew nothing about. I think this was John's way of putting me in my place and a not-so-subtle reminder that there were protocols in high profile investigations that needed to be followed, and I had gone off the rails. I could feel the redness rising on my face. I was angry and embarrassed.

All I could say was, "Well, I guess it's time for me to head back to the office."

Chief Dellicker and Detective Bedard simultaneously replied.

"Thanks for coming to New Bedford."

I took a quick step out of the Chief's office and headed toward the station's front door. I almost ran over a young female officer as I stormed past the bored looking desk sergeant. I'm glad I parked the caddy five minutes away. It gave me time to cool down as I walked. I had been sandbagged, but I deserved it. I needed to put my ego away. I knew that I had done most of the legwork to date, and it was paying off. I needed to be in Chelsea by 3:00 p.m. That gave me a few hours. I had a lot to think about. I briskly walked to my parking spot on Purchase Street. To top of my beautiful morning, I had a shiny orange ticket on my windshield. I would be contributing twenty-five dollars to the city of New Bedford's coffers.

CHAPTER FIFTY TWO

I had just gotten sandbagged by Chief Dellicker, and my supervisor was strongly encouraging me to be a team player. All instincts pointed in the direction of Route 195 and a ride back to Saugus, but I had a good feeling about Frank's wife. She was a sweet woman, and I thought we connected well when interviewing her husband. This grieving time would be a lousy time to call her. I was sure the New Bedford PD had already interviewed her. On top of grieving the death of her husband, she was making the arrangements for his wake and funeral. I wasn't even sure if the house had been cleared as a crime scene. I hesitated but decided to give her a call. I pushed Frank Medeiros on my contact list, and the phone began ringing. I fully expected my call to go straight to voicemail, but on the third ring, I recognized a soft voice with the ever so little remainder of a Portuguese accent on the line.

"Hello, this is the Medeiros residence."

"Ms. Medeiros, this is FBI Agent Robert Ragusa. I don't know if you remember me. I was at your house last week and interviewed your husband."

"Of course, I remember you, Mr. Ragusa. Why are you calling me?"

"First, let me say I am terribly sorry for your loss, and I was hesitant to call you, but I'm in the city and was hoping I could have a few minutes of your time. I would like to talk to you about what happened to Frank."

"Mr. Ragusa, I've already talked to the police for hours. I don't know what more I could tell you that I didn't already tell them."

"I'm sorry to bother you, but just a few minutes, if you can."

Her reply came slowly, "Ok, Mr. Ragusa, a few minutes but, I must make funeral arrangements, and my relatives are constantly calling me. Come by the house."

"Thank you, I'm only a few minutes from your home. I'll be right over."

I couldn't help feeling lousy about this. I had to convince myself that Mrs. Medeiros might be able to provide information that could help solve the murder of her husband. I pulled into the driveway of the Medeiros residence. I sat in the Caddy for a couple of minutes, trying to get my head together. I had faith that the New Bedford PD was conducting a thorough investigation, but I wanted to specifically focus on the relationship between Frank Medeiros and Gil Galloway.

As I approached the front entrance, the front door swung open. Mrs. Medeiros was standing in the entranceway with what looked like a basket of scones in her hand. Now I felt like a crap sandwich. With everything she's going through, she's going to offer me scones.

She looked like she had aged ten years since my last visit just a week ago. She greeted me cheerfully but with more than a hint of weariness in her voice.

"Hello, Mr. Ragusa. Please come in. I remembered from your last visit that you were a big fan of my scones. These just came out of the oven." She put the basket of scones, still hot from the oven, before me as I walked through the doorway.

"Thank you for seeing me. Do you have family coming over? I can do without a scone."

"I have some of Frank's family coming by later today. I guess they just want to see how I'm holding up. I baked plenty. Please have one."

I reached over to the basket and gently removed one of her delights.

"Please follow me."

I followed her into the expansive, sunlit living room. She pointed me toward a high-backed white velvet chair nearest to the coffee table. Mrs. Medeiros placed the scones on the coffee table. The full sweet aroma of the raisin hit my nose.

As I nibbled around the outer crust of the scone, I began what I knew would be a delicate conversation.

"This is delicious, as always. Thank you so much for taking the time to see me at what must be a difficult time for you. I know the police have been by and talked to you. I don't want you to have to repeat yourself to me. I'm interested in the relationship between your husband and Gil Galloway."

"Ok, Mr. Ragusa, what would you like to know?"

"Well, about their history together. From what I understand, they go way back to when they first started working on the docks."

She replied, "Yes, that's true. Gil and Frank first met in high school. They were both on the varsity baseball team. Frank used to tell me that they were friends but only on a casual level. Like now, back in the eighties, if you didn't go to college or trade school, the only jobs were low paying factory work or fishing. Both Frank and Gil began fishing right out of high school. Then they both moved up the ladder, eventually captaining and owning their boats."

"I shouldn't say this, but Gil likes to gamble, and he likes to drink. He and Frank were friendly, but they didn't run in the same circles. Sure, Frank would occasionally have a drink with the crew after unloading their catch. He played poker with Gil and a few other fishermen at the Portuguese Social Club, but Gil seemed to take it further than my Frank. My husband never told me much, but I overheard more than a few conversations between Gil and Frank, with Frank telling him he didn't want to get involved. I did not know exactly what he was refusing to get involved in. What I do know is that when Frank started spending more time hanging around the Widows Cove Tavern, his mood seemed to change. He started coming home later and was not in a good mood. I don't know maybe, it's nothing, but something about that bar still bothers me."

"There's no easy way to ask this, Mrs. Medeiros, but do you think your husband participated in something illegal?"

"My heavens no, my Frank was a good husband and a hard worker."

"Did he have a gambling problem?"

"He wasn't a very good poker player. That's all I know."

"I'm sorry, but I had to ask."

"You're not the first one to talk that way. The police asked me the same question."

"One more question, and I'll be on my way. Do you think Gil Galloway had anything to do with the murder of Frank?"

"No, but I'll give you some advice. Check out that bar, the Widows Cove."

"I will, Mrs. Medeiros. I'll let myself out."

CHAPTER FIFTY THREE

I jumped in the Caddy and thought about giving Gil Galloway a call. He lived only three streets over. I made a mistake by not initially considering him as being involved with the Emma Jean, but he wasn't looking so squeaky clean anymore. Why not? All he could do was hang up on me or let my call go to voicemail. So, I rang him up. The phone rang and rang. I figured I was headed toward voicemail when a man with a hoarse voice answered.

"This is Gil, who's this?"

"Captain Galloway, this is FBI Agent Robert Ragusa. I'm in the city. Can I come by and talk with you about the Emma Jean?"

"Well, agent, the short answer is no. My attorney's name is Mark Langella. Any questions about the Emma Jean go to him. His office is in Fairhaven. Look him up on his website." Click. The phone went dead. Well, I guess that was the end of my day in New Bedford. Time to go home.

I steered the Caddy back toward the ramp to Interstate 195 North. I was starting to doubt myself.

I had been with the FBI for two decades, but my instincts had been so wrong in this case. Things have gone progressively bad from being slipped a mickey at Mike's Restaurant to the beat down of Steve Poole and now having to go hat in hand to the New Bedford Police Chief after being dressed down by my boss. The FBI provides the best law enforcement training in the world. I wasn't a rookie agent, but I had made rookie mistakes with this case.

As I headed onto 195, my cell phone started buzzing. It was John, checking how the meeting with Chief Dellicker had gone. Had the chief already called John with an unfavorable opinion of me? With a little trepidation, I picked up on the third ring.

"Rob, I need you back at the office ASAP. I just got a call from Interpol in Washington DC. The National Crime Agency (NCA) in London raided an east end flat early this morning and arrested two men. The raid went off without a hitch. Their forensic team is going through the laptops they confiscated. It's early, but it looks like there is a direct link to a veterinarian's office in Hyannis. It seems like your tip on our missing fisherman, Hank Gonsalves, may have been right on the money. I'm coordinating with the lead investigator at London's NCA office and Interpol in DC. The NCA Cyber Crime unit is going through the laptops as we speak. The two men arrested are being questioned. The interview of these two men may break the case wide open. It looks like all your legwork and trips to New Bedford are finally paying off."

"It looks like this is much more than a local drug ring. Its tentacles stretch from London to Cape Verde to New Bedford and Hyannis. We need to get the Coast Guard up to speed. New Bedford PD, too. The Emma Jean case has become such a high-profile case that they even called Rick Raymond back from vacation. I want you, Rick, and Detective Bedard to find out how the veterinarian's office is tied into all this. Rob, I will be back in my office at 2:00 p.m. I want your thoughts on how to proceed. We can use the 3:00 p.m. meeting to get everyone up to speed and develop an operational plan. Can you get back by 2:00?"

"You know, John, it depends on traffic. I'll do my best to get there as quickly as I can."

I floated out a trial balloon to see John's response.

"John, I was a little taken aback in my meeting with Chief Dellicker and the detective he assigned to the Emma Jean case, Mosey Bedard. They both knew a lot more information than I did. They got me up to speed on the case, not the other way around." John's response was not immediate. Had I pushed him too far?

"Well, Rob, I know you're a team player. See you soon." That was it. I just had to suck it up and move on.

I ended the call and felt a sensation of relief washing over me. I was beginning to think maybe my career with the FBI was not going to come to an inglorious end. I had involved a civilian in the investigation and almost got him killed and myself suspended. Steve was going to be okay after some convalescing. An investigation about a kitchen fire on the Emma Jean and a missing fisherman led to a major international drug ring peddling the most dangerous new drug on the street. Multiple agencies, including the FBI, Interpol, London's NAC, the US Coast Guard, and local law enforcement, were all working together to keep this new deadly drug off America's streets.

My adrenaline kicked in, and I punched the gas pedal on the Caddy until the speedometer read ninety miles per hour. I was heading for a hefty speeding ticket. What the hell? I was feeling lucky. My day wasn't over. I pulled into the parking lot at 2:15 p.m. Traffic had been heavy on the Southeast Expressway. Bumper-to-bumper from the Dorchester gas tanks to the city. I threw the Caddy into the park and headed toward the front door. John expects punctuality but even the FBI can't make traffic move any faster. I waved my badge to the receptionist, who was on the phone. She nodded and buzzed me in.

I made my way to the end of the hallway. John's door was open. John and Rick Raymond were carrying on a heated conversation. The conversation ended abruptly when I entered John's office. Maybe I was getting paranoid in my old age, but I suspected they were talking about me. John and Rick got out of their seats simultaneously.

John said, "Rob, do you know Rick Raymond from the Portsmouth office?" Rick extended his hand and gave me a firm handshake, saying, the FBI office in Portsmouth, New Hampshire was a bit of a backwater.

The locals call New Hampshire "Cow Hampshire." It's a rural, beautiful state where not much crime happens. The Portsmouth office is a stepping off point for new field agents looking to get their feet wet. They are usually promoted to busier offices like Boston if they perform well. I didn't know Rick well but had met him briefly at a couple of seminars. He was known as a rising star after he and another agent broke a drug smuggling operation in Manchester, New Hampshire, a couple of years ago.

"It's nice to see you again, Rick. How are you doing? I guess we're going to be working together. Congratulations on that drug smuggling ring you broke up in Manchester. It made national news."

"Thanks, Rob. Usually, the most exciting thing that happens in New Hampshire is busting your boys from Massachusetts buying illegal fireworks across the state line for Fourth of July Celebrations."

I had to keep telling myself that the more experienced professionals assigned to this case, the more likely it would get solved. I knew I could get along with Bob. I wasn't sure about Rick Raymond or the hot shot detective from New Bedford, Mosey Bedard. I know it's stereotyping, but Bedard reminded me of Don Johnson's partner in Miami Vice, dressed in an expensive suit and a hundred-dollar haircut. I also had mixed feelings about the 3:00 p.m. meeting. I did want to hear what John had come up with. He was good at working with other agencies and local law enforcement, setting up joint efforts, coordinating operations, and smoothing over egos. I must admit, John was a more than competent supervisor and a talented politician.

John signaled Rick and I to follow him out of the office. Down the hall, the second door to the left was an unmarked office called the "war room." This room was where major operations were discussed and planned. As we entered, Bob Halloran and Mosey Bedard were already seated at the conference table. I settled into the chair to the right of Bob. John sat at the head of the table and began handing out spiral bound packets. John was meticulous in nature and, for major operations like this, would hand out detailed plans to those involved, complete with all aspects of the operation, including individual responsibilities and chain of command.

Once everyone was seated, John took the lead.

"Why don't we start first with introductions? Rob, how about you go first."

I stood up and introduced myself. Everyone else in the room followed. John went last.

"Mosey Bedard, Detective with the New Bedford Police Department."

"Rick Raymond, FBI field office Portsmouth New Hampshire."

"Good morning, I'm Bob Halloran, Investigator with the Coast Guard."

"I'm FBI Special Agent in charge John Ring. Well, gentlemen, now that we all know each other, let's get down to business.

"I don't think I need to remind you that anything said in this room stays here. Interpol is aware of this operation, as are the top brass at Quantico. We aim to intercept a shipment of high potency carfentanil that we believe will be dropped by air and retrieved by a New Bedford-based fishing boat, the Ruth Ann. Interpol has intel that the drop will happen at 0300 hours tomorrow night in Georges Bank. The coordinates are in your packet. The Coast Guard will be taking the lead on this operation as the drop site is outside US territorial waters. Bob Halloran has already briefed me on the specifics of the operation. Bob, why don't you take it from here."

"Thanks, John. Interpol and the FBI have intercepted internet chatter on a site that has been being monitored. This drug smuggling ring is based out of London. The leaders of the drug ring have paid off airport officials in Cape Verde. The carfentanil is getting through Cape Verde customs as a natural shipment to veterinarians in the United States. On paper, it looks legitimate. Veterinarians legally use carfentanil to anesthetize large animals such as elephants and lions. The problem is they're shipping enough carfentanil to knock out every animal over 100 pounds in the entire world. That was the red flag for investigators.

"We think that the carfentanil is being dropped by planes based in Cape Verde which then rendezvous with fishing boats off Georges Bank. The shipment gets picked up, hidden in the hold of the boats, and brought back to New Bedford at night. The shipment is then offloaded to a cut house in the city. Fishermen are known to have loose lips, especially when liquor is involved.

"Some intoxicated fishermen on the Ruth Ann have been running their mouths at the Portuguese Social Club and the Widows Cove Tavern. New Bedford Police have confirmed from undercovers and paid informants working the local fishing bars in the city that Ruth Ann participates in drug smuggling. A cutter out of Boston is ready to intercept them. The plane being used does not have enough fuel for the return trip to Cape Verde. They will have to refuel, either in Martha's Vineyard or Hyannis. Two Jayhawks will be following. The pilots will be in constant communication with the FBI on the ground. When the plane lands to refuel, FBI agents will be there to arrest them."

Bob looked around the room and continued.

"Rob, Mosey, and I will be aboard the cutter. The cutter's captain, Lieutenant Commander Nicholas Dutra, has been fully briefed on the operation as have the crews of the two Jayhawks. Due to this operation's sensitive nature, the cutter's crew have simply been told that they are looking for illegal scalloping in Georges Bank."

"Carfentanil is highly toxic and is only handled by me, Agent Raymond, Agent Ragusa, and Lieutenant Commander Dutra. We plan to take the boat by surprise after loading the shipment onboard. Two Coast Guard petty officers of my choosing will be briefed on the cutter and accompany us when we board the Ruth Ann. We assume that the fishermen will be armed. Everyone in the boarding party will carry a Glock 19M. If the operation goes south the 50-caliber deck gun on the cutter will be manned and ready to go.

"We are going to board under the auspices of a simple check. Rob, Rick, and Mosey will be dressed in civilian clothes. This disguise should not raise suspicion from the crew as sometimes civilians from other agencies such as the Fisheries Division accompany us on patrol. The plan is to get the crew on deck and then take them by surprise. Once the captain and the crew have been secured, the vessel will be searched for carfentanil."

John spoke up.

"Any questions? Everyone read your packets. All the details of the operation are there. Read them thoroughly. We meet tomorrow night at the Boston Coast Guard Station at 2300 hours."

That was it. I had some reading to catch up on tonight. On paper, it seemed like this would be easy to pick. But, in my heart, I knew from experience that no operation ever went exactly as planned. Well, the day was done. Everyone stood and shook hands and left the conference room. I had important reading to do, but that would have to wait. Benny and Mai Tai at Kowloon was the next order of business.

CHAPTER FIFTY FOUR

I pulled into the parking lot of the Kowloon around 4:30 p.m., just before the dinner rush. The regulars were all at the bar. One of the regulars, Biff, owned a small construction company. He had a wife, but nobody knew her. Now that I think of it, nobody knew his real name. He was just "Biff." He was pleasant enough; he always played in the annual charity golf tournament. Another regular, John Alvarez, a.k.a. "Johnny A to Z," had been a nightclub manager in Florida. His elderly mother had been diagnosed with Alzheimer's. His father had died three years earlier, and he was an only child. He moved back to Saugus to take care of her. He liked to relive the old days of working as a bar manager at the Copacabana in Miami. Hanging out with the stars, Frank Sinatra, Jackie Gleason, and others. Who knew if it was true? It didn't matter. Everyone would be enthralled after he had a few Mai Tai's and started spinning his tales. Then there was Mickey, an Irish tenor with a quick wit who would occasionally pull a few regulars off the bar, form a makeshift barbershop quartet, and break into Danny Boy.

Benny oversaw keeping the alcohol flowing and the bar under control. You never waited for a drink when he was behind the bar and man did it get busy! It was like he had a sixth sense. Benny would come over just as you were about to take your last sip and speak those magical words, "Would you like another?"

I had a date planned for tomorrow night with Sandy. I would have to cancel, and I didn't want to. I had been on dozens of major operations in my FBI career, some very dangerous. I had a bad feeling about this one. A sinking feeling in my stomach that I just couldn't shake. Maybe it was because I was getting toward the end of my career. I had made it this far without a scratch. Retirement was calling. I loved the FBI, but I was approaching mandatory retirement age. That was a fact. I had mixed feelings about retirement, an odd mixture of excitement and terror. I had hobbies, fishing, and golfing. I always wanted to own a boat. I had come close to buying an 18-foot Boston Whaler years ago. I decided against it then because I didn't think I would have enough time to use it to make it worthwhile. I had saved a fair amount of money, no debt. I owned the condo outright, and the FBI provided me health insurance and a good pension for the rest of my life.

I had seen other agents die shortly before they retired, heart attacks mostly. I also knew agents who had been killed in the line of duty just before they put in their papers. I was starting to care for Sandy. I felt she had feelings for me too. I needed to see her tonight. I had made a reservation for tomorrow night at Quincy Bay that I needed to cancel. I couldn't tell her why. She knew the nature of law enforcement and would put two and two together. It was a lot to ask but I needed to see her tonight.

Benny came by just as I reached for my cell phone.

"Mr. Rob. How are you today?"

"Good, Benny. Looks like another busy night for you."

Benny grinned and said, "Always busy at the Kowloon. You want the usual?"

"I sure do."

"Mai Tai, no fruit. Coming right up, Mr. Rob. You look tired. I will make it extra special for you."

"Thanks, Benny. I appreciate you."

Benny came back with just what I needed. He put a menu before me, but I waved it off. I needed to know if Sandy would be able to meet tonight. Maybe she would want to go somewhere else for dinner. My first call was to Quincy Bay. I canceled our dinner reservation. Then I called Sandy. The phone rang and rang, finally going to voicemail. I wasn't upset, just disappointed. She was working late or in traffic. I didn't want to go into detail in the message, so I just asked her to call me. I took a slow pull on my Mai

Tai, and my phone started vibrating. It was Sandy. I picked up on the first ring.

"Hi, Sandy. Thanks for getting back to me so quickly."

"Sure, Rob. Is everything okay?"

"I'm sorry, but I need to cancel tomorrow's dinner plans. Something has come up."

With a trace of disappointment, she replied, "All right. I can't say I'm not disappointed. I was looking forward to seeing you again."

"I know this is a lot to ask, but I need to see you tonight. It's nothing serious. I am just missing you. I'm at the Kowloon. No surprise there, right? I can meet you anywhere you want, even if it's just for a little while. What do you think?"

"I'm heading home on the Southeast Expressway just south of the city, heading home. I'll get off at the next exit, turn around and meet you at Kowloon. Twenty-five minutes. I think I'm developing a taste for Chinese food."

"That's great. I can't wait to see you."

"Me too, Rob. See you in a few."

I ended the call and went back to my Mai Tai. I hadn't felt like this in years. It had been so long since I had any romantic feelings for anyone. It felt wonderful. Like everything in the world was fresh and new. A world, thankfully, far away from the death and depravity I saw on a regular basis as an FBI agent.

Thirty minutes went by and in came Sandy. I was sitting on the bar stool closest to the door so I could keep an eye out for her. She looked great. Cream-colored knee-length dress, hair back in a ponytail. I felt like the luckiest man in the world. I signaled her over to the bar.

"Hi Rob. Your call caught me by surprise."

I got off the barstool and gave her a hug that almost took the breath out of her.

"Rob, are you going away to war or something?"

"Why would you say that?"

"Well, you just gave me a hug like that famous World War II picture of the sailor kissing the nurse in Times Square."

"No. I'm not going anywhere. I'm just glad to see you."

With a raised eyebrow Sandy said, "Somehow I think something else is going on."

"No, nothing really. Look, I really appreciate you seeing me on such short notice. I'll take you out to dinner anywhere you want to go."

The regulars were all looking at Sandy, smiling and waving.

"No, let's stay here. I like their Pu Pu platter for two. I think I'm becoming a Kowloon regular. I like that."

I paid my bar tab with Benny and the hostess took us to the same table (our table) in the back of the dining room. The same ancient waiter came over.

I ordered two Mai Tai's, one for Sandy and one for me, and a Pu Pu platter for two. The conversation started with small talk, the weather, and plans for the weekend. I had not met any of Sandy's family. She told me her brother, Cameron, was coming up in two weeks from Philadelphia for the weekend. Cameron was married and had two adult children living in New York City. He was an architect who had been involved in the planning of some of Philadelphia's modern skyline. She was close to Cameron, his wife Carla and both kids, Shane, and Liza. She had numerous cousins and extended family but didn't see them very often, only at the occasional family reunion. I would get a chance to meet Cameron when he was in town. That would be a big step in the direction I wanted this relationship to go.

Our Pu Pu platter arrived. There is something about cooking meat over an open flame. Even if it's a sterno. It brings out the caveman in me. Sandy was moving the conversation in a different direction, more prodding. She knew something big was up. She had been around law enforcement long enough to know when something was about to happen.

"So, Rob, it doesn't seem like you cancel at the last minute. Anything you want to share with me? I promise it won't go any further. I'm very experienced at keeping my mouth shut."

I hesitated. I looked her straight in the eyes. I really felt they were trusting eyes, so I did something

I've never done before. I broke protocol. I told her about Operation Wave Runner.

"There is a major drug smuggling operation out of London supplying carfentanil to the United States. They are using small planes, based out of the Cape Verde Islands, and making the drops onto fishing boats off Georges Bank."

Sandy leaned in closer. "Rob, What's carfentanil?"

I replied softly, "You've heard of fentanyl? Carfentanil is a thousand times stronger. If it hits the streets of the US, overdoses will go up tenfold. I'm involved in a joint operation that's going down tomorrow night. I can't tell you anymore. I shouldn't have told you what I just did. Please keep this quiet."

"Of course, Rob, I'm worried about you."

"I'll be fine. It's a well-planned operation and everything should go smoothly."

Sandy just stared off into space. The conversation had ground to a halt.

"Sandy, I'm sorry if I ruined your night."

"Not at all Rob, but I need to head back home."

We had made a decent dent in the Pu Pu platter. Our waiter bagged up the leftovers. Nothing better than cold Chinese food for breakfast. I paid the bill, and we headed out to our cars. I didn't want the night to end, but it was only our third date. Sandy had parked a couple of spaces down from my car. I walked her to her car, thanked her for joining me and leaned over to give her a peck on the cheek. She surprised me by grabbing the back of my head and pulled me into her body. A long, slow kiss ensued. I dropped the to-go bag in the parking lot, and we kissed like a couple of teenagers at the drive-in.

Sandy whispered in my ear, "It's a long drive back to Weymouth. Could I stay at your place tonight? I'll sleep on the couch."

"I can do better than that," came my quick reply. I pulled out of the lot for the five-minute drive to my condo with Sandy right behind me. My mind was racing. I hadn't been intimate with a woman for years. Was that really what she wanted? I've never been good at reading signals from the opposite sex. You need to hit me upside the head for me to get the message. She was tired and really didn't want to drive home. I felt like tonight could define the future of our relationship.

I was falling in love with Sandy. I knew she cared for me, but were we on the same page? I just figured I would take it easy and let Sandy take the lead. Women always dictate the pace of the relationship. I had learned that the hard way from prior relationships.

She followed me back down Route 1 to the condo complex. Sandy parked in a visitor spot and caught up with me at the lobby door. We walked arm in arm down the hallway toward my unit. I opened the condo door and Trixie was there to greet me. She was standoffish as usual. Now with another female to contend with, Trixie went into the bedroom and wouldn't come out. Oh well, she would just have to get over it. Sandy was staying tonight and hopefully many more.

"Rob, do you mind if I go into the bedroom to freshen up?"

"Of course not. The light is on the right near the door."

Sandy slowly closed the bedroom door. I pulled out a bottle of Chardonnay and uncorked it. I poured a couple of glasses and gave Alexa a direct order to play a Frank Sinatra medley of songs. Summer Wind came on as I sat down on the couch.

Sandy came out of my bedroom and my jaw hit the floor. The ponytail was gone, and her blonde hair cascaded down around her shoulders. She was dressed in one of my oversized Red Sox T-shirts and nothing else. "I hope you don't mind, Rob. I just wanted to get comfortable."

"No, don't mind a bit. That T-shirt sure looks a lot better on you than on me."

I handed her a glass of wine and she sat down on my lap. I started to talk, and Sandy stopped me in my tracks with a long, slow kiss. The two glasses of wine were simultaneously placed on the coffee table. Sandy laced her fingers in mine and tugged at my arm leading me toward the bedroom. This was going to be a night to remember. We made love as if the world was going to end tomorrow and this was our last night on Earth. I hadn't felt like this in years. Our relationship had gone to a whole new level. Wrapped in each other's arms, we both drifted off to sleep.

The alarm went off at 7:00 a.m. I wiped sleep from my eyes and went out to the kitchen to make a pot of coffee. Sandy looked like an angel, still sleeping soundly. Trixie had spent the night at the foot of the bed, trying to protect her turf. She was still getting used to having another female around. She followed me out to the kitchen and began purring and rubbing on my leg. This was her cue that she wanted to be fed. I put some wet food on her dish and started the coffee maker. The aroma of dark roast wafted through the condo. I hadn't expected Sandy to stay over. I didn't know what she ate for breakfast. All I had was white bread and eggs.

I could hear movement in the bedroom as I poured a cup of coffee. Then she emerged from the doorway. Even with her hair tousled and yawning, she looked beautiful.

I don't know why I said this, but I greeted her with, "Good morning, sunshine."

Thankfully, she laughed.

"Well, you've seen me at my best. Now you get to see me at my worst. I hope there will be another date."

"There certainly will. How do you like your coffee?"

"Black with two sugars, please."

"I can do that."

I poured Sandy a steaming cup of coffee and two sugars as she sat at the kitchen table. I hadn't had breakfast with anyone in years. Hopefully, she would bear with me as the menu was limited.

"I have orange juice and a little V-8. I can't vouch for the viability of the orange juice."

"Coffee is just fine, Rob."

"Well, welcome to Rob's House of Toast. Today's specials are eggs, any style, as long as they're scrambled, French toast, and of course, toast. How can I serve you?"

"I haven't had French toast in a long time. I'll give it a try."

"Very well, French toast it is."

I pulled out of the kitchen cabinet my aged black iron skillet, four slices of Wonder Bread, a tub of margarine, four eggs, and the remnants of a bottle of Aunt Jemima syrup. It looked like it was beginning to crystallize, but I could squeeze two servings out, with any luck. Pretty soon, the French toast was browning in the skillet. I looked over my shoulder, and Sandy smiled and nodded. She was impressed with my culinary skills. I poured out the remnants of the Aunt Jemima syrup and served. Sandy wolfed down her breakfast and finished her cup of coffee. I poured her a refill.

I started to clear the table when she said, "Rob, I had a wonderful night last night. Thank you for everything. I'm rushing things, but I want to be a part of your world."

"You are a part of my world. You passed the Kowloon test. Everybody there loves you. If it's up to me, you're not going anywhere."

"That's what I wanted to hear. I hate to be rude, but I'm meeting my brother today. I'm going to freshen up and be on my way."

"No problem. I need to prepare for tonight's operation anyway. I'm grateful for last night. I hope for a repeat soon."

Sandy slowly got up and walked to the bedroom. She changed and freshened up in the bathroom. I hated seeing her go but needed to keep my mind clear for tonight's operation. She gave me a hug and long kiss and headed out the door. I could feel the emotion in it.

"Bye Rob. Call me soon. Be careful."

"I will, don't worry about me. Everything will be just fine."

Will it be, Nona?

CHAPTER FIFTY FIVE

I spent the day reading through the details of Operation Wave Runner. It was a coordinated effort to intercept the airdrop of carfentanil to a fishing boat, the Ruth Ann off Georges Bank. Internet chatter had confirmed that a small plane would be leaving Cape Verde. Interpol had intercepted the coordinates where the drop was to take place. The plane would have to refuel for the return trip and file a flight plan with the local airport. The drop was to be made at 0300 hours. Interpol relayed information to the FBI office in Quantico that the airport to refuel would be Hyannis. However, Martha's Vineyard and Nantucket had small airports that could service the plane for its return trip to Cape Verde. FBI field agents would be surveilling all three airports.

A Gulfstream 200 was being used for the drop. It had a range of 3800 miles. With a full fuel tank, flying to Hyannis with 500 miles to spare would be enough. The cutter commanded by Lieutenant Commander Dutra would coordinate with two Jayhawks based out of Air Station Cape Cod and intercept the Ruth Ann. A boarding party from the cutter would board the Ruth Ann and search under the premise of a routine check on fishing and maritime regulations.

Will Garcia captained the Ruth Ann. A background check on Captain Garcia had raised no red flags. He had a good reputation on the waterfront. He had worked his way up the ladder to captain, having started his fishing career on one of the Codfather's boats. However, so had half the fishermen still working on New Bedford's waterfront. The Codfather had been imprisoned for illegal fishing and tax evasion. He was not known as a drug smuggler. Captain Garcia had been interviewed by IRS agents and the FBI at the time of the Codfather's investigation and had come up clean. He was an unlikely candidate to be involved in a major drug smuggling operation, but who knows what drives greed and desperation in people?

It was a cool night for a July in Boston. I put on my FBI windbreaker and headed for the Boston Coast Guard Station at 10:00 p.m. There will be a short briefing with all the agencies involved at the Coast Guard station. It was a moonless night with light fog rolling in from Boston Harbor. I passed through the North End. It was eerily quiet. A few delivery trucks making late-night deliveries and a few late revelers walking unsteadily down the brick sidewalks were about the only signs of life.

I pulled into the parking lot at five minutes to eleven. I reviewed John's operation plan multiple times. It was meticulous, as usual. The plan covered any contingency. I knew though, from past field operations, that plans could go awry. The fence that was supposed to be three feet high ended up being eight feet high, that type of thing. I have been involved in many multi-agency joint operations in the past, but never with the Coast Guard. I wasn't much of a mariner. The ferry to Martha's Vineyard for a weekend away was about it. I just hoped I didn't get seasick and embarrass myself. I entered the Coast Guard station. A skeleton crew was manning the station. The ship's crew was already aboard the cutter, awaiting orders. A select few officers had been informed that this operation involved intercepting a major drug smuggling ring off Georges Bank. The rest of the crew assumed this was a routine boarding of a fishing vessel for possible maritime or fishing regulation violations.

The conference room was on the first floor. Sitting around a large oval wooden table were John Ring, Bob Halloran, Rick Raymond, Lieutenant Commander Nick Dutra, Mosey Bedard, and the Boston Coast Guard Station commander, Dale Germond. I sat at the last open seat to the right of John Ring, who was seated at the head of the table. In these joint operations, interagency squabbles would often break out over who was in charge. The meeting was low key and cordial. John Ring went through every detail of the operation. Everyone in the room had already been briefed, so there were no surprises. Everyone knew their role. It was unlikely that there would be guns on the Ruth Ann, but no chances would be taken. The 50-calliber on the cutter would be manned and ready if the operation went south. The boarding party would also be armed with 9-millimeter handguns.

John concluded the meeting. Everyone shook hands and headed for the cutter. Once we were on the cutter, Lieutenant Commander Dutra ushered us into his stateroom. We were introduced to three junior officers who would also be part of the boarding party. After the introductions and small talk, I headed out on deck for fresh air. The cutter glided through the calm waters and out to see. I had been a part of many operations that, at least on the surface, seemed a whole lot more dangerous than this one. It was just one small fishing boat. My thoughts drifted to thinking about Sandy and our night of passion. I wanted a life with Sandy. I was hoping this operation would be just a nice boat ride.

Time will tell.

CHAPTER FIFTY SIX

It was a cloudy, moonless night with calm seas. The condition of the night was perfect for this type of operation. We headed to the coordinates at twenty knots. Except for the boarding party and the Lieutenant Commander, the crew of the cutter was under the assumption that this was simply a routine boarding of a fishing vessel that was under suspicion for probable fishing violations. Mosey Bedard, Bob Halloran, and I had been provided a cover story that we were investigators from the United States Marine Fisheries. We would be part of the boarding party to observe and document the search of the Ruth Ann. We had been provided official looking badges that, to the casual observer, looked totally authentic. Nobody should question us.

The three of us gathered on deck as the cutter sliced through the still water. It was quiet, and we were all lost in our thoughts. I knew Bob well. I had no doubts about his abilities. Mosey was a different story. He came across as cocky. That could be an asset sometimes, but I still had reservations. He had years of experience on the streets of New Bedford. The city has a rough edge, and I was sure he had had his share of encounters with gang members, rapists, drug dealers, murderers, and the like. Local detectives often work cases alone. Operation Wave Runner was a joint operation. Would he play well with others? What if things went bad? How would he react? I'd find out soon enough.

Lieutenant Commander Dutra was on the bridge monitoring the progress of the Ruth Ann. I had never been on a Black Hull cutter, so I decided to pay him a visit. I opened the door to the bridge, and it looked like Mission Control in Houston. There were blinking lights, red and yellow switches, and a green glow from the radar screen everywhere you looked. The captain turned around to face me as I entered.

"Agent Ragusa, did you drop in for a tour?"

"Well, sort of. I'm interested in how all this works."

The captain was in front of the radar screen and waved me over.

"This is the brain of the ship, Agent Ragusa."

"Please call me Rob."

"Ok, Rob, but I'm still Commander Dutra," he said with a wink. "I have a question for you. Do you know anything about radar?"

"Not really, commander."

"If you could come here, I want to show you something strange."

He pointed to the radar screen and said, "Do you see these two dots on the radar screen?"

I peered closely at the screen. I could clearly make out two dots. The commander was pointing at the dot closest to the center of the screen.

"See here? This dot is the Ruth Ann. We don't know what the other dot is. You didn't forget to tell me any details of this operation, did you?"

"Of course not, commander. Our intel has not indicated any other ships being involved in this drop."

"Well, our two Jayhawks have already left Air Station Cape Cod and are heading toward the rendezvous point. I hope there won't be any surprises. I'm assuming, then, that this is a coincidence. That this is just another vessel that is fishing in the same general area as the Ruth Ann. But the fact is, as you can see on the radar, the other vessel is closing in on the Ruth Ann at a speed that most commercial fishing boats cannot maintain. If this is not a coincidence, this obviously complicates matters. It's too late to change the plan. Interpol and our men at Coast Guard Station Boston are tracking the plane from Cape Verde. It's heading straight for the drop zone. Do you still want to proceed with the operation?"

"We've come this far, commander. I've been involved in many field operations where things don't go as planned. Everyone in the boarding party is highly trained. I am confident we can handle any contingency."

"Well, Rob, confer with the rest of your team. We'll back you up from here, but once you board the Ruth Ann, you'll be on your own. One of the Jayhawks will follow the drop plane to wherever they refuel. We can keep the other Jayhawk circling for backup. I've relayed this new development to the pilots. I suggest you get your boarding crew together and get them up to speed on this new development."

I had talked confidently about the game plan to the commander, but I was worried. We had no intel about another boat being involved. I made my way off the bridge and back on deck. The other two members of the boarding party, Ensigns Morrow and Edwards had joined Mosey and Bob on deck. As I approached, I could hear a casual conversation about Boston's sports teams, including the Red Sox's chances of winning the pennant this year.

"Well, fellas, we have a new twist." The talk abruptly stopped, and all eyes were upon me.

With a look of worry on his face, Bob Halloran said, "I don't like surprises, Rob. What's going on?"

"There might be a second boat involved." I had barely gotten the words out of my mouth when the responses came in unison. I heard a loud, "How can that be" from all four.

"Commander Dutra has spotted a second boat that is closing in on the Ruth Ann. With any luck, it's just another fishing vessel or pleasure boat that may be in the area. The commander is concerned because of the high rate of speed at which this boat is traveling, it may not be a fishing boat. It's highly suspect. We need to be aware that our intel may have been flawed and this boat is somehow involved in the drop."

Everyone was nodding. It was too late to change our plan. We would have to be extra vigilant and prepare for the worst-case scenario. The commander joined us on deck and gave me the thumbs up, our sign that the cutter was close to the rendezvous point. Everyone checked their weapons as we slowly made our way to the smaller boat which would take us to the Ruth Ann.

As I walked past the commander, he leaned over and whispered "We lost the second boat from radar. Not a good sign."

CHAPTER FIFTY SEVEN

Everyone was geared up as we boarded the RBS-1. The seas were smooth, and the RBS was an incredibly stable vessel that could handle a pounding in rough seas. The two Jayhawks had left Air Station Cape Cod. One would be providing cover for us, and the other would be tracking the plane after the drop was made. The boatswain mate fired up the outboard. The fore and aft 50 Caliber machine gun were manned as we headed toward the rendezvous point. The cloud cover hung low over the sky.

The moonless night, still air, and pitch blackness of the North Atlantic provided ominous overtones of what lay before us. As the RBS hit thirty knots, the roar of the twin Honda 225 outboards precluded any conversation. Everyone knew their job. In my experience from prior operations, the brief time before an operation begins is the time to clear your head. The team had been over the details of the operation ad infinitum. You had to count on your training, experience, and skill from here on in. Everything was going according to plan. The one loose end that lingered in my mind was the second boat. What was it, and how could it have just disappeared from the radar? We were proceeding with Operation Wave Runner, but I had real concerns. I don't believe in coincidences, and I don't like wild cards.

Above the roar of the outboard engines, Boatswain Mate Hubbard yelled, "Two minutes."

I rechecked my 9-millimeter, put a round in the chamber, and took the safety off. Bob signaled the boarding party to the fore. The plan was to stay back until the drop had been made and the drugs were on the boat. Unlike typical boarding, little notice would be provided to the crew of the Ruth Ann. We didn't want the crew to be able to exchange fire with us if they were armed, nor did we want to provide them the opportunity to dump the drugs into the vast ocean.

We had all been provided with night vision binoculars. Through my binoculars, an outline of a small jet was coming into view. The silhouette of the Ruth Ann could be made out half a mile off the starboard side. As we approached the Ruth Ann, the plane throttled back, and packages began to fall from the sky, landing about 100 yards off the port side of the Ruth Ann. The accuracy of this drop made me think this wasn't the first time these drug smugglers had done this. We sat low in the water, and the tension was building. Through my binoculars, movement on the deck of the fishing boat became apparent. The engine of the Ruth Ann could be heard as the boat headed toward the packages bobbing on the waves. Crew members using gaffs could be seen pulling each package toward the Ruth Ann. So far, so good. We waited. When the last package was pulled from the sea, Bob gave the boatswain mate the sign to move in. The twin 225's roared to life, and the RBS headed full speed toward the Ruth Ann.

A high-powered spotlight lit up the fishing boat as the RBS got within three hundred yards of the Ruth Ann. Bob Halloran got on the loudspeaker.

"Captain of the Ruth Ann, you are being boarded by the United States Coast Guard. This is a routine boarding. Cut your engines and have all crew on deck. Prepare to be boarded."

Boatswain Mate Hubbard slowed the RBS to five knots as we prepared to board the Ruth Ann on its starboard side. The engines of the Ruth Ann had been cut, but there was no movement on deck. The sound of splashes off the aft of the boat could be heard. They were dumping the drugs! Bob gave the signal for Hubbard to move in quickly. The RBS got within one hundred feet of the Ruth Ann when, what sounded like a nuclear explosion, blew the Ruth Ann right out of the water. Pieces of metal rained down. One hunk the size of a softball hit Mosey on the head, knocking him to the deck. My ears were ringing. Bob was bleeding from his left hand. Minor injuries, but everyone was okay.

The Ruth Ann was listing badly to port and would be under the waves in minutes. What had been a drug sting now had turned into a rescue operation. Bob got on the radio and was about to transmit a mayday to Commander Dutra when a powerboat, maybe thirty feet long, screamed in toward the aft of the Ruth Ann at forty knots. It was sleek like a cigarette boat and positioning itself to pick up the drugs bobbing in the small waves. This boat had to be the second boat that had evaded radar detection. Bob ordered the powerboat to cut its engines, no luck. The engines could be heard idling as the crew continued to pick up the bales of drugs. Bob gave the order to approach Ruth Ann from the starboard side. Because of the position of the sinking boat, the cigarette boat couldn't be seen clearly. This action was bold! The drug smugglers were sticking their middle finger up to the US Coast Guard.

We headed slowly past the sinking Ruth Ann and were met with a melody of heavy automatic machine gun fire. Bullets flew overhead and pinged off the RBS. Bob ordered Ensign Morrow on the fore deck to open fire with the 50-caliber. We were engaged in a gunfight with a cigarette boat. Just as the 50-calliber came to life, another explosion rocked the RBS on the port side. I grabbed for anything to keep from going overboard. A wall of spray hit me in the face. When I wiped the cold ocean water from my face, I could see a tall man on the cigarette boat holding what looked like a rocket-propelled grenade launcher. He quickly disappeared from the deck. The cigarette boat's engines roared, and it sped past our RBS toward the west. Ensign Edwards raked the cigarette boat with the aft 50-caliber, but it kept gaining speed. The silhouette of two men appeared on the aft of the cigarette boat. They opened fire on us. Bullets were pinging off the sides of the RBS. Everyone dove for cover, and the gun battle continued. Boatswain Mate Hubbard put the RBS in full throttle as we gave chase. The cigarette boat was 300 yards off our port side.

The 50-caliber rattled as shell casings rolled back and forth on the pitching deck. They must have been playing with us or trying to lure us into a trap. We were doing forty knots but not gaining any ground. The roar of the engines was deafening, and the RBS was slicing through the wake. The cigarette boat had been painted black, and our spotlight was useless. They were using evasive tactics to avoid us. The machine gun fire stopped, and the noise of the cigarette boat's massive engines began to fade as it pulled away.

One of the Jayhawks had taken chase, but communication on the radio indicated that the boat had slipped away under the cover of darkness. Commander Dutra was on the radio with Bob. The order had been given to end the chase. The commander had relayed the information to Air Station Cape Cod and US Coast Guard Boston. A full-scale search would be conducted. We had two men on the RBS that needed medical attention and survivors from the explosion of the Ruth Ann in the water. Boatswain Mate Hubbard set a course back to the site of the Ruth Ann explosion.

I felt defeated. We were so close to intercepting the largest known shipment of carfentanil to the East Coast, and now disaster had struck. We had two wounded men, and the drugs had slipped through our net. We would soon find out the casualty count of the Ruth Ann. How could anyone have survived that explosion?

The RBS cut through the humid night, and Bob signaled us all over to the port side. "We've been given orders to return to the cutter rather than the site of the Ruth. Anyone needing medical attention will board the cutter and report to the sick bay. Replacement crew will take their place, and we'll return to participate in the rescue operation. One of the Jayhawks is dogging the drop plane, and the other Jayhawk will take part, with other assets from Air Station Cape Cod, to search for the cigarette boat. I know this didn't turn out as planned. Keep your heads up. We'll find that boat."

I wasn't so sure. The Cape has innumerable rivers, bays, inlets, and estuaries where a boat could hide. The drug smugglers had a well thought out plan. The crew of the cigarette boat knew their destination. We didn't. They weren't going to dock unassuming into some marina on the Cape. There had to be people on shore who would hide the boat. They were going to receive the drugs. Who were they and more importantly, where were they?

CHAPTER FIFTY EIGHT

Boatswain Mate Hubbard glided up the port side of the cutter. Shrapnel hit him, and a bright red stain was growing on his right forearm. Commander Dutra was there to greet us.

He bellowed over the noise of the idling outboards, "Anyone needing medical attention should disembark and report to sick bay immediately."

No one moved. Commander Dutra looked at Boatswain Mate Hubbard and said, "You, Helmsman. I am ordering you to report to sick bay immediately."

Boatswain Mate Hubbard gave us a look of resignation as he climbed onto the cutter's deck. He quickly disappeared. Hubbard was a brave man. He had been operating on pure adrenaline during the chase. Nobody knew how badly he was injured.

Mosey Bedard had managed to stop the bleeding from the gash on his head, but the bandage he had covering his right temple indicated it was more than just a scratch. A reddish color was visible on the gauze bandage.

The commander barked, "Detective Bedard, get to sick bay and have your head looked at."

Mosey looked the commander in the eye and shook his head, no.

The commander said, "This is my ship. I told you to get to sick bay, now."

"No, sir. I'm not done here yet," was Mosey's reply. The Coast Guard had no authority over local law enforcement or the FBI, and the commander knew that.

The commander gave him a disgruntled look and replied, "All right, Detective Bedard, have it your way, but that gash looks serious. Have it looked at."

Mosey shook his head, yes. Commander Dutra then ordered a new helmsman to take the place of Hubbard.

The new helmsman pulled the RBS away from the cutter. We headed back to what was left of the Ruth Ann. Five hundred yards from the cutter was a debris field. The Ruth Ann was now at the bottom of the Atlantic, taking her secrets with her. I heard the explosion's blast from a distance and didn't believe anyone could have survived. We were joined by two other RBS's dispatched from the Coast Guard Station Boston to join in the rescue effort. A grid search was conducted through the night and into the early morning hours. Daylight brought no signs of life. The wreckage of the Ruth Ann bobbing on the waves of the North Atlantic yielded an array of fishing gear, life jackets, food containers, clothes, and one bale of carfentanil that the smugglers had missed. No bodies.

The bodies of the crew now lay at the bottom of the dark ocean. Recovery efforts would continue, but it seemed that Georges Bank had claimed yet another ship and its crew. Bob gave the helmsman the order to return to the cutter to offload and catalog what little was left of the Ruth Ann. It was going to be a long boat ride back to Boston. I still hadn't processed what had just happened. Our well-planned operation had turned to crap. I knew John would be at the Coast Guard Station Boston with many questions. I didn't really have the answers. Back to square one.

CHAPTER FIFTY NINE

The cutter was approaching Coast Guard Station Boston. The skyline was beautiful. The clouds had lifted, and a bright full moon silhouetted the city. The Prudential Building, the Custom House, and other skyscrapers all came into view as we approached land. I never get tired of seeing the skyline. I don't think most people consider Boston a romantic city, but it can be. Especially viewing Boston on a hot summer night.

My cell phone service kicked in as we got closer to land. John had left me a message. He had been in touch with the commander, monitoring the operation. He knew that Operation Wave Runner had gone badly and wanted a debriefing by the commander and every boarding party member. The sun was just starting to rise as the cutter docked at Coast Guard Station Boston. As the ship tied up, I had a few moments to reflect. I hoped that the Coast Guard, FBI, and local law enforcement would not play the blame game. Unlike on television, radar is not foolproof. Small boats sometimes cannot be monitored.

Nobody could know if the second boat in the vicinity of the Ruth Ann was another fishing vessel or pleasure boat. Obviously, it wasn't. It was nobody's fault. Perhaps our intel was flawed. All precautions that could have been taken had been taken. Bob Halloran had made the right call to go forward with the operation. I would have made the same call if I had been in charge.

Commander Dutra came down from the bridge and signaled everyone in the boarding party to follow him down the gangplank. John was waiting on the pier. He didn't look happy. John extended his hand to Commander Dutra.

The commander brushed right past him as he barked, "Everyone follow me."

I could sense that the blame game was about to begin. Everyone followed the commander like little kids about to be grounded for misbehaving. As the commander steamed toward the main entrance of the Coast Guard station, officers and enlisted men saluted and stood stiffly at attention as he passed by. Everyone scrambled to keep up with the commander as he stormed down the hallway to his spacious office.

The Station commander's boss, Evan Phillips, was in from Washington DC with other Coast Guard station commanders for several meetings. It was clear that Commander Dutra would be leading the briefing. He sat at the head of an oval, dark wooden conference table. Everyone else sat down, with Bob Halloran taking up residence at the first chair to the right of the commander. I was the last one in the office and closed the door quietly behind me. The tension in the room was palpable, and the malfunctioning air conditioning didn't help the mood. Commander Dutra looked slowly around the room and began to clear his throat. I was prepared for a tongue lashing, but his tone was surprisingly contrite.

"I'm not here this morning to assign blame for the failure of this operation. The Coast Guard lost the second boat from radar, and it was anyone's guess as to its intent. I agreed with Bob that the right course of action was to proceed with the operation in the hope that the second boat near the Ruth Ann was just a coincidence."

Bob Halloran was the first to address the commander.

"Sir, I take full responsibility for the failure of this operation. I gave the order to proceed, and it led to disaster."

"Nonsense, Bob," came the commander's swift reply. "A good leader must make split-second decisions, often without accurate information. You made the right call. Your men did a fine job of interrupting the drug smugglers. No one was seriously hurt or injured, at least on our side. We must look forward, not backward." The commander then focused his attention on John Ring.

"Do you have anything you want to add, Agent Ring?"

John responded, "Yes, commander, the FBI has just received plausible information that the drugs are heading to a safe house in Hyannis. I propose that we continue our joint operation with the Coast Guard and local law enforcement, including Hyannis Police. We need to find that cigarette boat and the smugglers before they distribute the drugs. Our information is spotty, but it seems a local veterinarian, Dr. Callahan is potentially using his oceanfront home to hide the drugs and his office in Hyannis as a front for the distribution of carfentanil. I want Agent Ragusa and Detective Bedard to surveil the Callahan estate. I've contacted the chief of police in Hyannis, who will assign a detective to the case.

Just then, Mosey bolted out of his seat.

"Look, I damn near died out there. I'm not turning this case over to Hyannis, so they get the glory."

John looked intently at Mosey.

"I understand, and I'm okay with that. But you'll have to clear it up with your supervisor. If we're surveilling in Hyannis, we will need to coordinate with the Hyannis PD."

With that, Mosey seemed to cool down.

The commander then rose from his seat, signaling an end to the meeting.

"Well, men, let's go finish the job."

Everyone slowly filed out of the commander's office.

John pulled me aside and whispered, "Do you trust Steve Poole?"

My reply came quickly.

"He's already put his life on the line for us providing information. Yes, I do."

"That's good enough for me, Rob. Go home and get some sleep. Tomorrow's going to be a busy day. I've set up a meeting with the Hyannis Chief of Police, Mike Mahan, for tomorrow at 9:00 a.m. I am expecting you and Rick Raymond to be there. You'll need to bring Chief Mahan up to speed.

"I also want you to contact Steve tomorrow and pay him a visit. Just you, let's try to keep this low profile. I don't know who I can trust."

Whoa, that was a strange comment by John. My mind was racing. What did he mean by that statement? If he couldn't trust anyone, who could I trust?

CHAPTER SIXTY

I had my orders. The next destination was my condo to get some much-needed sleep. I headed back to the Caddy and drove out of the parking lot. I told Sandy many of the details of the operation, and I knew she was nervous. I was just passing over the Tobin Bridge, when "Unforgettable" by Nat King Cole began playing on the radio. My cell phone suddenly lit up. It was Sandy. I picked up on the first ring.

"Rob, how are you? I've been so worried."

It was great to hear her voice. When the tracers were flying overhead, I wondered if this was the end and if I would never see her again.

"I'm fine, Sandy. I'm headed back to the condo. I need some sleep. It's been a hell of a night. I've missed you, Sandy."

"I've missed you too, Rob. Can I come over? I know you're beat, but I must lay my eyes on you. I won't stay long."

"Of course. I'd love to see you. Where are you?"

"I just left the Boston PD. I can be there in fifteen minutes."

"Okay, we should arrive at about the same time. Park in the visitor's parking spot. I'll wait for you in my car."

I pulled into the condo parking lot. It was going to be a warm, muggy day. Sweat was already starting to bead up on the back of my neck. Sandy was already standing by the lobby door. My excitement at seeing her was already building. I had just closed the car door when Sandy ran over to me and gave me the biggest hug I ever had. No words were spoken. I took Sandy's hand, and we walked together silently to the lobby door.

CHAPTER SIXTY ONE

We talked for hours about everything under the sun, except Operation Wave Runner. Around midnight we went to bed, and I was asleep before my head hit the pillow. Trixie woke me up the next morning with her usual wake-up call, purring and licking my face. Sandy was still asleep. It was 6:30 a.m., and the sunlight was beginning to light up the living room. I threw on my clothes from last night, brushed my teeth, and headed out the door.

I needed to get to the Hyannis Police Station by 9:00 a.m. The trip would take an hour and fifteen minutes in the winter, but this was July and the height of tourist season. It was "change day" on the Cape. Change day is the day when vacationers' week of summer bliss was ending and the new vacationing hopefuls would be arriving from New York, New Jersey, Connecticut, and a sprinkling of other states. It was too late to beat the rush, and getting over the Sagamore Bridge could take at least an hour.

We hadn't made love last night. Now I had to leave without greeting her and making her breakfast.

I had no choice; I left Sandy a note on the kitchen table. Not a very romantic way to wake up. Well, she knew the work of law enforcement, and I hoped she would understand. I grabbed the keys to the Caddy and quickly looked at my text messages. The first message I saw was from John about not being late for my 9:00 a.m. meeting with the Hyannis Police Chief Mahan and the fact that Mahan assigned a Hyannis Detective, Vince Almeida, to the investigation. The Hyannis Detective would be at the meeting as well as Rick Raymond. I hated to see the involvement of another police department. I was not a fan of joint operations. As the old saying says, "Too many cooks spoil the meal." I was just starting to feel comfortable with Rick Raymond and Mosey Berard and now two new players had been added to the mix.

The second text caught me by surprise. It was from Steve Poole. He texted me at midnight last night. The text read in capital letters: CALL ME ASAP.

I exited my condo and headed for the parking lot. I hated to leave Sandy. I desperately wanted to wake her with a steaming hot cup of coffee, bacon, and eggs in bed. The idea was much more appealing than sitting in a five-mile stream of traffic behind campers, SUVs, and motorcycles inching across the Sagamore Bridge. I fired up the Caddy and headed south through light traffic on Route 1.

I scrolled to Steve Poole on my contact list and rang him up. I knew even though Steve often closed the Widows Cove, he was usually up at the crack of dawn. He picked up on the first ring.

"Rob, how are you? Where are you?"

"Steve, you caught me by surprise. You usually don't text. I'm just crossing over the Tobin on my way to Hyannis. Why? Your text has me a little concerned. What's up?"

"Rob, the chatter around the docks is that the drug ring is being run out of Hyannis. New Bedford is also involved as a drop point and distribution. Word got around quickly about the raid on the Ruth Ann. Another fishing boat was in the area poaching and you know fishermen. A secret is never safe with a little Jameson flowing. I had a bunch of fishermen in here last night, and after a few rounds, they started talking about more than their last catch. The talk got onto how there was no way this drug ring could be operating without someone on the inside."

"What do you mean, Steve, when you say, 'the inside'? Like the Harbor Patrol?"

"Maybe. But more likely, the police department. Either Hyannis, New Bedford, or both. These guys have been around the docks a long time. They've seen a lot of dirty dealings going on. They wouldn't be talking like this if there wasn't something to it. Rob, I even heard about the cigarette boat and how it got away with the drugs. They must have been tipped off.

I didn't hear any names being dropped. But the word is, the guys on the cigarette boat are locals. I don't know how high this goes, Rob. Don't trust anyone."

I was stunned. Word had already gotten around the harbor about the raid of the Ruth Ann before the morning papers had hit the stand.

"Thanks for the heads up, Steve. Watch your back. How are you feeling?"

"I got released from St. Luke's yesterday. I'm a little banged up. I talked to Hal. He wants me to lay low for a while and recuperate."

"Steve, I don't want to be visiting you again at St. Luke's. The next time it could be at the morgue, not the ICU."

"I'm a little upset, Rob. I've known Hal for more than thirty years. I have been to his kids' graduations, birthday parties, and baseball games. He never came by the hospital to see how I was doing. I thought I knew him better."

"Yeah, that is weird, Steve. I'm surprised."

"Well, Rob. I'll keep my head on a swivel and ear to the ground. When I get back to work, stop by the Widows Cove. I'll have a cold Sam Adams on ice for you."

"Sounds good, Steve. Stay safe."

I trusted Steve's information. Fishermen were notorious gossipers. Nothing went down on the docks without word eventually getting around. Who could I trust in New Bedford other than Steve? The answer was nobody. I understand why John had his suspicions. Now, we are about to add Hyannis to the mix. I longed for the days when I was a solo act. I'd have a lot to think about, while sitting in traffic, crossing the Sagamore Bridge.

CHAPTER SIXTY TWO

Surprisingly, I had made good time. The Hyannis police station is located on Phinney's Lane, just off Main Street. I was an hour early, so I decided to park on Main Street, and grab a cup of coffee and a raisin bagel. My parking karma was holding. I found a space in front of the Bread and Roses Bookshop and Café. It was a beautiful summer morning. The weather was about eighty degrees and not too humid. I went to the hostess station and was greeted by a tanned, blonde woman, maybe early twenties, in better shape than I have ever been in my entire life. Her greeting was short and to the point.

"Inside or outside, sir?"

"Outside," came my swift reply. There was one open table on the patio. I grabbed a Boston Herald and sat down. My server came by—another tanned blonde, a little shorter—to take my order. Do they have a factory where they produce these people? They all look so similar. A lot of college kids spend their summers on the Cape. Without them, the restaurant business would cease to exist. They wait tables, tend bar, and go to the beach on their days off. Find a few roommates to share an apartment, and you might even manage to save a little tuition money.

Before she could put the menu in front of me, I blurted out, "Raisin bagel, cream cheese, and a large black dark roast."

She nodded, wrote my order down, and headed back toward the kitchen. I realized that I had been a little rude. I'd make it up on my tip. My order came quickly. The bagel was the size of a hubcap. Another example of the supersizing of America. A muffin used to fit in the palm of your hand. Now you can feed a family of four with one.

I ate half and wrapped up the other half for later. I finished my coffee and headed back to the Caddy. Main Street was starting to fill up. The souvenir shops were opening, selling overpriced Cape Cod T-shirts, sweatshirts, and coffee mugs.

The fiasco that was Operation Wave Runner was still burning in my brain. I had scanned the Herald, and there was no mention of the fishing boat explosion. Probably not enough time to make the morning edition. The FBI and Coast Guard would go into full damage control. The story to the press would be benign: "A routine patrol and subsequent explosion of the fishing vessel the "Ruth Ann" is under investigation." The foot solders like Bob Halloran and I would be leaned on to wrap up this mess quickly before the real story came out.

I was already apprehensive about another police department being involved in the case, especially now with Steve's information and John's suspicions. Now the Hyannis Police Department would be involved. I had heard through the grapevine that the Hyannis Police Chief Mike Mahan had a strong personality, shall we say. Probably not what was needed right now.

He had assigned his best detective, Vince Almeida, to the case. I knew nothing about him. Police work in Hyannis in the summer was mostly writing parking tickets and arresting drunk college kids. It wasn't all fun and sun, though. There is a darker, more seedy side to Hyannis. When the tourists go home after Labor Day, the hotel and motel rooms for $200 to $300 per night get rented by the month. Often a motley mix of drug users and the working poor. Legitimate people that just can't pay the sky-high rents on the Cape.

The Hyannis police station was five minutes from the coffee shop. I pulled into the parking lot ten minutes early. I left my 9-millimeter in the trunk, pulled out my FBI ID, and headed into the building. I planned to just lay low during the meeting. I didn't know how much of the failed operation was shared between John and Chief Mahan. Steve Poole's words were still ringing in my ears. I wasn't sure who I could trust. New Bedford and Hyannis were both small towns. The more I thought about it, the more convinced I was that Steve was onto something.

A middle-aged, balding sergeant was manning the front desk. He glanced up from his paperwork and looked over his horn-rimmed glasses at me. I pushed my badge up against the plexiglass. He took an uncomfortably long time looking at it. He acted like he was a bouncer checking for fake IDs at one of the nightclubs in town.

"I'm here for a nine o'clock meeting with Chief Mahan." He gave me a knowing nod and said, "Last office on the right." He buzzed me in.

I made my way past the phalanx of cops and administrative staff to the chief's office. Rick Raymond, Mosey Bedard, and a tall, thin man of about thirty-five were seated directly in front of Chief Mahan's oversized desk. I assumed the young man was Vince Almeida. He didn't look the part of a police detective. He had long sandy brown hair, a red polo shirt and tan pants. He looked like he had just stepped off the eighteenth hole at Cape Cod Country Club. On the other hand, Chief Mahan looked like he came out of central casting for Dragnet. He had buzz cut of graying hair, square jaw and not an ounce of fat. He was five foot eight inches tall but sinewy. My guess was he hadn't lost many fights in his life.

In a tone that projected authority, Chief Mahan said, "Come in, Agent Ragusa. We've been waiting for you. Please, have a seat."

I shook hands with all three and sat down. The chief went on.

"I've been on the phone with your supervisor, John Ring. Your joint operation with the Coast Guard did not go well. Agent Ring has informed me that the Ruth Ann exploded and that you were fired upon by a cigarette boat that has managed to elude capture.

The Chief continued.

"Let me get you all up to speed. There is some good news. The drop plane was followed to Plymouth Municipal Airport. Two FBI agents were waiting for the pilot and copilot. The two Cape Verdean Nationals knew they were in serious trouble. The nationals had to answer to not just from the FBI, but also from their bosses back in Cape Verde.

"The pilot and copilot were taken into custody. When the FBI agents boarded the plane, two packages of carfentanil were still on board. These guys know they are facing long sentences in a federal prison. Apparently, the older pilot was keeping his mouth shut. He lawyered up immediately. Agents separated the two, and the younger copilot, Ramone, started talking after being offered the possibility of a chance to plead to lesser charges. Ramone told the investigator that a veterinarian, Dr. Lewis Callahan, has a veterinary practice in Hyannis. He also owns an oceanfront estate on Bay Shore Road in town. Dr. Callahan is involved

The Callahan estate is five acres, with oceanfront access to Nantucket Sound. The main house is surrounded by tree cover. The entire estate has an eight-foot fence surrounding the perimeter and, coincidently, has a covered boathouse with a lift at the shoreline. Veterinarians make good money, but this estate is worth more than five million dollars. Unless he inherited the place, it would be out of his league. SAIC John Ring also mentioned that Interpol chatter had been linked to Dr. Callahan's staff at the Buttonwood Zoo in New Bedford. They think he has been using his position as the staff veterinarian at the zoo to smuggle carfentanil. How big this operation is and who else might be involved was anybody's guess. The carfentanil could be at Dr. Callahan's house, his office, cut houses in New Bedford or Hyannis, or all the above."

I had to pipe up.

"Chief, there are only four of us in this room. What you are explaining seems like an operation that will require more boots on the ground. You're talking about multiple sites. We do not know how many men are involved in the drug smuggling ring or their defensive measures."

Chief Mahan shot back, "Slow down, Agent Ragusa. I've talked with Special Agent Ring and Chief Dellicker in New Bedford. Everyone agrees that the operation needs to stay small, at least for now. The commander at Joint Base Cape Cod is up to speed. The Coast Guard will surveil the estate from the air and sea, blocking any escape routes.

Word on the street is that the smugglers are getting inside help. For now, the job for you three is to surveil the doctor's estate and his veterinary business. I went to the District Attorney, but we do not have enough for a search warrant yet."

Mosey had been sitting in silence with a slightly stunned look.

"With all due respect Chief, New Bedford had this case long before Hyannis. I've never worked with Agent Ragusa. I mean no disrespect Detective Almeida but until today, I never heard of you, and I know a lot of officers in Barnstable County."

"None taken," came the curt response from Almeida. I could understand keeping the surveillance team small. But, in my experience, joint operations often come with turf wars, clashing egos, and different ideas about how to execute an operation.

The Chief could sense the increasing tension in the room.

He interjected, "Look, I have faith in all of you, and Vince is my best detective. Agents Ragusa and Raymond, your respective supervisors, tell me you are their best field agents. I know you have not worked together before and that's difficult. You will have to get to know each other in a hurry. Detective Almeida's knowledge of the criminal elements in Hyannis will be valuable to this investigation. We do not think carfentanil has hit the streets yet, so time is of the essence. We need more intel to obtain a search warrant for Dr. Callahan's home and business. That will be your number one priority. If we get the evidence we need, we can detain Dr. Callahan and shake things loose. I doubt the good doctor has ever seen the inside of a holding cell. He may talk and break this drug smuggling ring wide open if we can get him into custody."

All four nodded in agreement.

The Chief added, "All right. I want Agent Ragusa and Detective Bedard to surveil the doctor's estate. Detective Almeida, you will work with Agent Raymond and surveil Dr. Callahan's office. I will have backup ready if you need it. I've been to the pizza place in the strip mall where the doctor's office is. There is a front entrance to the various businesses, and an alley runs behind the building. You can only access the alleyway from the parking lot. You will have to keep an eye on both the front entrances and anyone entering the alley."

"The doctor's estate is going to be more difficult. The estate is likely alarmed. We do not know what other protective measures are in place. There may be guard dogs and armed guards. Agent Ragusa, you, and Detective Bedard will enter the property under the guise of Animal Control Officers. If questioned, your cover story is a complaint of a loose dog biting a woman near the estate, and you have been sent to find and secure the dog. We have got the Animal Control van parked out front. You will go in Animal

Control uniforms. Do not enter the home without probable cause. We just want to get an idea of who is coming and going and any defensive measures we might face in a raid. Keep your eyes out for any boats on the property. Officer Reynolds has your uniforms at the front desk. You can change in the locker room. Hopefully, your uniforms fit. Any questions?"

The four of us shook our heads, and said no. We rose in unison from our chairs and exited the Chief's office in silence. Once in the hallway, everyone shook hands. Rick Raymond broke the silence.

"Well, I guess you two will be getting to know each other. I think you two got the plum assignment. Detective Almeida and I will sit all day in a parking lot, watching people with their pet pooches coming and going."

The four of us headed back through the station house toward the front desk. Sergeant Reynolds was waiting with our uniforms. As I reached for mine, a uniformed officer brushed past me on his way out the door. As he turned to respond, Sergeant Reynolds called out to him, and I saw his face. The hair went up on the back of my neck. He looked like the dark-haired guy in the car, who tried to take me out on the Tobin Bridge. It couldn't be, could it?

CHAPTER SIXTY THREE

Detective Bedard and I parted company with Rick Raymond and Vince Almeida and headed toward the locker room. Of course, Mosey's uniform fit perfectly. My pants were about two inches too short. The length was what we used to call "flood pants" back in high school. Oh well, they would have to do. We made our way past the front desk and into the parking lot. The Animal Control van was gassed up and running.

"Detective Bedard, do you want to drive?" Bedard responded, "Call me Mosey. No, you can drive. I do not do well with anything larger than a passenger car."

"Okay, hop in then. Let's get this show on the road."

We headed out of the police station's parking lot, down Phinney enroute to the Callahan estate. We were winging it. Everything had happened so fast. There was so little intelligence on the estate. Dr. Callahan had not been on anyone's radar screen until a couple of days ago. A background check had been conducted on the good doctor. He had no criminal record. Apparently, he was well regarded in the community and had been running a successful veterinary practice for many years in Hyannis. Dr. Callahan was also the staff veterinarian at Buttonwood Zoo in New Bedford. Why would a respected professional, making a very good living, get into drug smuggling? In my years with the FBI, I learned early on that crime has no typical stereotypes. All kinds of people commit crimes, sometimes heinous ones. The creep peeking into your windows at night could be the local librarian.

You have to keep an open mind. The motive could be greed, a debt owed to someone or just the thrill of it. Maybe Dr. Callahan just got tired of giving cats and dogs rabies shots and was looking for a little excitement in his life. Or he has a gambling problem. If he is involved in this, his excitement will be dodging the romantic advances of inmates at a federal prison.

It was a five-minute drive to the estate on Bay Shore Rd. A gate with an intercom was at the front of a long winding driveway. Thick foliage blocked any view of the house. During the briefing at Hyannis PD, we were provided with an aerial view of the estate. We knew the layout of the grounds but little about the home's interior. Town records showed that Dr. Callahan had bought the estate in 2010. The real estate market had tanked in 2008, and nothing was selling. The estate was almost five acres with two hundred feet of oceanfront. The doctor lived at home with his wife, Charlotte. They had no children. Public records showed the home was nearly 5,000 square feet with five bedrooms and four bathrooms. A small separate guesthouse near the main home was added five years ago.

I pulled up to the intercom and pushed the shiny silver button. No answer.

Three or four attempts later, a man with a gravelly voice growled, "Who are you, and what do you want?"

I responded, "We are from Animal Control. We had a complaint about a loose dog. A woman got bit on or near this property. We're in search of the dog."

"Not possible," came the reply. "Look, Sir, my voice rising and more authoritative, I am just trying to do my job. We are searching all the properties in the area. Our search will not take long, just a quick drive around the property to ensure the dog is not on these grounds."

"Hold on. I need to get the okay from my boss." Mosey sat in the passenger's seat, looking straight ahead.

"Do you think they're on to us?"

I replied, "I don't see how unless there's someone dirty in your ranks." I could see his face getting red from his neck and slowly creeping up to his forehead. "Screw you, Ragusa. What are you talking about?"

"Word on the street is that there is someone on the inside, possibly a cop. The only people in the FBI who know about this operation are my supervisor, John Ring, Rick Raymond, and the big shots in Quantico. If anyone gets tipped off, my money is on either the Hyannis PD or the New Bedford PD."

"C'mon Ragusa. I've been in the force for over ten years. The Chief runs a clean, tight ship. No way there is a dirty cop in our department." Mosey continued to give me a death stare.

"Look, Mosey. I hope you're right. But right now, we need to put this aside. It's just the two of us. I don't know what we're walking into here. I suggest you take a few deep breaths, put one in the chamber of your 9-millimeter, and take the safety off. I'll do the same. Let's just keep our eyes peeled. Are you a good shot?"

A smile came across Mosey's face, and, with pride, he said, "I'm number one in the department."

As we were getting locked and loaded, a gravelly voice came through the intercom.

"All right. The boss says it's okay but make it quick. There isn't any dog loose that I know of." The gate slowly parted, and I drove onto the property. I had never been involved in an operation with so many unknowns. I planned to take it slow around the grounds and get as close to the main house and guest house as possible. Mosey had a hidden camera attached to him and would take pictures, gathering intel. Chief Mahan had not provided backup, feeling that the fewer people who knew about our surveillance, the better. If anything went down, we were on our own. Memories of the firepower on that cigarette boat flooded my mind. 9-millimeters were not much of a match for rocket-propelled grenades and machine guns. If this went south, the bad guys would make quick work of us. No turning back now. I'm not particularly religious. Four years of High School at Gate of Heaven had cured me of that, but I mimicked Mosey when I glanced over and saw him give the sign of the cross. Mosey gave me a nod. I nodded back as we inched down the driveway toward the main house.

CHAPTER SIXTY FOUR

The driveway was long and winding, snaking around the outer perimeter of the estate. Lined by evergreen trees, it provided perfect protection from prying eyes. I kept the van at five miles per hour, pretending to scan the premises for our mystery dog with my windows rolled down. Mosey had the camera in full operation and was snapping away at nothing. It seemed like forever before the main house came into view. The main house was a towering brick Tudor mansion. The grounds were spectacular. I'm not much of a horticulturist, but the array of dazzling flowers and shrubs put the Arnold Arboretum to shame. A horseshoe-shaped, paved driveway allowed parking for at least fifteen cars. A newer white Ford 350 pickup and a Porsche Carrera were parked near the front entrance. Venetian blinds were covering every window in the home. Dr. Callahan was apparently no sun worshipper. All the blinds were closed. Unusual for a beautiful, seventy-five-degree summer day. Most people pay exorbitant prices for oceanfront real estate to enjoy the view and cooling ocean breezes. Why were the shades closed? My radar was up.

As I rounded the bend, passing the driveway on my left, I noticed a glimmer of light coming from a large picture window. The blind was pulled back ever so slightly, and the shape of a balding, middle-aged man came into view. We were being monitored. Chief Mahan provided us with a picture of Dr. Callahan. I had taped it to the dash. Mosey was looking in the other direction. I gave him a subtle jab and pointed to Dr. Callahan's picture on the dash then the round-faced figure poking his pudgy face out from behind the blinds. He looked intently at the picture and nodded no. So, we still weren't sure if Dr. Callahan was inside. Who else was in there? Our job was to surveil the property, not raid it. Seeing some bald guy in the window was nowhere near probable cause for entering the main house or a search warrant, but at least we were on the right track.

Mosey turned his body to get a good shot of the guy in the window's face and said, "Smile, you're on candid camera."

As I began to pass the front driveway, I could see the man in the window disappear as the blinds closed. We continued onto the main access road. The gravel road appeared to circle the entire property. I steered the van toward the right side of the main house and headed toward the rear of the property. A tennis court and in-ground pool were attached to the right side of the main house. A six-foot gated fence surrounded the pool. No one was swimming or sunbathing today.

The backyard expanse of the manicured lawn extended to the shoreline of Nantucket Sound. An enormous sunroom and deck off the back of the home provided incredible views of the bay. It was breathtaking. I could picture myself in a lounge chair and chardonnay in hand, watching the sun dip over the horizon. I wished I was here as a guest of Dr. Callahan. Instead, I was here to catch him as part of a major drug smuggling ring and end his life of luxury. Mosey kept snapping away.

When we entered the grounds, the conversation between Mosey and I had ceased.

Now, he turned to me and said, "Ragusa. Over to the left should be the boathouse."

I nodded in agreement. I could see the outline of a boat lift. The boathouse was enormous and could easily dock a fifty-foot boat. That, alone, was not suspicious. Fifty-foot yachts were commonplace in the summer on the Cape. A dock half a football field long stuck out into the sound. You could park three fifty-foot yachts on it. A twelve-foot dinghy tied to a cleat bobbed gently in the rolling surf. We needed to get a look into the boathouse. If the cigarette boat was there, it would be probable cause for a warrant.

With that information, any judge on the Cape would grant us a search warrant. It had to be Mosey that would conduct the search. He had the camera, and if I was spotted leaving the van, it would look suspicious to whoever may be monitoring us. I was very aware that we might need to make a quick exit. I didn't know Mosey from a hole in the wall. How would he hold up if things went sideways?

He turned to me and said, "I guess it's showtime, Ragusa. Keep the motor running." "Good luck. I'll cover your back as best I can."

His sarcastic response came quickly, "That makes me feel so much better. You might want to unholster your Glock. I'll do the same."

The passenger side door of the van creaked open as Mosey's feet made a scraping noise against the gravel driveway. Mosey was equipped with a high-powered pair of binoculars and was making his best impression of an Animal Control officer searching for a pooch on the loose. I had my right hand on my Glock, staring intently at Mosey as he slowly progressed into the boathouse. So far, so good. Another thirty feet, and he would have a clear view of the interior. Just then, I heard movement from behind a thick patch of shrubbery about fifty yards to the left of the boathouse.

Out came, at what I guess was full throttle, a golf cart of all things. It would have seemed comical as they headed toward Mosey, going all ten miles an hour, except for the two serious-looking guys on the golf cart with handguns drawn. The golf cart careened up to Mosey and came to a screeching halt. The driver jumped out. I had my window rolled down all the way and could hear him scream at him, "Who the hell are you?"

Mosey coolly replied, "Take it easy, man. Put that gun away. I'm from Animal Control. Your man at the front gate buzzed us in. We have permission to search the grounds for a stray dog who bit a woman." Mosey's 9-millimeter was concealed under his untucked shirt. I could see Mosey had his right hand on his waist, ready to pull his Glock if this got out of hand. It was, indeed, showtime, and Mosey was the star of the show. Hopefully, he was a good bullshit artist. I didn't recognize either the driver or the passenger. The driver looked like he had just come off the beach. He had sandy blond tousled hair, medium build, tanned. He would fit in at any exclusive country club on the Cape. The passenger was a different story. He was dark-haired, with a stocky build, and a salt and pepper mustache. He looked like the muscle, and the driver, the brains. The conversation got quieter, and both guys lowered their weapons. Lowering their weapons was a good sign. I could see Mosey waving his hand in a circular motion. Maybe trying to get across to these goons that we had to search the entire property.

I was so intent on watching Mosey that I nearly jumped out of my seat when I felt a hard tap on my left shoulder. Staring at me through my rolled down window was the pockmarked face of another member of the Welcome Wagon. I never saw him come. I had my hand on my Glock, but there was no way I could get into position to fire if this guy was armed and had bad intent. His voice was surprisingly pleasant.

"Nice day for a drive, eh?" I couldn't quite place the accent. It sounded maybe Canadian.

With my heart pounding out of my chest, I stammered, "Yeah, it sure is. Wow, you guys have a great job being able to have this view every day." I added, "You know, man, we're just doing our job. We don't want any trouble."

He panned the inside of the van and said, "Yeah. Sorry 'bout these two bozos coming on so strong, buddy. But you can't be too careful. There are a lot of thieves on the Cape in the summer. Sometimes people aren't who they seem. I'm Walt Gleason. I run security on the estate for Dr. Callahan."

Now was the time to introduce myself, but I was so thrown off that I couldn't remember the name on my badge. I pretended to sneeze and, out of the corner of my eye, caught a glimpse of my badge, Robert Stevens.

"I'm Bob, pleased to meet you. Sorry, just allergies, damn grass pollen."

Walt stuck out his right hand. I didn't know if this was a trick to get me to release the grip of my gun or if he was just being friendly. I didn't want to cause suspicion. I had no choice but to release my grip on my Glock and shake his outstretched hand. We shook hands as I spotted Mosey coming toward the van.

The two goons returned to the golf cart and headed toward the main house. Mosey said to Walt, "We won't be much longer. Just need to take a final sweep of the perimeter of the estate. No sign of any dog so far. The woman who called in was probably confused."

Walt leaned in and, again, scanned the inside of the van as Mosey opened the passenger side door and got in.

"Well, I guess you have a job to do. Do me a favor. Don't get out of your vehicle unless you see that dog. Understand?"

"Yes, sir, no problem. If there was a dog, he's probably taking a crap on your neighbor's lawn right about now."

Walt let out a chuckle as he backed away from the van. I put the van into the drive and slowly pulled away. He waved at us, and I waved back. Both Mosey and I let out a simultaneous sigh of relief. That was a close call.

CHAPTER SIXTY FIVE

I steered the van past the boathouse, following the gravel driveway along the property's perimeter. Mosey kept snapping away, trying to get any little detail that would indicate what was inside. We were both so busy looking at the back of the boathouse that we almost missed it. The sun was hitting in such a way that you could see the shadow of the bow of a boat on the water. The silhouette clearly looked like the shape of a cigarette boat. I was tempted to pull the van over and look, but we were clearly being watched, and another encounter with Dr. Callahan's security staff probably wouldn't go well.

The driveway meandered left as the guest house came into view. Mosey turned his camera toward the guest house. The clicking of the camera continued. There was a white suburban parked outside the front door. Shades covered all the windows. A common theme at the Callahan estate. There appeared to be no movement inside. The shadow of what could be a large power boat in the boathouse was incriminating but still wouldn't be enough for a search warrant. We were coming up empty.

Surveillance from the air or water would likely tip off Dr. Callahan that he and his cohorts were being watched. Trees and shrubbery were hindering any surveillance from the street. How many times could the FBI and local police put on a ruse to gain access to the estate? It was frustrating. I drove as slowly as I dared, not wanting to arouse suspicion. We turned to the left past the guesthouse and back onto the main driveway when I saw it. A black sedan was approaching us. My heart started pounding out of my chest. I hadn't been able to get the plate number of the sedan on the Tobin Bridge, but this vehicle looked very familiar. No need to panic. There are a lot of black sedans in Massachusetts.

I didn't know for sure if this was the vehicle on the Tobin. I didn't know who was in the vehicle or their intentions. I had a pair of sunglasses in the pocket of my shirt. I casually pulled them out and put them on before the vehicle passed. Mosey saw me put the sunglasses on and gave me a look like, "What the hell are you doing?" I ignored him. If this was the same black sedan, the driver or passenger might recognize me and blow our cover. If I pulled over to try and position the van to block their view of me, it would look suspicious. I had to drive past them. I needed somehow to see who was in that sedan without being recognized. Mosey was oblivious to what I was doing. Probably better that way.

The sedan was within ten feet. Mosey turned the camera on the car and snapped away. We both were moving at a leisurely five miles per hour. I could tell the windows were tinted. I could make out four figures inside the sedan. As I glided past the sedan, I pretended to adjust the left mirror. The faces of the four men came into view. I didn't know the driver. He was an older man with thinning white hair and an angular face. I looked at the picture of Dr. Callahan taped to the dash. It wasn't him. The other three put my blood pressure into stroke territory. On the front passenger side was Waxy. In the backseat was the shooter from the Tobin and another passenger whose body language and facial expressions reminded me of those hostage videos kidnappers make and send out to the media. It was Steve Poole.

Steve was looking straight ahead. He didn't see me. The driver was busy looking ahead, trying not to sideswipe our van on the narrow driveway. The shooter in the back seat beside Steve was staring intently ahead. I tried desperately not to make eye contact, but it happened anyway. Waxy and I locked eyes for a brief second. His reaction put me at ease. He smiled and waved. I hadn't been made. Once the sedan had passed from sight, I pulled the van over onto the shoulder of the driveway.

Mosey gave me a quizzical look.

"What's going on, Ragusa?"

"We've got a problem. That sedan we just passed has four men in it. I know three of them. Two of them tried to kill me on the Tobin Bridge. One of them I don't recognize. The other is Steve Poole, a bartender from the Widows Cove Tavern in New Bedford. He's a good friend of mine. Steve has been feeding me information on the Emma Jean case all along. Some thugs tuned him up a week ago and put him in St. Luke's Hospital. That was just a warning. I told Steve to back off, but I guess he didn't. He's not going to get out of here alive."

Mosey asked a question that shocked the hell out of me.

"What if he's in on it, Ragusa? Did you ever think of that?"

I wanted to backhand him, but he had a point. I pondered the question for a minute and said, "There is no way. I've known Steve for decades. He's a stand-up guy. Do you think the beating was just for show? I'll stake my reputation and my pension on him."

Mosey came back at me. "All right then, so what now?"

That was a good question. How long would it take for the cavalry to arrive? Even if they did, would we be ordered to stand down? Do we even have probable cause to go in? How much time did Steve have? I had to make a split-second decision.

"I'm going in. I can't take the chance that we'll be ordered to stand down. Not with my friend in danger. I know this is against protocol. I'll understand if you stay behind. Your job will be on the line. We're both going to be on the hot seat, even if things work out but I can't wait."

Mosey, staring out the van's front window, seemed to know he was making a career making or career breaking decision. He turned slowly toward me as he mumbled, "I can't let you go in there alone. I can't believe I am saying this, but I'm in."

We were both out on a limb. The protocol would have been to notify Chief Mahan and John Ring. They would make the call based on whether our observation of Steve Poole sitting in the rear of a sedan with three suspected drug smugglers was probable cause to enter Dr. Callahan's estate. I didn't think we had time. Chief Mahan, fearing our cover could be blown, had not put a backup team in position. Escape by sea was still possible. We didn't know what was inside the boathouse. The silhouette of a sleek boat within seemed to confirm that the cigarette boat involved in the gun battle during Operation Wave Runner was there, but we didn't know for sure.

One thing we did know, dogs didn't patrol the grounds. We hadn't heard any barking from inside the estate, but it was still possible there were dogs in the main house, ready to tip off the bad guys to our presence or rip us apart if we entered. It was a chance we would have to take. I've known Steve for more than thirty years. He had put his life on the line, providing key information on this case. He had been put in the hospital once. The thugs in the sedan were not taking him for a joy ride. My guess was if we didn't intervene, the bottom of Nantucket Sound would be Steve's final resting stop.

I ditched the van behind an overgrown rhododendron bush ten feet back from the road. Mosey and I approached the main house on foot, along the left side of the access road, along the tree line. We were out of view from the guard shack.

"What's your plan, Rob?"

Before I could answer, Mosey said, "Tell me you have one!"

"There's only one way we can get near the house without being spotted. We keep following the tree line and hope we aren't spotted. When we reach the house, we'll split up. I'll take the front door. You enter through the back door, off the back deck. We don't have flash bangs, and if the doors are locked, we'll have to shoot the locks off to gain entry."

Chief Mahan had provided us with the floor plans of the Callahan Estate. I pulled them out of my back pocket, unfolded them, and reviewed them with Mosey. As I pointed to the first-floor schematic, Mosey was following along.

"Steve could be anywhere in the house. Once inside, you clear the kitchen, library, and dining room. I'll clear the living room, bathroom, and first-floor bedroom. We don't have zip ties or handcuffs. If we come across any bad guys, disarm them, and use one of these pieces of dog leash to tie them up."

Bewildered, Mosey asked, "Where did you get those?"

I replied, "Well, after all, we are Animal Control Officers. They were in the back of the van." I pulled out my Swiss army knife and cut off four three-foot pieces of leather leash.

"Hopefully, we can keep the element of surprise on our side. We're going to have to move fast. If Steve isn't on the first floor, move to the second. I'll search everything on the left side. You take the right. I'm pretty sure the guy in the sedan's back seat was the same guy who shot up my caddy on the Tobin Bridge. You know he's not going down without a fight. I'm not sure about the others."

"Well, it's simple. I'll say that much about your plan. Even if this goes textbook, Ragusa, our asses will still be in a sling. Just so you know, I'm risking my career for your friend. I don't even know him."

"If this works, Mosey, I'll introduce you. Maybe Steve will treat us to a Sam Adams at the Widows Cove."

Mosey shook his head with amusement and said, "How about free beer for life. Let's just hope this plan of yours works."

Mosey was right. I had no business getting him involved in this. I had a good feeling about him. I was glad he had my back. We moved steadily along the hundred-foot oak and maple treelined perimeter. It hadn't been planned, but our Animal Control uniforms were forest green and provided perfect camouflage in the dense overgrowth. I took point and Mosey positioned himself on my right shoulder. We made steady progress and were within fifty feet of the front of the house.

Trying to stay out of view and keep moving forward wasn't easy. Unlike the nicely manicured lawn and shrubbery, Mosey and I were essentially bushwacking through the brush. The tree line had not been cleaned out for years, if ever. It was a minefield of fallen branches, remains of what once was a stone wall, and green prickly briar rising from the forest floor like a serpent. It seemed more like the jungles of Vietnam than Cape Cod. It had rained last night, and mud puddles of various depths had to be traversed while constantly slipping on the soggy forest floor.

We had gotten within twenty feet of the main house when a cacophony of angry voices could be heard coming from the living room. The blinds were closed, but the windows on the first floor were open. The sounds emanating from the house seemed to be directed at Steve Poole. I only recognized two of the three voices from inside the living room. One was Steve Poole and the other was Waxy. Waxy's tone was more measured than the other voice. In a menacing loud pitch, Steve was being screamed at. It was a barrage of accusations in which every other word seemed to be "motherfucker." The harangue would occasionally be punctuated by Steve pleading, "Just let me go. I will pretend this never happened. I won't say a word." His pleas went unheeded, and the harangue continued.

As painful as it was to listen to, it was helpful. Two of the thugs in the sedan and Steve were in the living room. I could only make out three voices, leaving the fourth guy, the driver, unaccounted for. We also didn't know who else was in the house. Walt and his two partners in crime were still somewhere on the premises and unaccounted for. I didn't know how many armed men Mosey and I would be facing.

The screaming continued, muting the sound of the constant cracking of undergrowth as we plodded forward. We had finally reached the house and passed just to the left of the bay window in the living room. The screaming had intensified. The low growl had turned to a roar. The screamer seemed to be coming unglued.

I signaled Mosey forward and whispered, "You got a watch on?" Mosey rolled up his sleeve, exposing a vintage Rolex.

The look on my face said, "Whoa, they must pay better in New Bedford PD than the FBI."

Mosey saw the look on my face, a gift from an old girlfriend. I replied in a slightly sarcastic tone,

"The one that got away?" Mosey nodded his head up and down.

I pointed at my Timex and raised my index finger. "Two minutes, and we go in together."

I gave Mosey the "go" signal, "mark." We didn't have walkie talkies, and, like a couple of rookies, we left our cell phones in the van. We would have to time our entrance the old-fashioned way. Mosey made his way to the back entrance while I waited at the front. The second hand on my Timex clicked away for what seemed like an eternity. I unholstered my Glock and racked a round in the chamber. My heart was pounding out of my chest.

I made my way along the bay window and reached the stone steps of the entryway with five seconds to spare. The ornate wooden door looked too sturdy to kick in. If it was locked, I'd have to shoot the lock off and kick the door in. The only glitch would be a deadbolt inside. Then I would be screwed, and so were Steve and Mosey.

Mosey, I sure as hell hope you're in place. It was go-time. I turned the handle of the front door, and it gave easily. My lucky day. Hopefully, the back slider was unlocked as well. The door creaked as I entered the front hallway. I crept down the hallway past what must have been family pictures lining the walls. Dr. Callahan and who, I assume, was his wife on their sailboat, in the pool, playing tennis, nice life. The door to the living room was closed. I could still hear yelling as I slowly approached. As I was about to turn the gold doorknob, I could hear footsteps coming in my direction from the kitchen. I had nowhere to hide, so I got into a crouched position with my Glock ready.

My hands were sweaty, and the grip on my Glock was slipping. Beads of sweat were forming on my forehead. The footsteps were getting closer. I lowered my Glock to aim chest high. My training from Quantico and years of experience kicked in. In my mind, I kept repeating in my head, "center mass, center mass." The kitchen windows provided enough backlight to make out a figure heading straight down the hallway. The top of a brown boot became visible. I recognized the brown work boots. It was Mosey. We made eye contact at the same time. I signaled him over to my position.

I whispered in his left ear, "Did you clear the downstairs?"

He nodded yes.

"Steve and at least three others are in the living room. The third bad guy from the sedan may be there too, but I'm only hearing three voices. They could waste Steve any minute. The shooter from the Tobin seems to be running the show. We'll go in together, subdue and disarm the crew and clear the scene. Hopefully, without a shot being fired. If all goes well, you can watch our guests, and I'll clear the second floor."

"Ragusa, what about trying to negotiate with these guys? They don't know that it's only the two of us. Maybe we can bluff them into surrendering or at least releasing Steve?"

"No, Mosey, I saw the look in that shooter's eyes when he tried to kill me on the Tobin. He's a stone-cold killer. He'll kill Steve for sure. We need the element of surprise."

"All right, I trust your judgment."

I gave Mosey a final piece of advice. "If anyone points a gun, shoot to kill. All right then. On three. Ready? One, two, three."

At three, I kicked in the door. The shooter had a gun pointed at Steve's head. Waxy was to his left, and a third guy was sitting comfortably on a chair in the left corner of the room.

Mosey and I were both screaming at the top of our lungs, "FBI put your hands up."

Steve made eye contact with me. He was white as a ghost, scared out of his mind.

"Show me your hands," I screamed. "Show me your hands."

Waxy wore a black oversized T-shirt, and his right hand wasn't visible. The guy in the chair had his hands in his lap, covered by a newspaper. I could tell by the look in Waxy's and the shooter's eyes that they recognized me. The shooter and the guy in the chair seemed shocked. Buy Waxy was cool as a cucumber. I couldn't believe it, but he was smirking. My head was on a swivel, trying to keep an eye on everybody. Suddenly, the shooter wheeled to his right and fired in what seemed like slow motion.

The noise was deafening. The round had found a target. Not me but Mosey. He was falling to his knees. Blood was seeping out of his chest. Mosey managed to get off a couple of rounds before slumping to the floor. Both rounds went high, scraping plaster off the ceiling. I opened fire and put a full clip into the shooter. The impact of the rounds hurled him backward onto the couch. A pool of blood stained the white silk upholstery. Steve bolted from the couch and flew past me and out the living room door.

Waxy called out to the third guy, "Larry, you all, right?"

Well, now I could put a name to the face. During the shootout, Larry had gotten out of his chair. The Boston Herald had fallen to the floor, revealing his hands. He had a revolver pointed at my head. His hands were shaking. I knew Mosey was bleeding out, and I had to end this fast.

I hollered at the top of my lungs, "Put the gun down. Put the gun down!"

Waxy had his right hand in his pocket. My face turned a bright red shade, I screamed at him, "Show me your hands. Show me your hands right now."

No reaction; Waxy just stared at me. Larry wasn't in good physical shape, maybe thirty pounds overweight, so his next move surprised me. Before I could react, he darted across the living room and took cover behind the couch.

I yelled at Waxy not to move as I made my way to the right of the couch. I never saw the gun. Larry shot through the back of the couch, the bullet striking me in my right forearm, knocking my Glock from my hand. The bullet had only grazed me, but the pain was searing, blood leaking onto the oriental rug. The Glock was only two feet in front of me, but it might as well have been twenty. Before I could go for my gun, Larry emerged from the back of the couch with a smug look of triumph. He was approaching me to finish me off. Waxy was to my left and still had his right hand hidden. I was confused. I assumed he must be carrying. With my gun on the floor, why didn't he pull his gun out and get in on the fun with Larry?

"Well, well, well, Agent. I guess this is it."

The words were sinking into my brain. This was it. The only thing left to do was pray. Thoughts of my parents flooded my mind. Childhood memories of the beach at Castle Island, getting a hot dog and fries at Sullivan's. Going to my first Red Sox game flashed before my eyes. Larry raised his revolver for the coup de gras. At least it would be quick. Then Waxy spun to his left, and the shiny blade of a knife appeared from beneath his shirt. Waxy hurled it in Larry's direction. With the ivory knife handle sticking out of

Larry's pot belly, he fell backward onto the floor with a thud. What just happened?

I looked at Waxy in stunned disbelief. He made his way toward me. I reared back in a defensive posture.

"Don't worry, Agent Ragusa. I'm on your side."

He took a red handkerchief from his back pocket and applied pressure to my wound.

"Keep pressure on your wound."

I stared at Waxy as he stood up and pulled out a cell phone. I could hear Waxy saying to whoever was on the other end of the line.

"Send everybody you've got. There are two men injured."

Waxy put his arm on my shoulder as if to comfort me. What was happening here?

"Agent Ragusa, you're probably not going to believe this, but I'm a confidential informant for the New Bedford Police Department. I was facing a five-year stint in Walpole State Prison for drug dealing. The District Attorney made me an offer I couldn't refuse. I could plead to a misdemeanor if I became a paid informant and helped infiltrate the carfentanil drug ring. Everyone in the city knows my history, so getting access to the cartel and gaining their trust wasn't hard. Dr. Callahan was in way over his head. He has a gambling problem, and his share of the carfentanil score was going to pay off his gambling debt. A raid on his estate and his office was already planned for tonight. You and Mosey were only supposed to gather intelligence, not be cowboys."

While Mosey was bleeding out on the living room floor, Waxy felt it was more important to provide the details of his undercover work. I crawled toward Mosey's crumpled body and yelled at Waxy to help stem the bleeding. Finally, the wail of sirens screaming down the driveway seemed to snap Waxy out of it. He had moved to Mosey and was applying pressure to his wound with another handkerchief when the living door burst open and an army of cops and EMTs poured in.

Chief Mahan was right behind the first EMT. The look on his face said "pissed," but it quickly turned to concern with he realized how badly Mosey was hurt. Two EMTs rushed over to Mosey and started working on stopping the bleeding. I thought I saw one of them shaking his head. That is not a good sign. The EMTs had him on a gurney, blood everywhere. He had an IV in his arm when they wheeled him past me. I had a painful ringing in my ear. I could hear a muffled voice Chief Mahan yelling at me.

"Where is Dr. Callahan?"

"What did you say, Chief?"

"I said where Dr. Callahan is."

I was fading, but I got out, "The second floor hasn't been cleared. Maybe the doc is up there hiding in a closet."

A uniformed Hyannis officer suddenly appeared.

"Chief, we've cleared the house. Nobody else is here."

"Okay Officer Delgado. Cordon off the grounds. Nobody but first responders come or go without my permission."

The young officer snapped off a quick salute, "Yes sir," and walked briskly out of the room.

Walt and his two underlings must have heard the gunfire and the sirens and hightailed it out of here. But where were they now, and where was Dr. Callahan?

An older female EMT entered, approaching the chief. She had traces of blood staining her white uniform. She walked up the Chief Mahan and began whispering in his ear. I interrupted the conversation.

"My partner, is he going to make it?"

She responded, "He's in bad shape, but it looks like he's going to make it."

I could make out the whoop, whoop of helicopter blades. She added, "He's stable. They're taking him by helicopter to Mass General."

My mind was racing a million miles an hour. Of course, I was concerned for Mosey but what about Rick Raymond and Vince Almeida? They were on a stakeout at Dr. Callahan's office. Chief Mahan had not shared the details of the raid planned for tomorrow with either Mosey or me. My guess was Rick and Vince were in the dark as well.

CHAPTER SIXTY SIX

Rick Raymond and Vince Almeida sat in a nondescript Crown Vic in the strip mall parking lot, lamenting.

"I can't believe we're sitting here, watching Fluffy, Fido, and the occasional guinea pig come and go. The real action is going be at Callahan's estate."

Dr. Callahan did seem to have a thriving practice. In two hours, maybe ten pet owners had come and gone.

Most stakeouts involve two FBI agents. Under pressure from Chief Mahan, John Ring reluctantly agreed to let the FBI conduct surveillance on Dr. Callahan's office with a team comprised of an FBI field agent and a detective from the Hyannis PD. Both John and Chief Mahan had suspicions that an officer or officers in either the Hyannis or the New Bedford Police Department were involved with the drug ring. Rumors spread like wildfire in a police department, and word was circulating that the bad guys were being tipped off. The drug ring always seemed to be one step ahead. Our cover had been blown in Operation Wave Runner but by who? The New Bedford Police, Hyannis Police, Harbor Patrol, who knew.

Rick had parked in the rear corner of the parking lot. The car was in a perfect vantage point to cover the front entrance and anyone walking or driving down the alleyway in the back of the building. There was no exit from the alley, so a car or a person would have to loop around back to the parking lot to leave.

It was getting hotter outside, and the air conditioning in the Crown Vic was struggling to keep up. The air in the car hung heavy, and we had to keep wiping the sweat from our foreheads and necks. Dr. Callahan's powder blue Beamer was not parked in the lot, but the steady stream of pet owners led me to believe he had to be in the office. He didn't have a partner, and a veterinary assistant can only do so much.

An older model sedan, driven by a middle-aged man, pulled into the parking lot and began creeping along the sidewalk toward the office's front entrance. Larry had dark, curly hair with a few flecks of gray. He was looking around like he was casing the place. What do you steal from a Vet's office? Something was off. My pulse was getting a little quicker, and a dull ache was forming in my stomach.

"I don't like it, Rick."

Vince seemed to have that sixth sense that something bad would go down. We were both on high alert.

The sedan crept past the nail salon, the pizza joint, and then the front door of Dr. Callahan's clinic. Then left the parking lot and turned past me and disappeared down the alleyway behind the strip mall. The minutes ticked by and nothing, no sedan, nobody on foot, nothing. Obviously not a delivery driver, so what was up? I was about to put the Crown Vic in drive and peek down the alley when the radio crackled. I must have had the oldest car in the fleet. It was a ten-year-old piece of junk. Nothing worked right, including the radio. I could tell it was Chief Mahan, but he was breaking up. Something about two officers being shot.

I went to pick up the transmitter when a loud explosion rocked the clinic. The front door flew open, and a stream of people with dogs and cats in their arms poured out into the parking lot. Smoke billowing out of the front door. The dazed throng took refuge wherever they could. I frantically called dispatch to send ambulances and backup ASAP. I grabbed the 12-gauge shotgun and took off across the parking lot toward the clinic's front door, with Vince trailing me.

People were coughing, dogs were barking, and cats were screeching. For all the chaos, it didn't seem like anyone was seriously injured. I quickly scanned the chaotic scene and couldn't see anyone bleeding or with any obvious injuries. Vince followed me across the parking lot. I signaled him to cover the back alley.

As I gingerly moved toward the front door, I counted a dozen people in the parking lot. I turned to my right as Vince disappeared around the corner of the building into the alley. I had been there when the front door opened, and ten people had gone in. I took a quick count, twelve people, two with lab coats on, and neither one was Dr. Callahan. Most likely the veterinary assistant and the receptionist.

I pumped the shotgun, loading a solid slug into the chamber, and made my way to the front door. I couldn't see a damn thing through the cloud of smoke.

"FBI, Hello, anyone here?"

I could hear faint moaning coming from the back room. Back up would be here any minute, but I couldn't wait. I made a racket tripping over chairs and knocking over an end table as I passed the front desk and made my way toward the exam room. I took the safety off and slowly opened the door.

The smoke began parting, and a figure hanging from the ceiling appeared. It was Dr. Callahan. He was hanging from a beam in the ceiling, gasping for oxygen. I leaned the shotgun against the door as I moved toward him. I pulled out my Swiss army knife and cut him down. As we made eye contact, sheer terror filled his eyes. I was there to save him. All he knew was that a strange man was holding a knife and coming toward him. The doctor probably weighed 160 pounds, but he was dead weight. I grabbed him around the waist with my left arm, raising him an inch, taking pressure off the rope around his neck. With my right hand, I pulled out a knife from its sheath. The blade of my knife made short work of the rope, and we both crashed to the floor. I loosened his collar as he gasped for air.

A nasty looking bright red line crossed his neck. The color seemed to be returning to his face, and his breathing started normalizing.

"You all right, Doc?"

Dr. Callahan moaned and reached for his neck.

"He tried to kill me."

"Who tried to kill you?"

The doctor's trembling right hand began to rise, and he pointed directly behind me. I jumped to my feet and turned around. The barrel of my 12-gauge pointed right at my face. It was the driver of the sedan.

"You should have stayed in the parking lot. Yeah, I spotted you a mile away. Nobody but the police drive Crown Vic's. You need a new ride. You spoiled my plan. Kind of ironic getting killed by your own gun. You must have been asleep during the gun safety course at the academy."

I was trying to think fast. I knew backup was on the way.

I tried to bargain, "Give me the shotgun. Nobody has died yet."

I was reaching for the barrel of the shotgun when he turned the gun around and slammed the stock into the bridge of my nose. The blow sent me careening into the back wall. Blood poured like an open faucet out of my nose. The cold stare on his face said it all. He was going to kill both of us. A 12-gauge shotgun at point blank range will take half your head off. Seared in my brain were images of two suicide victims who had taken their lives by eating their shotgun. What I couldn't get out of my mind was that my family wouldn't be able to have an open casket.

His voice wasn't menacing but measured.

"Sorry it's got to end this way, but I can't let you live. You've seen too much. I was going to make it look like the good doctor had taken himself out rather than go to prison, but you spoiled my plan, wrong place wrong time."

Dr. Callahan pleaded to deaf ears, "Please don't."

"Sorry, Doc, you were just a pawn in this whole thing. You're no longer of use to us."

As the driver started to raise the shotgun, he gasped. Like a giant redwood falling in the forest, he stumbled forward, tripping over the doctor's legs, and dropped dead at my feet.

Vince had been covering the back door. It was a heavy metal door. The explosion hadn't budged it. I could hear Vince screaming my name as he pounded furiously, trying to gain entrance. My ears were ringing from a combination of the explosion and Vince's incessant beating on the door.

I looked at Dr. Callahan, who suddenly regained his voice and composure.

"We got to get out of here."

He pointed to a door half hanging off the hinges.

"The carfentanil was stored in that room. The explosion probably made it airborne. He must have breathed it in. If we don't get out of here, we'll join him on the floor."

I helped the doctor to his feet and we both made our way to the back door. I turned the deadbolt and pulled hard on the door. The explosion had bent the metal, and the door was stuck.

Now it was my time to pound on the door.

"Vince, push on the door," no reply. Suddenly the door came flying almost off its hinges right into my face. I staggered back as Vince, who had lost his balance, came tumbling through the door onto the floor. I helped him to his feet, and the three of us headed out the door into the alley.

"Quite an entrance Vince."

"Yeah, not so graceful, but it got the job done."

As we returned to the parking lot, I thought I would see if Dr. Callahan was in the mood to talk.

"So, you know the dead guy in your office, Doc?"

"Yeah. He was an enforcer on the lower end of the ladder. He went by the name of Buzzy. The cartel stationed him at my estate, mostly to keep an eye on me."

We walked down the alley toward the parking lot side by side. I didn't bother cuffing him. Dr. Callahan knew his fate. No more fancy cars or oceanfront homes.

I asked, "Doc, why did you get involved in drug smuggling?"

His reply came quickly.

"Greed. I have a gambling problem and a wife with expensive tastes. I know what carfentanil can do. My conscience finally got to me, and I tried to get out, but the cartel said they would kill my wife. I knew I was in over my head. I contacted the New Bedford Police Department yesterday and talked to a detective there. I told him about the smuggling operation, the carfentanil, everything, but he seemed skeptical. Then Buzzy shows up today, puts a noose around my neck, and tries to hang me. Make it look like a suicide."

Doc Callahan had come close to meeting his maker.

"Doc, do you remember the name of the detective you spoke to?"

"No, I don't, but he had a high-pitched voice; struck me as unusual for a cop."

We turned the corner and into the parking lot as what seemed like every cop car on the Cape came screeching into the lot. Ambulances, the bomb squad, the SWAT team, everyone was there. I walked the doctor over to a squad car.

I cuffed the doctor and as I put him into the back seat, he turned toward me and said, "Thanks, agent, I'm actually glad it's over."

I got back on the radio with Chief Mahan.

"Rick, are you and Vince all right?"

"Yes, Chief, there is one fatality in the clinic. There was an explosion. The people in the clinic cleared out. I was able to get a good look at them as they headed out the front door. No one seemed seriously hurt but, the EMTs can better determine that."

"Okay, Rick."

"Chief, get the bomb squad and the hazardous waste guys over here pronto. There is a stash of carfentanil stored in the back office."

"Okay, Rick you and Vince head back to the station. I'll meet you there for a debriefing in an hour."

"Chief, are Mosey and Ragusa, okay?"

"I'll fill you in when I see you in person."

"See you soon, Chief."

I haltingly put the radio back in its holder. A feeling of nausea suddenly came over me as I returned to the Crown Vic and pulled out of the parking lot.

CHAPTER SIXTY SEVEN

Mosey was on his way to Mass General. Larry was on his way to the morgue. I made my way through the maze of police vehicles and ambulances on the grounds, searching frantically for Steve Poole. He was nowhere to be found. As I passed the last ambulance parked in the driveway, I caught the attention of a young EMT sitting in the driver's seat.

He yelled out to me, "Sir, you're bleeding. Let me look at that arm."

I waved him off, but he jumped out of the ambulance and approached me.

"Let me look at that."

Reluctantly, I extended my right arm. He opened the ambulance's back door and came out with some antiseptic spray and gauze bandage. The gash had stopped bleeding, but the dark red stain on my arm extended from my hand to my elbow. After wiping off the blood, a two-inch cut was visible where the bullet had grazed the top of my hand.

The EMT asked me to move my right thumb and fingers. It hurt like hell, but I could do it.

"That cut could use a few stitches. I can do it right now."

I asked him, "What's your name?"

"Connor Klemmey, sir."

"Please stop calling me sir. You're making me feel old. Thanks for helping me out. I'm FBI Agent Rob Ragusa. Nice to meet you. Call me Rob. I appreciate your assistance, but if you've got a butterfly bandage in that bus, which should do it."

Connor went into the ambulance and came out with a butterfly bandage.

"Sir—sorry, Rob—I really think a couple of stitches are in order."

"I appreciate your concern, but this will do just fine."

As he unwrapped the bandage and began applying it to my arm, I asked "Listen, I asked all the other first responders, so I might as well ask you. When you were pulling into the estate, you didn't happen to notice a tall, maybe six foot two, older white male with bushy white hair, did you?"

His response startled me.

"Yeah I did now that you mention it. A guy matching that description was getting into a blue pickup truck. He looked disheveled. I pulled over to check on him, but the pickup truck took off."

"Can you give me a description of the pickup?"

"Yeah, it was a beater. It had to be at least ten years old, with one of those cabs on it that covers the bed of the truck."

"Did you get a look at the driver?"

"No, not really, it was a big guy that's all I remember. After the pick-up took off, I put it in drive and turned into the driveway."

I looked down at my arm. The bleeding had stopped.

"Nice work, Connor. That should do the trick."

I nodded my approval and headed back to the main house.

After being kidnapped and barely escaping being killed, why would Steve Poole get into a pick-up truck and take off? If the man Connor had described was even Steve Poole. I doubt he is the only tall, older guy with curly white hair in Hyannis, but it seemed a hell of a coincidence.

Chief Mahan approached me as I brushed past his cruiser.

"How are you doing, Rob?"

"I'm fine, Sir. A nice young man just finished patching me up."

I showed Chief Connor's handiwork.

"Mosey's on his way by helicopter to Mass General. From what I'm hearing, he's going to make it."

"Thank god for that."

Chief Mahan asked, "Did you hear what happened to Rick Raymond? There was an explosion at Dr. Callahan's office. There's one dead inside. Dr. Callahan is in custody and is being transported back to the station for booking. Rick said at least ten people were in the office when the explosion happened. We've got every available ambulance over there. The bomb squad and our Haz-mat guys are there too. Apparently, Dr. Callahan was storing the carfentanil in a back room. We don't know if it exploded, or a bomb was set off. We've evacuated the area and cordoned off the strip mall. I've contacted John Ring. He's sending some of his agents to the scene to assist with the investigation. You should call and get him up to speed on what happened here."

The chief added, "I told Rick I wanted to meet with him and Vince at my office in an hour. What about you? It looks like a trip to the emergency room to get checked out is in order."

"No, Chief, I'm fine. The bleeding stopped. I can swing by the emergency room after the meeting. "This may seem strange, but I could really use a cup of coffee right now. I'm going to stop at Dunkin before I head over to the station. Can I get you anything, Chief?"

"No Rob. I'm good. I'll catch up with you in an hour."

CHAPTER SIXTY EIGHT

I hopped back into the van. I guess my brief career as an Animal Control officer was ending. I took a deep breath and slowly exhaled. The gravity of what had happened began to sink in. Mosey had been shot, his prognosis for recovery was still unsure. I had gotten lucky; a few more inches to the left, and the bullet grazing my right hand would have gotten me in the stomach. Steve Poole had gotten out alive, but where was he? A thought kept nagging at me. Why would Steve get into a pick-up truck and just vanish? He had been through an ordeal, kidnapped, possibly beaten, tortured, and drugged. I just didn't know. Maybe he was disoriented, or just that fight, or flight response psychologists talk about had kicked in, and it was "flight" for Steve. Maybe he had just flagged down the first vehicle that came by, trying to get the hell out of Dodge. I knew Steve. And even under extreme duress, I just didn't see him getting into a vehicle with a stranger. Could he possibly have known the driver?

I turned the ignition and skirted the van around the phalanx of ambulances and police cruisers with their blue and red lights lighting up the sky. I pulled out onto Bay Shore Rd. The nearest Dunkin was on Bearses Way, near the police station. I was just about to pull into the Dunkin drive-thru when my cell phone rang. I didn't recognize the number, but it was a text message.

All in caps, it read WIDOWS COVE!

Suddenly the light went on. I remembered that Hal drove an old blue pickup. I hadn't told Steve about the surveillance operation Mosey and I were on at the Callahan estate. If Steve didn't know, how would Hal know, and was it Hal's pick-up that Steve had gotten into? How would Hal know Steve would be at the estate? The whole thing made no sense. I didn't know what was happening, but I knew I needed to get to the Widows Cove ASAP. I wheeled the van back, screeched to Bearses Way, and headed back to New Bedford.

CHAPTER SIXTY NINE

I flew down the Mid-Cape Highway back over the Sagamore Bridge and onto the access road that parallels the Cape Cod Canal. There were no hands free in the van, so I drove with my left hand, calling with my right hand, John Ring and Chief Mahan. Both calls went to voice mail. I left somewhat cryptic messages that something had come up, and I was going to the Widows Cove Tavern. I didn't know who had sent the text, but if anything was going down at the bar, I didn't want the cavalry arriving until I knew what was happening.

The Canal access road is usually packed in the summer, but I got lucky. The traffic was moving along at a steady clip, and I got to the ramp for 195 in ten minutes. I was trying to keep my eye on the road and scroll down to Steve's name on my contact list. I almost hit a kid on a bike and rear ended a minivan. I kept hitting the green button and getting the same result, voicemail.

"Hi, this is Steve. I hope you're having a good day. Leave a message."

No sense leaving a message. If Steve had his phone with him, he would see my name pop up and call me. If Steve was with Hal, why hadn't Hal called? Nothing was adding up.

I flew down 195 to Route 18 and headed up Union St. I parked in a metered spot a block down Union Street and from Widows Cove. I didn't have any quarters for the meter. Oh well, if I got a ticket, the FBI would have to pick up the tab. The neon open sign was flashing, and the lights inside were on. I walked to the front door and gave it a pull. It was locked.

I could hear voices inside. It was normal business hours, but if customers were inside, why would the door be locked? Someone was inside but who? I backed away from the front door and headed to the side alley. The side alley led to the back of the bar and the kitchen door. Nerves on edge and radar up, I unholstered my Glock and took the safety off. I could see seagulls picking at the dumpster from last night's garbage in the back lot. As I turned the corner of the building, I saw Hal's pickup. The kitchen was in the back of the bar with swinging doors connecting the bar to the kitchen. Anytime I was near the Widows Cove, the smell of burgers cooking, or shrimp Mozambique was always in the air. Today the air seemed as sterile as a hospital.

I walked slowly past the overflowing dumpster and up the concrete steps to the landing. I made my way around a couple of cases of empties and got to the rusting metal door. I ever so gently gave it a pull. It was open. I opened the door with a crack and scanned the kitchen. No one was there. I could hear voices from the bar but couldn't make out what they were saying. I needed to decide quickly. Do I fall back, call the police, and wait, or go in alone? For all I knew, maybe some customer had locked the door by mistake, and Hal was pouring beers and shots. If Steve hadn't shown up for work, that could explain why the kitchen wasn't open. During the slow periods, Steve tended to the bar and cooked. As I recall, if Hal was filling in as a cook, he wasn't much of a chef. Well, I had to find out. No contact from Steve or Hal. It didn't add up, and what about that text? Who sent it and why? I decided to go forward.

CHAPTER SEVENTY

I inched my way past the grille, stepping on the remains of a baked potato, past the cooler, and got within a couple of feet of the bar entrance. The voices were louder. I could hear what was being said. It was Hal doing the talking.

"Steve, we go way back. I didn't want any of this to happen. You know business has been off. What with all the new restaurants opening in the city. I've got five kids, and they are all involved in something. I'm like at an ATM that ran out of money. At first, it started with me buying fish at the fish house that were being sold through the back door. Bycatch that was being sold for cash at cut rate prices. Then one day at the fish house, I'm approached by Hank Gonsalves. He had just come into port and was offloading the catch from Emma Jean. He asked me to meet with him and a couple of friends at the end of the day about a 'business proposition.'"

I hear another voice, and its female. I recognize the slow drawl. it's Cocoa Brown.

"Steve, I love you, but you screwed up a beautiful thing. These junkies are always looking for a better high. We were just going to provide it for them. If we didn't, someone else would have. Carfentanil is coming to these shores, whether we like it or not. You have got to give the people what they want. We had the Stash Houses all set up, and distribution up and down the East Coast. Carlos had managed to pay off the harbormaster."

I could hear Steve respond. His voice was a mixture of anger, sadness, and bewilderment.

"Carlos? Wait. Are you talking about the Codfather?"

A high-pitched male voice piped in.

"Yeah, Mr. Bartender. The Codfather is still running the docks. Nothing happens in the harbor without his say so. With the Federal Hill mob out of the picture and Frankie Costa living a quiet suburban life, there was a power vacuum. The Codfather was happy to fill it. You'd be surprised how much business you can conduct from prison. He still has connections in the old country. The Cape Verdeans provided the product and the planes. We brought in Frank Medeiros and Hank Gonsalves to smuggle the carfentanil in at night. All the pieces fit together. That was until that two-bit drug dealer, Waxy, turned on us. Ragusa was getting too close to figure out what happened to the Emma Jean."

"Hal, your bartender friend here was a fly in the ointment. Word got back to me that he was helping the FBI. We can't have that. I thought roughing him up would be enough, but no; he's a slow learner."

Someone cleared their throat, and I could hear Hal's voice.

"Wolfie, the Feds aren't on to me. I'll keep my mouth shut. Leave Steve and me alone. I was never really involved anyway. I introduced you to Cocoa and Waxy and let you move some money through the bar and my bank. There's no way they can tie this back to me."

Whoa, so this is Wolfie. Steve had told me he had a bad feeling about the guy and his crew from that one encounter at the bar.

It was Hal again saying, "Wolfie, let Steve go. He has a 40-foot sailboat out in the harbor. Let him sail off into the sunset. Head to the Caribbean, some island where they don't ask many questions. It's believable. I mean, he's done it before. Everyone in the city knows Steve is a wanderer. If anyone asks about him, I'll just tell them he told me that he needed a change. It is a believable story."

"I'm afraid not Hal. I got my orders. The Widows Cove is soon to be under new management."

Things were going south. It was time to make my move. Before I could break through the door, I couldn't believe it. My phone buzzed. I looked at the screen.

It was a text from Chief Mahan: Sit tight; help is on the way.

Every cruiser in New Bedford would be surrounding the Widows Cove in a minute or two. With my right hand, I clumsily texted back: Stand down. I could hear sirens in the distance getting closer. The cavalry was on the way. Without the element of surprise, it was likely someone would get killed or end up as a hostage situation. I was staring at my phone, praying.

Finally, a reply: You have five minutes.

The sound of the sirens started to fade. The word must have got out.

With my Glock in my right hand, I slammed my shoulder into the door with everything I had. A tray stand with plates and empty beer bottles was in front of the door. The door violently swung open, and plates, glasses, and beer bottles went flying.

My eyes scanned left to right. Cocoa and Wolfie were sitting against a table near the front door. Hal and Steve sat on bar stools at the end of the bar, next to each other.

I bellowed, "Everyone put your hands where I can see them."

I was trying to keep my eyes on everyone at the same time. The only one I didn't think might want me dead was Steve. Cocoa was screaming at the top of her lungs. Wolfie lunged to his right and grabbed Cocoa by the throat. He held a .38 Special to her head. Wolfie seemed to be surveying the scene, deciding his next move.

"Agent Ragusa, you're getting to be a real pain in my ass."

"Yeah, you're not the only one who feels that way," I shouted back.

Then Wolfie said, "Listen. I will have to let your two buddies go and that's a shame. Cocoa and I are going to take a little boat trip. Carlos has plans for her. She is going to be visiting Hank Gonsalves and Frank Medeiros. And, Agent, since we're all sharing, if you're still wondering about the Emma Jean, Frank Medeiros set that fire. Unfortunately, he had a conscience and decided he didn't want to be in the drug smuggling business. He was going to collect the insurance money and retire. Oh well, he was a loose end that needed to be tied up. Now he's on permanent retirement."

Cocoa was struggling to break free. She was a street-smart girl. She knew what Wolfie meant. Wolfie started backing up slowly, waving his gun frantically. He reached back and opened the deadbolt on the door.

He screamed at Cocoa, "Shut up, or I'll kill you!"

"Let me go, you asshole."

With that, he tightened his grip on her neck. I didn't want Wolfie getting out onto Union Street. God knows what would happen, but I didn't have any options. I didn't have a clean shot, and Steve and Hal were easy targets.

The door creaked open, and Wolfie walked backward with his right hand pointing the gun at me and his left hand gripped like a vise around Cocoa's neck.

"Stay put, Ragusa. I'll be on my way."

I inched forward as he stepped backward onto Union Street. The two then disappeared from my line of sight. I opened the door and saw Wolfie pushing Cocoa into the passenger side of a black sedan.

Before she was in, I heard a familiar voice saying, "Stop. FBI. Drop the weapon."

It was Rick Raymond. He stood in the Weaver Stance, fifteen feet from the sedan. This prompt must have surprised Wolfie because he gave Cocoa a hard push into the car, wheeled to his left and raised the .38 Special with one motion. A shot rang out, and I saw a Wolfie rock backward as a bright red spot began to form in his chest. He slumped against the sedan and fell onto the sidewalk, Wolfie, a.k.a. New Bedford detective, Affonso Ferreira. was dead.

Rick ran up to the dead body and kicked the gun away. By now, I had made my way onto the street. Rick saw me and waved.

"Everyone all right, Rob?"

"Yes, Hal and Steve are in the bar, unharmed. I'll check on Cocoa."

I opened the car door, and Cocoa fell into my arms. Now I could hear the scream of sirens as they came up and down Union Street. I got Cocoa to her feet.

"You saved my life, Rob. Wolfie was going to kill me."

"I always liked you, Cocoa. I never thought you'd get wrapped up in something like this."

"Sorry, Rob, I mean that."

She looked like a sad puppy. I felt some sympathy for Cocoa, but carfentanil was going to kill many people. I guess she somehow had rationalized her role in that. People can rationalize a lot. I put the cuffs on her and led her to a New Bedford Police cruiser.

Rick had entered the Widows Cove through the front door to clear the scene. I followed him in and quickly cleared the bar and kitchen. Steve was sitting on the barstool next to Hal. He looked shell shocked as he stared not at me but through me. It was tough to see a couple of old friends like this. Rick gave me a thumbs up as he led Hal out of the bar to a waiting cruiser. As Hal approached the front door, I saw him turn to Steve and mouth the words, "Sorry." Steve said nothing. He just looked at him with a blank stare as Hal exited the Widows Cove Tavern in handcuffs.

This case had taken so many twists and turns my head was still spinning. Some of the bad guys ended up being good guys, and some of the good guys ended up being bad guys. I remembered some families growing up in Southie. One brother grew up to be a priest, the other a bank robber. Who knows why people do what they do? I plopped down on a bar stool next to Steve, the neon open sign blinking in the background. My phone buzzed again. It was a text message from Rick Raymond. It read: Two fishermen just found Hank Gonsalves floating in Hyannis harbor, a bullet in the back of his head.

Alone for a moment in my thoughts, I realized it was over. I had solved the puzzle, but I had this nagging feeling of emptiness. I turned to Steve, who was staring at the floor. I didn't know what to say to him. It just came out.

"Well, just like old times, Steve?"

He raised and slowly nodded his head.

"Yeah, Rob, just like old times."

We got up from our bar stools in unison. I would transport Steve and myself to the New Bedford Police Station. He would have to undergo interrogation there. I knew he wasn't involved, but it was protocol. We walked out the front door together, past an army of police officers. I pointed Steve toward the van. We both were silent as I pulled out slowly onto Union Street. One piece of the puzzle was still unsolved. Who was that blonde at Mike's Restaurant with the rose tattoo?

EPILOGUE

Operation Wave Runner essentially ended the carfentanil drug smuggling ring. Three members of the drug ring were arrested in Hyannis. FBI agents arrested the pilot and copilot of the drop plane at Plymouth Airport. All five were charged with Federal Drug Trafficking in Boston Federal Court. All five were tried and convicted. They are currently serving twenty years to life sentences at Administrative Maximum prison, ADX Florence. Commonly known as "Supermax," it houses some of the more notorious criminals in the United States, including the Unabomber.

With the assistance of Interpol, the Metropolitan Police conducted a late-night raid on a flat on Brick Lane in London's east end. Five men were arrested there, including the mastermind of the operation, a Cape Verdean National, Manuel Lopes. All are facing drug trafficking charges in the United Kingdom.

Acting on information provided by Cape Verde Interpol, Cape Verdean Police raided a hangar at Praia International. In the hangar, the police confiscated

100,000 pills laced with carfentanil. Although no suspects were on scene, a Gulfstream 2, parked in the hangar, was impounded. Interpol linked the carfentanil drug ring to the Eser crew in Cape Verde. The crew was rounded up by Interpol and local police. Thirteen drug ring members are languishing in overcrowded jails in Cape Verde, awaiting charges. In a joint televised news conference, the DEA and FBI announced this bust as ending the carfentanil drug trade in the United States. It has been estimated that if the carfentanil had hit the streets of the US, millions of lives would have been lost.

Robert Ragusa and Mosey Bedard recovered from their wounds. Agent Ragusa was awarded the FBI's Medal of Valor in a ceremony conducted by SAIC John Ring. The ceremony was held at the FBI's office in Washington, DC. Agent Ragusa considered retirement but has decided to continue his FBI career for at least another year. Mosey returned to the New Bedford Police Department. Detective Bedard received the Hanna Award Medal of Honor, the highest honor the Commonwealth of Massachusetts bestows on a law enforcement officer. Vince Almeida transferred into the Hyannis Police's Vice Squad. He recently broke up a child prostitution ring operating in Eastern Massachusetts. Bob Halloran retired from the Coast Guard after thirty years of service. He and Rob meet once a month for coffee at Dunkin Donuts in Saugus. New Bedford

Police Officer Alfonso Ferreira, a.k.a. Wolfie, was laid to rest at Oak Grove Cemetery in New Bedford. His pension was forfeited.

Sandy sold her small bungalow on the South Shore and moved into Rob's condo in Saugus. They are regulars at Kowloon. Benny has given his thumbs up on Rob's new love interest. Sandy started painting again, focusing on street scenes. She has several pieces for sale in a Boston's Back Bay gallery. Trixie is slowly adjusting to having another female in the home.

Rick Raymond was promoted and transferred from the Portsmouth New Hampshire, FBI field office to the Boston Field Office. He was awarded the Chief's Award, the department's highest honor. Hal Naworski pleaded no contest to a federal charge of money laundering. He is serving a five-year sentence at the minimum-security federal prison at Fort Devens in Ayer, Massachusetts. Due to a lack of evidence, he was not charged with drug smuggling. Steve Poole makes the two-hour drive and visits him often.

Steve Poole was interrogated by the FBI Coast Guard and the New Bedford Police Department and cleared of criminal wrongdoing. The FBI lauded him for his assistance in bringing down the carfentanil drug smuggling ring. His legend has only grown since the drug bust. Hal transferred the Widows Cove liquor license over to Steve. You can find him behind the bar at the Widows Cove Tavern, regaling customers with his exploits. Dr. Callahan accepted a plea deal from the Feds. He is serving a ten-year sentence at a minimum-security federal facility. His veterinary license was revoked. Wayne Barrett (Waxy) entered the Federal Witness Protection Program. He was relocated to an undisclosed location in the United States.

• • •

Separate services were held for Frank Medeiros and Hank Gonsalves at Our Lady of Assumption Church. Gil Galloway gave the eulogy at Captain Medeiros's service. Both were well attended. The Bristol County Medical Examiner removed .38 caliber bullet slugs from both bodies. The FBI forensic lab in Chelsea matched both bullets to the 38 Special belonging to Officer Rogers. No charges were brought against Cocoa Brown due to a lack of evidence. She is still a frequent patron of the Widows Cove.

New Bedford continues to evolve from a hard-edged fishing port to a genteel tourist town. More craft breweries and upscale restaurants have opened on Union Street. The cobblestone downtown is filled with art studios and trendy bars. The city still has its rough edges, but "The times are ever changin.'

GLOSSARY

Vince Almeida	Hyannis Police Detective
Sandy Atlas	FBI agent Rob Ragusa's girlfriend
Henry Avena	FBI Arson Investigator
Wayne Barrett (Waxy)	New Bedford-based drug dealer
Mosey Bedard	New Bedford Police Detective
Cocoa Brown	Patron Widows Cove Tavern
Whitey Bulger	Boston-based gangster
Dr. Lewis Callahan	Veterinarian
Vinny Chen	FBI Computer Scientist
George, (Cookie) Cooley	Helicopter Pilot
Frankie Costa	New Bedford-based gangster
Christian DeJesus	Crewman Emma Jean Captain Medeiros's boat
Ron Dellicker	New Bedford chief of police
Peter Duenas	Rob Ragusa's roommate, Quantico
Nicholas Dutra	Lieutenant Commander United States Coast Guard
Robert Edwards	Ensign United States Coast Guard
Lara Engalls	Coast Guard Health Services Technician
Robert Halloran	Coast Guard Investigator

WIDOWS COVE

Bryce Harper	Coast Guard Rescue Swimmer
Affonso Ferreira (Wolfie)	New Bedford Police Detective
Will Garcia	Captain of the Ruth Ann
Gil Galloway	Captain of the Olivia Rose
Barry Gomes	Crewman Emma Jean
Harold Hale	Helicopter Pilot
Henry Gonsalves	Missing Crewman Emma Jean
Jason Ludowsky	Coast Guard Commander Air Station Cape Cod
Michael Mahan	Chief of Police Hyannis
Roger McCloskey	Coast Guard Investigator
Frank Medeiros	Captain of the Emma Jean
Eric Mallory	Chief Warrant Officer, Coast Guard station, Boston
Hal Naworski	Owner Widows Cove Tavern
Lenny Page	FBI Forensic Specialist, Boston Field Office
Steve Poole	Bartender Widows Cove Tavern
Carlos Rafael	The Codfather
Rick Raymond	FBI Special Agent, Portsmouth New Hampshire Field Office
John Ring	FBI Special Agent In Charge, Boston Field Office
Robert (Rob) Ragusa	FBI Special Agent Boston Field Office
Manny Sousa	Crewman Emma Jean
Benny Wu	Bartender at the Kowloon Restaurant

ABOUT THE AUTHOR

Dr. Paul Rooney is a first-time author. He has a private psychotherapy practice in New Bedford, Massachusetts. He lives in Wareham, Massachusetts with his wife Paula and their dog, Rory.

IT'S JULY IN BOSTON, The humidity drapes over the city like a wet blanket. FBI Special Agent Rob Ragusa is nearing retirement. When the phone rings and he is reconnected with an old friend from his days in "Southie," Coast Guard Investigator Bob Halloran. A New Bedford-based scalloper has caught fire, and a fisherman is missing. What first seems like a simple fire investigation will lead him back to New Bedford, a city that holds fond memories and a long-lost friend from the nineties. Times have changed for the better in the port city, but New Bedford has always been a dangerous place. Like the city of New Bedford, the Widows Cove Tavern has changed. But old friend, Steve Poole, is still behind the bar. On the docks, no one can be trusted. Desperation, greed, and murder will test long-standing relationships. Rob will have to rely on his experience, newfound teamwork, and courage to save the lives of his inner circle and solve a crime with far-reaching tentacles that threaten to shake the city and the country forever

DATE DUE

Printed in the USA
CPSIA information can be obtained
at www.ICGtesting.com
CBHW071049090824
12949CB00007B/130

9 798822 932319